PILLARS
OF LIGHT

and passion as two faiths and many sub-cultures grind against each other is rather wonderfully crystalised into the union of architectures that results in a great cathedral for one religion built using the ideas and brilliance nurtured in the world of the other. It's a big, diverse book with a lot to say. A great read!' Mark Lawrence, internationally bestselling author of *Prince of Thorns*

PRAISE FOR PREVIOUS NOVELS:

'*The Sultan's Wife* is full of intrigue, deceit, skulduggery and murder. It has romance in it, but also heartbreak and personal tragedy. It's deeply evocative of North Africa – the sights, the smells, the culture, but there are also great depictions of London at the time, and the court of Charles II. I really enjoyed it, most especially because of Nus-Nus, a well-drawn, stand-out character who deserves to appear in another tale.' Ben Kane, author of *Spartacus: The Gladiator* and *The Forgotten Legion*

'Jane Johnson's bewitching new novel *The Sultan's Wife* is far more than a rip-roaring read: it's a true work of art. Deftly recreating the court intrigue of the tyrannical Moroccan Sultan Moulay Ismail – with all its trappings . . . of superstition, black magic and torture – it sucks you down through interleaving layers steeped in blood, sweat and raw adrenalin, to a mesmerising bedrock of real history. *The Sultan's Wife* gets inside you, conjuring its magic long after you read the last line.' Tahir Shah, author of *The Caliph's House* and *In Arabian Nights*

'*The Salt Road* is an exhilarating ride. Part historic and part contemporary, with universal themes of betrayal, love, and the anguish caused by human greed, it has an ending rich and fulfilling enough for those who like all their questions answered.' *Toronto Globe & Mail*

Jane Johnson

PILLARS
OF LIGHT

uclanpublishing

Pillars of Light is a uclanpublishing book

First published in Great Britain in 2017 by
uclanpublishing
University of Central Lancashire
Preston, PR1 2HE, UK

978-0-9955155-5-0

1 3 5 7 9 10 8 6 4 2

A CIP catalogue record for this book is available from the British Library.

Printed and bound in Great Britain by Clays Ltd, St Ives plc

For Abdel

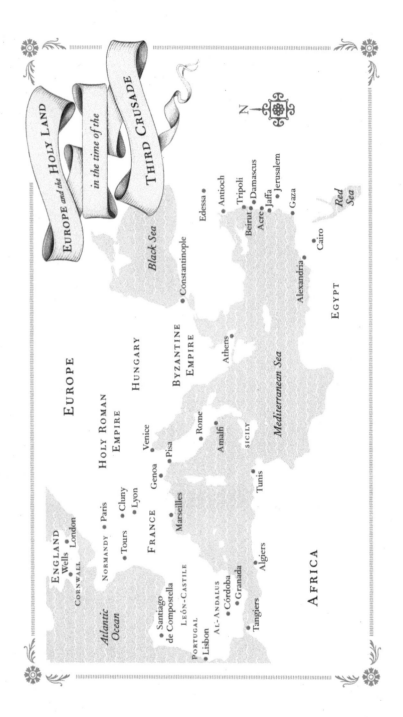

EUROPE and the HOLY LAND in the time of the THIRD CRUSADE

Lovers find secret places within this violent world
wherein they may make transactions with beauty.

RUMI

Dramatis Personae

IN ENGLAND

The Moor, traveller (origins unknown)
John Savage, foundling
Enoch Pilchard, also known as Quickfinger
Mary White, also known as Plaguey Mary
William of Worcester, also known as Red Will
Michael and Saul Dyer, twins going by the name of Hammer and Saw
Edward Little, also known as Little Ned
Rosamund, also known as Ezra

Reginald de Bohun, the Bishop of Bath and founder of Wells Cathedral
Savaric de Bohun, also known as Fitzgoldwin: cousin to Reginald

Abbess of Wilton, presides over the shrine of St. Edith and the Nail of
    Treves
Eleanor of Aquitaine, wife to King Henry II of England and mother to
    his sons, including Richard, known as the Lionheart

IN ACRE (also called Akka)

Emir Beha ad-Din Karakush, Governor of Akka

Baltasar Najib
Nima, his wife

Sorgan, their eldest son
Malek, their second son, serving Sultan Salah ad-Din
Zohra, their daughter
Aisa and Kamal, youngest twin sons

Yacub of Nablus, a doctor
Sara, his wife
Nathanael, their son

Various aunts, uncles, cousins, neighbours, soldiers.

THE ARMY OF THE FAITHFUL

Salah ad-Din Yusuf ibn Ayyub, Commander of the Faithful and Sultan
    of Egypt, known by the Christians as Saladin
Imad ad-Din, the Lord of Sinjar, brother to the sultan
Al-Adil, the sultan's younger brother
Al-Afdal, Salah ad-Din's older son
Al-Malik az-Zahir, Salah ad-Din's younger son
Baha ad-Din, the Qadi (judge and senior officer) of the Army
Imad al-Din, the sultan's scribe
Taki ad-Din, Prince of Hama, the sultan's nephew
Saïf ad-Din Ali al-Mashtub, a warlike Kurdish chieftain
Keukburi, known as the Blue Wolf, an emir from east of the Euphrates

Various messengers, commanders, soldiers.

THE CHRISTIAN ARMY IN SYRIA

King Philip Augustus of France
Guy de Lusignan, deposed King of Jerusalem and the Latin Kingdom
Conrad of Montferrat, Lord of Tyre, an Italian nobleman: his rival
Count Henry of Champagne
Gerard de Ridefort, Master of the Temple
Robert de Sable, knight of Anjou

Archbishop of Auxerre
Bishop of Bayonne

King Richard I, known as The Lionheart and by the Muslims as Malik
    al-Inkitar
Ranulf de Glanvill, Chief Justiciar of England, also known as the
    King's Eye
Geoffrey de Glanvill, his brother
Baldwin of Forde, Archbishop of Canterbury

IN THE MOUNTAINS OF SYRIA

Sidi ad-Din Sinan, known as the Old Man of the Mountain, Grand
    Headmaster of the Hashshashin, a sect of Nizari fundamentalists,
    often called the Assassins

City of Akka,
known by the Christians as Acre,
Syria

✺

SUMMER 1187

S o much temptation, and never enough money. Over the ordure of the livestock and the acrid stench of too many sweating people in the marketplace, Zohra Najib could just make out the first nose-twitching delights of Sayedi Efraim's perfume stall. She felt her heart beat faster as her brother Sorgan forged a passage through the crowd. He made a useful battering ram, at least, on busy souq days.

As they neared the stall, she pressed a coin into his hand. "For sugared almonds." He knew where the dainties were sold and would linger there, unable to make up his mind, until she came for him. She saw him bring his palm up to gaze at the silver piece, watched his face break into a slow grin. Then his hand formed a greedy fist around the coin. He could hardly get away from her fast enough. More than one shout of protest went up as shoppers were shouldered aside in his headlong rush for sugar.

She slipped between a pair of women bent almost double under the weight of overfilled baskets, the carry-straps biting into their foreheads, and almost cannoned into two big Templar knights patrolling the crowds. Her second oldest brother, Malek, an officer in the Syrian army, had warned her about the Christian warrior-monks. "They take vows of chastity, but they do not always stick to them," he'd said, his handsome face stern. "Be sure to keep out of their way."

But the knights were not interested in her: their wolf-like gazes roamed the crowds.

At the perfume-seller's stall Zohra let her eyes run hungrily over the wares. Some of the incense—frankincense, white benzoin, myrrh—was beyond her purse, but there were other, less expensive options. She loved spending time here, rubbing the patchouli leaves till they gave up their scent, sniffing the crystals and resins, rolling the shards of aromatic wood and dried rose petals between her palms, losing herself for a while in a world of gorgeous possibility before the dullness of her life swallowed her once more.

Sayedi Efraim, the stallholder, was a tiny man in a crumpled brown robe and a crocheted skullcap. He had one good eye and one closed and withered socket, but that single eye was beady and astute: it was often said it could see money wherever it was hidden. He beamed at his customer, radiating back at her the joy he felt at the presence of her silver. "Take your time, little bird. Take all the time you need."

Zohra knew it was good for business for him to have a pretty girl at the stall: it attracted other clients. She smiled back at him. "Show me something less expensive, *sayedi*."

He spread his hands. "How to place a price on a house that smells like a palace, or a girl who smells like a princess? Expense is all in the mind, little bird."

She fixed him with what her mother would have called "a straight look." "Expense is in the pocket, *sayedi*. I have a single dinar and a great deal more than perfume to buy." She opened her palm and the silver coin glinted seductively in the sunlight.

The coin had a cross impressed into its centre: it had been minted in the Latin Kingdom, as the Franj called their embattled realm. Not that it mattered: Zohra knew the trader was happy to take any coin—Christian bezants from Cyprus and Tripoli; silver dirhams from Aleppo, Sinjar and Baghdad; deniers minted in Antioch and Jerusalem . . . Akka was a city that had always prided itself on its cosmopolitan nature. Situated as it was on the edge of the Middle Sea, it was a trade crossroads: merchants came here to sell gold and spices, silk and saffron, fish eggs and resin, glass and songbirds. From north and east and west they came, from Venice and Marseille, India and China, Trebizond and Sarai.

The Bay of Haifa offered respite during the notorious winter storms, and its deep, safe anchorage gave shelter to a fleet of ships. To the north lay the fortified city of Tyre; to the east the road to Nazareth and Jerusalem and the rich lands between. Akka was a strategic gem, and so the city changed hands often, but business went on much the same as usual, no matter who was in charge. Goods were traded, money circulated—everyone was happy. Well, maybe "happy" was an exaggeration, she thought, remembering the Franj knights pushing through the markets with their swords at the ready and their surcoats emblazoned with huge crosses, an affront to every good Muslim. If you listened, you could hear the squeal of pigs in the livestock market, and every day the bells that the Christians had sacrilegiously hung in the minaret of the Friday Mosque rang their hideous summons to Shaitan. Every day she prayed that Salah ad-Din would one day retake the city and melt down those wretched bells.

The stallholder selected a piece of frankincense—an opalescent, crystalline bulb—and held it beneath Zohra's nose. The initial strong, musky scent was followed by the much prized balsamic undertone. She inhaled in a sort of daze.

"This is my best *hojari*," Sayedi Efraim said. "The first cut of the resin, all the way from the sacred trees of Dhofar, brought through the Empty Quarter and then the Great Desert by caravan. Just think of the dangers those brave cameleers endured to bring this frankincense all that way so that an old man could make a pretty girl very happy. Is their courage and enterprise not worth the small price I ask?"

"Stop your song and dance, Efraim! Can't you see she doesn't want to buy your expensive frankincense?"

Zohra turned and found a young man standing there. He was tall and lanky, with a long, mobile face and a mass of black hair that his small, precarious skullcap did nothing to confine. He had a determined set to his chin, eyes of a deep, mysterious brown, and his grin was lopsided and mocking. "Wait till some fat merchant's wife comes by with her husband's purse. Besides, frankincense is too heavy for such a beauty—maybe orris root or cassia?"

Zohra opened her mouth to speak, but the man leaned forward and placed a finger on her lips. Greatly affronted, she took a step back.

The man caught Zohra by the arm. "No need to run away, pigeon. Here, this is what you need. Amber, like your eyes." He chose a square of amber-musk from Efraim's bins and rubbed it between his fingers. "Close your eyes," he instructed, warming the wax in his hands to release the essential oils. "Blow all your breath out and then, when I tell you to, breathe in."

Zohra did as she was told, though she was not usually so biddable. At once, the sweet perfume flooded her senses. She put a hand out to steady herself, opened her eyes wide, found that she had clutched his arm. What was she doing, touching a man in public? She snatched her hand back. But the man smiled, a smile that lit his whole being; and at that moment the sun struck him full on, turning his pale skin almost as opalescent as the frankincense. The scent of amber enveloped them like a cloud: they might at that moment have been the only two people left on the face of the earth.

"I'll buy four pieces," the man told the stallholder, and then he haggled furiously till he'd paid less for four than Zohra would have paid for two. "Wrap them separately," he instructed, and when this was done, he took Zohra's hands in his own and closed his fingers over two of the bits of amber. She stared down at their interlocking flesh, feeling the blood beating through his skin, pulsing against her own. Suddenly, it seemed impossible to breathe.

Then, just as suddenly, he released her, and when she looked up, blinking, it was to see that his attention was no longer on her, for he was craning his neck, staring out across the crowd. She experienced a moment of disappointment before her ears registered the shouting. Angry voices, loud and insistent.

Oh no, was her first thought. *What has Sorgan done?*

But it was nothing to do with her brother. Words became distinct: "Hattin," "defeat" and then "Saladin," spoken the Franj way, a curt mangling of their sultan's name. Her heart clenched. Had the Muslim army been defeated? The idea of her brother Malek hacked by enemy swords was for a moment so distressing she lost her breath again.

"What are they shouting?" she asked at last.

By way of response, the stranger picked up her basket and took her by the arm. "We must get you out of here. Right now."

"My brother is in the bazaar."

"Your brother can look after himself."

"No, you don't understand!" She began to pull away. "I have to fetch him, I must . . ."

But he didn't let go. His eyes were shining, but she could not tell whether it was with anger, or fear or some other emotion. He hustled her on.

Around the corner, out of sight, someone screamed and an angry buzz rose like bees. The stranger hauled her so hard it was as if her feet barely touched the ground. At last they were on the fringe of the market where the press of folk was less intense. He let her go.

5

"I had to get you out of there quickly."

Zohra, angry at being manhandled, snapped, "I can take care of myself!"

"It's not some market brawl. There's been a huge battle. The Christians have been routed. The Bishop of Akka is dead and the True Cross has been captured by Salah ad-Din."

Zohra stared at him. "Our sultan beat the Franj?"

"At Hattin, yes, a great victory: twenty thousand dead and their king taken captive. There will be reprisals, bloodshed. It's not safe. Where do you live? I will take you home."

"I can't go without Sorgan." Zohra willed her brother to come lumbering out of the bazaar. But there was no sign of him.

"Your brother can find his own way home."

"Sorgan may look like a giant, but he's barely got the wits of a child."

His air of control wavered. "I'm sorry, I did not realize. Look, stay here, keep out of sight and I'll fetch him." He ushered her into a doorway. Zohra described her brother, told him how he had gone to buy sugared almonds, then watched as the stranger in his dark robe became a shadow among shadows within the eaves of the covered market.

Sorgan would never come away with a stranger: there would be a scene. He could spend hours at the sweets stall, devouring it with his eyes, before making his immense decision. He was as stubborn as a mule, and just as immovable once he had an idea in his head. Surely, it would be quicker if she went back in to fetch him . . .

But now a stream of people was running out of the market, women clutching purchases and pulling small children, youths with bloodied clothing and wild eyes. From the street behind her a detachment of Franj militia appeared, swords glinting in the late-afternoon sun. Turning back, Zohra saw Sorgan emerging from the bazaar, looming over the stranger, who had him by the arm.

Her big, simple brother was grinning and grinning, hugging an enormous bundle to his chest.

Zohra's relief turned at once to consternation. "What have you done? What have you taken?"

Sorgan's eyes darted. He said nothing.

"He wouldn't come away easily," the stranger said, his eyes on the retreating militia. "So we bought half the stall, didn't we, Sorgan?"

Her brother gave his throaty, infectious laugh, but Zohra glared at him, appalled. Sorgan dug into the parcel. "Would you like one?" Between his giant fingers gleamed a single sugared almond, proffered not to his own sister but to the nice stranger. Zohra had never before seen him share his treats with anyone. This in itself was oddly disturbing; more so was that in the crevice of his palm she glimpsed the silver coin she had given him.

The young man took the almond solemnly and popped it into his mouth. "Thank you, Sorgan. You're a gentleman. But we must get you home now."

"You're coming too, aren't you?" Sorgan asked, alarmed.

"I am."

"You are?" Zohra was even more alarmed by this prospect than her brother had been by the young man's likely disappearance. What would the neighbours say to see her accompanied by a strange man, and a Jewish man at that? What would her father say? But they were walking so quickly that there was no time to address the matter in any polite way.

She waited until they reached the top of the hill, two streets away from the family house, and there she stopped. "We can get home safely from here. Thank you," she said, sounding ridiculously formal. To make it worse she dug in her coin-purse, picked out two large pieces of silver and held them out to him. "For your trouble. And for the amber and almonds. We really can't accept gifts from a stranger."

The young man gave her a sardonic look. Then he picked the coins out of her fingers and returned them to her purse. In the guise of an extravagant bow (which dislodged his precarious skullcap), he bent over her hand and pressed his lips to her palm. Straightening, he jammed the cap back on his head.

"My name is Nathanael bin Yacub, known all over town as 'the doctor's son.' You'll find my house at the end of the Street of Tailors. Knock at the door with the hand on it. And if you don't, I will send my djinns out to look for you."

He gave her his lopsided grin, told Sorgan to be sure to look after his sister, and then walked quickly away, leaving Zohra staring after him, the burning impression of his wicked mouth against her skin.

PART ONE

The Miracle Men

I

Priory of St. Michael on the Mount,
Cornwall, England

✳

SUMMER 1187

I was born a godless creature.

Two mendicant friars walking the pilgrim's way towards the Benedictine priory of St. Michael on the Mount found me among the ancient hut circles on the moors overlooking the bay, living off worms and berries and covered head to toe in dark whorls of fur.

Perhaps that was why my mother abandoned me, thinking me more animal than child. Or perhaps I grew that pelt as a defence against the elements. Either way, the friars decided to carry me off to the priory, to raise me in God's house and make a civilized man of me. I kicked and fought all the way. I heard later they debated dropping me over the side of the boat in which we made the short crossing between the mainland and island. There have been times when I wished they had.

They gave me a scratchy hessian robe and a name: Savage. John Savage. I was taken into the priory as an oblate, although I had not been formally given up by my parents (if I even had any). The order of Saint Benedict forbids a child to be dedicated before the age of ten. No one knew my age: they made of me a servant and used me at their will.

Set upon by the older boys, I would snarl and give battle and prove myself the animal they called me, but whenever I tried to run away they would find me and drag me back before I could escape across the causeway that rose magically out of the sea at low tide. Novices, being the lowest in the order, love to have someone lower on whom to vent their frustrations.

When the falling fits came on me, they thought I was possessed by a devil. When I fell, frothing and talking nonsense, I was unable to fight back: that was when their kicks fell thickest. I would rise an hour later to find bruises all over my body and the afterimages of strange visions in my head.

Pillars of light and soaring arches, accompanied by the scent of roses. They haunted me, those visions. They haunt me still.

The day I dropped the reliquary, spilling Saint Felec's foot bones all over the chapel floor, Brother Jeremiah hit me so hard his hawthorn stick broke in half.

I'd been in the priory fourteen years by my own reckoning, so no doubt the stick had been weakened by repeated acquaintance with my recalcitrance. I felt exultant, till I realized he now had two weapons. Covering my head, I fell to my knees on the rough slates, cowering amid the shards of bone and wood.

I swept them towards me. "I'll mend it so you'll never be able to tell the difference! And there are always more bones in the graveyard where these came from!" I remembered very well that October morning when the prior had sent the sacristan out into the churchyard to dig up the skeleton of an unknown monk and cut off its foot in order to create the relic of "sacred Saint Felec," ancient king of drowned Lyonesse.

I realized too late my error in mentioning this shameful secret, for Brother Jeremiah flew from a state of anger into one of apoplexy.

"You foul little demon!" he roared. The first stick fell. "Liar! Ingrate!" *Whack!* Shoulder. "You're a wild thing, possessed by unclean spirits." *Whack!* Shin. "And if I can't pray them out of you . . ." *Whack!* Arm. "I must beat them out!" Spittle shimmered in his grey beard.

I curled in on myself like a dying wasp. "*Mea culpa*, brother, *mea culpa!*"

He grimaced and raised both arms as if to beat a giant drum. I prepared myself for the agony to come, but it never did. Instead, a thin, dark man appeared at the door of the chapel and came towards us, the skirts of his black habit kicking up as he ran.

"Stop! He's just a boy! Leave him be!"

Brother Jeremiah gave the newcomer a ghastly smile. "Being a foreigner, you won't understand our ways, brother. He is a fallen being. We must chastise such a sinner in this world, for else he will not mend his ways, and his soul will be tormented in the next." When he raised his arm again I ducked and waited for the blow to fall.

When it did not, I glanced up and saw that the dark man had taken hold of Brother Jeremiah's arms and was pushing him back against the wall. The monk struggled wildly, calling his attacker *infidel, unbeliever, blackie, wretch, ignotus*. But for a thin man the stranger was remarkably strong. Brother Jeremiah was subdued; his weapons clattered to the ground. Over his shoulder the dark man called, "Get up, John, and go outside."

But I knelt, rooted. I had seen Brother Jeremiah strangle one servant and bash the brains out of another. He might have been old but he was as grim as Death. Even the prior was frightened of him. Who was this stranger who knew my name, and must therefore have been here long enough to know the evil power of Brother Jeremiah? I risked a glimpse at his face. Fine-boned, ascetic: like a saint in an illumination. Except that his skin was as dark as leather. A vague memory stirred. Some weeks back, during the winter storms, there had been a wreck off the rocks of Tater Du, west along the coast towards Land's End. Sailors brought three men in that wild night, to the hospital here at the priory, all as limp as knouts of wet kelp. The two bigger men died. Was this the third? The only survivor?

I forced myself to my feet and shuffled outside. Night was falling. The sky and sea were the same deep shade of grey, the horizon merging into cloud. The distant mainland was a black whaleback in the gloom, tiny lights flickering from fires and candles in the village across the water. How often had I wished myself inside one of those tiny houses, away from the monks and the novices? But there was no escape from this place, except in death.

Around me in the falling dark, small upright stones marked the passage between worlds of previous inhabitants: the priory's grave-yard, each man's resting place memorialized in the same way as his neighbour, no difference in rank or degree made between them, as Saint Benedict decreed in the second chapter of his Rule. I had always thought I would join them there, sooner rather than later.

I shivered in the rising breeze, then crept to the chapel door and pushed my head around the door jamb.

Brother Jeremiah was on his knees in front of the altar, motion-less, eyes closed, hands pressed together, palm to palm in prayer, like a good child. And beside him, the dark man, visible in the shadow only by the gleam of his eyes. As if he had intuited my presence by some minute shift in the air, he said, without turning, "Brother Jeremiah has passed away, and we should leave, too."

❄

I left St. Michael's Mount with the stranger, who told me to call him simply "the Moor," in the small hours of that summer night.

At last I was going to escape this hated place, and no mean-spirited novices would stop me. We left with some of the prior's gold, but the Moor said that was all right, because we were going to put it to better use than that corrupt old churchman ever would. The first use we put it to was to bribe a young fisherman to row us across the narrow strait between the island and the Cornish coast. Then we walked the pilgrim's way by night, and slept in the rough embrace of furze and bramble in the day.

We kept out of the sight of other travellers, though the Moor did not appear anxious.

"How did Brother Jeremiah die?" I asked at last.

He did not answer for a long time. Then he said, "Best not to ask, John."

"Will they seek us as murderers?" I had seen men hang, could imagine the scratch of the rope around my neck.

"There is no mark on him. God called him home. He was not a young man."

Might I, too, be unexpectedly called home one night as I slept beneath a gorse bush? I decided I had better make a friend of the Moor. I had never had a friend before, and I did not know what to do. I made a nuisance of myself, asking eager questions. In the end he told me he had been travelling with a master mason when their ship had been caught in the storm and gone down on the rocks. He said he had come from Cordoba, a city far to the south, where he had spent years copying manuscripts in the library of a great man.

"Are you a scribe?" I asked.

"I'm a bit more than a scribe," he said with an enigmatic smile.

"I like to draw," I said. I had watched the monks in the scriptorium at the Mount. Their scribblings fascinated me, and when they were gone for the day and I cleaned the room, I would gather up the pieces of vellum and broken quills they had discarded. I poured gall-ink into whelk shells I had brought from the beach and tried to copy their work. I made lines on the paper—like writing, but not like writing. My lines looked like wiggly worms. I drew a wiggly worm, added eyes and a mouth. It made me laugh. Then a crow flew past, and I drew that, too. Soon I was drawing all sorts of things: black-backed gulls, arch-backed cats and bare-branched trees. Gargoyles with saints' faces; saints with gargoyle heads. Caricatures of the monks, hoods up, scythes over their shoulders: Death's army. And the strange visions that came to me in my falling fits. Those were the hardest images of all to draw. I could never master the trick of capturing in miniature the immensity of what I saw in my head. It frustrated me to the point of fury.

The Moor regarded me with interest. "You are more than you seem, John. I like that."

No one had ever said anything like that to me before. It made me flush with pleasure. I decided I would follow him anywhere.

"Where are we going?"

"We are going to see the things we must see and do the things we must do. But travelling the world does not come cheap."

"We have some gold now," I said brightly.

"It will not last forever. Nothing ever does."

We were standing on the edge of Bodmin Moor in the early-morning sun when he said this. A buzzard passed overhead on slow, steady beats of its broad wings, and then it was gone. I blinked and looked back at him.

"The monks always seem to have a lot of gold," I said.

"People give it to them for the favour of the saints whose relics they own—to grant their prayers, cure their ills or cancel out their sins."

I thought about that for a while. Somewhere in the distance there was a brief, agonized cry. It sounded almost human, but it was probably a rabbit, lost to the buzzard. Then I told the Moor about the "relics" of Saint Felec.

A gleam came into his eye. "Bones," he echoed speculatively. "Well, that is interesting."

A few nights later we found ourselves beneath a yellow moon at a charnel pit on Slaughter Moor. I blew on my hands, stamped some life into my feet. How could it be so cold in the middle of summer? "Hurry up, can't you?"

A laugh rumbled up from the pit. "There are some things, John, that can't be hurried, and that includes the dead. If you want it done quicker, you'd best come down here yourself."

I wanted to please him more than anything in the world, but the thought of all those unquiet spirits . . . "I en't coming down there for love nor gold."

He shifted soil carefully. Unearthing a skull sliced clean across, he held it for a moment, examining it in the golden glow cast by the oil lamp we'd bought from the fisherman. The flickering light picked out the hollow orbits and the triangular nasal cavity. Then he put it aside, tenderly, as though he knew the owner, and bent to his task once more. Not many would dare desecrate such a place, especially after dark, but the Moor said the dead were dead, and the body was no more than a vessel from which the soul wings free. He said spirits did not linger, and bones were only bones.

"Those who owned them may have existed long ago, but before their carcasses were thrown down here like so much rubbish their lives were full of passion, sorrow and delight." He sighed. "War is madness, John. Fighting never achieved anything of value."

The hollow we were in was full of vapours that twisted in the moonlight like phantoms. There were strange lights here, the sort of lights that would lead you into the bogs and drown you in the deep brown water where the piskeys lived. I shivered and sat down on the edge of the hole, dangling my legs. The Moor looked up at me, his eyes gleaming like half-moons.

To confound him, I jumped down, and was rewarded with a wry smile. "We'll be here all night else," I said shortly. With loathing, I laid hands on a bone and tried to dislodge it, causing a tumble of earth.

"Go easy," the Moor admonished.

I was determined to hide how terrified I was. Together, we shifted soil and rotted cloth, stones, bones and bits of rusted metal. After a while, a large bone came clear and I hauled it out. "What about this?"

The Moor brought the lamp closer. "Scapula," he declared.

"What's a scapula?"

He touched my back. Beneath the rough weave of my shirt, my skin tingled. "There. A shoulder blade."

"Who ever heard of a holy shoulder blade?"

"Far stranger items are found in your Church's golden reliquaries. The Pope in Rome keeps Isa Christ's sandals and foreskin beneath the altar in the Lateran basilica. In Venice, I saw a molar from the mouth of Goliath, and in Constantinople I hear they have the axe Noah used to make his ark and a phial of the Virgin Mary's breast milk."

"It would be long curdled to cheese!" I snorted. "What fool'd fall for such hogwash?"

"Never scorn the faith of believers, John. But it's true that a scapula is not ideal."

At last he uncovered an arm, the bones pitted with age but still intact. I thought—*one day my arm will look like this*—and shuddered. He brushed earth away. Still clutched in the weird fingers was the crossguard of a hilt decorated with twining beasts, leading to a long, lean blade.

I had never held a sword before. He passed it to me, and as I held it, it was as if power flowed through the metal into my arm. It made me feel like a king. Yes, just like a king . . .

"Careful, John." The Moor stepped back as I flourished the weapon clumsily.

"Behold the bones and sword of good King Arthur, saviour of the English!" I said. "The hero who drove the heathen from our shores, before falling in the Last Battle." The locals had told us this was the site of the battle of Camlann, where the English army had made its last stand against the invading Saxons.

The Moor looked thoughtful. "This King Arthur is not a saint, though. Will monasteries pay good money for parts of a dead king?"

"Everyone loves the hero of Monmouth's tales, from the poorest ploughboy to the richest knight. They'll queue for miles to touch his bones. The monks en't fools—they'll take popularity over sanctity any day of the week if it brings in trade."

The Moor sighed. "It is the same the world over, John."

2

Glastonbury

❄

FESTIVAL OF ALL HALLOWS,

1ST NOVEMBER, 1187

The Moor tilted his head to examine the complex carvings above the door of the chapel. "Just three years to create this. Remarkable."

I gazed up, smelling in the air the scent of winter: woodsmoke and cold earth.

The old church, originally raised by Joseph of Arimathea, had burned down; they'd built this Lady Chapel with almost miraculous speed. We had arrived in time for the consecration. All Hallows is when the saints are at their strongest and can hold back Satan's power.

Word had travelled far and wide of the marvellous relic making its way to Glastonbury: King Arthur's arm, still clutching the sword that saved England. Spurred on by curiosity, desperation and hope, some of the pilgrims had made journeys of more than a hundred miles to see it. There was a huge crowd milling about, waiting for the procession to complete its circuit.

"What'll they do to us if they realize it's a fake?" I had asked over and over as we trudged through Devon and into Somerset. But the Moor had just laughed. It didn't reassure me.

A chill breeze came out of nowhere and I ran a hand over the unfamiliar baldness on the top of my head. I hated having a tonsure, but the Moor had insisted: we had to play our part. I was wearing a white robe given to me by the abbey's monks, the traditional colour for the All Hallows mass. Used to Benedictine black, I felt exposed. The Moor, on the other hand, was in startling Pentecostal red. "I stick out like a sore thumb as it is," he had said as he put on the vestments. "People will remember a black man no matter what he wears, but they are less likely to question a black cardinal."

Quiet had fallen for the arrival of the guests of honour. First, the justiciar, Ranulf de Glanvill, known as the King's Eye since he watched over the kingdom when Henry was in France. I hoped that eye wouldn't fall upon me. Beside him, his brother, Geoffrey. He had the face of a butcher, red and fleshy, and the meaty fists of a born bully. The justiciar had eyes of winter-blue, sharp and penetrating. They grazed me and came to rest on the scarlet Moor, and my heart stopped. But the Moor just nodded, equal to equal, and the two men passed on.

Behind them, with a head of grey woolly hair, like a sheep in purple robes, was the Bishop of Bath, Reginald de Bohun. We had already met; he looked at us, then quickly—too quickly— looked away.

The lesser gentry were in overly bright clothing, flaunting their fortune and lack of taste. Wealthy merchants' wives displayed their flashiest jewels to advertise their husbands' success. I thought: *Ned and Quickfinger will have their eye on those.*

Quickfinger we'd found in Launceston. I'd watched him disappear under a trestle table where people were busy eating a harvest feast. When they rose to go they found they were all wearing mismatched shoes. While I was laughing, I saw how Quickfinger moved among them, quietly robbing a purse here and there. I nudged the Moor. He grinned and nodded, having seen it all for himself, and shortly after that, Quickfinger became the first member of our troupe. He was from the north.

"York?" I remember asking him.

"Farthern tha'." Quickfinger had pointed up into the air as if to suggest he fell from Heaven.

His accent was so impenetrable that I couldn't always understand him, and he'd claim the same of me, mocking my West Country vowels with such a mangling imitation that I'd want to knock him down. Twice we'd nearly come to blows, but he was as fast on his feet as he was with his hands. Then he'd grin and grin as if touched in the head. It was an act he'd developed to distract people. You don't tend to make a lot of eye contact with someone who grins in such a lunatic way. And that was when he'd rob you, take your purse or your belt-knife or whatever else he could lay hands on. Life was a huge joke to Quickfinger. It made him likeable and dislikeable in equal parts.

Ned was small and dark and rat-like enough to pass for the cripple he pretended to be. He'd fastened himself on to the growing troupe as we passed through Tavistock. I did not much want his company, for he had a sly, weaselly look, but he showed us tricks that were breathtaking: producing gold from the Moor's ear, and fitting himself into a tiny hole in a tree you'd think not even a cat could squeeze into before disappearing altogether and reappearing on a branch above our heads.

Tricksters and thieves—impossible to trust at the best of times. I felt my skin prickle.

On the outskirts of the congregation, the servants, smiths and rustics, penitents and cripples gathered, looking overawed. Kept at a safe distance by the constables, their hideous faces hidden by hoods, clutching their clappers and bells, were the lepers from St. Mary Magdalene's, poor souls suffering Purgatory on Earth, let out of the lazar house to seek the only known cure for their affliction: a miracle.

The procession reappeared, led by a monk carrying a great jewelled cross worth a king's ransom. Then came the prior bearing the Corpus Christi, and a line of canons cradling the relics that had survived the fire. After this came the big oak-and-silver box containing "Arthur's" arm and sword. The doors to the chapel were thrown open and in they went, commemorating Christ's triumphant entrance into the Holy City of Jerusalem, and the sacristan waved us to follow.

Inside, the Lady Chapel was pitch-black, the thick darkness and animal smell oppressive. There began at once a cacophony of unearthly howls, the clanging of metal. The Glastonbury monks banged and stamped and screeched, playing their parts as Hell's minions. It was the one time in the year when the disciplined quiet of the Benedictine life could be set aside and they could behave as badly as they liked, reminding the congregation of the demonic punishments that awaited their sorry, sinning souls in the afterlife if they didn't do what they were told and give Mother Church all their money. Those who'd never before experienced the Ceremony of Light shouted in terror.

I turned and saw the Moor grinning in the darkness, revelling in being a Saracen, a heretic, an intruder among the enemy, a wolf in the sheepfold. His grin did not fill me with confidence. If all this went wrong, we'd never get as far as being hanged, I thought. They'd rip us apart. I added my own voice to the demonic choir: it was a relief to howl out my terrors.

At last the windows were unshrouded, candles lit. The Lady Chapel was flooded with light. Hell was banished for another year. In its place, pillars bursting with carved foliage, arcades decorated with crimson, gold and blue. The sun and moon together, defying the natural order, hovered above the head of a smiling Virgin Mary, the Christ child cradled in her arms. Bright friezes of saints, martyrs and apostles gazed down. I felt their eyes on me.

I looked out over the congregation. Somewhere amongst the merchants was the rest of our troupe: Red Will; Hammer and Saw; and Plaguey Mary, farther back among the peasants.

Hammer and Saw were twins, small and dark and wiry. They spoke a shared language when in their cups that none of the rest of us could understand. We'd seen them in a village on the edge of Dartmoor, juggling. We later discovered they were out-of-work carpenters, clever with their hands. Quickfinger soon taught them to pick pockets.

Red Will and Plaguey Mary we'd found on the outskirts of Exeter. Will was playing a flute, badly, and Mary was laughing at his lack of skill. She gave us an assessing look. We soon disabused her of the idea we might be customers. Despite the name she went by, Mary was a hale and healthy whore, one possessed of a robust sense of humour and a ready laugh. We passed them by, but Mary came after us, sensing a better opportunity than her usual trade, and Will followed.

Travelling players, a terrible minstrel, jugglers, out-of-work carpenters, pickpockets, a whore—how I enjoyed their company after the mealy-mouthed monks and the mean novices and their snide violence. We laughed and shared stories, and soon I felt for the first time as if I was part of a family, and not the runt of the litter, and that by our ruses and clever tricks I was taking some sort of revenge on Mother Church for all I had suffered at her hands.

From the edge of Dartmoor to the Somerset Levels, our ragtag band had gone from church to chapel, priory to abbey to marketplace, faking a cure here, a resurrection there, gaining renown and money along the way. People were so willing to believe. They wanted miracles to exist. And the clergy we approached were all too happy to play along. Miracles brought money in, in the form of offerings, but Canterbury had been piling up its gold in the thirteen years since Thomas à Becket's canonization, leaching away funds from all the other saints. We were rarely turned away when offering our authentications and testaments. This grand fraud here in Glastonbury was to be our swan song, after which we would disband and go our separate ways, once the abbey's bursar had divided up the spoils with us.

At least, that was the plan . . .

During the sermons, one of the fettered mad folk started to cry out like a squallyass and had to be removed next door, into the patched-up ruins of the nave. The prior, sensing he was losing his audience, declared: *"Miraculum magna videbis!"* "Now miracles will be seen!"

The relics were announced: from Saint Aidan and the Lindisfarne saints, Saint Indracht and Saint Beonna, Saint Patrick of Ireland . . . the list went on and on. We'd been told at dinner the previous night that before the canonization of Thomas à Becket, Glastonbury was the richest in relics, with twenty-two entire saints (well, almost entire—a half of Saint Aidan was claimed by the monks of Iona, and another bit was in Durham, but almost half of such a powerful saint was better than a whole minor martyr), and so its coffers used to overflow. But following the rise of the cult of Saint Thomas, and the great fire, Glastonbury's fortunes had been on the wane. And you could see how the congregation hung back, dissatisfied with the array of worn-down saints, waiting as the reliquaries were disposed about the chapel under the watchful eye of the warden. Pilgrims had been known to try to steal a souvenir here and there; one man got caught with a mouthful of Saint Beonna after bending to kiss the bones.

Finally, out came the ornamented box that our clever carpenters, Hammer and Saw, had made. Amazing that tin, shined up right, could look so much like silver.

The canons opened the reliquary so that the pilgrims could view the bones of Arthur's strong right arm. All round the Lady Chapel there was a great intake of breath. Rumours of the cures the hero-king had brought about, all the way from Cornwall to the Somerset moors, had been reaching them for weeks. At Newton St. Cyres a dead boy who had fallen down a well was restored to life. In Ottery St. Mary a pox-struck woman was instantly cured. In Chard a deaf man was suddenly granted the gift of angel-song. In Charlton Mackrell all manner of ailments had been cured by the drinking of water that was run over the bones. Agues and poxes, quinsy and falling sickness: all banished by the king's sword-arm.

And so here they were, the hopeless and helpless: those for whom doctors had achieved nothing but a miraculous lightening of the wallet; those who had tried remedies, from boiled snails to dog spit and everything in between; who'd been bled and leeched and covered in foul-smelling poultices; who'd prayed to all the saints for babies, for straight limbs, a stiff prick or a cure for baldness, all to no avail. Now it was down to King Arthur.

The pilgrims poured forward. Squabbles broke out. The Moor made a signal, and a twisted little man who had been pushing himself around on a wheeled trestle with hands shod in wooden pattens suddenly untwisted his distorted limbs, got up from his handcart on legs that now appeared sound and walked into the crowd. People touched him for luck, the next best thing to the holy bones being someone in whom the mana ran strong.

A man blind from birth, as he had sworn in the catalogue of penitents, stared about with an idiotic grin. "Ah, the colours! The colours hurt my eyes! Praise the Lord! Crimson and gold, azure and green. Are those trees that grow out of the pillars, or have the stones come to life before my new eyes?"

Don't overegg the pudding, Will, I thought.

A possessed man came to his senses and started to sing the *Te Deum*.

A leper peeled foul sores from his arm, revealing unmarked skin beneath.

All was going beautifully, the merchants and nobles pressing ever greater oblations upon the overwhelmed church officers. The money was pouring in. A commotion behind me caused me to turn, to find another erstwhile blind man crying out ecstatically, "I can see! I can see!" Then he ran into a pillar and fell down as if struck by a knacker's mallet.

The Moor caught Plaguey Mary by the arm. "He isn't one of ours, is he?"

She shook her head. "Some fool who's got carried away by it all."

The man was beginning to writhe, blood pouring from his split skull.

"For God's sake, create a distraction."

Wailing as if possessed, Mary whirled away, unlacing her bodice. "Save me, King Arthur! There is a demon inside me, curled up between my teats. Do you see him? Oh, he is black as night and wicked as Satan. Cast him out, I beg of you!"

Husbands stared as her opulent breasts sprang free; wives cuffed their husbands. No one paid any attention to the blind man, now groaning and clutching his head at the foot of the pillar.

Into the midst of this chaos, a man came running through the doors and shouted something. The Moor whispered urgently in my ear. I watched the red robes flicker like a Pentecostal flame and then he was gone. I tried to follow, but the press of folk was suddenly so tight around me that I couldn't move.

The justiciar's brother caught the messenger by the elbow and made him repeat his news. His great, red, slab-like face turned ashen. The messenger took a big breath, then cried out, "By God's grace and on the orders of Henry, *Rex Angliae, Dux Normaniae et Aquitainiae et Comes Andigaviae*, bear witness to my words. Jerusalem has fallen!"

I went cold all over. Good Christ, what timing.

The messenger strained to make himself heard. "Jerusalem the Golden, the City of Solomon, the Navel of the World, has fallen into the hands of the great devil Saladin and his pagan horde! Its people are slaughtered or scattered to the four winds. The Sanctuary is defiled and the True Cross has been captured by the Saracens. The flower of Christianity has been destroyed. All is lost!"

Around the Lady Chapel, faces became still. Mouths hung open, dark caves of despair. Some people crossed themselves and prayed. Then one woman wailed, "Jerusalem the Golden! Jerusalem the Golden!" as if she had lost a child. And that broke the spell.

The heart of Christendom had ceased to beat; it was at this very moment being desecrated by the heathen. And here were these Christians, helpless and continents away.

In such a world, who could believe in miracles?

The golden glow of hope was lost. What had seemed illuminated and transformed by the glory of the saints now showed itself a shoddy illusion. As if a veil had been dropped from her eyes, a woman stared at the leper—a small, dark man we knew as Saw, a twin to Hammer—and frowned. I knew the hideous sign of leprosy to be no more than a paste of coloured flour and water, dried to a repulsive crust. The woman leant in and with sudden boldness peeled the sore off his face, revealing a cheek that had never been afflicted with anything worse than pimples.

At the same time, someone else discovered the true blind man, blood running in runnels down his face; another rounded on Red

Will and accused him of never having been blind at all—whoever heard of a man blind from birth knowing the difference between colours and the names of each one?

In rising panic, I tried to blend into the background, just one appalled monk among the rest. Little Ned's trolley was found to have a hidden compartment for his not-so-shrivelled legs, and inside it, a string of pearls he had slipped off some fat neck. One of the merchants' wives began to scream, "My jewels, my jewels!" and suddenly Jerusalem the Golden was forgotten as people patted their necks and their belt-pouches and realized they lacked much of what they'd come in with—not pains and ills, or even sins, but purses, rings and necklaces . . .

Shit. Now our heads are in the noose.

"Run!" I screamed at Quickfinger and Hammer, and they made a dash for the door. I swam through the crowd after them, shoving people out of my path. Angry churchgoers pursued the members of the troupe. Quickfinger went sprawling, bringing Hammer crashing down on top of him, spilling booty. Ranulf de Glanvill shouted, "Close the doors!" Just before I could reach them, the great wooden doors banged shut, and suddenly the justiciar's brother was standing in my way. I cannoned into him. It was like running into a wall.

"Running a ring of thieves, are you?" He grasped the collar of my robe and hauled me upright. "Who the hell are you?"

Who was I? Just a wild boy, a savage, dressed up as a monk. My silence was construed as defiance. De Glanvill hit me, the great ring on his finger mashing my nose. I felt something in it burst; blood cascaded down the front of my white robe.

"What's your name, you bastard?" he repeated, shaking me as if I were a rat.

I started to laugh, out of terror. "I—I, ah . . ."

A muscle twitched in my cheek. The scent of roses bloomed in my head. Powerful and pungent and hot as summer, the scent scalded my nose. My knees gave way, leaving me hanging from his fist, my legs beginning to jig. I saw the look of disgust on his face, and then the gates in my head opened into a sky of gold, revealing pillars and arches that soared higher by far than those in the Lady Chapel, and I was lost.

3

City of Akka

❋

"Equal sizes, Zohra!" Nima Najib peered over her daughter's shoulder as she failed yet again to make the *ma'amul*— a delicate pastry filled with a mixture of chopped dates, pistachios and walnuts, orange blossom water and spices—to her exacting standards. "Look, this one's twice the size of the others. Don't be so slapdash!"

Zohra's cousins loved tasks like this—precise, repetitive— but she lacked patience. "I'm trying, Ummi, I really am." What did it matter if the pastries weren't all alike? They tasted the same in the end.

They had been preparing food all morning to celebrate the reuniting of the Najib family. The occupation was over; Akka was liberated, and Jerusalem recaptured from the infidel. It was the first family gathering in long years. Zohra's father, Baltasar, had been down to the livestock market on his way back from the mosque and bought a fine black ram and three chickens. Indulgent towards his simple eldest son, Baltasar had allowed Sorgan to lead the ram while he and the twins—Aisa and Kamal—had each carried a flapping chicken. When they returned, Sorgan had been sent to feed the pigeons on the roof terrace to keep him occupied while the butchery was carried out in the courtyard. Sorgan had a soft heart, and no one wanted to explain to him the connection between the blood on the tiles, the missing animals and the meat on his plate.

While Sorgan stroked the soft feathers on his favourite birds, Baltasar had shown the twins how to cut the ram's meat from the bone. They were twelve years old—five years younger than Zohra. Kamal, who had a tendency to act like a small child, got smacked for running around with the horns on his head and getting blood all over his clean tunic; and then Aisa tried to stop Kamal from retaliating and caught a blow in the face, which resulted in more blood and washing.

As the only girl, it had fallen to Zohra to get her brothers into clean clothes, a task she undertook with gritted teeth and the necessary degree of no-nonsense brutality. Then she had returned to help her mother in the kitchen. They had been working for five solid hours now: washing the mutton, rubbing it with freshly ground cardamom and cinnamon, loading it into the biggest pan and setting it to poach over the fire. They had sliced a dozen onions, plucked and jointed the three chickens, rubbed saffron into the meat and set it aside to marinate in lemon juice and garlic while getting the rest of the feast underway. While Nima griddled aubergines until their skins burned and filled the kitchen with smoke, Zohra had made the bread dough and left it to prove, then gathered armfuls of herbs from the courtyard garden. They'd mashed the aubergine flesh with garlic and lemon juice and sesame paste and chopped the herbs and cucumbers and radishes for the salad. Only then had they turned their attentions to the fiddly, infuriating pastries.

"Oh my," Nima said suddenly. Her cheeks were flushed; sweat beaded on her forehead. She ran a hand through her hair. *Were those grey streaks there yesterday?* Zohra wondered. *Well, of course they were. No one goes grey overnight.*

"Take a rest, Ummi. Go, sit in the shade in the courtyard, out of all this heat."

"No time for that. We must finish these and then get the *qidreh* on." Nima wiped her forehead, then carried on cutting and filling and crimping like a woman possessed.

Zohra felt powerless. There had been nothing she could do to dissuade her mother from hosting the feast. Nima had been insistent, partly because she wanted to impress her sisters-by-law. Their husbands were well-to-do importers, whereas Zohra's father was an invalided veteran, and they had to scrape by on whatever Malek sent home from his wages as a soldier in Salah ad-Din's army. But really, who cared what the aunts and cousins thought of them? Zohra didn't.

She found her thoughts drifting to the man she'd met at the perfume stall. Nathanael, the doctor's son. What a strange-looking creature he was. All that curly black hair and that bold, bold look in his eyes. And the way he had laid a kiss on her palm! No one had ever touched her like that. A Muslim girl was sacrosanct: to be touched by any man was *haram*, forbidden. And yet the doctor's son had behaved as if it were entirely normal, and no shame at all. He was a mystery, a fascinating, disturbing mystery . . .

"Zohra, wake up! It's as if you've been in a dream all morning. And, oh! Look at the mess you've made of those. Well, it can't be helped now. Quickly, take them down to the oven, and don't forget the dough."

Zohra loaded up a tray, made their symbol in the dough and, with it held precariously on her head, ran to the communal oven down the road to leave the *ma'amul* and flatbreads to bake, only to find that the oven was full: everyone was celebrating. The next oven had a queue that stretched around the corner, and so she ran down the hill to a third bakery she located only by the spiral of woodsmoke that rose from its fire.

"Leave those with me," an old woman said, taking hold of the tray. Zohra recognized her with despair as the Widow Eptisam, an incorrigible gossip. She had an eager, rabbity face with protruding teeth, and eyes that constantly darted from one thing to another. "I'll put them in as soon as my own come out, it would be my pleasure, *binti*."

"No, it's fine. I'll wait." Zohra didn't want to be beholden to her. But the widow had a firm hold on the tray, so in the end, rather than have to stay there and be talked at for half an hour, she left the pastries and dough with the old woman and turned for home.

As she passed a junction of alleys an idea nagged at her: if she followed one of them down the hill she would come to the Street of Tailors, where the doctor's son, Nathanael, lived. The idea of his proximity made Zohra flush.

All this time—the best part of three months since she had encountered him in the bazaar—she had toyed daily with the possibility of following his impudent instruction to come to his house, and daily, she had retreated from imagining what might happen if she did.

Zohra had been brought up to believe that a good angel sat on one of her shoulders and a bad angel on the other, and that every decision involved a struggle between the two. So far her good angel had prevailed—during daylight hours, at least—but she could feel the pull of the bad angel now. Or perhaps it was the djinns with which Nathanael had threatened her.

When Salah ad-Din's army had reclaimed Akka there had been chaos for a while, and she had barely dared to set foot outside. But it had not stopped her thinking about Nathanael bin Yacub before she went to sleep each night, and in her dreams. Wicked thoughts, wanton thoughts. Thoughts that shamed her in the light of morning. She prayed for the strength to stop thinking about him, but it seemed that Allah had his mind on more important matters than one girl's perverse infatuation.

She gazed in the direction of the Street of Tailors. You couldn't see the top of the street from where she stood, just a confluence of roads where half the houses lay empty, while others were in the process of being rehabilitated. Salah ad-Din, generous to a fault, had offered safe passage to any Christians who wished to leave Akka and make a life elsewhere—and not just safe passage, but also a purse of gold so they might re-establish themselves outside the caliphate. There had been rich ransoms acquired when Jerusalem fell, many gold treasures appropriated and melted down for coinage. Still, it was hard to imagine any other conqueror being so magnanimous in victory. And so, many Franj had taken up the offer and abandoned their homes, leaving whole neighbourhoods half-empty. Merchants and traders, or functionaries like her cousins Rachid and Tariq, had swooped on the vacated houses like locusts on a cornfield and were now all puffed up with self-importance, as if grabbing what they could made them better than those who stayed where they were. It was one of the reasons Zohra was not looking forward to the family gathering: the women would spend all their time discussing the bargains they had made in the market over this carpet or that set of copperware for their new quarters. They were so boring, Zohra could happily have seen them all carried off, kicking and screaming, in the back of the Franj carts.

The thought of the trials to come fed her bad angel the strength it needed to sway her decision, and suddenly her feet were carrying her down past the little street market, past the spice trader, and the old man who sold chickpeas and flour and rice, and the one who gave you a bunch of fresh herbs for nothing if he liked the look of you, past the tea shop where old men sat outside all day long, nursing their glasses while their conversations—like their tea—turned increasingly bitter. It irked Zohra that men could sit around while women's chores stretched to infinity. They had so much more freedom. Aisa and Kamal didn't have to clean the house or help with the laundry. They weren't expected to prepare meals or even to fetch the shopping, and they were praised for their smallest efforts, like spoiled princes. As for Sorgan, all he did was eat whatever she and her mother cooked, sleep, then demand more food. *Still*, a little voice inside her reasoned, *if you were a boy from a military family, you'd have been sent off to war like Malek, expected to kill or be killed*. There wasn't even one small part of Zohra that hankered after that.

She turned the corner and there it was: the Street of Tailors, though there had been no tailors here for years. All the houses were residential, most occupied by Jewish families, and for that reason alone Zohra had never walked down here before. But it did not appear forbidding—quite the opposite. Pretty wrought-iron balconies jutted from the walls in a way you would never see in the Muslim quarters of the city, where the women preferred to keep their gaze turned inward to the courtyards. Bright flowers cascaded from these balconies: bougainvillea and hibiscus. Pungent geraniums splashed red as blood against the sunlit walls. A tortoiseshell cat lazed in the shade between doorways, yawning widely as Zohra passed.

The door with the hand on it.

Her recollection was a bit hazy, apart from the feel of his lips, hot against her palm. Even now, remembering, her knees felt shaky.

She came to a halt. A blue door, paint flaking in the sun. She walked on. A studded wooden door. On the other side, a recessed door painted a dark red, its knocker in the form of a lion's head. The end of the street was in sight now. Had he given her the wrong address on purpose? He had seemed so sure of himself. Perhaps he accosted girls all the time. She almost turned around, feeling like an idiot, hoping no one had seen her. But she had come this far. *I'll just walk to the end*, she told herself. *Then I'll go back and wait for the bread and pastries to come out of the oven.* It was almost a comfort to know there was something so ordinary to follow this absurd excursion.

The last house had looked abandoned; someone had nailed a piece of wood across the door. She hardly dared look beyond it. Her heart began to beat faster. If it looked like the right door, would she dare to knock? And if someone opened it, what would she say? She walked on, in a sort of dream. A tall, narrow window with a curved, decorative iron grille overtopped a large studded door, and in the middle of it was a brass knocker in the shape of a hand, fingers hanging down, like a *hamsa*, the Muslim good-luck charm they often called the Hand of Fatima, to commemorate the Prophet's daughter. That couldn't be right. Even so, she reached towards the knocker. But before she could lay a hand on it, the door swung outward and a woman came out. She had a handsome figure and a mass of springy black hair tied back in a spangled red kerchief, revealing long, silver earrings. Dark, almond-shaped eyes fixed themselves upon Zohra, who gave a little yelp of surprise.

Now she wished desperately she could be anywhere else in the world. So he was married. Nathanael was married, and playing a game with her. And suddenly she realized to whom he must have given the other two of the four pieces of amber-musk he had bought at the perfume-seller's stall. What a fool she was.

The woman stepped out into the sunshine. "Hello," she said. "Were you looking for the doctor?"

When the light struck the woman, Zohra saw at once that she was older than she had at first seemed, maybe the same age as Nima, for although there was no discernible grey in her hair, on her pale skin was a wealth of tiny lines, lines that told of decades of laughter and worries.

She shook her head. "I was looking for Nathanael." It was done, and her fate was sealed. She waited, rooted by leaden legs, for destiny to unfurl itself.

The woman smiled, a wide, frank smile, her eyes merry crescents. "Ah, I see. But my dear, you are too late. You should have come before."

Zohra felt a chill. What did she mean? Was he dead? Surely not. She seemed so cheerful.

"You must be the girl Nat met in the marketplace, on the day the news of Hattin reached the city."

Zohra nodded dumbly.

"We expected you weeks ago."

"I . . . I couldn't come." What was she supposed to say? She wasn't sure whether to be flattered or dismayed that Nathanael had talked about her to this woman.

"Come in, out of the sun. It's too hot to be standing in the street."

Zohra followed her into the cool shade of the house. It smelled different to her own home, not of cooking and boys, but of sharp, acidic, medicinal scents that stung the nostrils, and of something pungent and waxy. Out of the harsh sun, it took a while for her eyes to adjust. She took in carved wooden chairs, colourful wall-hangings, a tatted striped rug, a huge jug of flowers. Tasselled cushions lay here and there; candles in ornate silver holders were clustered on a low table; piles of books and scrolls were scattered as if they were simple debris rather than rare and precious objects. This home was like a palace—a small but perfect palace.

"What is your name, child?"

"Zohra."

"I am Sara, Nathanael's mother. Zohra and Sara—the same names in different languages. Isn't that lovely?"

The woman took Zohra's hands between her own. Zohra felt the calluses on them: working hands, big and practical, warmth flowing from them. Suddenly, she felt quite at ease, not a Muslim girl intruding into a Jewish house but a welcome visitor.

"How old are you, my dear?"

"Seventeen," Zohra said. Then, "Is Nathanael here?" she asked.

Sara shook her head. "I'm so sorry, no, he's not. Sit down. I'll bring some tea—or would you prefer something cold? Some pressed lemon, or some watered wine?"

"A little watered wine would be lovely." This woman seemed so sophisticated, she did not want to seem gauche by refusing.

By the time Sara returned, Zohra was already regretting her choice. She took the glass with trembling fingers and touched her lips to it. The wine tasted both bitter and sweet, but not unpleasant. She swallowed and felt it slide coolly down her throat, leaving a burning tingle behind. Wine was like nothing she had ever tasted before. She was reminded that in the *Thousand and One Nights* bad women drank wine often, and then came to grief.

"Nathanael is in Jerusalem," Sara said. "He left yesterday."

Zohra's tongue stuck to the roof of her mouth. She could think of nothing to say, the disappointment was so keen. Jerusalem was a week's journey away. She took another huge gulp of the wine and almost choked. "When will he come back?" she managed at last.

"He's gone to study at the institute. Medicine, like his father. I expect he'll be back for visits." Sara smiled.

They sat quietly for a while, Zohra trying not to cry, drinking her way steadily to the dregs of her glass because she didn't know what else to say or do. Then she got to her feet and handed the empty vessel back. "I must get home."

"Come back any time," Sara said. "Now you know where we are. I'm sure Yacub would be delighted to see you again."

Zohra promised that she would visit, though her voice sounded faint and distant even to herself. At the front door, she touched the *hamsa*.

"Why do you have a Hand of Fatima?" she found herself asking. "I mean, I thought only Muslims had them . . ." She wanted to bite her tongue off for saying something so clumsy. It must have been the wine.

"We call it a Hand of Miriam," Sara said. "And if you look you'll find them on the doors of old Christian houses, too. They'd call it a Hand of Mary. You see, we're none of us so different, are we? Do come back and see us, Zohra. You're always welcome."

Zohra ran nearly all the way home, reaching the corner where the Armenian sisters spent the day on their doorstep, their sharp eyes on the lookout for anything they might trade as gossip, before realizing she had forgotten to collect the bread and pastries and had to run back down to the third bakery and endure the scolding of the Widow Eptisam.

The house was in chaos by the time she returned, for her cousins had all arrived early and were milling about the kitchen. Nima was flustered, having been caught in her work clothes with her hair askew and smears of oil and flour on her face, while both her sisters-by-law wore immaculate robes glittering with embroidery fresh from the best seamstresses in Damascus, heavy gold earrings and alarming quantities of kohl, as if they were attending a wedding rather than a family meal. Zohra held out the tray of baked flatbreads and pastries, but Nima pushed it back at her, eyes flashing. "My daughter will entertain you while I change!" she said sharply, then lowered her voice so that Zohra alone could hear. "Make them tea and settle them in the guest salon, and don't waste another second."

Zohra sighed and accepted her punishment. "Aunt Mina, Aunt Asha, Cousins Khalida and Jamilla, come and sit in the cool, and I will bring you mint tea."

Khalida and the aunts let themselves be bustled out of the kitchen—they did not want to spoil their expensive silks—but Jamilla hung back, and turned burning eyes upon Zohra.

"Have you heard from him?"

Zohra felt her heart stop. How could she know about Nathanael? "What?"

"Have you heard from our burning coal?"

The Burning Coals of Islam. After the Battle of Hattin, Malek's heroism had been recognized: Zohra's brother was now a burning coal, a member of Salah ad-Din's personal guard.

She shook her head. "No, we've not heard from Malek in a while. There was a messenger last month." The messenger came every month with a pouch of coins; the last one had come all the way from Jerusalem. It was all that kept the jackals from their door. "He was fine then. The messenger didn't mention him taking any wound." In fact, he hadn't mentioned anything at all; the money had arrived without a note.

Even the thought of Malek had a physical effect on Jamilla. She caught her breath, her eyelids fluttered, colour caught in her pale cheeks. It was such a shame about her arm, Zohra thought. She would have been almost pretty if it hadn't been for the withered limb that hung flaccidly at her side. You could hardly tell under the stiffened silk of her sleeve, but when they were children her brothers had teased her mercilessly, calling it her "witch arm" and pretending to be terrified lest it touch them. And yet Jamilla had always idolized Malek, making excuses for his cruelty or thoughtlessness: *he can't help it, he's a boy; he can't show his real feelings, it's unmanly . . .*

"I wish he were coming." Jamilla looked down, smoothed the silk at her slim waist with her good hand. "I put on my best robe."

Zohra felt a flood of sympathy. "He would compliment you were he here, I'm sure. Here, help me with the tea."

They made mint tea and carried it through to the guest salon. Zohra poured it from a great height towards the little decorated glasses—but the wine, or the feelings her visit to a forbidden house had stirred up, made her hand unsteady. Tea splashed everywhere, making the aunts exclaim and shield their skirts. She served them in order of seniority. Aunt Mina. Aunt Asha. Jamilla's elder sister, Khalida. Jamilla. A glass for Nima. One for herself. Then she fled away to splash cold water on her face and try to calm down. She changed into her good kaftan—the sky-blue silk with the silver trim—put her hair up under a white scarf and went to the kitchen to dust the pastries with sugar and powdered cinnamon. She was trying so hard to make them as pretty as Ummi did that when a pair of hands encircled her waist and an unmistakably male body pushed itself against her she bit her tongue, which always protruded when she concentrated. Before she had a chance to scream or fight free, a pair of hands travelled to her breasts and squeezed hard. Just like that—as if testing fruit at the souq.

She turned, ready for a fight, thinking it was Kamal or his horrible friend Bashar. But instead she found her cousin Tariq grinning at her defiantly. The wine rose to her head once more. In a fury she flung herself at him, hitting him hard on the chest, leaving fist-shaped marks in powdered sugar on his smart damson robe.

Tariq laughed and caught her wrists. "You'll need to get used to it, cousin. When we're wed I can do to you whatever I want. And I shall want to do a great deal. I like a girl with a bit of fight in her." His eyes travelled over her lasciviously. Then, with her wrists imprisoned in one of his big hands, he ran the other down over her abdomen to her crotch, jamming his fingers hard between her legs.

Zohra wanted to cry out, but it would shame her family. She backed away till the worktop dug into her spine, and clamped her thighs shut on his invading hand, but still he kept pushing at her, his tongue between his thick lips, his black, expressionless eyes watching her.

"Get away from me, you filthy pig!" she hissed. "You are disgusting. Disgusting!" She squirmed and fought until sweat trickled down her ribs. Had he smelled the wine on her? Was that what made him think he could treat her like a whore?

"Zohra?"

Tariq's hold on her relaxed and she sprang away from him, and there was Sorgan, her big, simple brother, framed by the doorway, half stooped beneath the lintel, his face creased in consternation. He looked from his sister to Cousin Tariq, whom he disliked, and his face darkened.

Zohra stepped to his side. "Sorgan, perfect timing!" She squeezed his arm. "You can help me carry the food through."

Sorgan's gaze swept the pastries, the piled flatbreads, the dishes of olives and hummus, the spicy salads and *baba ghanoush*, and puzzlement dissolved to a slow grin. He held his hands out for the tray.

"Take it to the big salon," Zohra told him, "and ask Baba and Cousin Rachid and the uncles to take their seats." As Sorgan's enormous fingers closed over the sides of the tray, she added, "Cousin Tariq is coming with you to make sure you don't eat anything before you get there."

Sorgan's gaze travelled up to her, hurt. Then he said, "Your dress is dirty."

Zohra looked down. Tariq's hands had left sweaty imprints, unmistakable—on her breasts, at her crotch. Sweat stains were impossible to get out of silk, and her family could not afford to replace the kaftan. She glared at Tariq with loathing. "Even if you were the last man in Akka, I would never marry you."

"As if you will have any say in the matter, stupid girl." Then he pushed past her, knocking her shoulder dismissively.

She watched him stride down the corridor, a man complacent about his own position in the world, confident in his future. She thought of Nathanael, a hundred miles away in Jerusalem, gone without a word. And then she looked around the little kitchen, at all the luxuries and care brought together for this family gathering—at the chicken steeped in expensive saffron, at the towering steamer full of *qidreh*, all evidence of her mother's determination to impress her husband's family. She thought of Jamilla's trembling adoration for her brother, of oblivious Malek, caught up in a war waged by men, and felt as if she had stumbled upon a deep and terrible truth.

That when it came to the world of men—with their weapons of iron and their quest for knowledge and power and gold and plea-sure—the feelings of a woman weighed as light as feathers.

4

John Savage, cell in Bath Gaol

❄

NOVEMBER 1187

I woke to find myself in prison, my head throbbing from the after-effects of my falling fit and de Glanvill's brutality.

Where the rest of the troupe was, I had no idea: Quickfinger, Little Ned, Hammer and Saw, Red Will, Plaguey Mary. Thinking of them made me miss them all keenly. It had all been going so well, but now it looked as if we would all hang. I sat there, tears pricking my eyes, trying not to cry.

"John?"

For a moment I thought I was dreaming, but when I looked up there was the Moor, alive, outside the bars of my cell! Shooting to my feet, I reached through and we clasped hands. I could feel the whole of my heart in my eyes. Then I remembered where we were.

"For God's sake, they'll hang you, too!"

The Moor laughed silently, his half-moon eyes merry with some unspoken secret. "Don't worry about me. I am invisible." He touched my face, suddenly solemn. His fingers were flames on my skin. "Your poor nose, *habibi*," he said softly. "I am sorry, John. I tried to warn you to come away sooner."

"I couldn't hear you." It was half true.

He pushed through the bars a flat loaf and a piece of hard yellow cheese.

"Is this the condemned man's last meal?" It was all too good to be true: the Moor, here, free, his hands full of gifts. Between bites I said, "Listen, here's what I've been thinking—" I swallowed, coughed as the morsels went down the wrong way, and finally continued. "See here?" I pointed an inch or so above my Adam's apple. "Give the hangman his price and tell him to place the knot just there. If he does it right it'll choke me, but it shouldn't kill me, not right away, won't break the neck. Saw it happen to a man hanged in Market Jew: they cut him down after half an hour, more dead than alive, wry-necked as a half-strangled chicken and making a wretched noise, but even so, he was alive. They had to give him a royal pardon. That's what they do here, see, if you survive a hanging." I was gabbling with bravado, but I couldn't stop. "Just make sure the hangman knows what he's doing, and give him only a bit of the money up front. Show him the rest, right? To encourage him. If you're still my friend you'll do this one thing for me. You are still my friend, aren't you?"

There was a long silence. Then he began to laugh, a rich sound that filled the cell and the corridor beyond, until I was sure the guards would come running. "Ah, *habibi*," he said. "I love you as a brother. More than a brother. But sometimes I think you are quite mad."

I found myself laughing, too. The Moor had this power, a sort of glamour that touched everything. He radiated confidence and grace. It was the utter sincerity in that dark, solemn face that made him such a fine liar—the sort of liar you loved even as he beguiled you.

Now he said, "Do you want to save your own life, John Savage?"

Was the question a trick? I nodded.

The Moor's grin widened. "I have a proposition for you."

I had the feeling this might be worse than a hanging.

In the dead of night I was removed from my cell, transported across town in a covered wagon and led into a luxurious room where three men waited.

There were tapestries on every wall, brass sconces, rich carpets, many books—it was a veritable palace. I turned to one of the three men: it was the Moor, dressed head to toe in scarlet. Gave him a sarcastic nod. "Cardinal." Then, to the man sitting at the table, "Bishop." Reginald de Bohun, purple robes and sheep's-wool hair. We had met before.

The man standing by the fire had stout shoulders and a fleshy face. The red veins of his nose spoke of too much good wine (and indeed a large goblet was in his hand), but the mouth was full and loose and generous, made for smiling rather than scowling. He was not smiling now. He regarded me with an intent interest that made me uncomfortable.

"My cousin, Savaric de Bohun, sometimes called Fitzgoldwin," the bishop said briskly. He motioned for me to take a seat: a wooden stool. "This gentleman tells me you are prepared to participate in our plan."

I stared, incredulous, at the Moor, who looked back blandly.

Savaric took a swig of wine. "So, John Savage, time to throw the dice." His cousin tutted, but Savaric took no notice. "I apologize for the secrecy, but for now it's necessary. Let me get straight to the nub of the matter. Jerusalem has fallen to the heathen horde. War will be declared upon the Saracen. The heads of state across the Holy Roman Empire must act to recover what is lost. Already Prince Richard has taken the cross, and others will follow him: an army will be assembled to go to war in the Holy Land. But this is no easy thing, nor cheap, either. Soldiers must be enlisted and trained; funds must be raised. Many men; lots of funds. War is a costly business.

"Your . . . exploits between Cornwall and Glastonbury interest me."

I could feel the Moor watching me, as enigmatic as a cat.

"That sort of artistry and invention is just what we need in a new venture I have in mind. Between us, we can save Jerusalem and our own souls." Savaric strode forward. "We need you to create the spectacle to end all spectacles, and take it on the road." As he said this he thumped his goblet on the table and flung his arms wide so that the gold chain he wore bounced, the vast ruby hanging from it flashing in the candlelight.

"What manner of spectacle?" I asked. "And to what end, exactly?"

"*Negotium crucis*, the business of the cross," the bishop said. "Like Pope Urban's tour in the last century. A fundraising drive for the holy cause." His voice dropped. "I do not greatly approve of the means, but the end is undeniably just."

Savaric's eyes shone. "We will carry the relics of the great King Arthur before us, symbolic of the struggle between the goodness of Christendom and the wicked heathen. With your help, word will spread. We will set up a stage in every major town. My cousin and I will preach and conduct mass. You and your players will demonstrate with action what the common folk cannot comprehend in words. We shall be trumpeted by angels, hymned by choirs, welcomed by all, and we shall leave laden with funds for the king's war effort and the parole of thousands to take the cross." With his hands planted on the table, he added, in a false-whisper, "And, of course, where crowds gather, there is always the potential for . . . shall we say . . . a little extra trade?"

I couldn't quite believe what I was hearing. "Thievery?" The bishop, at least, had the grace to look shame-faced, though maybe that was just a trick of the candlelight.

"A little light-fingered byplay wouldn't be frowned on. You and your troupe will, in addition, be paid a generous stipend for your work."

The Moor detached himself from the wall. "Actually, I was thinking more along the lines of a share of the takings." He grinned, wolfish. "A fraction, agreed between us." He smoothed out a sheet of vellum on the table, picked up a quill, rattled it in the inkpot on the desk and sketched a swift mathematical working. "If x represents the total sum of money taken on the day in offerings, donations, tithing . . . and other means, and y is the expense incurred in laying on the show—the cost of travel, servants, accommodation, repast, materials, and other sundries . . ."

As they haggled, my mind drifted. This morning I had been calculating my chances of surviving a hanging; now I was being offered a part in an ecclesiastical fraud inspired by the very fakery for which I'd been arrested. It was hard to get my head around.

"Stop!" I said abruptly, and the room fell silent. "I haven't yet said I'll do it."

They all stared at me. A walking dead man throwing away his only chance of survival?

"This venture. It's big, complicated, expensive . . . and dangerous. Why would you entrust such a thing to people like us?"

Bishop Reginald leaned forward. "We need your expertise—"

"The expertise of liars and thieves?" I laughed. "I'd have thought you had plenty of that on tap. What is religion, when all is said and done, but smoke and tricks?"

The bishop looked uncomfortable. "What we do, we do for the greater good of the Church."

"So you would connive with one of the very Saracens against whom you would take up arms?"

The Moor raised an eyebrow, then said, "I've been called many things in my time: Arab, Berber or 'barbari,' as the Romans termed it, and now, incorrectly, a Saracen. I am just a man, John, like any other. This is a good offer. Our paths run parallel for a time at least. We lose nothing by doing this, and could gain much."

I made a show of mulling it over, but really, what choice did I have? "All right, then," I said. "I'll be a part of your mumming-show."

The bones of the accord were agreed to; I left the details to the Moor and applied myself to the roast chicken that was brought to me from the kitchens. Then I pulled my stool up to the fire, took off my boots, wriggled my toes and allowed a little bliss to steal over me.

I must have dozed, for suddenly there was a hand on my shoulder and someone was saying, "Come along, John. Time to go back now."

Groggy with sleep and wine, I groaned. "Back?"

"To your cell, as if you had never been away."

"I'm not going back—"

"*Habibi*, it's necessary."

The bishop smiled, but it did not reach his eyes. "I'm very much afraid, Master Savage, that you will still have to undergo the trial." As I began to shout, he held his hand up. "Geoffrey de Glanvill and his brother are pressing for a death sentence for the entire troupe. We cannot be seen to associate our enterprise with felons. You must prove your innocence."

I looked to the Moor, but he wore his most inscrutable expression. "It's true, John. You must go back and face a trial. Declare yourself the headman of the group and say that you stand for all of them, guilty or innocent."

Savaric's face glowed in the mutable light of the candles. "Trial by ordeal. You'll cite your right to claim it under the 1166 Assize of Clarendon, which states that anyone on the oath of the jury accused or notoriously suspected of robbery, theft or receiving may be put to the ordeal. Then you'll undertake their test and walk away a free man, as will the rest of your troupe. An innocent man, whose fame precedes him. The best possible example to both believers and unbelievers. We have it all worked out, don't we?"

The Moor turned his shining half-moon eyes upon me. "Trust me, *habibi*. I have a plan."

5

JANUARY 1188

On the day after Twelfth Night I found myself on trial at the Bath Assizes.

The witnesses shuffled past, a good-sized crowd, so keen to see me hang that many had travelled all the way from Glastonbury: burghers and millers, butchers and pardoners; a merchant in Flemish red and his wife, with a pearl necklace making deep, round indentations in her fat white neck; the blind man, with another guiding him—the wound on his forehead had almost healed, though the bruise still showed yellow.

The business of the court was tedious and the judge's clerk had a droning voice that stopped me from paying attention to his words. At last it was my turn to speak.

"I am an innocent man!" I lied. "And I claim my right to trial by . . ." trying to recall the exact words, "ordeal. I cite my right to trial by ordeal under the 1166 Assize of Clarendon."

At once there was furious muttering. Geoffrey de Glanvill thumped the table, and the ring that broke my nose winked in the light. "Outrageous!" he roared. "How dare you try to escape your just punishment by such lawyer's tricks! You are a thief, a liar and a heathen, and I shall see you swing!"

The assize judge, having conferred with his clerk and the sheriff, leaned across to whisper into de Glanvill's ear and there followed a furious exchange of whispers. Then de Glanvill sat back.

"John Savage," the judge announced, "you are entitled to trial by ordeal in answer to the charges laid against you." He looked at de Glanville. "The baron has requested that the test be the ordeal of oil."

Oil? My stomach turned over. Boiling oil burns down to the bone. I had heard of murderers made to stand on burning coals until their feet were blackened ruins. The Moor had once told of an ordeal practised by the desert peoples: "A ladle is heated in the fire and then laid upon the tongue of the accused. If the man is lying, the tongue will shrivel and he will not lie again. The Bedu call this rite 'the true light of God.'"

"Christ on an ass!" I had blasphemed. "That's barbaric."

The judge was speaking again. ". . . However, the assize decrees that the ordeal for the crimes of which you are accused should be the ordeal by water."

Water was surely better than oil, wasn't it? What was the Moor's plan? Terror flooded in again. My knees buckled and I had to be caught by the guard. I hardly registered the moment when the officials returned with the pitcher of boiling water, but suddenly there was a lot of steam in the air, and I thought, *It's January and very cold—maybe with every moment that passes the water will cool and be less likely to do me damage.* Then another man pushed through the crowd and set a brazier full of glowing red coals beneath the pitcher.

The mechanics of the trial were explained to the audience. The correct temperature of the water would be tested by lowering an egg into the liquid: if the egg cooked, then the defendant's right arm would be plunged into the vessel and held there for the duration of the Lord's Prayer. If his arm scalded—*my arm!* a voice in

my head cried—and the flesh sloughed away from the bone—
my flesh, my bone!—then he was clearly guilty in the eyes of the
Almighty and he would have his right foot severed and be hanged
forthwith. But if at the end of the prayer the prisoner revealed to the
world an unscathed limb, then not only would all charges against
him be dropped, but any sin he might have committed in his time
on this earth would be forgiven.

How I wished I had stayed on the Mount and taken my beatings
like a dutiful oblate.

The egg was dropped into the pitcher. Time passed. It felt like
years. I began to think about how much I liked my right arm. It
had fed me and defended me. Given me enough pleasure to damn
me for lustfulness. It had swept the refectory and drawn a hundred
likenesses and wiped my arse. It had been very useful, my arm. I
was quite attached to it.

A bead of sweat ran down my back, the Devil's finger tracing
down my spine.

The egg came out. Its shell was cracked. The white was boiled
hard.

"John Savage," the judge intoned, "you are accused of running
a criminal gang, of larceny and deception. Do you maintain your
claim of innocence of these charges and do you stand for . . ."
He looked at the parchment the clerk handed him, read out the
names of the troupe one by one: William of Worcester, Michael
and Saul Dyer, Edward Little, Enoch Pilchard, Mary White. My
befuddled brain had trouble making sense of the proper names of
the members of our troupe. My mouth was so dry I could not find
the words. I nodded.

"And will you now prove your word with your deeds, in the
view of God Almighty and all people here gathered, and undertake
this ordeal?"

My arm was going to be boiled off. And where was the Moor?

I remembered the way he had turned his half-moon eyes upon me, told me to trust him. Did I trust him? He was possibly a murderer, most certainly a trickster. But those eyes, and the way he had touched my face so tenderly through the bars of my cell . . .

I swallowed, aware of Geoffrey de Glanvill's burning, hate-filled gaze.

"I will."

One of the guards grinned in my face, his teeth yellow as a rat's, then took rough hold of my right arm and rolled the sleeve up to the shoulder. I'd never felt so naked. As I approached the table, the heat from the brazier crisped the hairs in my nose. The air hung still as the spectators anticipated pain and damnation.

"Our Father, who art in Heaven . . ." the officers dutifully chanted, so slowly that each syllable crawled into the next.

Trying to blank out the panicking creature that chattered in my head, imploring me to push through the crowd and run like a rabbit, I closed my eyes. *May I see the Moor in Hell if he fails me . . .* And I plunged my right arm into the pitcher of boiling water.

Shock engulfed me. I could not tell what I felt. The sensation was so brutal it transcended the definition of "hot."

"Thy kingdom come . . ."

A foul odour bloomed in the courtroom—pungent, sulphurous—and a man in the audience made a joke about it smelling like his wife's cooking. "I ain't taking a bowl of soup at your house again!" his neighbour quipped. People laughed.

I bit down on a scream. In my mind I saw my limb withdrawn into the light, revealing a vile mutilation, the flesh scarlet and melting . . .

"And forgive us our trespasses . . ."

My poor arm. What would I do without it? Then I remembered that it wouldn't matter. If I failed the ordeal I'd not be needing the arm anyway, because I'd be getting hanged forthwith.

"For ever and ever . . .

"Amen."

"Remove your arm from the pitcher."

The voice of the judge broke into my cruel reverie, but I was so lost in my horrid imaginings that I simply stared at him.

"The ordeal is over!"

Slowly, I took my arm out of the pitcher. Little curls of vapour twisted up from the surface, spiralled lazily to the ceiling. The crowd gasped. The arm was pink—not a savage, raw red, but the pink of skin gently warmed in a salving liquid, the pink I saw the one and only time I ever willingly took a bath at St. Michael's Priory—glowing, healthy, unmarked pink. In fact, I thought, my arm looked better than when it went in. Cleaner, certainly.

Geoffrey de Glanvill stood for a better look. "God's eyes, this is some trickery!" he growled.

The judge reprimanded him for his blasphemy, then turned his attention to me. "John Savage, you have undergone the trial by ordeal of water and God has judged you and yours innocent of all charges. Your associates will be released. You are free to go."

I was carried from the courthouse on the shoulders of the crowd, who, in their fickle, superstitious manner, had decided that I was to be treated like a living relic, the beneficiary of God's miraculous intervention. I was touched for good luck, bought ale—horrible, thick, porridgey stuff they had to skim the barley out of—and offered tarts, both edible and female.

It was late evening before the Moor found me in an alley, alone at last, with a bellyful of ale.

"What was in the pitcher?" I asked him as he helped me to the dormitory.

"Water."

"Water and what?"

He tapped his nose. "A substance that makes it smoke. A little trick I picked up from a sorcerer in Marrakech." It was all he would say.

"Are you a sorcerer?" I asked.

He tipped his head back and laughed. "I've been called such in my time, among much else. But believe me, John, I would have let no harm come to you. You must always remember that, and trust me."

Through ale-glazed eyes I scrutinized him woozily. "How can I trust a man who won't tell me his name?"

His face became very still. Then he leaned towards me and whispered something close to my ear. I felt his breath, hot against my neck. But I was too drunk to catch the words, and seconds later I passed out.

PART TWO

Taking the Cross

6

On the road
England

❧

On a bit of waste ground on the edge of Bath, we staged our rehearsals under a leaden sky.

"Scream, Mary. Really scream! Clutch your bodice like a woman trying to preserve her last shred of decency."

Plaguey Mary waved an arm at her rapist—Red Will, hunched with embarrassment, the blacking on his face smeared by sweat. "He's hopeless. You should make *him* the ravisher." She winked at the Moor.

"Do not ask me to play a Saracen as some brutish villain." The Moor turned away.

I took the curved wooden sword from Will's hand. "Look, like this." I brandished the weapon, snarling horribly. "You've just slashed your way into Jerusalem and now it's time to take your prize. You're going to sow your seed in every infidel woman you can lay hands on. It's your right as a conqueror."

The Moor looked at me, slowly shook his head, then walked away.

Will nodded uncertainly. He'd only ever lain with two women, he'd admitted to me late one night on the road. One of them was his friend's sister when they were both off their faces on mead, and he couldn't even remember if he'd managed to put it inside her. And the other was Mary, when he'd plucked up the courage to offer her his pennies; and then she'd laughed at his poor, nervous offering and deemed it too small to be a "William," maybe just a "Bill."

He took the scimitar back and waved it overhead, pulling a face.

"Grimace, don't simper! And Mary, don't flash your dugs. Remember, you're a God-fearing woman who's just seen her sons cut down by a pack of Saracens. Look terrified and pray for deliverance."

Mary snorted and tossed her unruly shag of hair. For the past decade she had been living off her wits. She didn't care what any man thought of her; she knew perfectly well what she thought of them.

"Much good praying ever did anyone. She'd be better off belting him with her piss-pot."

"For shame, Mary!" Will growled. He might have been a penniless minstrel and a thief, but still he prayed three times a day and meant every word of it.

"It's very simple," I told them. "If you play your parts well we all make money, and if you screw it up we'll be back in the gaol waiting for the rope."

This seemed to focus them for a while.

Savaric and Bishop Reginald came to watch us rehearse. The bishop stood there with the corners of his mouth turned down when the play-acting got too coarse, but Savaric cheered us on.

"You can't underplay these things, Reggie. The populace doesn't understand subtlety. The mummers aren't here to appeal to their better natures—that's down to you and me—it's their blood they've got to rouse." He leapt into the square we had marked out to represent the dais and he acted out both parts—Saracen marauder and abused woman—with unseemly gusto.

"You're remaking the world for them," he explained, panting. "Here they are, tucked away in their safe little villages. For them, Jerusalem may as well be on the moon, or under the sea. It's your job to make Jerusalem come to them. You've got to make them care enough that it's lost that they'll give up all they hold dear to go and win it back. When you," he said to Red Will, shifting from foot to foot, "ravish Mary here, you have to make a man believe the Saracen could be beating down his door at any minute to carry off his wife!"

He spun around to confront Hammer and Saw, who had come to practise their own scene. "And when you two piss on the True Cross, you have to make them want to kill you for it."

Saw looked to his twin. "That shouldn't be too hard."

"You, Michael, yes?"

Hammer nodded uncomfortably, not liking that anyone with authority should know his proper name.

"Do it with a real flourish, right?"

Hammer hoicked the length of sheep's intestine out of his breeches and swung it about with suitable abandon.

Bishop Reginald tapped the Moor on the shoulder and they went aside to sit on a bench. I watched them with their heads bent together as if they were sharing secrets and felt a raging jealousy. When it became clear that Savaric had usurped my role as rehearser of the troupe, I crept away to find out if they were talking about me, just in time to hear Reginald ask of him, "You did not like the Lady Chapel?"

I watched the Moor hesitate. "It is fine work. But something about it is . . . unsatisfying. The colours are visionary, and the arcades are lovely. But even with all the candles it was dark in there. The windows are too small, the pillars too thick. It does not lift the soul. The prayer hall in the Great Mosque in Cordoba, on the other hand, with its bicoloured pillars and infinity of arches, combines great power with a delicacy of effect. And I have heard that the Umayyad Mosque in Damascus, based on the Prophet's own mosque in Medina, is even more perfect in its design. I would dearly love to see it for myself one day."

The bishop leaned back, musing. "I have such plans for Wells, you see. The foundations are laid, but I want to be sure . . . not to repeat the mistakes of the past. The problems of combining height and the need for light with sufficient strength in the structure . . ." He dipped his head so that I had to strain to hear and by a pro-digious effort caught "fountains of light" and "soaring pilasters," "great arches reaching skywards."

My skin began to tingle. Blood rose in my cheeks, beat in the tunnels of my ears. When I succumbed to my falling sickness, I would smell the scent of roses and see a pair of tall doors opening before me, beyond which impossibly tall pillars, joined at their apex by sharp arches, rose into a light-filled dome or a golden sky. The sensation that overtook me at these times, after the initial panic, was one of intense serenity that enfolded me like angels' wings. I had no control over these fits, or of the images that accompanied them. How were a churchman and an infidel privy to my visions? I had never spoken of them to anyone.

The Moor's brow smoothed as if he had solved some puzzle in his mind. "To make a place where contradictory elements may be reconciled."

The bishop sat back with a look of fierce bliss upon his face. "To invite the immanence of the transcendent."

"A place where earth touches Heaven." The Moor looked right at me with a gaze so penetrating that I felt my soul peeled naked. "John, fetch your drawing things."

I had been drawing—little caricatures and portraits of the troupe, trees and churches, bits of building—for some weeks, but secretly, fearing ridicule and reprisal. I had hidden my poor efforts from everyone beneath my pallet. But one day, a few weeks ago, I had come upon the Moor with my tattered drawings spread before him on the floor of the dormitory at Bath Abbey while the others were at prayer—or more likely in a tavern.

"These are good," he'd told me, a curious expression on his face.

I tried to gather them up, but he put his hand on my arm. His touch made my heart thunder. I shook him off in another sort of terror, grabbed my drawings and ran away, down the stairs and outside, where I dropped them down the well.

The next day, like a man attempting to charm a wild animal, he'd found me when I was alone and held a small packet out to me.

No one had ever given anything to me without expecting something in return.

"Go on, take it."

It was a bit of old oiled cloth. "What have you given me this for?" I was disappointed and angry.

"Open it!"

Inside the cloth were leaves of creamy white, bound with fine silk. I touched them with wonder—so soft, so smooth. "What are they?" I had never seen anything so white—it was like being given pieces of the moon.

"Paper," he said. "For your drawings. And this, too."

Out of his satchel came a small stoppered bottle and a reed cut into the form of a pen. He dipped the reed in the ink and ran a black line down a page, spoiling it. Three more strokes, four, then he turned it to me. It was his face, but it wasn't. I laughed out loud. The proportions were all wrong.

I took the pen from him and did what he'd done, but I had only used quills before: I used too much pressure, and made a hole. The next time I left a blot. The third time in a few swift lines I drew his profile: his long, straight nose, cheekbones like carved wood, strong chin. It was not difficult, I had drawn his likeness about a hundred times before.

He stared at it, astonished, then at me. I held his gaze, trying to be the man I hoped I had become, but then quailed and looked away. We never spoke of this moment after—of either the drawing, or the touch.

The next day, on a pretty sward of land at the foot of the Mendip Hills some miles to the southwest of Bath, back on the road towards Glastonbury, we pulled up our horses and dismounted, in my case with some relief.

Bishop Reginald spread his arms wide. "This is Wells, the Place of Many Streams," he told us, beaming with pride, "where all the holy springs meet and join as one. It is the most beautiful and blessed place in all of England."

Between the willow trees, over a gleam of water, I could see some small stone houses, a cluster of ecclesiastical buildings, a jumble of cottages and some barns and pigsties. There was also a great pile of rubble and evidence of what must once have been an ancient church, now no more than ruins, a scurry of men with barrows and picks, and innumerable trenches and holes in the ground. It looked more like a battlefield than a blessed site.

"Here I shall dedicate to Saint Andrew a wonderful new church, the largest and most beautiful ever built in England."

I'd never seen the bishop so animated. He ran from one place to another, pulling the Moor along by the sleeve, pointing up and down and sideways, talking, talking. Dawdling behind them, I saw the Moor stop suddenly and describe an arch in the empty air, his hands flowing up to a point, then sweeping down again. Then they were off, chins wagging, heads nodding, leaping over the trenches into the centre of the sward. Dodging a pair of workmen staggering under the weight of a huge stone, I ran after them, my satchel banging against my hip.

"The cloisters are extraordinary," the Moor was saying as I caught up to them. "I have visited the Qairouan Mosque, and at Puy they have experimented with new forms influenced by Islamic designs, a method of spreading the weight of the walls in such a way that the space between them may be opened high and wide. It is quite breathtaking. Something about the angles of the *sekonj*, which support the vaulting, setting it at a diagonal between two walls. And the formation of the cupolas. Domes like a golden sky."

"Puy is one of the points of departure for the pilgrimage route to Compostela," the bishop said.

"I have read the *Kitab Ruyyar*, describing the route." The Moor nodded. "But I have not yet walked the Way. You know the old story is that they brought Saint James's body back from Jaffa in a ship made of stone? I have always believed that image to be symbolic of the church there."

A mason was summoned and another earnest conversation ensued. The mason called a new man over and he went running off, to return a few minutes later with a flustered-looking greybeard. Then the whole long conversation was repeated, with the Moor making wild gestures in the air and the old man furrowing his brow.

"John, if I describe something to you, can you draw it for me?"

I had been kicking at a stubborn tuft of grass, bored by their chatter. A beetle was burrowing its way into the earth, away from the disturbance of my boot. I looked away from it unwillingly. "I doubt it."

"Come here, John."

His eyes locked on mine. I walked towards him, drawn by the dark lodestone of his gaze. Quite against my will I found myself saying, "I can try."

It took several attempts, for I couldn't visualize what he meant, but at last we had a sketch of what he was trying to convey.

The old man clucked his tongue. "Ah, you mean squinches."

"*Sekonj.*" The Moor grinned. "Yes!"

The greybeard shook his head. "Can't be done."

There followed a protracted argument, during which my attention wandered. Light and strength; strength and light. In my head danced a procession of pillars and arches. Fair white stone, hard as iron, gave way to softest petals. The scent of roses.

The edges of my vision began to haze. I swallowed, braced myself. I would not fall, I would not shame myself . . .

When next I was aware of myself I found that my lap was full of drawings. Sweeping lines, elegant curves. Had some angel entered my body and guided my hand? For once it appeared that I had not measured my length on the ground and jerked and jinked, but had sat quietly, sketching like a man possessed. Once conscious, I drew on, letting the Moor's words push the charcoal across the surface.

"That's it, John. But even taller. Up to the sky!"

We ran out of paper. A boy was dispatched to fetch it from the church stores, and I sketched some more.

"It'll never hold," the greybeard opined, shaking his head grimly over my drawings.

"It will," cried the Moor. "It's stronger than the Roman arch, see?" He made an adjustment to a sketch.

By the end of the day they all seemed very excited.

"And then a great window here, and tall, pointed inlets of light . . ."

"But I can't work from mere sketches," the greybeard warned at last. "It's all very well striving for something so new, but it carries a great risk if it goes wrong. Towers collapse, and if there's a congregation gathered beneath . . ." He spread his hands. "I'll need mathematical plans, master masons used to working with these foreign forms. It'll be costly. Very costly." He sucked his teeth.

Bishop Reginald patted him on the shoulder. "We will get you masons and mathematical plans, good Adam. One way or another."

The old man squinted at the Moor. "And what's to say this Saracen here don't mean to undermine your entire scheme, on purpose, like?"

"I am not a Saracen," the Moor said.

By the time we were ready to set off it was almost summer, though you'd never have guessed it. As we crossed the River Parrett, a freezing wind blew horizontal rain in across the Somerset Levels, soaking us to the skin. The Bridgwater docks were busy, but the workers showed little interest in the show, and the grim weather kept most folk indoors, so there were blessed few to witness the shambles of our first public performance.

Having missed his cue, then forgotten his single line, Quickfinger stumbled off the edge of the stage, blinded by his helmet, and with unerring aim fell on top of a well-built woman, who went down under him like a capsized ship. Her husband beat Quickfinger off her, a fight broke out, and Savaric's steward was robbed of his purse in the ensuing melee. No one could be induced to take the cross, and the few who had let curiosity overcome the rain suddenly drifted away as soon as the collection pots came out.

I looked at the Moor. "Christ's breath in a bottle, we're all going to hang!"

The players were searched, but of the steward's missing purse there was no sign.

The next day, after travelling to the wool town of Taunton, the sun came out and we put on a better display. We came away having signed fifteen young men with the cross, much to the distress of their wives and mothers.

We were rewarded by a stay at the local Benedictine priory, during which time the Moor and I went carefully through the troupe's possessions until the purse turned up in Ned's boot. Miraculously, the second morning, after mass at the high altar, the steward found his purse again, caught in the deep hem of his cloak. Savaric apologized to us all, though it was clear he was suspicious. Later we took Ned outside and delivered a painful reminder of the rules of the contract. That evening, his bruised ribs well strapped, Ned was surly but biddable, like a chastened donkey, but in the days that followed I sometimes caught him watching me through narrowed eyes.

Under the shadow of Rougemont Castle at Exeter, we managed a roistering performance, after which the bishop led the faithful in prayer and launched into an exhortation to action. Savaric then took over the stage, telling in ringing tones how that chief devil of the enemy, Saladin, had broken down the holy walls of the city and massacred the good Christians within. How babies were murdered one by one.

Out charged Ned, in blackface, with several ragdoll babies threaded onto his lance. "Ten thousand heads were severed! Blood ran through the streets in a torrent. Those who did not flee or were put to the sword were barricaded into churches and burned alive, their souls carried to Heaven in a pillar of smoke!" He squatted by a make-believe fire formed by blowing red and orange silk scraps with a bellows and pretended to roast and eat the babies, and a woman in the crowd fainted. The Moor had been persuaded against his conscience to put his knowledge of chemistry to good use and now burned minerals in a brazier out of the sight of the crowd so that a great cloud of green smoke swirled up. People gasped, never having seen anything like it before.

In the end they were queuing up to take the cross—young men

and old, singly and in roistering groups. One mother came rushing out of the crowd at the sight of her son being signed on the forehead by the bishop and dragged him away by his belt. "What will I do on my own, with your father gone?"

"It is his duty, goodwife," Savaric roared. "Let him go, and be thankful you have raised him well enough that he can repay his debt to God, king and country!"

She would not to be put off. "My Alfred is in the ground for king and country, I will not lose my boy Jamie as well."

There were sympathetic murmurs in the crowd. Savaric took a determined step forward. "Madam, we passed through Taunton a few days back and a woman there tried to deny us her son. The next day she was struck deaf and blind."

You could see the fear in her eyes. Reluctantly, she let go of the lad's belt and burst into noisy tears.

Savaric took the lad firmly by the arm. Every soul counted; each carried a handsome price. A moment later, the clerk wrote his name in the register: if he defaulted now, he would end up flogged and in gaol. The boy—barely thirteen, by the look of him—bowed his head and tramped away, but the euphoria had ebbed: we took no more converts that day, though donations kept flowing.

Later, when no one else could hear, I said to the Moor, "Do they really eat babies? The Saracens?" It was a serious question I had been pondering for days, but he looked at me as if I'd lost my wits.

"Do *you* eat babies?"

I recoiled. "Of course not."

"And yet there would be more truth in accusing your people of being cannibals."

"What?"

"You eat the body of your god. Wafer and wine: body of Christ, blood of Christ."

"That's different!"

He said no more, just gave me a look, and walked away.

More lies, I thought. It was all we did: peddle lies.

7

❋

aybe my doubts infected the other players, because our performances gradually lost conviction, and by the time we got to Crewkerne, takers for the cross were so reluctant we had to resort to spiritual blackmail to get them started, reminding them of the eternal punishments of Hell that await sinners: of the fires and tortures, the demons and succubi. Then we sent Hammer amongst the crowd with his hair and beard whitened with flour and wrinkles drawn on with charcoal. When Savaric roared, "Will no one here heed the call of Christ?" Hammer stepped forward and bleated, "I would gladly do so, sir, were I forty years younger!"

He was invited to come up to the front to touch the bones of the saints, and as he bent to do so, the Moor sent up a flash of light that had the audience reeling and blinking, and in the confusion Mary hastily wiped Hammer's face and beard with a wet cloth and he sprang upright, hale and twenty-three once more, and declared that he was willing to take on Saladin and his army singlehanded.

After that, everyone wanted to touch the bones, and we signed another thirty.

In Salisbury people were keener to donate money than to go to war, even when Mary went amongst them handing out distaffs of wool to the able-bodied, saying they were good only for the work of women. Even this didn't shame them, and in the end we resorted to offering an amnesty to the prisoners in the local gaol. Bribed with a decent lunch and the promise of atonement for their sins, they were released as long as they took the cross and whipped up the crowd. Unfortunately a number of them escaped.

Savaric shrugged. Their names were in the register, and it was on the numbers he'd be judged and rewarded. "If they're caught, we'll sign them up twice." His cousin clucked his tongue disapprovingly.

We moved on to Wilton, the largest town in the region, which boasted a fine abbey that the bishop wished to visit because it was reputed to house not only the bones of a major saint but also a nail from the True Cross. "I hear they paid a hundred pounds for it," he said in awe.

The Moor and I exchanged glances. We had sold two such nails, to the abbeys at St. German's and Tavistock, on our journey north, but it seemed we had undercharged.

On our way we also sold: some straw from the stable in which the Christ child was born; a bottle of Christ's breath; a flask of Mary Magdalene's tears; the strap of Saint Peter's sandal. It was amazing what people would buy from two indigent priests newly arrived from the Holy Land.

The Abbess of Wilton had a sharp eye and an impressive bosom. She greeted Bishop Reginald warmly, but Savaric she looked up and down, taking in his sumptuous robes and conspicuous chain. She said, "I've heard about you," then pursed her lips primly.

When the Moor was introduced, he placed his hand on his heart and bowed deeply. She was immediately charmed. They walked together and shared a long conversation about herbs and their uses, and yet again I marvelled at his ability to find common ground with everyone he met.

After supper in the abbey's refectory, the abbess boomed, "I shall now take our guests to see the Nail of Treves and the bones of Saint Edith."

"Wilfrida, the mother of our blessed Saint Edith, was forcibly abducted from this very abbey by King Edgar," she recounted. "He got a daughter on her, but she refused to marry him. Her piety so moved the king that as penance he did not wear his crown for a full seven years.

"Wilfrida returned to Wilton, and it was here that young Edith grew up and took the veil. In turn she became abbess here. Great marriages she was offered, lands, riches and powerful alliances, but she preferred a life dedicated to God and the protection of our abbey." A secret smile stole across her face, as if she thought herself a very Edith.

We walked a little way in silence. Overhead, a barn owl ghosted on outstretched white wings. We heard its screeching call as it disappeared into the moon-touched trees. I shivered, but that might have been because the Moor's hand brushed my own.

Inside a pretty, well-made church, we found the shrine to Saint Edith: of solid gold, artfully ornamented, huge. Savaric gasped, then said aloud what we were all thinking. "It must be worth a fortune."

The abbess placed her hands on the shrine in a proprietary fashion. "Within a week of Edith's death, miracles were being proclaimed in her name. People had visions of her breaking the Devil's head! King Canute himself endowed Wilton Abbey with this excellent shrine."

"Well, what a very warlike saint!" Savaric chortled. "Clearly, we need Saint Edith with us to take back Jerusalem."

The abbess gave him a look that suggested she would like to break his head.

The Nail of Treves, by contrast, was rather less impressively housed, in a clear glass phial mounted in a small silver reliquary, yet I noticed that while the rest of us were transfixed by the huge slab of gold surrounding the good Saint Edith, the Moor was drawn by the more modest relic. His face had a sly, closed look. Or perhaps it was just an effect of the jittering candle nearby.

"This is Egyptian rock crystal, a thousand years old," the Moor said softly, gazing at the phial.

The abbess came to his side. "It is very ancient," she replied, "but I do not know whence it came."

"I have seen perfume sold in the markets of Cairo in phials just like this."

"It is not the container that is valuable," she admonished him, "but the content. That is one of the nails used in the crucifixion of our Lord Jesus Christ."

"The Church of San Salvatore in Spain has some of the bread with which Isa Christ fed the five thousand," he said, pretending a great interest in this piece of infidel lore. "By divine intervention it remains miraculously fresh, and the two pieces of broiled fish from that same feast have no stink to them. The church also boasts the dice used by the Roman soldiers at Golgotha to cast lots for Isa's tunic—though the garment itself is kept by the cathedral in Trier."

As we walked back to the nunnery, he continued to regale the abbess with tales of some of the more extraordinary sacred objects he had come across in his travels, while Bishop Reginald and his cousin, troubled by the sight of so much gold, talked in low voices about the need for us to raise our game as we continued towards London.

After Compline I lay dozing, unable to fall asleep. Even though this place was a nunnery, I still found myself uncomfortable. The pallet I lay on appeared to be vermin-free and was covered with good wool. Nor did the snores of others disturb me too much; sleeping men can't do you much harm. But my senses were always on alert in a dormitory. I couldn't help it—fifteen years of needful vigilance will do that to a man.

So when the Moor slipped out of his bed and padded catlike across the floor, I was instantly awake. When he reached the door, he looked back to see if he had attracted attention, then lifted the latch with such stealth that I was confirmed in my suspicion that he was up to no good.

I watched the door close behind him and for a moment lay still, heart pounding. He wouldn't like to be followed. For a few seconds longer, I stayed, fighting my curiosity. Then I crawled out from under the blankets and went after him, my leather socks silent on the flagstones.

Outside it was dark, the moon hidden by clouds. It took a long moment for my eyes to make out his tall, straight figure disappearing through the arch in the courtyard wall, heading towards the chapel.

The shrine! Was he going to try to carve a piece off the reliquary, or to stagger away with the whole thing? You could never sell a piece of gold that large. But then I thought about the woods behind the chapel, the barn owl's destination: where there were woods there were always charcoal burners, and charcoal burned hot enough to melt gold. You could divide it into portions, bury what you could not carry, take what you could to sell to a goldsmith somewhere far enough away to avoid suspicion—Bristol, say, or London, where there must surely be other dark-skinned foreigners like the Moor and he could pass for a gold merchant.

I quickened my pace. When I reached the chapel the door was closed. I twisted the round iron handle. The devil! He had locked it from the inside. A hot surge of jealous fury rushed through me. I banged on the door. "Open up! It's me, John!"

There was a deathly hush, then soft footsteps. The grate of iron on iron. The door opened and with a single, swift action I was caught by the collar and dragged painfully inside. The door clicked shut again. The Moor turned the key in the lock; we were together in the gloom.

"What are you doing following me?" His black eyes blazed.

"I . . . ah . . . I thought you were stealing the shrine. I thought you were leaving me behind . . ."

His grip relented. Then he started to laugh, soundlessly, a breathy rush and catch of air. "You really must think me some sort of magician, *habibi*. Look." He opened his hand. I saw what looked like one of the old nails we had dug up in the pit on the moors and sold along the way. But no, it was not one of those small nails. It was as long as the palm of his hand. It was the Nail of Treves.

"What are you doing? Put it back!"

"I needed to see it again," he said. He leaned past me and unlocked the door, stuck his head out, looked around. "Go back to bed. I will come back in a little while. It wouldn't do to be seen together."

The corners of his mouth curled up—a private joke. When I hesitated, he ducked his head, kissed me once, firmly, on the lips, then pushed me back out into the night.

And so back to the dormitory I went, feeling like a fool.

My lips burned as if brushed by flame.

8

❈

King Henry imposed a tax requiring that every man give one-tenth of all his income and goods to the war effort. The "Saladin tithe" it was known as. The only way to avoid paying it was to take the cross.

The mood was ugly wherever we went. People were taking to the forests to avoid the tax collectors, and as we passed through Eartham Wood near Arundel we were set on by bandits. Hammer clubbed two attackers and sent a third away dragging his foot. Saw fought with a dagger in each hand. Little Ned produced, as if from nowhere, a pair of small throwing knives and dispatched another two of the bandits in quick succession as they bore down upon Savaric and his jewelled chain. Quickfinger charged after the fleeing men, bellowing his own name—"Enoch Pilchard! Enoch Pilchard!"—which alarmed them mightily. He came back with a small purse from which he removed a couple of coins. He then tossed it to Mary, who stowed it away in her cleavage. Interesting. I wondered how long they had been a couple.

Over the following days I noticed that Mary looked at Quickfinger more often than he looked at her, and that Will watched them both sourly. Will put his hands on Mary in the rape scene in such a way that she fought him off for real. One day the Moor stepped in, the peacemaker as usual. "Time for a change of roles," he suggested. "Why don't you take Will's place, Michael?"

The Hammer looked dubious.

"Ye shud mak 'im t'wench." Quickfinger grinned nastily at Will. "'E'll mak a reet gud un." He pursed his mouth into a simper until there was a wicked resemblance to the minstrel.

Will's face went purple. Then he put his head down and charged at Quickfinger. Just before Will's skull looked set to make contact, Quickfinger stepped aside and Will barrelled into Hammer instead, who was bowled over. He was a small man, Hammer, but wiry and tough. He sprang to his feet and held Will's flailing arms easily to stop him going after Quickfinger.

Will's eyes were red and there was snot dripping from his nose. "You don't love her!" he shrieked at Quickfinger. "You don't care about her at all!"

Mary folded her arms. "Shut up, Will," she barked.

Will was openly crying now, the tears running down his chin. "He . . . he . . . he lies with other women. Wherever we go, he goes sniffing after a new one!" He stared at Mary, his eyeballs bulging with desperation. "He's . . . he's . . . a fucking pig!"

No one had ever heard Will swear. It was his prissiness more than anything else that made him so disliked by the others.

Quickfinger was grinning like a fiend. "I canna help it if all the wenches chase me." He waggled his hips obscenely till the rest squawked with laughter. "Word goes round, y'know how 'tis. They all want a piece."

Mary's face went still. Her eyes sparked fire as she looked from one man to the other. "You're all a load of pricks and I want nothing to do with any of you. Fuck off, Enoch." Gathering her skirts, she stalked away, more the lady than we had ever seen her.

Will slept apart from the rest of us that night and looked so forlorn that the very sight of him set Quickfinger and the twins to laughing. At last, the Moor took him aside, and after that we dropped the rape scene from the mumming, but whatever camaraderie had glued the group together had been lost.

Mary turned her back angrily on Quickfinger when he tried clumsily to make amends. She talked only to the Moor and to Little Ned, and then not much. She was coolly polite with me. I missed the Plaguey Mary of old, with her ribald wit and devil-may-care ways, and all of a sudden I could see she was older than I had thought.

At Winchelsea, we were rehearsing a new scene outside the church late one afternoon when we heard a scream and a girl came running towards us with her dress in tatters. She was spattered with blood, a knife in her hand.

"They raped me!" she cried. "I was only defending myself!"

Hammer stepped towards her, palms out. "It's all right—"

She swung wildly, ripping his sleeve.

"Fuck me," breathed Hammer, stepping smartly of out her path.

The Moor touched Mary on the arm and said something quietly. Mary nodded, then stepped towards the girl. "Come with me!" She beckoned her towards the church. "Quickly! Sanctuary—you can claim sanctuary."

The girl had a plain, broad face and a plain, broad body; it was her hair that was her beauty. Luxuriant and dark, it fell to her waist, and the dying sun lit red fires in its curls. She grimaced, then fled up the steps and into the church.

At the door, Mary turned back to address us all. "You haven't seen her. You tell them you've seen her, I'll personally rip your balls off." Framed by the Norman archway, she was more fearsome than any gargoyle. Nobody said a word. She whirled inside with the girl. The door slammed shut.

Running footsteps, a man came huffing into view—barrel-chested, richly dressed and flashing gold, but blood stained his tunic. My heart stopped. It was Geoffrey de Glanvill, brother to the King's Eye. I remembered him in the Lady Chapel, with his red butcher's face and air of command, the way he broke my nose with his ring, how he held me like a rat as the fit came on me; how angry he was in court when I escaped my punishment. As inconspicuously as I could, I stepped behind the Moor. The air felt charged with danger.

"Hoi, you! Where is the bitch? That little harlot stabbed my cousin in the neck!" De Glanvill addressed Savaric, whose face transformed in an instant from shocked to inexpressive, the large, heavy-lidded eyes wide and glib.

"I do not know what 'harlot' you mean, sir," Savaric answered. He looked lowborn in his fustian robe, so it was no surprise that the noble did not recognize him. "We have seen no one, save the sexton half an hour past, and I swear he had no tits."

De Glanvill looked disbelieving. "But she ran in this direction, from between the pauper dwellings there!" He gestured to where a row of low almshouses fronted the green. "You must have seen her."

Savaric shrugged, insolent.

The man's face darkened. "Who are you, sir?" he demanded. "I shall be making my report to my brother, Chief Justiciar of all England."

The churchman gazed back blandly. "You may report my name as Savaric de Bohun, erstwhile archdeacon of Canterbury, whom your brother took great pleasure in removing from office."

De Glanvill took a step backwards. Then he sneered. "I should not be surprised to see you in such reduced circumstances, my lord. Gamblers never thrive." He turned curtly on his heel and marched back the way he came.

I was surprised to see the Moor fall into step with him. "Bring my apothecary bag, Will," he called over his shoulder.

In perplexed silence we watched him go. Then Savaric beckoned to me and together we walked up the steps to the church. Inside it was dark and musty, the candles unlit. There was a smell of stale incense, dead mice and that greasy, animal smell that hung around long after the last mass when tallow candles were used rather than beeswax. For a moment I stood in the grip of an unwanted memory.

I had been just a lad, cleaning the floor of the chapel at the Priory of St. Michael on my hands and knees. It was early morning and I was barely awake, yawning so hard my jaw cracked, still in a dream of pulling up a string of mackerel, breathing in the sharp, salty air, feeling the rough line between my fingers, watching the flash and spin of silver in the green water as the fish were drawn to the surface.

Then suddenly a hand had gripped the back of my neck. "You're just a little savage, hardly more than an animal. Can't even speak the king's English, let alone make confession. Eh? So you won't be telling anyone about this, will you?" Another hand lifted the back of my robe. "Do you believe in God, then, boy? No? Well, believe in this."

I struck out at my attacker, but he hit me with the censer. Incense spilled, surrounding me with the scent of roses. It was the first time I'd suffered a falling fit.

Savaric's voice brought me back to the present. "Over there."

Mary crouched by the high altar with her arm around the fugitive. The girl's eyes were black holes in the mask of her face.

Savaric took a step towards her and she scrambled to her feet. The knife caught a ray of red light falling through a window high up in the nave. He sat down on the nearest pew. "It's all right," he said softly. "He's gone. We told him we hadn't seen you."

The girl subsided as if her knees had given way, and suddenly you could see there wasn't much fight left in her, just bravado.

"Tell us what happened," Savaric continued. "No more harm will come to you."

Her name was Rosamund and she was the fuller's daughter, promised to a boy from a farm outside Rye.

"Not that I want to marry at all," she said. "Babies and housework and doing a man's bidding—I've had enough of all that."

Her tale was familiar: two drunken lords, thinking they had the right to take what they pleased; one held her down while the other raped her, but when they changed over they did not count on her quick reaction. She grabbed her rapist's belt-knife and stuck it in his neck. "Right to the hilt," she said fiercely, miming the stab. "He wasn't expecting that."

Good girl, I thought. I wished I'd had a knife, back at the priory.

"Is he dead?" she asked. "I hope so, even if I hang for it."

"You won't hang," Savaric told her. "I offer you my protection."

"You can travel with us," Mary offered. "As one of the troupe."

It was difficult to put an age to the girl: maybe sixteen or seventeen. She was sturdily built, not fat, but muscular—a girl used to manual work.

"That'll have to go," I said, pointing to her sumptuous hair. "And you'll have to dress as a boy, play a man's part on stage."

She tilted her square chin at me, then handed me her knife. "Men are the lucky ones in this world. I'll be happy to trade my hair for a man's freedom."

9

❄

The Moor and Will returned a while later, Will's eyes as round as wheels.

"The Moor saved him! De Glanvill's cousin. Honestly, if you'd seen all the blood, you'd never have believed it possible. He was as pale as a fish belly, looked dead as dead."

"Neck wounds can be nasty," the Moor admitted. "The man will survive, at least till we're well away, though I doubt he'll speak again." His gaze travelled to the newest member of our troupe. "You must be Ezra, from Gosport, son of a fisherman. Family boat gone to the bottom, lad has to make a living as best he can. Your mother's name is Mary, and your dear drowned father was Joe. Can you remember all that?"

Rosamund, who from that moment forth was called Ezra, nodded solemnly.

We travelled on to Rye, leaving the people of Winchelsea uncrossed. The town of Rye was the victualling point for vessels along this stretch of the south coast and one of the royal cinque ports. Here we were to roll out our more sophisticated repertoire, one that preyed on men's consciences rather than on their baser instincts. "Rich men always have a great many sins lying heavy on their souls," Savaric said with feeling. "They will be anxious about what will happen to them after they die and keen for an easy promise of Paradise."

But before we could get started a royal herald jumped up onto the stage and announced that King Henry was dead, three days ago, God rest his soul.

A mass was said for his soul in the magnificent St. Mary the Virgin, which stood on a rise overlooking the marshes and the River Rother. It was an impressive piece of architecture, and the bishop walked around it with me and the Moor after everyone had gone.

"It's in the French style," the bishop said. "But it's so . . . earthy." He shook his head. "Not what I want for Wells, not at all. I have dreamt . . ." He turned to the Moor, his eyes alight with a burning enthusiasm, and the pair of them walked apart, exchanging dreams of poetry in stone.

I took myself down into the town and took an ale or two in the Mermaid. The tavern was packed with drinkers, all raising a tankard to the dead king and wishing the new one well.

"I know a man who met Prince Richard," one said, and a group formed around him.

"What's he like?"

"A fine-looking man—tall, red-haired and pale-eyed, and very fair of face, with a true kingly air to him."

None of this was surprising. No one was likely to say the new king looked like a hobgoblin, even if he did. The speaker related that Richard was a great warrior, won all the tourneys, could compose poetry and sing to a lute. I yawned: such a paragon.

Behind me, another man said quietly, "They say the king's corpse bled from the nose when Richard paid his respects."

His neighbour asked, "You mean he caused his father's death?"

I pressed my way through the crowd towards the door, intent

on pissing away some of the ale in order to make room for more. Out in the alley, I almost fell over a man slumped over, weeping copiously.

I touched the poor chap on the shoulder. "You all right?"

A great moon face turned up to me. It was Savaric.

"He was my friend."

His shoulders heaved violently, then he reached up and clutched my arm, opened his mouth to speak and out came a great billow of fermented honey, which told me all I needed to know.

"Come on," I said, trying to haul him up. "Let's walk down to the sea, get some fresh air. You'll catch some awful contagion sitting here."

The Moor glided around the corner at that moment, a shadow among shadows. I was grateful to see him.

"Help me get him up on his feet."

Savaric wasn't a small man, and dead drunk he was a dead weight. We heaved him upright, the churchman swaying unsteadily, fumes of mead wafting off him.

On a rise of shingle overlooking the sea we sat down in a row and stared silently out at the black waves and the trembling silver line of the moon's path upon it.

"I loved Henry," Savaric choked out at last. "He was a great man. Headstrong and rash sometimes, but his anger came like a thunderstorm—noisy and furious but passing quickly. We would have been friends again, had I just had the time to pay him back what I owed him." His great lugubrious eyes gazed out over the dark waters. "He was a lion, with his tawny hair and that big, bold, open face. None of us could keep up with him, he had such energy. I took his money . . . and now I'll never have the chance . . ." His hands fell and flexed. "I am damned, damned forever. If I cannot make restitution for my sins with he whom I wronged, then I must find another way of buying my way into Heaven."

The Moor waited for the spasm to pass, then put an arm around Savaric's shoulder. "They say his son is much like him, this Richard."

Savaric turned to him. "They do say that, don't they?" A pause. "I will do my utmost to raise funds for his holy war. And in doing so, perhaps I can save my soul."

He hauled himself to his feet, and at once the Moor stood to steady him. Savaric waved him away. "Leave me be. Where is my cousin? I must talk to him right away!" And he lurched off into the gloom.

"I will see you to the path, at least," the Moor said. "We do not want you falling into the marsh."

I sat there freezing on the chilly shingle, wishing I still had the fur the monks had shaved off. Such a bright moon: it was like an eye, the eye of God, beaming down on me. What did it see? An unworthy soul, a half-wild thing pretending to be a civilized man? A man who loved another? Unnatural, absurd.

Shingle crunching underfoot.

I turned so fast I cricked my neck. The Moor was looking down at me, his gaze more penetrating even than the silver eye above. Then he folded his long legs and we sat there in the darkness. I could feel a tension between us that had never been there before and I was suddenly tongue-tied. All the hairs on the back of my neck prickled, and my mouth burned as it remembered another time we were alone together in the night, when he had pushed me out of Saint Edith's chapel all those months ago. I wished I could take him by the arm now, brotherly, casual. Say, "So, that kiss you gave me in Wilton. Tell me, what was that about, eh?" But of course I couldn't. And so I sat rooted like some big, dumb plant, its leaves trembling at every touch of breeze, waiting desperately for the sun to shine on it again.

At last he turned to me. For one terrifying, delicious moment I thought maybe he would kiss me again. But all he said was, "I think we shall soon be heading for foreign climes."

A minute later he stretched and rose, pulled me to my feet, and together we walked in silence back to the abbey.

The next day, fervour was in the air. There was to be a new king: the first prince in Europe to take the cross. There was money to be made, and Richard's favour to be won.

Bishop Reginald held forth in ringing tones, reminding the crowd of the terrors that await the sinful soul when it descends into Hell, of the demons with their pincers and tridents, of the flames that burn to the bone but never devour, of the howls of the tormented and their never-ending trials. Beside me, Savaric groaned and hung his head.

"You are a blessed generation!" Reginald cried. "You are blessed to be alive in this year of jubilee. This chance will not come again. To you who are merchants, men quick to recognize and seize a bargain, let me point out the advantages of this offer. Do not miss out on this great opportunity to buy your way into the Kingdom of Heaven. Take up the cross and vow to fight for the Holy Land and you will be rewarded with indulgence for all your sins. I, Reginald of Bath, second in the intercessionary line after only the Archbishop of Canterbury himself, will take your confession and ensure that God hears your vow. Sign for the cross today and all will be forgiven. The cost is so small, the reward so great—the firm promise of entrance to Paradise forever and ever, amen."

There was a sob behind us, and Savaric pushed past us to fall on his knees before his cousin.

"Take me for the cross!" he cried. "God knows, my sins are great. I was close to the king, foremost among his nobles, but I transgressed. Oh, how I transgressed! I drank and swore and I gambled. Oh, how I gambled! As God is my witness, I loved the dice better than my Bible. I carried my favourite pair with me at all times . . ."

He held up his great gold chain and the crowd fell hushed and attentive. Then he clicked open the great ruby bauble on the end of it and from this tipped a pair of dice into his palm and held them up to the crowd.

"I have won and lost fortunes with these two mites of wood." He paused, considering. "Mainly lost." He bowed his head, turned the dice over in his palm, then cast them far out into the crowd. "I abjure my wicked ways!" he cried, "and I hereby take the cross."

I stared at the Moor, who seemed transfixed. "We never rehearsed this," I said uncertainly.

Bishop Reginald looked confused, but he gave his cousin the Bible to kiss, signed him with the cross and handed him his token.

Savaric held it aloft. "For King Henry, God rest his soul! And for Richard, who has vowed to retake Jerusalem, I pledge my allegiance to the cause, and that of all my associates, who will accompany me!" And then he turned to survey us, his "associates."

"Is he still drunk?" I asked.

There was no answer. If the Moor was ever shocked by anything, he masked it so well you would never know. But now a vein pulsed on his forehead and his face looked full of blood.

"Come along, my friends!" Savaric exhorted us. "Fall on your knees beside me."

Astonishingly, it was Rosamund, or should I say Ezra, who was the first to answer his call. Having just played the role of a Saracen, she came galloping past us all onto the dais in blackface to lay her wooden sword at his feet and cry out, in as manly a voice as she could manage, "I take the cross!"

The crowd cheered—there was something about her youth and passion that moved them.

The twins, Hammer and Saw, followed with a shrug. "What else is there to do once the tour is over?" Saw asked. Like Savaric, they waved their wooden crosses, the crosses they had so roughly carved sitting on the back of the wagon.

"Ah, fook," said Quickfinger, looking forlorn. Then he pushed past me and knelt at Bishop Reginald's feet.

Will gazed at Mary with a plea in his eyes. She looked away. I saw him set his jaw, and then he too mounted the dais, which left only the Moor and me.

"They can't hold you to it, can they, the vow?" I asked. I thought of all the criminals we sprang from gaol in Salisbury. I was willing to bet none of them was planning on taking ship for *Terra Sancta*.

"It's your immortal soul," the Moor said. He put his hands on my shoulders and regarded me steadily. "This is where our ways must part, John."

I stared at him. "What? No! I don't want to go to war. I want to go . . . wherever you are going."

"You cannot come where I am going, John. You're not ready for that. Stay with the troupe—they need you, especially Ezra. She's not as tough as she thinks she is. Look after her." He touched me lightly on the cheek. "We will meet again."

Then he turned and walked away with all the dignity of a prince, leaving me exposed and alone, my knees trembling like the fool I was.

What could I do? I should have run after him in full sight of the crowd, should have caught him by the arm and demanded to accompany him, told him I loved him and cared about nothing else. But instead I stood silent, in desperate confusion, wailing inwardly, once more an abandoned child. The scent of roses bloomed all around me but there were no doors to Heaven opening before me.

As if in a trance, I found myself walking slowly up the steps and dropping to my knees before the bishop.

That night, on our return to the dormitory, thick in the head with the gallons of ale I had drunk to drown my desperation, I found tucked carefully beneath my drawing satchel a pouch of soft leather. When I picked it up, it lay heavy in my hand. Inside were about twenty silver coins, a small fortune. Surely this was all the money the Moor had amassed for his part in our unholy charades these long months.

There was something else in the bottom of the pouch. Wrapped in a square of green silk was a heavy length of crystal hanging from a leather thong. And inside the crystal was the Nail of Treves.

PART THREE

Love Behind Walls

10

City of Akka

❀

JULY 1189

Zohra yawned and stretched out the crick in her back. She'd been up and working since before first prayer. She had prepared the day's dough, taken it to the oven, made a sweet barley porridge, swept the downstairs rooms and watered the plants—all those small tasks that men could not be expected to do themselves. Then she had changed her mother's linen, turned her, washed her, brushed her hair and smoothed rosewater over her face. Her father's sisters had often come to offer their help with her mother, but Baltasar, too proud to admit to the extent of the disability caused by his old war wounds, had turned his face away from them.

Zohra propped her mother's head up on the yellow silk cushion to help the water go down her throat. For the past week Nima Najib had stopped swallowing of her own accord, but just lay there, breathing through her mouth, her brow furrowed as if deep in dream she was concentrating on some insoluble problem.

She stroked her mother's cheek, so dry and diminished, and suddenly felt a wave of anger. How could she deteriorate so quickly and leave Zohra to do everything? Nima was not an old woman, was maybe in the middle of her fourth decade, but ever since catching that fever she'd been getting weaker all the time. Zohra sensed this new phase was no longer the normal exhaustion of a suffering patient. But she was too young to die. Wasn't she? Zohra took one of the lax hands in her own and shook it in a sort of rage. But her mother did not stir.

The call to *dhuhr*, the noon prayer, rang out across the city. Zohra looked through the window-grille to the city beyond. Under a turquoise sky a clutter of ochre roof terraces, seemingly piled one on another, stretched all the way to the sparkling sea, punctured here and there by slender turrets, cupolas and the great minaret of the Friday Mosque, and finally by the Tower of Flies at the end of the breakwater.

"Is she still asleep?"

Her young brother Kamal was a troublesome boy, much given to outbursts of temper—the last thing you needed in a household in which one parent was sick and the other crippled.

"Yes, she's still asleep."

"Is she going to get up today?" His light eyes, so like her own—more gold than brown—blazed at her.

"Maybe later, *insh'allah*."

Kamal stared at his mother. "She's drooling."

"I just gave her some water."

He laid his head down beside Nima's, then jerked back. "Her breath stinks! You should give her mint leaves to chew."

Nima could no longer chew but there was no point in saying so.

"I want her to be well again!"

"You just want her to fuss over you." She ruffled his hair. Kamal was their mother's favourite, despite his petulance. "Have you seen Aisa?" she asked.

At once his twin bristled. "Why?"

"I have to go to the bazaar. I thought he might sit with Ummi."

"He's up on the roof with Baba and his pigeons." He wrinkled his nose. "Filthy, smelly things."

The year before, Kamal had stolen a pair of Baltasar's precious birds and sold them to a butcher in the souq. Only Zohra knew the truth about the missing pigeons: when she'd come to do the washing, she'd found guano all over Kamal's sleeve. He'd sworn it was from the gulls—an unlucky hit—but Zohra knew pigeon shit when she saw it.

"I'll watch over Mother. Don't you trust me?"

She smiled, but he was not far wrong.

He stood there, looking down at Nima, his face dark. "If she does not get well soon, I will hate God and all mankind."

Visiting the bazaar meant running the gauntlet of neighbours' good intentions. There were only so many ways of saying "No change" without giving offence. Neighbours wanted to chatter about their own sick relatives, or people they'd heard of who had survived the sweating sickness. They wanted to reassure and offer support, but their kind words felt so hollow that Zohra could not face them and had taken to wearing a full veil whenever she left the house. It was not the only reason she wore the veil. Disguise was sometimes necessary.

She kept her head down and walked quickly past the friendly baker on the corner and his portly son, Brahim. Past Widow Eptisam with her eager rabbit face and darting eyes. Past the Armenian sisters who sat on their doorstep all day, watching the world go by. Past the fierce, blind imam and his stone-faced daughter, Fatima.

But now as Zohra passed the road that led to the eastern ramparts, she felt a sense of doom settle over her. Great changes were coming, none of them good. She had a terrible feeling that Ummi was not going to survive this latest bout of illness. And then Zohra would be forced to marry her rich cousin Tariq. A family must look after its own: that was what everyone said. She had no power to refuse the union. Other girls would be happy to marry Tariq; she had heard them say as much at the hammam. But the idea of being wed to her cousin, forced to submit to his pleasure, to bear his children, was the worst thing she could imagine.

She had come to the edge of the bazaar now, could see the reed roof of the *qissaria*, the covered market, which led into its shady depths. But instead of taking her usual route she turned aside and walked through the copper-workers' quarter, where the men sat outside on their stools, dinging away at great pans and vessels with their little hammers. Other girls might dream of an "outfit" of kettles, pots and pans made here for their dowry, but not Zohra. She could admire the workmanship without coveting the object and all it stood for: a life of servitude.

But passing through the woodworkers' quarter, she stopped to admire a collection of nesting bowls, very finely made and burnished to a rich honey-gold by the sun. She picked up the topmost bowl. It sat as sleek as a kitten in her palm. The band of decoration around the rim was made from a tiny mosaic of different-coloured woods arranged in a geometric pattern.

"Do you like it?" The speaker wore a complexly woven turban and had a foreign accent; the bazaar had an ever-shifting population of traders and customers.

"It's lovely work," she said. "But I was only looking."

"I'm afraid we charge for that, and more because you touched the piece."

What effrontery! She put the bowl down. "That's absurd!"

The stallholder grinned. His long fingers picked up the bowl. He held it out to her again. "Here, take it. You won't find workmanship like that from here to China. I'll give you a very good price: a single qirat."

Zohra's eyes lingered on the little bowl. How pretty it would look full of beads or small coins. "It is a beautiful thing, but no." There was no money to spare.

"Take it. Please. For no more payment is as valuable as a compliment sincerely given."

She surprised herself by reaching out to take it. But he did not let go. Instead, he closed his hands over hers so that the bowl, smooth and fragile, was held between them. For a brief, heady moment she felt an illicit thrill rush through her, which somehow had nothing to do with this man, but had to do with the magical transactions that took place between all men and all women. Then she realized that the stallholder still held her hand. She pulled away.

"Just lift your veil for a moment. It is the only price I ask for the bowl."

Zohra had been tricked. But instead of showing her anger, she laughed. What had come over her? Was it that he was a foreigner, a transient in the city, and almost as old as her father? Or maybe it was because she was already bound upon a dangerous adventure, one that rendered this small transgression as nothing.

Zohra unpinned the black cloth that veiled her face and looked him boldly in the eye.

The man touched his heart. "Beautiful," he said. "A good craftsman always recognizes beauty, even when it is hidden."

Zohra hastily restored her veil, then tucked the bowl into her basket and ran from the scene.

The stallholder called after her, but she did not turn back.

At a brass-studded door at the end of the Street of Tailors, Zohra stopped. She looked quickly back over her shoulder, then gave three sharp raps with the Hand of Miriam doorknocker. A face appeared at the window overhead, a tall, narrow window fretted with ironwork. She heard a grating sound, and then a set of heavy keys came flying down from the grille that had opened in the window's base. Zohra made a grab for them, juggled them awkwardly and dropped them with a clang at her feet.

"Hell and salt!" Zohra retrieved them and swiftly let herself into the house, locking the door behind her.

"When did you get so clumsy?"

She looked up and there was Nathanael, sitting on the stairs, smiling gleefully, the light from above making a nimbus of the dark hair tumbling around the pale moon of his face.

"Father says the inability to coordinate is the first sign of senility."

"I'm only two months older than you," Zohra protested, disarmed as she always was by the laughing brown eyes that could go from candour to wickedness in an instant.

"You're late. I thought you were never going to come."

"Nathanael." Reproachful now. "Don't I always manage to come?"

A snort of scandalized laughter. "Such a temptress! Now, quickly, upstairs with you before the djinns magic you away again."

"I can't stay for long. There's still the shopping to be done."

"Ah, now that's where the djinns are so useful. They've brought me chicken and saffron, figs, pistachios, goat's cheese and rice. And those little red chili peppers your brothers like so much. Onions, honey, balsam and white benzoin. Did they forget anything?"

Zohra cocked her head. "Sometimes I think you are in league with the Devil." She shook the contents of a pouch into her hand and Nathanael extracted a number of coins, then folded Zohra's fingers over the remainder.

"No more? That seems a remarkable bargain!"

"The honey's my own, and since I look after the damned bees, I'll give it to whom I please. The balsam and the benzoin are from the storeroom. Now stop your chattering or you'll make my little helpers hungry, and then we'll all be in trouble."

There were times when Zohra was convinced the doctor's son was able to summon demons and djinns. But she could not seem to help herself; she came back again and again.

The room upstairs was in its usual untidy state. Books and scrolls were piled everywhere, gathering dust that Zohra itched to sweep away. On the shelves lining the walls were yet more arcane items: glass bottles, bundles of dried plants, stones, birds' wings and bits of bone, even two or three skulls that made her shudder whenever she looked at them. They didn't look human but she did not like to think where they might have come from.

On a low table in the middle of the room, paper, ink and reeds had been set out; beyond this a wide divan was spread with a patchwork of covers in a riot of hues and fabrics. Zohra made to sit down, but Nathanael took her by the arm. "Which lesson do you want first?"

"I, well, I may not be able to come for the next two days, so perhaps the letters . . ."

"Foolish girl, wrong answer. Must I punish you?" He pulled Zohra's veil away, took hold of two handfuls of lustrous black hair and, silencing her with his tongue, pulled her down onto the divan, then twisted and straddled her.

Between the two of them, something made a cracking sound. Zohra drew away, feeling something sharp jab into her ribs. "Oh . . ." She investigated the contents of the cloth bag she wore across her body, then held the victim out to him. "It was a gift. For you."

In her hands lay the little bowl from the woodworker's stall. It had cracked cleanly in two.

11

The pigeon struggled in Aisa's hands, attempting to flap its wings. He knew he was not good with the birds, not like his father or his big brother Sorgan. He was too afraid of hurting them so he tended to hold them too loosely, and, recognizing his lack of confidence, they would try to get away. Now he tightened his grip.

The pigeon stretched its neck with a squawk, and at last Aisa's father, Baltasar Najib, could hold his tongue no longer. "Hold her gently, no need to squeeze. Like this." He took the bird from Aisa, caging his fingers loosely around its breast, and at once the bird stopped struggling. It bobbed its head as if to bring the man into focus. The high sun lit its black neck feathers to an iridescent green tinged with pink and purple.

"She's so beautiful. I'm sorry I squashed her. I thought she was going to escape." Aisa stroked the bird's head. "All those little bones."

Baltasar smiled, and for a moment his craggy face was transformed. "Never mistake delicacy for weakness, son. Females of a species are often tougher than the males."

Aisa frowned, uncertain as to what his father meant. He was fourteen, on the edge of manhood, but being fine-boned and small for his age, like his twin, he often looked younger. No more so than now.

"She will get better, won't she?"

They were not talking about birds any more.

His father did not answer. Instead he turned the pigeon over and inspected its feet. The bird was a handsome creature with extravagantly feathered fetlocks. It was hard fitting a message to the thin little leg hidden amidst those ridiculous plumes, but Baltasar was sentimental about his birds and proud of their looks. He'd never trim their plumage. Besides, he always said dewlaps were the best fliers, better even than his adanas.

Aisa watched his father make several attempts to tie the piece of red wool in place and itched to do it for him. Among the many other wounds Baltasar had taken at the Battle of Ramla he'd lost a couple of fingers, and even though the bird was quiet it was a fiddly job. At rest, the tendons in his father's hand would sometimes contract till he was left with little more than a claw. Aisa's mother, Nima, used to massage her husband's maimed hand for him with almond oil, but she had not been well enough to do that these past weeks, and the old man would not suffer anyone else to do the job. To pass the task to someone else—to his sister Zohra or to him— was a betrayal, Aisa thought, as if doing so was to accept that Nima would never get better.

Finished with the wool, his father cast the bird into the bright sky. "Off you go, my lovely girl."

For a moment the pigeon hung over them, its spread wings radiant in the sunlight, then it wheeled away northwards. They watched it go till even the speck of its silhouette was invisible. By the time Baltasar turned back to his son, his eyes were wet and his voice was breaking.

"Sometimes it's hard to believe there can be such beauty in the world."

Aisa didn't think the remark was meant for him, but before he could think of a response, his father had limped across the terrace and was busying himself among the nesting boxes, row upon row of them lining the shelves against the highest wall, his grey head bent over the cooing birds.

They worked in companionable silence, cleaning out the guano, sweeping the floor, refilling the seed-trays, making small repairs to the woven reed covers and perches, until a tall, spare figure appeared suddenly in the doorway. The man stepped into the light.

Aisa's eyes widened. "Malek, Malek! You're home!"

His brother was austerely handsome, with high cheekbones and an aquiline profile, a solemn set to his mouth, until he smiled, as he did now.

"Who is this, then? A cousin visiting from Aleppo?"

Aisa giggled. "Have you forgotten me so soon?"

Malek pretended shock. "Aisa? No, it can't be."

"But it is!" Aisa felt alarmed now. Had he really forgotten in the two years since he'd last come home?

"How you've grown! And gained some muscle, too."

"I swim every day. I can hold my breath underwater for a count of two hundred now. Soon I'll be able to join Salah ad-Din's army too!"

"You'll do no such thing, not while I breathe." Under his shock of grey hair their father's face looked as if it had been carved out of wood by a man who had not yet mastered the tools for delicate work.

"Father." Malek inclined his head, placed the flat of his hand over his heart.

Aisa could feel the tension filling the air between them. Then, as if breaking through an invisible barrier, Baltasar strode forward and wrapped his eldest son in a close embrace. "Allah be praised for sending you safely home to us!" He stood away. "You aren't wounded, are you?"

"Sound in every limb, *alhemdulillah*." Malek ran his hands down over his face, kissed the palms, touched his chest. He hesitated, weighing his words. "The fortress at Shakif Arnun is proving stubborn. I'll not be able to stay here long. The sultan was concerned when he heard Ummi was so ill, but I must return to my duties shortly—"

"If the sultan was so concerned, why could he not have released you once the Franj were trounced?"

Malek drew himself up. "The war is never over. From one end of the empire to the other there are insurrections. And there have been attempts on the sultan's life by the *hashshashin*, though praise be to God he has thus far escaped unharmed. But as his protection and his shield I must go back to him as soon as I can."

"The life of Salah ad-Din is clearly more important to you than your own mother's."

Aisa looked from one man to the other, his loyalties torn. He did not understand the root of the anger between them, but he felt he must somehow intervene. He grabbed his brother's arm. "Tell me again about the Battle of Hattin!"

He never tired of hearing about the famous rout of the Christians—how their great general Salah ad-Din had prevented the invaders from reaching the wells and water sources along their route, and delayed the battle until the sun beat mercilessly down on the heads of the infidel and all they could see behind the shoulders of their foe, stretching like a sheet of cool silver, was Lake Tiberias, that the Franj called Galilee. How the Christians had rushed into the fray with the sun in their eyes and their minds ravaged by the promise of water, and been herded and slaughtered like sheep at Eid. It was a thousand times more exciting to hear such events from your own brother's lips than from the fat old baker or the water-seller.

"Another time, little brother. I did not come here to tell war stories." Malek stole a look at his father, his glance resting on the telltale traces of the cruel wounds the old man had suffered in a battle with a less fortunate outcome. "How is she, Baba?"

Baltasar sighed. "The doctor says the hand of death is upon her."

"Dr. Abas? That old fraud. Have you let Yacub of Nablus see her?"

The older man looked away. "He's a Jew," Baltasar said shortly, as if this was explanation enough.

"Yacub attends the Emir Karakush. The emir is known to be very difficult to please, so, Jewish or no, he must be good."

"If he's so good, why hasn't he cured that damned eunuch? Tell me that!"

Malek took a breath. "At least let him take a look at Ummi. What harm can it do?"

"You've been away for two years, and within ten minutes of being back you think you can tell your father what to do in his own home, with his own wife?"

Malek held his father's angry gaze for a long moment, then he spread his hands and took a pace backwards. "I am sure you know best, Baba," he said.

Behind them, Aisa stole a surreptitious glance over the wall of the terrace. From up there you could see right over the city— the Friday Mosque, with its green-tiled roof and tall minaret, the reed roofs of the covered market and the great bazaar beyond, past the whitewashed houses of the Genoan and Venetian merchants to the boats bobbing in the inner harbour, and beyond that to the narrow spire of the Tower of Flies, rising stark against the glinting sea beyond. Somewhere down there was the house of a renowned Jewish doctor by the name of Yacub of Nablus, and he intended to find him.

A rattle of feathers broke the stillness of the air, and the black dewlap returned, wings and feet spread wide for a landing.

"Good girl," Baltasar crooned. "What a good girl you are,

Ayesha." He had names for all of them, and could tell them apart in a second.

Aisa ran across the terrace. "Look, look! She's carrying a message!"

Attached to the pigeon, above the red twine, was a curl of paper. Baltasar carefully teased it off the bird, but unwinding it without his missing fingers was difficult, and when he dropped it for the third time Aisa could bear it no longer. Bending his head over the tiny scroll, he squinted, then pulled back, disappointed. "I can't read it."

Malek peered over his shoulder, and grinned at the series of dots and dashes. Malek held it out to Baltasar and the old man laughed, a creaky sound like a rusty gate, as if laughing was a thing he had forgotten how to do.

Aisa looked from one to the other. "What? What is it?"

"He knew I was coming home." Malek smiled, a flash of delight that brought a light to his eyes.

Aisa looked puzzled. "Is it a code?"

His brother nodded. "We devised it when I was about your age."

"What does it say?"

"Hello from Sorgan."

Aisa was disappointed. Then he brightened. "Will you teach me the code? Will you, Malek, will you?"

His elder brother ruffled his hair. "Perhaps, little pest. If you are good."

That night Zohra lay awake beneath her cover on the divan opposite her mother, listening to the ragged draw of her breath. With her eyes closed, she conjured Nathanael's dark, laughing eyes, his long, clever fingers. A thrill of heat raced through her core.

No! She must not think about him and the things they did together. He was Jewish; she was Muslim. For them even to be alone together was wrong. And if her father ever found out, he would assuredly kill them both. The honour of their family was at stake. The trouble was, it was this very transgression that made their liaisons so thrilling.

And so she lay there beneath the covers, trying not to touch herself in the way Nathanael touched her, trying not to think of the sounds he made when she touched him, trying not to think at all.

The next day she overslept past first prayer and failed to wake in time to prevent Nima soiling the bed. She had to strip and wash her mother, then quietly fetch Aisa to help her move the patient across to the other divan. After that she had to manhandle the wool-stuffed mattress out into the courtyard to be washed and then dried by the sun, which refused to come out from behind the clouds. This meant the mattress was still wet by the time the ram had to be slaughtered, and she feared the djinns would be drawn by all the spilled blood and would creep into the mattress.

Kamal came in to see his mother and threw a tantrum that she was not able to see him in the beautiful white robe Malek had bought for him. "I hate you!" he shouted at his father. "I'm not coming to the mosque—I don't want to be seen out with you. You're such a hypocrite! You don't care about Ummi at all. All you care about is your goddamned pigeons!"

And then he fled Baltasar's clutches and ran from the house, weeping.

Through it all, a pebble in a stream, Nima slept on.

Malek and Zohra exchanged glances. Her elder brother's face settled into its habitual cast, with lines deeply graven on his brow and hollowed cheeks, and a natural expression of gravity rather than lightness. He had gone away a boy of nineteen, but he had returned a man, bearing the marks of battle—little white scars crisscrossing his tanned forearms. She wondered what would happen if he found out about Nathanael, and had to push the thought away for fear he would read it on her face.

Malek waited until Baltasar, Sorgan and Aisa left for the mosque, saying that he would catch them up, then asked, "How long has he been like this?"

"Ever since Ummi fell ill, really." She stopped. No, it had been longer than that. Even as an infant he had been given to terrible rages, biting his twin for stealing his toys, flinging his food around if he didn't like it. "He's always been troublesome."

"It's more than that," Malek said, frowning. "Maybe you don't see it, because you're with him every day, but he's changed. There's a nasty edge to him, a hardness that wasn't there before. He wouldn't have said such a hurtful thing to Baba before."

"He's very upset about Ummi."

"As we all are. Especially Baba. He's looking thin."

"I do my best!" Zohra cried. "It's hard running the household all on my own." Then she, too, burst into tears.

Malek shifted uncomfortably. "Yes, well, I want to talk to Baba about that." And before she could ask him what he meant he turned and walked quickly upstairs to change.

While the others were at noon prayers, Zohra took her frustrations out on the carcass of the ram, hacking the chitterlings out of its belly and hurling them over the washing line on the first floor roof terrace to dry. But when she came to marinate the meat for the meal, the scent of the honey ambushed her and she stood there, dazed, remembering how Nathanael had once dribbled honey over her bare skin and licked it off again with a tongue as neat and rasping as a cat's. It had been at once disgusting and ecstatic. It thrilled her now, remembering. How could she give him up? Surely she deserved a little happiness amidst all the turmoil and gloom, a little reward for all her hard work?

The atmosphere over dinner was strained. Zohra could feel the tensions like the over-tightened strings of an oud, each word spoken striking a discordant note. Kamal had not returned from wherever he had run to in his fit of temper, and Malek and Aisa had been unable to find him. Sorgan was carefully concentrating on his food. Even the usually irrepressible Aisa was quiet. The conversation was left to Baltasar and Malek, and it soon became combative.

"Salah ad-Din made a big mistake with Tyre, not winkling Conrad out of the city when he had the chance. He had all the luck running for him after taking al-Quds." Baltasar refused to call Jerusalem by anything other than its Arab name.

"He could not have expected the Egyptians to be so lax."

"Egyptians!" his father shouted. "Who would trust an Egyptian? If it hadn't been for the Egyptians, we would never have been routed at Ramla, and I would still be in the army teaching green boys like you the way to do things!" He waved his damaged arm at Malek. "The sultan does not learn his lessons. After that fiasco everyone knew you couldn't trust an Egyptian to do anything right. You have to give them orders three times, and then put a good Syrian in charge of them."

"It was their navy," Malek pointed out mildly. "You can't just catapult your own commanders in over the top of their officers. Granted, they should have been on better guard, and not taken the words 'night watch' at face value, but it was a daring raid. You can't prepare for every eventuality."

"Hark to the hero!" Baltasar looked around the table in mock astonishment. "Seven years in the army and he talks as if he's a veteran of thirty campaigns! Salah ad-Din lost us a navy and the port of Tyre that day. He should have stuck to his task and taken it when he had the chance. Instead he gave Conrad a year to strengthen the city's defences, and if the bloody Franj decide they want their holy city back, now they've got a safe port for a beachhead."

Malek applied himself to the communal dish of lamb and apricots. "This is very good, Zohra," he said stiffly.

She gave him a tight little smile. "It's Ummi's recipe."

But Baltasar was not to be deflected. "And on top of all that, he shouldn't have let their so-called king go free."

"The King of Jerusalem was ransomed for a great deal of money," Malek said. "His wife pleaded piteously for his life."

"Some perfumed Franj chit falls to her knees before your beloved sultan and his heart melts like sugar in tea."

"Sibylla is a queen, and the sultan is a man of mercy. And Guy gave his word never again to draw a sword against the sultan, and always to be his faithful bondsman—"

"The word of a Franj! I'd sooner take the word of a dog! He is too trusting, Salah ad-Din, a fool."

Malek sighed. "The Guardian of the Faithful is a very great man. I feel honoured to be one of his burning coals."

"Burning coals! What crap." Baltasar glared at his eldest son, then looked away. Malek clenched his hands in his lap.

Kamal did not return until the next morning. When he did it was in the company of Bashar Muallem, a narrow-faced lad Zohra did not like. She had once overheard him talking nonsense with the twins—extremist rubbish about murder and martyrdom—and he and Aisa had got into a heated argument. Bashar had picked up a stone and hit Aisa in the mouth with it, and Aisa had lost some teeth: an unpleasant encounter. But at least Aisa had had the wisdom to avoid Bashar since then.

For Kamal, however, this assault on his twin had the opposite effect: he began to dog Bashar as if he were some sort of hero. One day, Zohra had turned a corner on her way to the bazaar and found the pair of them crouched in an alley, their backs obscuring whatever creature was making small whining sounds. Had they found an injured animal? she wondered, but only for an instant. Bashar looked up, alerted to her presence, and said something to Kamal, who started and leapt to his feet. The next thing she knew a small feral dog shot past her, one eye a gory hole. She wanted to believe her brother did not hurt the animal, but all she could remember was the surreptitious way Kamal wiped a hand on his robe when he thought she was not looking.

The two boys were in the courtyard now. As she passed them on her way to the kitchen, Bashar raised his head and his eyes followed her, assessing her. His knowing eyes stripped her naked, not with desire but with a cold cruelty. His gaze made her feel unclean.

A moment later Kamal came into the kitchen. "Tea, with plenty of sugar. And some honeycakes. We've been up all night and we're starving."

She turned. "Up all night? What have you been doing?"

"Nothing."

Kamal looked guilty, but under the guilt she could detect glee. She put her palm on his forehead. "You look feverish."

He swiped her hand away. "I'm fine, woman. Just bring us the tea." And he turned on his heel rudely and went back outside.

"Make your own!" she shouted after him.

In the end she made tea, but not for Kamal and Bashar. Instead, she made up a tray of tea, bread, oil and olives and the last of the baklava and took it to her father and Malek in the upstairs salon. Even before she got to the top of the stairs, she could hear raised voices. The air was hot with anger.

"It's not a matter of what I say, it's what sources are telling us. There's a big army on the march under the command of the Holy Roman Emperor Barbarossa. They say it's the largest fighting force the Christians have ever mustered."

"If the sultan is the general you say he is he'll stop them before they reach Antioch."

"Even so, you'd be much safer in Damascus."

Zohra startled so badly she almost dropped the tray. Damascus? She couldn't leave Akka. Panic made the blood beat so loudly in her ears she could hardly make out her father's response, and then her brother was talking again.

"Zohra is run off her feet—you only have to look at her. She's worn out trying to run the household with no help—"

"What would you know about it? You've been away for two years. Zohra is doing a fine job, and the boys, they help as much as they can."

Zohra wanted to go in, but at the same time she wanted to hear the discussion.

"Besides," Baltasar went on, "your mother is far too sick to be moved now."

"She would have a better chance of recovery in Damascus. I could arrange a litter to carry her, with guards to accompany you all and a doctor for the journey. The cousins will pack up the house here and keep it safe while you're away. Until she's better. Or, if you decide to stay in Damascus they'll arrange to send everything to you in the city."

Baltasar's face darkened. "You spoke about this without my permission?"

"Do I need your permission to speak to my own cousins?"

"I am still the head of this household, cripple or no!"

There was a long, charged pause. Then Malek said, "There's another reason. The Pisan navy has joined the siege of Tyre and is blockading the port."

His father snorted. "Conrad's no fool. He's reinforced Tyre's defences and he'll not give the city up. The king with no king-dom will be made to sit outside the walls till his army starves itself to death and his brigand Pisans desert." He shook his head. "Salah ad-Din should have cut the head off the man when he had the chance."

Malek sighed. "Having offered the King of Jerusalem hospitality, that would have been a dishonourable act. It's easy to judge the actions of the past. But Guy will need a port as a beachhead for his forces and supplies. If he decides to give up on Tyre——"

"He will come for Akka next? Is that what you mean? Spit it out, boy."

Wearily, Malek acceded.

"Well, he won't take it. With the arsenal and treasury here, the eunuch has made the city near impregnable. I'll take my chances against the cur and his band of snapping dogs. We are staying put—here, in this house—and there's an end to it."

Into the heavy silence that followed this pronouncement Zohra stepped. Malek, looking defeated, got to his feet and took the tray.

"Thank you, sister. It's very good of you."

"I heard what you said. About moving to Damascus."

"You were listening outside the door?"

"You were shouting to high heaven. It did not take much spying! I'm not sure we can move Ummi. She's very weak. It would be a great upheaval."

The two men exchanged a long look. The argument was brewing again, so Zohra left them to it.

Later, Zohra was sitting with her mother, some mending lying idle in her lap, not quite dozing, when Malek came in. Her head snapped up.

"Sorry. I didn't mean to disturb you." He watched his mother for several long moments. Then he said, "Is there nothing you can do to persuade him to move to Damascus?"

Terror stirred again. "He's a very proud man. He can't bear

anyone to say he can't take care of his own family, that he needs help. He chased Jamilla and Khalida out of the house when they came bringing food for us when Ummi first fell sick. Honestly, he roared at them like a lion. But it's true what I said: I don't think she can be moved. Well, you've seen her, how weak she is. And it's a long way, Damascus."

She watched as he set his jaw. "Zohra, it's not only Ummi I'm thinking about. I have to go back in a few days. It'll be harder if I have to worry about you here. Look, I've spoken to Rachid and Tariq. They'll assemble an escort and a litter for Ummi, and Uncle Omar will find a reputable doctor to accompany you. The family in Damascus will have everything else you need. But if there's anything you need sent, Uncle Omar will arrange to have it sent on."

"But, Baba—"

"He must choose to come or stay as he will. He's head of the family, but, Zohra, he's not in his right mind. Pain and grief are fogging his judgment. I must act for him. How could I ever forgive myself if anything were to happen to you?"

Zohra felt her mouth go dry. She had been sure Baba would have the last word, that Malek would bow his head to his decision. It was not her place to make her opinion heard—but what if she did not? She wet her lips. "Just look at her. Does she look like a woman who can survive even two miles in a litter?" When it seemed as if he might still press on, she said quickly, "And you know Baba will never leave. He has his pigeons. And Aisa and Kamal have their friends, and their studies—"

"Kamal's 'friends' are one of the reasons I urge you to go to Damascus. Bashar's brother joined the *hashshashin* last year, got himself killed in Aleppo in some crazy assassination attempt. Bashar was talking about joining them and carrying on where his brother left off. I don't want Kamal around him. He's too impressionable. He needs a firm hand, or he'll take a wrong turn. I fear for him, Zohra."

"I do my best!" she cried defensively.

"I know you do, but he needs good men around him. The cousins in Damascus will take him under their wing, teach him the business, set him on the right path. And you will have help with Ummi, and can share the chores with the girls. And Ummi can receive proper medical care. Baba too, if he will only let someone help him."

Zohra knew Malek had the best of intentions, but suddenly she could bear this no longer. "If you can't persuade Baba to move to Damascus, I don't know how I can, as a mere woman! And now I have a woman's chores to see to, so please excuse me." She stood up, dropped the unmended robe down on the clothes chest, dusted her hands down her skirts and gave him a firm look.

Malek sighed. "If you need me, I'll be with Tariq and Rachid." He looked down at his sleeping mother. "Goodbye, Ummi. May Allah grant you peace." He kissed her forehead, then turned and left the room without looking back.

Zohra watched him go, seeing how his back was rigid with tension, and was assailed not only by guilt but also the overwhelming feeling that she would never see him again.

❄

T hat afternoon, Nathanael lay with Zohra in his arms, dozing sweetly with the air from the open window drying their sweat. She sighed. "I wish we could do this all the time."

"You would kill me within a fortnight, little wildcat!"

A lazy smile. "More like a contented butcher's cat. I wish . . . I wish there were just the two of us in a house of our own and all the time in the world to be together. And I would make it beautiful and always clean because it would be my pleasure and no chore. And I would cook for you—oh, what I would cook! Capons stuffed with almonds and coriander; lamb roasted with honey and garlic; tarts of goat's cheese and onions cooked in sugar cane; bread studded with olives; parcels of saffron chicken; fruit poached with cinnamon and cloves—"

"And then when I was so fat I could no longer move, you would roast me whole and eat me up!"

"I would never want to eat you." She turned and caught Nat's eye, gleaming provocatively. "Well, there is eating and eating!"

"Wicked girl: I am your slave." He had never felt like this before. Her amber glances pierced him like knives. Any absence of more than a day felt like a physical pain.

"Well then, lie still and let me eat you up, slave." Zohra grabbed his hand and started to nibble at his fingers, and they fought and rolled like beasts in the tangle of fabrics until Nathanael managed to straddle her with a knee on each wrist to keep the marauding hands at bay.

His face became solemn. "I want you to promise me that if we are ever starving and likely to die that you will eat me." And as Zohra began to protest, "No, I mean it."

Zohra screwed up her face in disgust. "You are gruesome. I expect it's what comes of being a doctor's son and having to deal with death and bodies all the time."

"I am a doctor myself. For a year in Jerusalem and a year back here, in case you'd forgotten," he chided. "Anyway, they say that human flesh tastes no worse than pork."

"And how would you know about that?"

"I have tried a little pork. I believe in trying everything once. How else are we to truly know the world?"

Zohra flung him off at last. "Ugh, to eat a pig! You are atrocious. Whatever made you bring up such a horrible subject anyway?"

He hesitated, not wanting to tell her of the unsettling dream he'd had. She would think him strange. It would cast a shadow. Instead, he tried for briskness. "Come now. Get up, lazy lump, and show me you have retained what I taught you the last time you were here—no, not that, little wanton!"

They were laughing so hard they never heard the first knock at the door. Then Nat put a hand over Zohra's mouth. "Shh . . . shh. Stay. Be quiet."

The knock came again. Crawling across the divan with the patchwork cover pulled over his loins, he peered through the jalousie, then drew back swiftly. "It's a boy. He must be looking for my father. Maybe I should go down in case it's something urgent."

"If it's urgent he'll knock again."

They waited, and through the wooden blind Nathanael saw him move away. He sat back on the divan, but the spell was broken now.

"Come on. Your letters. I am beginning to wonder whether you ever actually wanted me to teach you how to read and write, or if it was just some ploy to keep coming here for other reasons."

Zohra chewed her lip as she dressed. "My father believes only boys need to be educated. Ummi took my side and even talked with the *ma'alema* to give me lessons, but she's been too ill this past year to take an interest in anything so trivial."

"There's nothing trivial about education," Nat said fervently. "It's the only way anyone develops their own thoughts, becomes a real person, not just some reflection of their little world. And no woman will ever be independent without some learning, unless she's as wealthy as the Queen of Sheba."

"Well, I'm never going to be that." Zohra unwrapped the little leather-bound book and set it on the table, then shook the inkpot and dipped a sharpened reed pen in it. After much deliberation, she formed a long row of markings upon a new piece of paper.

It had thrilled Nat to teach her the connection between the sound of a word spoken or chanted and the shape made to represent it with ink, to see what a revelation it had been to her. Although she had in the beginning found it difficult to memorize the Arabic characters, now her struggle was more in the form of the exercise, making them flow elegantly across the page without constantly having to lift the pen and chew the end and think hard. He was surprised by how profound a pleasure it gave him to be able to give her something so intangible, yet with such infinite value.

He watched her for several minutes as she concentrated, frowning slightly over her letters. The choice of exercise had been deliberate: to copy a love poem by Ibn Hazm, that great classical Arabic poet. But he rather suspected she had not taken in the import of the lovely words, being so caught up in the difficulty of the transcription.

Nat waited till she lifted the reed-pen then pulled the paper towards him. "You'll never make a calligrapher: your hand is uncommonly poor, and your spelling, too! 'I would cut open my . . .' What on earth does that say?" He pointed to a formless squiggle.

"'Heart.' It's quite clear to me." Zohra threw the pen down, much put out. "You can read what it says, can't you? Isn't that all that matters?"

"What, are you only going to write little love notes to me all your life?" He tousled her hair.

Zohra smoothed it down again. "It's not a little love note to you, it's just a poem by some man in some other time that I'm copying as an exercise. I'm no scholar. I just want to be able to understand writing and to make myself understood." She yawned and stretched. "I should go back. I've been longer than I should. It's not fair on the twins."

Nathanael felt a little affronted. Was she punishing him for his criticism? Did she realize she held such power? "You're always complaining they don't do their fair share. Still, I expect Abi will be back from the citadel soon, and if he catches you here you'll never get away." The equanimity with which his parents had accepted Zohra's frequent presence had at first disturbed him. Were they being deliberately dense? He wondered at first, but then one day he had heard them talking quietly in the salon when they'd thought him upstairs.

"I'm thinking of Zohra. If her father finds out there will be hell to pay. And he'd be within his rights to denounce Nat to the judge." His mother's voice.

"If the qadi comes we will talk to him. He will see we are decent people, not out to cause trouble. There are worse matches to be made. Look at the two of us." There had been a smile in Yacub's voice. Sara, Nat's mother, had also been born to a Muslim family and given the name Zohra. When she converted she took the Jewish version of the name.

"You think everyone is as accepting as my family were?" she said. "It's only because my mother and her sisters were romantics to the bone that I was not killed on the spot." This was not the full truth. The family ran a farm. For Zohra to marry a doctor—Jew or no—was a huge step up the economic ladder, and they all knew it.

A pause. Then Yacub said, "The heart knows no bounds, my love. If we break them apart, they will only be in greater jeopardy, meeting one another in secret, in places of lesser safety. They do no one harm."

"You say that now, but what if he gets her pregnant?"

"If he gets her pregnant, he's a poor student of anatomy, my dear, and no son of mine!"

Nat, listening, had winced and coloured. So they knew the whole of it. And so did he. He knew full well that every day they met, every time they touched, he put Zohra in danger. A Muslim girl's reputation was fiercely guarded by her family. Any hint of scandal and she would be unmarriageable in the eyes of her community. But he could not have stopped, not even if he'd wanted to. And he did not want to. The very idea turned him cold from the inside out.

Zohra laughed now. "Your father could talk the legs off a mule!"

"He's always like this when Mother's away visiting her sisters." Sara's sisters still lived on the family farm outside the city walls. "You'd think he didn't pass a word with his patients all day long."

"My father hardly talks to me at all. And Sorgan, he just sings to himself, and the twins are . . . well, they're young. As for Malek, I don't think he'll ever speak to me again."

Nat put a hand to her cheek. "I'm glad you didn't go to Damascus, sweetheart. I think if you had, I would have died."

Zohra stared at him, and at once he could see he'd overstepped the mark. In all their time together he had never made anything but light of the way they were with each other, and so she was able to make light of it too: a friendship, just a loving friendship, but not something that would drive you to despair or death—that was for the tellers of tales only, the men who sat in the marketplace and told stories of love-fraught emirs and beautiful, merciless maidens; of girls forced to marry ugly old men, girls who pined away for the love of a young carpenter.

Zohra looked uncomfortable, and when he leaned in to kiss her she laughed and ducked her head away. Nat felt wounded.

He watched her pick up the little volume and rub a thumb across the soft, worn leather. "Can I borrow the book?" she asked, surprising him.

"Of course. Keep it as a gift."

When they parted company at the door to the alley he caught her by the arm, pulled her roughly back and kissed her full on the mouth. It was something he felt he had to do—somehow she seemed to have slipped away from him, and he needed to lay claim to her once more.

"Zohra!"

The cry caused them to spring apart. Out of the shadows on the other side of the alley stepped a young man. For a moment he looked like a total stranger, older than his years, unfamiliar in this context. Zohra recognized him with a shiver—of shame, and fear. "Aisa—what? What is it?" But suddenly she knew with a horrible certainty who had been knocking on the door earlier and why. "Ummi." A statement, not a question.

"I was looking for the doctor, Yacub . . ." He was uncomfortable, would not meet her eye.

Nathanael took charge of the situation. "I'll come with you." He stepped back into the house and seconds later re-emerged with a large leather bag over his shoulder.

Aisa was bewildered. "We need the doctor, old Yacub—"

"I am the doctor," Nat told him firmly.

They ran through the narrow streets of the medina, avoiding the impenetrable crowds in the bazaar by skirting the market on its shortest side, a route that took them past the leatherworkers, the furniture makers and the woodworkers' stalls. They had just come within sight of their street when a bloodstained figure came running towards them.

Zohra turned and stared. "Kamal?"

He did not stop.

"Kamal!"

The volume of her own scream shocked her, but he did not even look back. Dread gripped her now. "Allah, Allah . . . what has happened?"

The door to the house was wide open. Inside, distantly, the desolate lowing of an animal in unbearable pain could be heard. And someone else was singing, a child's song, sweet and melancholy. The two sounds merged into something nonsensical, something jarring and discordant.

Zohra ran up the stairs, shoes and all, towards her mother's room. Just outside, in the corridor, Sorgan sat on the floor, rocking from side to side, his eyes closed, his arms around himself, singing. It was an unnerving sight to see a grown man so, but worse were the noises from up on the terrace. Her father, Baltasar, bellowing as if possessed. She was about to charge on up the stairs when she glimpsed through the half-open door her mother, arms outflung, on the divan.

She ran to the bedside. Nima's face was turned towards her, mouth open, features contorted. Her eyes stared into space; her hands were claws. Zohra sank to her knees. "Oh, Ummi. Oh no, no . . ."

Just moments behind her, Nathanael crouched and pressed his fingers against Nima's neck. Then he bent his head and placed an ear against her belly. At last he straightened up.

"She's dead, Zohra. I'm so sorry." With a practised hand, he closed the lids over the staring eyes.

Aisa, propped against the wall beside the door as if it were the only thing holding him upright, made a small, inarticulate sound.

"This is a hard thing to say, but I'm afraid she did not die naturally."

Zohra looked up at Nat, uncomprehending.

"I'm sorry, my love, but someone hastened her end." Nathanael picked up the yellow cushion from the floor, the one Zohra used to prop Nima up in order to ease the passage of food and water. He turned it over, frowned, held it out to her.

The yellow silk bore a damp stain the size and shape of a mouth.

PART FOUR

Besieged

13

The Syrian hills

❈

Malek Najib was unaware of the drama unravelling at his family home as he rode out of Akka. All that he had come to do there he had failed at. He had been so determined, this time, not to rise to his father's bait, not to lose control, to put the case—so clear to any right-thinking person—coolly and rationally. He had planned to introduce the subject of moving the family back to Damascus gradually over the course of his visit, to let the idea take root in his father's stubborn mind, then to shore it up with unassailable argument and soothing reason. But he had reckoned without Baltasar's savage, wounded pride and contempt for the man Malek held highest in his esteem, the Commander of the Faithful, Salah ad-Din.

He should, he knew, have allowed Baltasar to voice his criticisms without reaction, as the sultan himself would have done. Faced with the bitter fury of the broken veteran, Salah ad-Din would have listened to what the old man said with that grave smile on his thin, intelligent face, his eyes pinned on the speaker, as if weighing every word. And then he would have nodded, conceded the validity of Baltasar's opinion and quoted some apposite verse from the holy Qur'an that turned the attack aside. He would have re-engaged the man the next day, patiently, before slipping in a quiet doubt here, a gentle cavil there, until at last—even if it took many days—Baltasar would have announced he was moving the family back to Damascus after all, and any man who told him not to he would call a fool.

Malek sighed deeply. The sultan had given him permission to make this visit, having urged his lieutenant to move his family back to the capital. He was not sure which was worse: that he had not succeeded in his mission, or that he had to tell Salah ad-Din and see the disappointment—fleeting, well-masked but indubitably present—in the sultan's eyes.

He was oblivious to the beauty of the day, to the artistry of the ancient city gates he passed through, to the soft ochre limestone of the city walls, to the bounty of the orchards through which he passed—the oranges and apricots glowing in their nests of luxuriant green leaves, the lemons shining like stars, the plums and figs swelling on the branch, the pomegranates just beginning to take on their blush—and, beyond, to the olives and dates growing by the river, to the swoop of swallows over the crops and the call of larks in the brilliant blue bowl of the sky. He took no pleasure in the smooth flow of his horse's gait, the sheen on its chestnut coat, the intelligent carriage of its head, or in the smart figure he cut in his green tunic, embroidered with fine silver thread; the curved, damascened sword at his waist in its scabbard of figured leather; the supple riding boots that had cost him two weeks' pay. All was as ash in his mouth.

He took the old road along the coast, skirting the marshland, then turned north and west towards the uplands. Tell el-Musalliyin, the Hill of Prayers, loomed on the skyline to his right; to his left, the sea stretched turquoise and sparkling, its waters plied by shipping on its way to dock in Akka's spacious harbour, bearing trade goods from every corner of the world. Usually, this would have been enough to lighten his heart, the idea that the markets were full to bursting, that his pay bought his family all they needed. But riding out that morning, he could not help but feel misfortune was brewing. At the moment it was a storm far out at sea, but soon it would sweep inland, and there would be nothing he could do to avert it.

Perhaps this was why he tarried rather than take the fastest route, up through the Toron range, north-east back towards Salah ad-Din's camp. The thought of the sultan's displeasure, no matter how courteously masked, was too painful to contemplate; he thought he might take the longer route and consider the words he would use to explain away his failure.

He took his rest that night curled into a hollow on the side of one of the tawny hills, woke with the dawn, made his prayers facing away from the sea, brewed some strong thyme tea to put strength in his bones for the ride ahead and ate the bread his cousin had baked for him before he left Akka, unaware of the yearning sighs Jamilla had given as she pummelled her frustrations into the dough, or the kiss she had bestowed on the final baked item.

When he saddled up the chestnut it seemed more skittish than usual, throwing its head and blowing hard for no reason. Wrestling it into some semblance of obedience, he pointed its head uphill towards the ridge and put his heels to its barrel, hoping that the extra effort required would render the animal more complaisant. It was the most handsome horse he had ever owned, taken during the surrender of the Hospitaller fortress of Kaukub, called by the Franj Belvoir; but it was also the most contrary. He had had bare weeks to convert it from its infidel ways, and it had proved resistant. On the ride down to Akka he had thought it more responsive, but now here it was again playing up, jigging in a circle, flicking its ears as if spooked by something. He hauled at its head as it tried to jaunt right again and at last fought it to a standstill as he scanned the uniformly brown scrub for the cairn that marked the trail. But then the contrary animal circled again, pulling at the bit, and that was when he saw it.

A flash of silver to the north, down near the sea. Shading his eyes, Malek gazed into the distance but saw nothing but heat haze and a solitary hawk riding a current of hot air. He was about to wrestle his mount back towards the track when it came again: the sun winking off something far away, where Akka's coast road turned north towards Tyre.

Malek's chest constricted. Then, with sudden compulsion, he drove his mount hard up to the top of the highest part of the ridge, and while it puffed and blew, fat and out of condition, he stood up in the stirrups to get a better view. There! Dust rising like a cloud, and through it little flashes of light. A lot of men on the move. Had the sultan broken the siege at the fort and brought the army down out of the hills? For a few moments his breathing stilled and settled. But then he remembered the easier route would be by Tiberias and the great west road. To have come down from the Qala'at al-Shakif to the position he surveyed now, where the dust was stirred up and metal caught the sun, would have meant a precipitous ascent of the range, followed by an equally steep descent, farther to the north than was necessary.

He rode along the ridge, parallel to the sea, never taking his eyes off the ominous dust cloud until, twenty minutes later, his worst fears were realized.

By the time he saw the fires of the encampment below the Castle on the Rock hours later, Malek could hardly stay upright in the saddle. But the chestnut had been magnificent, running all day without respite, galloping along the upland tracks as surefooted as a goat. As they came down out of the hills guards ran to challenge them.

"*Allahu akhbar,*" he croaked, and half fell from his horse.

"It's Malek," the first sentinel declared. "One of the burning coals." Recognizing him, they helped him up and dusted him down and took the chestnut to the paddock.

"Why in such a state, lad?" asked an older guard. "Couldn't you stay away? Did you miss us that much?"

They laughed a little. But they had seen the state of the chestnut, its coat rimed with salt stains, and when he shook his head wearily and looked as if he might collapse, they stopped laughing.

"Take me to the Commander of the Faithful," he said, and they escorted him to the sultan's war tent.

Within, Salah ad-Din sat cross-legged on cushions, a book spread open in his lap. On the low table before him was a tray bearing a silver teapot, steaming fragrantly into the night air, some glasses and a wide bowl of fruit—damsons and apricots, black plums with the bloom still upon them, brought from gardens in the capital that very day by a series of couriers. Beside him, illuminated by a glass lantern casting out through its tinted shades a spill of coloured light, sat his friend Baha ad-Din, the qadi of the army, his hands curled around a beaker of tea as if for warmth, though the braziers glowed red in the corners of the tent, and curls of frankincense wound their way through the dim air between. There was a third man in the tent, apart from the group of servants gathered discreetly to the side of the wooden alcove wherein lay the sultan's bed. Reclining on a pile of cushions with a platter of chicken bones discarded at his side was the master of the fortress they besieged: Reginald of Sidon.

Malek swayed, light-headed. He concentrated on not pitching nose-first into the table, then prostrated himself with as much grace as he could muster. Only when he was down on the floor with his hand in front of his face about to grasp the sultan's robe to bring it to his lips did he remember his filthy state. Dust had adhered to his sweat and dried to a crust over his exposed skin. He could smell his sweat, acrid, as he raised his arm, and felt suddenly like a savage. He lay there trembling, trying to form the dire news into a cogent sentence, when a hand touched him lightly on the shoulder.

"Get up, Malek. It is Malek, isn't it? Though it is a little hard to tell beneath the grime of the road." A note of gentle reproof. To be dirty was an affront to God, rather than to himself.

"My lord, forgive me, I did not think the news could wait for the luxury of a bath." He rose unsteadily, aware all the time of the Franj lord's eyes upon him. He slid a glance in the man's direction. Malek could not get used to the sight of beardless men, especially with such pale skins. They seemed more like ghosts. He had seen small children burst into tears at a glimpse of them.

Salah ad-Din smiled. "Lord Reginald is my honoured guest. You may speak in his presence as you would with me alone." Bending forward, he poured tea in a gleaming stream from the silver pot into a small decorated glass and held it out to Malek. "Drink this down and then tell me what could not wait for a bath."

Malek tried not to gulp the tea greedily. So dazzled was he to have been served by his master's own hand that he almost forgot the words he had been so carefully preparing. "My lord," he managed at last, "the enemy is moving south from Tyre upon the city of Akka. At their head they fly the banner of the King of Jerusalem, Guy of Lusignan."

The sultan's expression did not change. Malek might as well have said that the sea was blue, the tide was coming in or that the moon had risen. Not by the flicker of an eyelid did he betray how unwelcome this news must be, when his army was already stretched from Aleppo to the Moab. Instead, he pushed the bowl of fruit towards Malek, and when the young soldier did not immediately react he selected a soft, black plum, turning it carefully in his long, bony fingers, scrutinizing it for any sign of blemish before passing it to Malek.

"You have ridden all day. You should eat something."

Pinned by that brilliant stare, Malek was shocked to see how frail his master appeared: older, his sun-seamed cheeks sunken, white hairs salting the once-black eyebrows and beard. He thought of how his mother had looked, shrunken and inert in her narrow bed, her skin like paper, her face fallen in to reveal the skull beneath.

Salah ad-Din steepled his fingers, his face mild and patient, as Malek ate the plum and then choked out the rest of his information: a great army—like a swarm of locusts—the banners of a thousand knights mounted on huge chargers, a company of Templars, another of Hospitallers, and many thousand foot soldiers. "Forgive me, my lord, but I am not trained in the art of estimating such a host."

Baha ad-Din glared at him as if this news was his fault, while the Lord of Sidon's eyes gleamed like those of a fox that has seen some new and unexpected escape route.

"Worse, my lord, I saw many sails on the horizon, warships entering the Bay of Akka. Forty or fifty of them, big ships, not merchant vessels . . ."

Now the scribe got to his feet, huffing loudly, for he was a big man and had been comfortable. "That snake Guy of Lusignan, God curse his name! I knew we should have left him chained in Tortosa. Just so much is a Christian's word worth." He flicked his fingers dismissively, a man ridding himself of filth. "They are all the same." And he glared at Reginald of Sidon. The wily old nobleman gazed back at him through half-lidded eyes, a basilisk stare.

The sultan beckoned to one of the young pages. "Have some water heated and add thyme and rosemary to fragrance it. My burning coal has ridden far today." He reclined into his cushions and arranged his burnous over his knees as if he felt the cold despite the warmth in the tent. "And tell me, Asfar, is she in the same condition as her rider, all covered in dust and sweat and half dead on her feet?"

Malek nodded dumbly, astonished that the sultan should even consider the welfare of a horse at this time, let alone remember its name and gender.

"She is a fine animal," Salah ad-Din continued, "of the Jaran bloodline, I believe. A strong arch to the neck, small head, neat fetlocks. You should breed from her when the time is right." He prided himself on his knowledge of all the finest Arab horses, their ancestry, strengths and weaknesses, and had been almost as delighted to liberate those they had come by at Belvoir from their Franj masters as he was at the freeing of the Muslim prisoners held at the fort. "Make sure the horse is well attended to," he told another page. "Give her grain from my own store."

"Shall I summon your generals?" Baha ad-Din asked.

The sultan closed his eyes for a long moment. Then he said gravely, "There is no immediate hurry." He turned back to Malek. "And your mother, dear boy, how does she fare?"

Malek swallowed. "My mother remains very ill," he said, for he was unaware that, long miles behind him and less than a day ago, Nima Najib had passed away. It seemed wrong to be bothering the sultan with such trivial matters in the face of this new, immense crisis, but still he ploughed on. "My father—"

Salah ad-Din nodded. "Baltasar Najib, a valorous man. Severely wounded at the ford of Ramla, as I recall?"

"My father is a stubborn man, my lord. He deemed my mother too fragile to be moved."

"Well," the sultan said, "in light of these new circumstances he may well have proved himself wiser than I."

Malek bowed his head, cursing his own foolishness. Of course, who could leave Akka now? The city was surely under siege.

❄

They decamped from the Qala'at al-Shakif two days later, leaving a force sufficient to continue the blockade of the fortress and its master, held under lock and key, and they marched by night and day down the easy route by Tiberias. A contingent of troops was sent along the Toron ridge to watch the enemy's movements, with orders to rejoin the main army above Akka. Taking the ancient road from Nazareth, the Muslim army advanced on the port city from the south-east past Khafar Kenna, that the Christians called Cana, and from there made for the peak known as the Hill of the Carob Trees.

There, Salah ad-Din surveyed the scene impassively, even though the enemy covered the plain like locusts upon a field of wheat, blotting out the sere grass and the green crops, obliterating the bright streams and orchards. They had made their headquarters less than a mile from the city's east gate, upon the Hill of Prayers, which Malek had passed just a few days earlier, his only worry at that moment being how to break the news to his commander that he had been unable to win an argument with his father. How long ago that seemed.

Akka protruded south into the bay like a beard upon a jutting chin, its face fronting the sea, the hollow between chin and neck formed by the harbour. Two sides gave onto water; the landward perimeters rose in great golden walls topped by crenellations and guard-towers. It looked strongly defended, and it was.

The Franj battalions fanned out from the Hill of Prayers all around the city, from the ramparts of the old Templars' ward to the north, to the farms beyond the Accursed Tower and all the way around to the eastern wall. From their mass, standards fluttered on the breeze, a rainbow of colour. As if in defiant answer to the jaunty banners of the Franj, the golden-ochre ramparts of the city were lined with the banners of the caliphate, a crescent moon emblazoned on apricot silk. In the inner harbour a forest of masts marked out the vessels that rode there, safe at anchor. The iron chain would have been raised to keep out hostile ships, stretching from the harbour wall out to the rock in the open sea upon which the Tower of Flies stood, named for the place where long-ago pagans had made sacrifices to their gods, where blood had spilled and stunk and blue-bottles had swarmed. Thinking of this made Malek shiver: would those flies soon circle the island once more, buzzing with excitement at the stench of spilled blood?

He remembered when they had retaken the city from the Franj, not much more than two years ago. He had fought grimly at Salah ad-Din's side with the rest of the sultan's personal guard, his teeth gritted so hard as he swung and parried and chopped and battered his way through the defenders that his jaw had ached for days afterward, worse than any of the countless small wounds and bruises he had taken. All the while he had thought of his mother and sister inside the walls, whose lives would depend on their success that day, for if they failed in their attempt to take the city, reprisals against the resident Muslims would be cruel. There was no knowing to what depths Christians would sink in their vengeance and hatred: they had no honour. He remembered the stories he had been told about their taking of Jerusalem in the last century: the babies slaughtered, their heads displayed on pikes; old men and women tortured; hundreds burned, locked into synagogues and mosques; the streets running with blood . . .

In the end, capitulation had come swiftly and with relatively little bloodshed. The Franj had surrendered Akka more or less intact, and since then the city's defences had been reinforced under the eye of Karakush, the sultan's deputy, who had designed the defences at Cairo and made that city impregnable. He hoped they would be able to save his family for a second time.

As if the sultan sensed his young lieutenant's thoughts, he said now in a quiet voice, which carried just as far as he wished it to,

"Fear not, the city is strong and well provisioned. Her people are in the safest place while we deal with these dogs, *insh'allah*."

Those within earshot echoed "God willing" and added their own prayers. They included the other members of the sultan's personal guard—his burning coals—men who shared Malek's rank and devotion: Imad al-Din, the Lord of Sinjar, a man with the beaked face of a desert tribesman; the sultan's son Al-Malik az-Zahir; his handsome nephew Taki ad-Din, whom he loved more than all his sons put together; and behind them a company of mamluks out of North Africa, their skin as dark as aubergines. Around their heads they did not wear the usual mail coif or helm but just a long strip of red or white cotton cloth wound round and round to form turbans like great onions. They prided themselves on needing nothing more: "Our heads are like rocks!" their captain, Aibek al-Akhresh, would joke. "Nothing can split them."

When the sun was high the call to prayer was heard shimmering through the air, and they all dismounted, cleansed themselves as best they could, knelt in the direction of Mecca and prayed. Then they ate their dates and bread and drank water from the skins at their saddles. The sun beat down, and still more Franj arrived by land and sea, and still the sultan sat his horse, watching and saying hardly a word.

At last the scouts and spies returned and they rode to where his war tent had been erected on Tell Keisan. There they made their reports, and Salah ad-Din nodded, and the qadi of the army, Baha ad-Din, watched, and the sultan's scribe, Imad al-Din, took notes.

At last the sultan passed the word that they would outflank the Christians, extending their lines in a large crescent by which to venerate Allah himself, the horns of the moon to encompass the whole Franj army from north to south.

"And so," he said softly, "the besiegers become the besieged."

14

London

OCTOBER 1189

T he coronation of Richard, Duke of Aquitaine, eldest surviving son of Henry and Eleanor, took place in the abbey church of St. Peter in Westminster on the nones of September, and even though many rich and powerful men of the kingdom were excluded from the ceremony, I was there, attending upon Savaric de Bohun, crammed in with all the nobles of the court—lords and earls, bishops and barons. Not a woman or a Jew in sight, both banned as bringers of bad luck.

I stood in the crowd, thinking rich men smelled no better than poor men, as we waited for the heir and his lords. A rich purple cloth had been laid all the way from the church entrance, up the aisle to the high altar.

"Tyrian purple, the colour of emperors!" Savaric fairly swooned at the sight of so much of it. "So costly only kings can afford it, for they say it never fades. Such a purple is obtained from a dye called argaman. Do you know how it is made?"

I sighed. "I am sure you are going to tell me."

"It is made by the crushing of a million tiny snails, and those snails are to be found only in the seas off Tyre. Twelve thousand of them would be sufficient to dye your cuff, and for the best effect the creatures must be harvested only after the rising of the Dog Star. I read this in Pliny, so it must be true. When I return from the Holy Land, I shall bring back a quantity for my use, mine and Reggie's— our robes will be the most resplendent in all the kingdom."

I watched Bishop Reginald take his place alongside the Archbishop of Canterbury, Baldwin of Forde, his arms full of the robes of state. The two churchmen exchanged a cursory nod; you could see they didn't like each other. I was surprised at the arch-bishop's advanced age. I'd heard while he and Gerald of Wales went on their preaching tour he'd forced his retinue to march hard up and down hill to get them into training for the coming war in the Holy Land, so intent was he on triumphing over the heathen horde. White-haired and scrawny, he didn't look to me like a man who could bear such rough treatment.

The congregation were for the most part overfed and ugly as sin. Pallid and overweight, past middle age: the flower of England and France! It seemed a sad indictment. And then suddenly my eye was snagged by a figure lurking near the back. Was it the shadow of a pillar that gave the man's face a darker cast? I craned my neck, feeling my heart thud.

"Stop gawking!" Savaric dug me in the ribs, but his continuing complaint was interrupted by the heralds' trumpets.

Through the doors came the procession, led by an ermined lord bearing the gold crown on a cushion. Behind him, beneath a white silk canopy supported by four long lances borne by men in flowing robes, strode the heir to the throne, too fast for his nobles, who had to skip to keep the canopy over him. Richard, whom the English called the Lionheart, had reddish hair and a big, rangy frame. He walked with his hands at his sides, fists balled, looking like a wild animal caged in by ritual.

The recitations of oaths were all in Latin, but in any case my mind was on the dark figure at the back of the abbey. When Reginald bent to place the golden sandals on the new king's feet, I turned, trying to pick the man out again. It couldn't be the Moor. How could he have got into the coronation of an English king? I remembered, though, how wily he was, how confident in his disguises, with what brazen delight he'd played the cardinal. But the space by the pillar was nothing but shadow; the figure had vanished.

Had the Moor been there, watching? Had he seen me? I hadn't seen him since the moment he'd walked away from us at Rye, but he was in my mind constantly. I was reminded of him by the oddest things at the oddest times. The monks' signs at our silent dinners— tapping one finger on another for the pepper, stroking three fingers across the palm for the butter to be passed—could make me suddenly splutter with laughter, remembering his wicked subversion of the signs in the *Monasteriales Indicia*. The smell of wet earth brought back that night in the pit on Slaughter Moor; even the mention of an owl could make me shiver. And of course every day I touched the Nail of Treves, hidden beneath my shirt, and thought of the giver.

It must have been him! If I didn't follow at once I'd lose him again in the vastness of London. I made to leave, but Savaric caught me by the arm. "Stop fidgeting!"

"I feel sick," I lied.

He looked at me in disgust. "Well you'll have to hold it in till they've crowned him. They won't let anyone in or out till then."

Through the rest of the ceremony I seethed and fretted, but I was not the only one willing the tedious ritual to be over. Suddenly Richard reached out and grabbed the crown from its gilded cushion. For a moment it looked as if he might jam the thing on his own head and be done with it, but then he thrust the crown at the archbishop, who took it and with unseemly haste set it on his head. As if this were not unsettling enough, something stirred in the gloomy air above the high altar, then flapped wildly past the archbishop's mitre. It flitted between the pillars like a lost soul, its black wings beating demonically, returning time and again to circle over the golden crown.

"A bat," someone said in awe. "A bat in daytime, that's an ill omen if ever there was one."

"A bat in a house is a sign of death."

"This isn't a house, it's a church."

"A church is God's house."

"This king's reign will bring many deaths," someone else whispered and was told to shut up.

More than anything else, the bat convinced my superstitious soul that the man I'd seen in the shadows was the Moor. Two dark strangers, two ignoti, intruding where they should not be. When at last they opened the doors, I wrenched myself free of Savaric's grip and pushed through the crowd, but outside there were hundreds milling around, waiting for the king to emerge and bless them. Of the Moor there was no sign.

Through the feast that night I found it hard to eat, even though the food was extravagant. Ridiculous, even. All manner of unnameable things stuffed inside each other, roasted with so many spices they might as well all have been chicken. I drank far more than I should have and was still feeling the effects the next day when we attended the king's gift-giving at Westminster Hall.

Reginald and Savaric had brought a gift for the new monarch. The choice had required much debate and I had caught enough snippets from their conversation to make me ill at ease.

"But it's a fake. He'll have us beheaded."

"It's not a fake. It's as ancient as you like."

"It's old, I'll grant you, but that's as far as it goes."

Savaric sighed. "Cousin, you are taking this far too literally. It represents a lost age, an age of chivalry and heroism. That will appeal to the warrior in him. He'll cherish the gesture as much as the object. He's his father's son—canny and mercenary—he'll fully understand the worth of it, and what it has cost us to give it to him in terms of its earning potential. It will be the best gift he is ever given, and he will remember us for it. Trust me on this, Reggie."

The conversation preyed on me, and when Savaric emerged the next day, clad in his finest and with a long bundle wrapped in his arms, I knew my instinct was right. I felt sick.

Beneath the arching hammerbeams of the hall, the noisy carousing of the court made my head ring. One by one the barons and earls presented their gifts—chalices of crystal and plates of engraved gold; candlesticks and robes of ermine, bearskins and bolts of silk; a pair of elegant hunting dogs so fine-boned they looked as if they would fly at their quarry like hawks. When Savaric knelt to lay his gift at the king's feet, I found myself imagining the three of us— Savaric, Bishop Reginald and myself—hoisted up on crosses like Christ and the thieves, or burned at the stake, with our guts hanging out like sausages and sizzling in the flames.

"Behold the sword of King Arthur of the Britons, the great hero-king who stood against the pagan Saxon army and drove it back into the sea!" With a flourish, Savaric unwrapped the weapon.

A woman laughed.

Richard leaned forward and picked up the sword, weighed it in his hands. "How did you come by this?" he asked.

Savaric looked to his cousin. Bishop Reginald looked at me. I studied the floor, willing one of them to speak. I could understand more of the nobles' language than I let on, but how could they expect me, a wild boy off the Cornish moors, to speak French with a king? At last Savaric said, "This sword came from the site of the great king's last battle in the West of England, isn't that right, John?"

There was no avoiding it. I looked into the face of the Lionheart, a face framed by fiery hair. A small, hard mouth tucked neatly away beneath a cropped moustache; the long chin close-coated by a wiry beard. The mouth smiled at my discomfort, but the smile didn't reach those wintry eyes. I'd come across many men with such colouring—tawny hair, fair skin, light eyes. Red Will, for one—but where in Will it gave the sense of a man weak and not quite formed, in Richard the effect was unsettling, like a pale fire that would burn you to the bone.

"It was retrieved from the ... ah ... site of the Battle of Camlann, at Slaughter Bridge on the Cornish moors," I said in English, forcing Savaric to translate. "The battlefield is well known by the local people to be the place where Arthur fell, defending their land."

Savaric had to explain what and where Cornwall was in the king's newly acquired realm. Richard asked at once if it was rich country, how many lords it had, what lands and castles and monasteries. Savaric spread his hands. "Alas, majesty, it is a poor, wild region, its people little more than savages."

Richard looked disappointed. Then he turned that chilly regard on me again. "And how do you know this to be the sword of the great king?" he said to me in English, shocking the life out of me—everyone said he had not a word of the language.

My guts crawled. "I didn't, lord. I ... ah ... that is, we, ah ... were looking for old bones that might be sold as relics. To the monasteries and suchlike. They pay well for these things, even if they know they're not real." Beside me I sensed Savaric flinching. But still I carried on, pinned by the king's cold gaze. "People believe such objects can work miracles." I stood condemned by my own mouth, waiting for judgment to fall. And there was no Moorish magician this time to save me with his cunning tricks.

Savaric started to speak, but the commanding woman sitting beside the new king said sharply, "*Assez!*" Everyone fell silent. She wasn't a hag, but neither was she a young woman. Her skin was lined and seamed, especially round her thin lips, but her eyes were sharp and bright and full of life, as if a witch had swallowed up a maid. She leaned forward. "This lad is sharper than the rest of them put together! People believe such objects can work miracles. And the Church gets fat on the back of lies and deception." She turned her gimlet stare upon Bishop Reginald, who quailed. "Well, there's nothing new in that." Now she regarded the king steadily. "Belief is a powerful thing, perhaps the most powerful thing of all. Belief is very useful to those who wield power. Tell me, Richard, when is a sword not just a sword?"

"You speak in riddles, Mother!"

Mother? So this was the she-wolf Eleanor. Wife to two kings, soldier of God. There was something terrifying about her—steelier even than the Abbess of Wilton. And suddenly you could see where he'd got that small, hard mouth from.

The thin lips curved into the semblance of a smile. "The people need heroes as a focus for their belief, and a hero needs a legendary weapon. Saint George used the lance known as Ascalon to slay his dragon; Perseus used Harpe to behead the Medusa; Charlemagne bore Joyeuse, the Sword of Earth; and Roland carried Durendal, the very same sword Hector carried at Ilium, if you believe the troubadours."

Richard grinned his lion-grin. "You put the scholars to shame."

"The sword this ancient king used to scourge the unbelievers from these shores confers an almost magical aura upon the man who bears it. But it must have a name."

"Caliburnus." I turned, and there was Archbishop Baldwin, scrawny as a chicken in his oversized robes. "In his silly tales Geoffrey of Monmouth named the ancient king's sword Caliburnus."

"In Cornwall we know it as Excalibur," I blurted.

The Lionheart raised his eyebrows. I didn't know who was more surprised that I should have the gall to enter the discussion—the king or me—but he let it pass. "Excalibur," he said quietly. He brushed his hand along the ancient blade, caressed the pitted hilt with its decorated quillons. Then he wrapped it back in its cloth and handed it to a servant. "Tell the armourer to make a good copy of this sword. Not a perfect copy, but of a length better suited to my reach. He'll know what is needed." He puffed his chest out, threw back his mane. "I shall carry it into battle against the heathen horde, just as Arthur did. We shall forge a new legend." He looked to his mother for approval, but she just glimmered at him.

"I have another riddle for you: when is a piece of wood not just a piece of wood?"

Richard folded his arms and waited.

"When it is the wood on which our lord Jesus Christ was crucified, that the blessed Helena excavated out of Jerusalem, where now stands the Church of the Holy Sepulchre, shamefully fallen into the hands of the infidel."

Richard laughed. "The True Cross! Wrapped in gold and studded with gems!"

"It is not the rich casing that makes it valuable," Baldwin said sharply. "It is Christ's Rood, the Wood of Life—the *Lignum Vitae!*"

"Quite so," agreed Eleanor. She turned a shoulder, shutting the annoying archbishop out of their conversation. "It may just be a piece of old wood, but it is not the gold that encases it nor the jewels that encrust it that make it valuable. It is the symbolic value it bears—"

Archbishop Baldwin could not help interrupting. "It is the cross on which Christ suffered his passion, on which he was crucified to save our souls—"

"Its symbolic value is what matters," Eleanor went on severely. "The appearance of things is important. I look at you, my son, and I see a handsome, well-made man. But a man, just a man. Put a crown on that head and you have a king. Put that sword in that hand and you have a hero." And now her eyes narrowed and her sharp chin jutted so that she looked the witch many had named her. "Let him ride into battle against the Saracen horde and take back from them the one True Cross, the holiest relic in Christendom . . . let him take that in his hands and you have not just a king, not just a hero," and here she dropped her voice almost to a whisper, "but an emperor, maybe even the Holy Roman Emperor . . ."

"Mother!"

She spread her hands, sat back. "I jest. Well, a little. But my point remains. Recapture the True Cross, my son, and the whole Christian world will open to you as easily as a whore spreads her legs."

I gazed around to see if anyone else had heard this extraordinary exchange, but everyone was talking and drinking. Even the archbishop had a large goblet in his claw-like hand. Reginald was looking at the ground in a thoughtful manner. I caught Savaric's eye. Out of sight of the rest, he gave me a lupine grin, well pleased with reception of the sword.

The feasting and gift-giving continued. Much wine was drunk and the noise in the hall became ever more oppressive. When a delegation of Jews brought their gifts through the crowd, insults broke out, followed by pushes and shoves and laughter.

"Go away, you dogs!" one lord cried.

The Jews filed in in their dark robes, dignified and quiet. They had brought sumptuous offerings—golden candlesticks and chains of office, caskets of jewels and crystal goblets. The king wanted the gold and ordered the guards to let them through. The nobles, full of drink and bile, catcalled and jeered, and as soon as the Jews had presented their offerings they were shoved rudely out of the great hall.

"I'll see you back at the abbey," I told Savaric, meaning Bermondsey Abbey where we were staying, east down the river on the other side of London's bridge.

A large crowd had gathered outside in the hope of catching sight of the king. Clearly, they'd been waiting for hours; the mood was ugly. Seeing the Jews expelled by the guards they took it as a sign of the new sovereign's shared loathing, for a knot of the black-garbed men was surrounded by a baying mob.

"Filthy moneylenders!"

"Christ-killers!"

It was beginning to sound like All Hallows—demons' voices raised in chorus. And then, without warning, insults turned to blows. Fists and clubs rained down on men who had come only to honour the Lionheart.

"Get out of our country!" others howled. "Bloody foreigners! Thieving devils!"

I remembered the Moor telling me how one man makes of another a stranger in order to render him an enemy he can kill without conscience. How, before he encouraged me to think for myself, I was so ready to believe that Saracens ate babies . . .

I couldn't just walk past. A young man in a black robe was bent double in front of me. I pushed away a brawny fellow with a stick. "Gerr'an! Leave him alone!" I cried.

The bully glared at me. Then his lip curled. "Another fucking Jew!" he sneered, and too late I realized my error. I'd fallen into my native Cornish tongue.

"I'm no Jew!" I cried, though something in me felt wrong to say it.

It didn't do me any good: they beat the two of us indiscriminately, till I could no longer fight but lay on the ground amid the filth, curled up to protect my vitals, while the man down beside me stopped even grunting in pain.

Had Savaric not come out of the hall at that very moment and roared with his patrician voice for the guards to intervene I'd surely not have survived. Many didn't, that evil night.

The violence spread, they told me after, from Westminster into Old Jewry, that collection of streets to the west of the White Tower where the Jews live and where they bury their dead, and there were many dead that day. Those who survived retreated into their houses, but the mob set fire to the ghetto, and when the inhabitants ran out into the streets with their clothes aflame, they were set upon by a baying crowd and torn apart—men, women and children, it made no difference.

They say that night the sky was lit as with an orange fire, as if Heaven witnessed the burning and held a mirror to it for shame.

15

City of Akka

❖

Zohra was coming from saying prayers at her mother's grave when the baker from the corner came running past the cemetery. "The Franj are coming!" he cried, great floury patches on his cheeks where he had clutched his face in horror.

"Not now," she said, aghast, but he had already run on to spread the panic. She subsided onto a patch of weeds beside the cemetery wall. How could life be any worse than these past few days had been? She had not slept, so tormented was she by flashbacks. The yellow cushion bearing the imprint of Nima's mouth. The single bloody handprint on the frame of the terrace door. Her father covered in blood, his eyes like dark holes in a mask of gore. The prized black dewlap lying dead in his hands. The smashed and overturned cages, the drifts of feathers and spattered blood. Kamal, pale and bloodstained, running away . . .

Her little brother had not come home. A neighbour reported that Kamal's friend, Bashar Muallem, had disappeared as well. "And good riddance," the man had added darkly.

The atmosphere in the house was unbearable. Baltasar could not look at Aisa without oozing tears; as a result, poor Aisa crept about the house as if he wished he could vanish like his twin. And Zohra blamed herself for everything. If she had been at home, where she should have been, looking after Ummi, her mother would still be alive, and so would Baba's pigeons, and Kamal's unstable, dangerous nature would be something still to be guessed at, and they would still be a family and not this ragged bundle of hurt bound together by guilt and need. It was God's punishment on her.

And now the Franj had come. She hoped Malek had made it back to camp safely. To lose him as well . . . she shook her head.

A shadow fell across her and she looked up and caught her breath. Then Aisa moved so that the sun hit his face. Like hers, it was gaunt with sorrow. "Come to the wall with me," he said.

She stared at him. "Why?"

Aisa held a hand out to her and she took it and hauled herself upright.

"It's our story," he said. He sounded odd, older. "History's being made here, just as it was at Hattin. In years to come, we will be the ones to tell the story of Akka and say we were there. We must bear witness."

And so she let Aisa pull her through streets and alleyways towards the northern ramparts. They ran past the ward where the Templar knights once had their headquarters, past the citadel walls, past the foot of the looming fortress known as the Accursed Tower, the place where had been minted, it was said, the silver coins Judas Iscariot was paid to betray the prophet Isa Christ to the Romans.

"This way!" Aisa climbed without fear up a broken part of the wall to the north of the keep as only a fourteen-year-old boy could do, and Zohra followed stiffly, testing every hold, the sun hot on her back, her heart pounding. At the top Aisa pulled her over onto the ramparts, where quite a crowd had gathered, craning their necks all along the battlements.

The Christian horde was masked by dust clouds and heat haze.

Then coloured banners and mounted knights came into view, the horses' hooves a rumbling thunder on the sun-baked ground. Infantry and archers, then hundreds of wagons, and finally massive timbers pulled on carts that could surely only be the makings of siege engines.

"See the blue banners bearing the great gold cross? Those are the banners of the King of Jerusalem!" someone cried, only to be shouted down by others: "There is no King of Jerusalem. He's just some jumped-up poulain bastard!"

Others swore they picked out Conrad of Montferrat and the Master of the Temple, Gerard de Ridefort, but in truth it was impossible to pick out any individual. Aisa wormed his way between two burly men and shouted back to Zohra, "Their horses are wearing armour too! I didn't know horses wore armour. They are huge!"

Zohra, suddenly feeling weak, sank down to the hot stone. She did not know why she had allowed herself to be led here at all. To see the Franj was to put a face to the foe, to make real what until now had been only rumour. Her chest felt tight with dread. All she wanted was to run to the house on the Street of Tailors, to crawl beneath the covers on Nathanael's divan and burrow her head against his hot skin and pretend that time had stopped. But she knew there was no going back to the little paradise they had made between them, the heat and the honey, the sweat and groans and kisses. She had to make amends for her sins of the flesh; she had to keep what was left of her family together. It was the biggest sacrifice, the greatest submission she could make, to Allah.

But she realized with a force that shocked her that the vast army moving to encircle the city, the disappearance of Kamal, the death of her mother and all the chaos and horror that was about to ensue was as nothing in the face of the loss of Nathanael.

❋

On the Street of Tailors, Nathanael greeted the news of the siege with a sort of mental shrug. What difference did it make if he could not leave the city? He felt more trapped inside his own skin than by Akka's walls. After her mother's death, Zohra would not open the door to him, would not read the messages he scrawled and left for her beneath the pot of basil outside the door. She had once walked past him where he waited for her at the end of the street, with her veil up and her head down, not even glancing at him, as if he did not exist. He felt his world had ended, but all around him everyone went about their business as usual. He did not care whether he lived or died, and people in Akka seemed determined to ignore the siege, as if by doing so they could make it go away. "All is written," they said. "Allah will protect us." He wished he could believe in a benign fate. But he was beginning to feel that his love for Zohra was cursed.

The next day he was called upon to tend to a defender who had taken a stray arrow in the shoulder. The distant strains of a Latin hymn drifted up over the walls, and he remembered quite sharply passing the Church of St. Anthony one summer morning four or five years before Salah ad-Din had retaken the city and hearing the same song sung by the congregation inside. He wondered how many of those the sultan had allowed to walk free were outside the walls with the enemy army. There was such a thing as too much mercy, he thought bitterly.

He looked out over the wall. In the hazy distance he could make out the tents and banners of the Muslim army on the hills, encircling the besieging Christian army but apparently doing no more than surveying it. There didn't seem to be much evidence of conflict. In fact, the only sign of action around the vast enemy encampment appeared to be hundreds of men with shovels producing enormous mounds of earth. A man wearing a striped camel hair robe leaned on the wall next to him. "They're digging in," he said. "They're planning on being here for a long time."

"Till they starve us out," another man added.

Nathanael went straight home and found his mother in their courtyard garden amongst the herbs they cultivated for medicines, a handful of lemon balm held to her nose. Her eyes were closed. She looked sad, yet serene, with the light falling gently on her face through the leaves of the vine that twined overhead. Bunches of fat black grapes weighed down the branches; no one had yet harvested them. *Better do that soon*, Nat thought.

His mother's eyes were the same deep, languorous brown as his own. She smiled up at her loved and much-indulged only child. "How are you today?"

Nat shrugged. He knew what she was asking, but he could not talk about it. "Where's Abi?"

"Up at the citadel, as usual. The emir's been struck down by one of his headaches."

"I saw his headache," Nathanael said. "Outside the walls. Stretching for miles and miles. People say this siege will go on for months."

Sara's smile faded. She looked around at their lush little garden: at the orange trees laden with fruit, at the fragrant spikes of thyme amongst which the bees made themselves so busy, at the hives and the vigorous chili plants. At the rows of herbs that would be rendered down to tisanes to treat all the little everyday maladies that people suffered from under normal conditions. But these were not normal conditions. They were at war.

"Perhaps we should go to the market," she said. "A bit more flour and rice wouldn't go amiss."

The market was so thronged it was almost impossible to enter the narrow paths between the stalls. Of course, everyone had seized upon the same idea, and were out trying to buy whatever they could stock up on. Already there were stallholders shutting up shop, their goods sold out.

"*Balak, balak!*" The grocer's boy struggled to get through the press of bodies. "Make way, make way!" He pushed his handcart against people's legs till they grudgingly gave way and let him through, only to surge forward like a wave in his wake, all trying to gain an extra inch or two of ground towards their goal.

Sara shook her head. "This is hopeless. Maybe we should wait until tomorrow."

"If we wait till tomorrow there will be nothing left," Nat said firmly, and he pressed ahead, making his body a shield behind which his mother could shelter, weaving as best he could through whatever gaps he could find. People trod on his feet. Hardly anyone acknowledged the trespass or said sorry, which was unusual.

Some obstacle had presented itself up ahead: the crowd came to a sudden standstill. Nathanael found himself pressed up against the rough raffia basket and ample buttocks of the woman in front of him; someone else elbowed him painfully in the side, spitefully, he thought, as if they blamed him for the holdup. The crowd was so tight that he could not turn to deliver a sharp rebuke or a sardonic look. He could not move at all.

We could die right here, trampled underfoot, and never have need of the flour we are queuing for, he thought.

16

✻

From the Muslim camp up on the hills above Akka, Malek surveyed the infidel host. The sultan and his personal guard had ridden to the edge of the escarpment so that the commander could assess the deployment of the enemy forces. For now the Muslim army might have outnumbered the enemy Franj, but the Christians were being reinforced every day as ships put in up the coast or anchored offshore and sent troops in by smaller boats between Akka and Haifa in the south. They came from all over the world, from throughout what they called the Latin Kingdom—from Poitou, Aquitaine and Anjou; from Pisa, Genoa and Naples; from Denmark, Holland, Swabia and Thuringia—places Malek had never even heard of. And they stood between him and his family.

For weeks now, they had watched the enemy setting up their trebuchets and ballistas around the Accursed Tower and pounding the walls, to little obvious effect. Every so often one of the engines was scorched by fire pots hurled from the city, or the engineers were picked off from above by the garrison archers. The Christians had dug their trenches and diverted into them the streams that had once fed the orchards and sugarcane fields that surrounded the city, creating moats and pits to impede the sultan's cavalry. It was frustrating to sit up here above them, doing nothing but watch. Malek itched to charge down the hillside at them, wreaking havoc. Their general was a cautious commander—he would do nothing until he had considered the possible outcomes of any action. But today Malek could sense the tension in Salah ad-Din's taut stance as he sat his horse beside him, watching the enemy with his hawk's eyes.

Malek knew that despite his straight back and unwavering attention he was in intense discomfort. For the past few days the sultan had been afflicted by a malady that had produced painful swellings the length of his torso, to the extent that off his horse he found it impossible to find a position in which he could rest. The doctors were perplexed. They had tried everything from leeches to tisanes, all to no avail. At the best of times he was a frugal eater, barely taking meat at all, but now he ate hardly anything. Word had spread, though as yet no further than his personal guard. They were all worried about him, but it was important their anxiety did not infect the wider army, or reach the ears of his officers, who bickered constantly amongst themselves.

The Lord of Sinjar was apparently similarly afflicted; he lay in his tent, moaning and calling upon God to end his woes.

"I'll end his woes myself," Malek's comrade Hicham said tightly, "if he doesn't shut up."

They were generally unimpressed by the Sinjar and Dyar Bakr troops, who had come unwillingly to the sultan's summons and spent their entire time complaining about the heat, the flies, the long trek over the hills to water the horses, the distance from their wives, the tribal unrest in their own region. But they were Kurds, as was the sultan himself, so perhaps that made them feel they had special licence to voice their complaints.

The Franj had begun to form up their battle lines, from the shore to the north of the city to the River Belus in the south. Salah ad-Din watched and said nothing, though his mouth was drawn down hard, the lines graven deeper than ever. Already the sun was beating down. Malek put a hand to his helm and found it hot to the touch—hardly the best conditions for a man with a fever, even without a heavy mail coif and the steel helmet above it.

"They will attack today," the sultan said at last.

They waited for him to say more. He did not. At last his son Al-Afdal asked, "What shall we do, sire?"

"We will let them attack us," Salah ad-Din said. He had consulted the Qur'an the night before in expectation of an assault, and now he set about arranging his forces. He would himself command the centre, with his sons to the right, and beyond them, carefully placed within view, the levies from Dyar-Bakr and Mosul, reaching almost to the sea. On the farthest right he set the troops of Hama under his dashing nephew Taki ad-Din. These men would not run, no matter what happened. To the left he stationed the Lord of Sinjar, the Emir of Harran and the other Kurdish forces. When their hearts were in it, they were fierce fighters, tempered by innumerable tribal wars. But out on the far left wing, to be sure the formation held steady, he placed his North African mamluks—the best of all his troops, the men with whom he had conquered Egypt. They lined up with their scarlet turbans and their fierce white grins, and Aibek al-Akhresh waved his scimitar in the air, keen for the fight. "Let us send them to their god, boys!" They cheered back.

Now Malek and the burning coals milled around the sultan as he rode back and forth, delivering his orders, and with them rode pages trying fruitlessly to hold a canopy over the commander's head to keep the worst of the sun off him. *At last*, Malek thought, *we shall see some action.*

At that moment Salah ad-Din's horse shied as a ground squirrel ran beneath its hooves. Malek noted the sultan's hastily disguised grimace. Worrying about his master took his mind off the battle to come. He was a veteran now, despite his youth. He had seen much, and sometimes knowing the dangers made them harder to bear. It was easy to charge into battle blithe in your ignorance; true courage came from knowing the worst and standing your ground anyway.

Thus far, Malek had been lucky. Or, rather, his time was not yet written, *insh'allah*. He had his own ways of taking his mind off the inevitable fear. They all did. Some prayed, seeking oblivion in the comforting repetition of the sacred words. Some sang softly to themselves. Others talked with loud bravado of past heroics, to reinforce a sense of their invulnerability. One or two furtively put out offerings to the djinns, to persuade them to fight alongside them; it was understood that a well-bribed djinn might throw dust into an enemy's eyes or unsettle a horse at a crucial moment.

Malek did none of these things. Instead, he took the sultan's sword and honed it to a lethal edge. *This is the sword of Islam*, he told himself. *This is the blade of Allah*. The sultan was unlikely to use it, for he rarely fought in the thick of the battle but instead directed proceedings at a distance, where he could best assess the movement of the opposing forces. When Malek returned the weapon he watched as his commander took the sword and examined it, saw the small smile of appreciation as he ran a thumb along the edge. For Malek, that was the finest thanks of all.

Four hours after sunrise the Franj army began to advance, the archers and crossbowmen out in front, then a vanguard of foot, the huge mounted knights, and the rest of the infantry at the rear. In the centre the banners proclaimed the presence of Conrad, the Count of Montferrat and Lord of Tyre; to his right, preceded by a canopy of white silk over what must have been some holy object, came the man who had been ousted from Jerusalem, Guy of Lusignan. Malek remembered him being taken prisoner after his war tent had been overrun at the Battle of Hattin—a blustering man with frightened eyes. Hard to believe such a man could be King of

Jerusalem. And to his left the Templars were arrayed under their great banners of white emblazoned with red crosses. These were the men who had cut down pilgrims on the road to Mecca, who had slaughtered women and children without mercy. That they called themselves "warriors of God" filled Malek with disgust.

Salah ad-Din raised his fist. Behind them the drummers started to pound out a battle rhythm, and then the long brazen trumpets joined them to produce a cacophony of sound. An attack was imminent.

Malek watched as orders were dispatched to the Prince of Hama and his column charged down the hillside. The Franj surged to meet and then apparently engulf them. For a moment it seemed the Muslim cavalry would be overwhelmed, but then Malek smiled. This show of weakness was an age-old tactic. As Taki ad-Din's force appeared to give way before the Franj, the enemy were drawn out of their disciplined formations, whooping and screaming. Down into the sea marshes the Christians pressed them, surging with violent glee, unleashed from their weeks of tedium behind their stagnant moats full of hungry mosquitoes. Swords and axes, maces and halberds flashed in the bright sunshine, and the cries of the wounded carried faintly on the hot currents of air drifting up from the shore like the cries of seabirds. Perhaps their frailty was more than show, and beside him, Salah ad-Din's brows drew together in consternation. He turned to his son. "Go support your cousin." Al-Afdal signalled to his troops, and they galloped down the hillside.

The sultan's bay pirouetted, unnerved, and almost unseated him. Salah ad-Din was a fine horseman, but Malek heard him stifle a groan. He spurred his chestnut in close to the bay and laid a hand on its bridle. It was not something he would normally have considered doing, but compassion drove him beyond thought of courtly custom. "Sire, your horse is out of sorts. Take Asfar. She has a gentler temperament and will not jar you so."

The sultan's mouth became a long, flat line. "Thank you, no."
He set his heels to his horse's barrel and urged it up the slope, the
better to view the scene below.

Down there, Al-Afdal's cavalry clashed with the Franj, laying
into them without mercy, forcing them sideways and separating
them from the rest of their forces, while the sultan's archers shot
down upon the foe, picking off the lightly armoured infantry. But
from his elevated vantage point, Malek could see that the central
block of the Christian army was still advancing, taking advantage
of the perceived weakness of the gap left by Al-Afdal's men, a solid
wedge of knights and infantry. The first rank of crossbowmen ran
before them, stopped and shot uphill. Their quarrels skimmed the
ground before the Muslim army, but the second rank had their
range. To the left of the sultan a man screamed and fell, clutching his cheek. Blood spurted around the shaft protruding from
between his fingers. At once, Malek put himself between the sultan
and the enemy. Now the lug-bowmen were taking aim, shooting
into the sky. Their arrows arched upwards and then rained down.
It was hard to know where to put his shield—over his head or
across his body. Men were falling to left and right, horses too,
screaming and tumbling.

Malek turned to make sure the sultan was unscathed and saw
how sweat beaded on his face from the effort of raising his shield,
but there was no time to say or do anything because now the archers
and infantry had parted and the armoured knights were upon them,
thundering up the slope on their huge chargers.

"For God and Islam!" Salah ad-Din cried, and raised his sword
to signal that the centre should advance.

For a long time it was hard to tell who had the advantage as
the currents of battle flowed back and forth, but about an hour into
the conflict the tide turned abruptly and the Muslim centre was
overwhelmed. Quite suddenly there were enemy knights in clear

view, and then they were coming at them, sensing an advantage, rapacious and unstoppable.

"Retreat!" Salah ad-Din cried, but his words were lost in the din.

Malek tried to shield his commander, but a grey warhorse came out of nowhere, blocking his way, rearing up in front of him to batter him with its massive hooves. Asfar skipped sideways, as nimble as a goat, and Malek stuck the big horse with his lance. He sensed rather than saw the huge beast falling, but he heard its scream and the cry of its rider. Before he could follow the sultan, another knight was before him and he had to parry a blow from the right, feeling the shock of it run up his sword-arm, jarring it to the bone, which set up a wild, trembling ache, almost causing him to drop his weapon.

Asfar turned, as if she saw the next threat coming before he did, and more by instinct than judgment Malek ducked as a man came at him with an axe. My, but his horse was fast! Malek spun and buried his sword in the man's unprotected back, shearing through cloth and mail, the blade snagging for a long moment in the warrior's spine and then coming free.

At last there was a gap. He stared through it, seeking out the sultan's retreating banners, but all he could see was a chaos of battling knights.

There! A flash of apricot silk. Up the slope, heading for the tents.

Evading another challenger, he wheeled Asfar around and pressed through the fighting men, riding down a pair of Franj infantrymen, leaving one clutching the place where his arm had been; the other simply disappeared beneath his horse's pounding hooves.

"Those bastards from Dyar-Bakr!" a man growled in Arabic, and he recognized through a mask of blood one of the sergeants from the watch, the man who had helped him when he had fallen exhausted from Asfar's back on his return from Akka. "They gave way at the first sniff of the enemy, ran bawling back to their wives!"

The sergeant raised his sword, spurred his mount forward in an ungainly leap and neatly skewered a man who was coming at Malek. "Get back to guard the sultan!" he called to Malek. "The centre's caved in—it's slaughter. You need to get him away from here."

Now there was a big Flemish knight coming at him, the green cross on his white surcoat splattered with red and brown. Malek faced him, but the warhorse ran past him a little way up the hill, then turned and charged at him. He gritted his teeth and hacked upwards and his sword met the Fleming's with a screech. Malek felt the fearsome power in his opponent's arm and knew he was done for. He dodged to one side, trying to set the Fleming off balance, but the man was wise to the manoeuvre and grinned, showing a row of strong yellow teeth. He drove his charger into the side of Malek's slighter mount, bulling her backwards till Asfar whinnied and reached out to bite, her feet skidding on grass now slippery with blood.

Malek thought they were both going down and freed his feet of the stirrups, aiming to jump clear, but then suddenly the sergeant popped into view. So intent was he on his prey, and with no peripheral vision in his heavy helm, that the Flemish knight did not see the man coming, knew nothing about it until the sergeant stabbed him in the side. Blood ran from the Franj's flank, and Malek saw a gap and took his chance, no time for thanks or pleasantries, pressing his knees sharply into the chestnut's ribs till she shot forward as if propelled from a slingshot.

Up the hillside they ploughed, heading for where he had seen the sultan's banners, but now there was no sign of them except for scraps of orange silk trampled into the ground. Discarded drums and instruments lay crushed among dying horses, dead men. And then he was upon the commander's war tent, that oasis of calm well above the battlefield, and there were Franj there, rooting through it, a pair of big Templar knights at the doorway and others he could glimpse moving about inside.

Where was Salah ad-Din? Malek urged Asfar on past the pavilion, on up the hill until she was blowing. He should never have allowed himself to become separated from his master. Somehow he had let the battle impose its own will on him, rather than keeping his discipline and maintaining his place. He pushed on, dispatching a man who was examining a wooden chest he had looted. The man's blood flew in an arc, and was lit for a single, almost beautiful, moment by the sun, before the headless corpse collapsed over its booty.

Now he was passing Muslim soldiers, writhing and dying: one man with his arm attached only by the tendons; another with his guts spilling between his fingers. With a shock he realized the second man was Hicham, his fellow burning coal. He turned back, intent on doing something—what? Everyone knew a belly wound like that was slow death, but even so, he had to try. But by the time he got there a Christian soldier had stabbed him through the throat and was helping himself to Hicham's helmet. Malek yelled at the enemy and ran him through. "Salah ad-Din!" he cried. But the shout was lost amid the moans of dying men, the Franj and the faithful, calling on their god or for their mothers.

Malek found himself thinking about his own mother. Poor fragile Nima, who had succumbed to her illness even as he was making his way back to Qala'at al-Shakif all those weeks ago. Just a day after they had set up camp here outside Akka, a bird had flown to the Hill of Carobs, a piece of scarlet wool affixing a scrap of paper to its leg. When the pigeon was caught and the message unfurled it appeared to have been written in some sort of code, which caused consternation. Was someone trying to harm the sultan by sending an evil spell? Was the bird a djinn? When Malek heard about the curious message his heart stuttered. Seeking out the man who had the pigeon, he demanded to see the scrap. In it he read, in the code he had devised all those years ago, "Ummi died. Sorgan." That was all it said.

He told no one but the sultan, who said, "God ever takes first those he loves best, for he cannot bear to be without them." Malek tried unsuccessfully to hide his tears, and Salah ad-Din looked aside until he had mastered himself. Then he asked, "Are there more birds trained like this one to fly here?" and Malek, who knew nothing of his brother's avian massacre, said yes, many. At this, the sultan looked thoughtful.

At the crest of the hill the fighting was at its worst, for the Christians, seeing the Muslim retreat towards their sultan's banners, thought them in flight and saw the chance of a rout. Malek found himself swept into the fray and beset on all sides. How long he fought he did not know. Weariness became a second skin, dulling all sensation. The necessity of concentration and reaction subsumed all else. He did not even feel the blade that caught him in the shoulder, or the arrow that nicked his thigh, or the myriad smaller wounds he sustained as he swept his sword high and brought it down again and again, on horse or man, shield or blade, mail or jerkin, helm or spear. He became aware of other Muslims fighting beside him, of cries of *"Allahu akhbar!"* and *"Y'allah islam!"* and more than once he drew back his blade at the last moment, realizing the man before him was one of their own.

Details leapt out at him, vivid and surreal—an eye knocked from its socket, hanging by a skein of fibres; the beautiful gold embroidery on the cuff of a dead man's tunic; a notched blade; the plaited mane of a piebald horse; coins spilling bright from a dropped purse. He saw a warrior with yellow hair and eyes the colour of the sky, and another with a red beard plaited in peculiar patterns.

When at last he emerged on the other side of the conflict he was covered in blood, and so was the valiant Asfar. At the top of the hill, forming a protective battalion in front of the apricot standards of the sultan, he found the mamluk soldiers, and what was left of his fellow burning coals. Their ranks opened for him and closed behind him. He had never been so relieved in all his life, for inside was Salah ad-Din, without visible sign of harm, sitting his bay, sword in hand, delivering orders as he had so many hours ago when Malek had last seen him.

More Muslims rallied to the standard as the day wore on and the sun began to dip. The Christians charged wildly and the sultan's army drove them back. The slaughter was terrible, but after a time the tide of violence lessened and gave way to the taking of prisoners, of whom there were many, among them the Master of the Temple, Gerard de Ridefort. Malek was surprised to see this beast of a Templar offered mercy by Salah ad-Din, given the opportunity to accept Islam and be ransomed back to his people. But the warrior-monk refused to save his own skin and accepted his death like a man, bowing his head to the sword. Other Templars were less resolute in their faith and gabbled the *shahada* as fast as they could.

Sick of the sight of blood, Malek went to tend to Asfar, washing her clean and dabbing on her wounds a salve he had bought for his own use from Yacub of Nablus. Her wounds were not life-threatening, though some projectile had skinned her right hock, laying it open to the bone. With a needle and silk thread that he carried always in his pack, Malek sewed the skin shut, and Asfar stood trembling all the while but never kicking. "You are the best horse in the world," he told her, and laid his cheek against her flank and wept.

Later, much later, he sat at the campfire of what remained of the sultan's personal guard. They had, it seemed, lost almost half their number. "They are probably at other campfires," one lad said hopefully. "I saw how Hicham and Yusuf went charging down the hill together. They may be with Taki ad-Din even now, eating goat stew and rice."

Malek remembered, painfully, his last sight of Hicham. "I do not think so," he said.

One of the mamluk officers approached out of the gloom, all that was visible of him the white of his teeth. His name was Ibrahim, a Nubian from the southern banks of the Nile. They passed some time in talking of where they had grown up, of their wives and children, or their sweethearts, or which battles they had seen.

Malek sat silently, overwhelmed by the sights of the day, wishing he had a wife or sweetheart on whom he might lavish his love, whose image he might hold in his heart as a refuge from all the horror. Still the sound of clanging steel, screaming horses and shrieking men echoed in his head. Still the memory of blows dealt and blows avoided came at him over and over again. It would be worse when he lay down to sleep.

At last, forcing himself to take part in the conversation, he asked Ibrahim, "Where is your captain, Aibek al-Akhresh, he of the head harder than any stone?" and they all laughed.

The Nubian had become very still. By the light of the leaping flames his eyes looked bloodshot. Then tears brimmed and spilled and he let them fall without shame, for his people's ways were different from those of the Arabs. "Aibek died a martyr's death," he told them, his voice as deep and as low as thunder. "His horse was killed under him, but he set his back against a rock and continued to fight until his quiver was empty. Then he defended himself with his sword and killed many of the enemy, until he was overwhelmed at last."

It was not the only tale of heroism and disaster Malek was to hear that night; at every campfire, similar stories were being told. No doubt the same sort of tales were being recounted down the hill among the campfires of the Christian army, and when he considered this he felt a terrible sadness fall over him. *We are all just men*, he thought, *yet God asks so much from us.*

17

✳

"What is your name and where do you come from?"

"Why are you here? Who sent you, Salah ad-Din or the Prince of Hama?"

"How did you find the High Path? We do not welcome visitors here."

Kamal Najib shifted uneasily from one foot to the other while his friend Bashar gave the answers they had prepared. The journey to this remote fortress had been long and hazardous, the mountains appalling. He had never seen anything like this terrible region before. The tawny hills outside the city, where they had spooked his brother Malek's horse and nearly been discovered, were the highest things he had ever climbed—higher even than the minaret of the Friday Mosque—but these mountains in northern Syria were of another order altogether. Most of the time their peaks were shrouded by cloud, but he still felt their presence towering high above him, and the sensation of such weight and mass looming there crushed his soul. To walk up and up into such a wilderness defied all logic, each pace a step into madness, a step nearer oblivion. A dozen times he had thought he would freeze to death, drown crossing a tumbling stream, be hit by rockfall; a hundred times he had near-wept at the sound of jackals crying in the night, hugging himself as their howls shivered through the chilly air. A thousand times he had wished he'd never left Akka at all, never followed Bashar on this terrifying expedition.

But then he remembered what he had done, and how he could never go back.

Now the scary guard was standing in front of him, prodding him forward. "Prostrate yourself to the Grand Headmaster of the Order and speak your name!"

Trembling, Kamal threw himself to the ground; touching his forehead to the cold stone floor, he pushed his name out through chattering teeth and waited for judgment to come upon him.

But no sword kissed his neck, and the sky did not fall. Instead, the old man who sat on his throne like some ancient, bearded prophet bade him rise.

"Come here, boy. Look me in the eye and tell me why you have come to Masyaf."

And Kamal, recalling with difficulty the words Bashar had drilled into him all this long, long way said, "Sidi ad-Din Sinan, I have come to offer myself as one of the *fida'i*, to be among the foundation of the faithful, to serve you and the Order in whatever fashion I may be of use, even to the death."

The old man smiled, but the fire that burned in his dark eyes had a cold, cold flame. "To the death, you say? Are you sure you know what you offer?"

Bashar had not prepared him for this. Kamal swallowed but no saliva went down, his throat was so dry. Unable to get the words out, he nodded dumbly.

Grand Headmaster Sinan—known to the outside world as the Old Man of the Mountains—leaned forward, fixing Kamal with his glittering black eyes. "I don't believe you do."

He made a tiny gesture with his right hand and a man stepped forward. He was clothed in a plain white robe and headcloth to denote his rank among the faithful, but his feet were bare, the soles offering a glimpse of tender pink in contrast to the polished wood-brown of the sunburned upper. He moved like a young man, but as he came close Kamal stared up into his face and was surprised to find grizzled streaks in his beard, even though his face was smooth and unlined, his expression one of perfect serenity.

"Walk into the flames," Sinan commanded, indicating the fire that burned in the central hearth. He spoke so nonchalantly it was as if he were suggesting the man merely fetch him a drink of water.

Without a beat of hesitation, the adherent turned and walked purposefully towards the fire. Kamal watched as the man's leading foot planted itself firmly amongst the glowing embers.

Beside him, Bashar let out a yelp, as high and feeble as the sound the feral dog had made when Kamal put out its eye.

Coals grated and spat, but the man stood where he was, still and silent. The fire took hold around his ankles, making the air shimmer above its new fuel, but still the man's expression remained serene, unchanged. The air was filled with an acrid stench, then with the smell of roasting meat. Something in Kamal's mind found this second aroma hard to make sense of; for a second his stomach remembered that it was empty. It rumbled, and saliva flooded his dry mouth, and then he was reminded of what had caused the smell, and Kamal felt something in him give way. There was a sudden warm, liquid sensation at his groin, and looking down at the dark stain spreading across his breeches, he realised he had wet himself. Shame gripped him: the blood rose in his face, and he was thinking he might further disgrace himself by vomiting, when there was a loud thud and he saw the adherent lying face down on the floor. The fire had burned his feet away from under him, leaving nothing to balance on but the bones.

Grand Headmaster Sinan clicked his fingers and a group of white-garbed men stepped forward and dragged the body away.

The Old Man transferred his impassive gaze to Bashar, who looked sick and sallow, then to Kamal. In those cold black eyes Kamal knew he had taken note of the tangible marks of his fear.

"That's what I expect of my *hashshashin*: that they act upon my orders without question or delay, knowing that their fate is written, and that they are as nothing before the will of God and will receive their reward for their obedience in Heaven. So must you be, if you are to be accepted as one of the faithful. So I ask you again, do you know what it is you offer? Are you ready to be one of my *fida'i*?"

They will kill me where I stand if I say no, Kamal thought. *And yet I must die horribly at some day in the future if I agree.* The realization was piercing, awful.

He was without hope, without home, without a future, and his only clothes were soaked in his own piss. Everything was already lost. He croaked out a single sound.

Na'am.

I am ready.

18

❋

"You're so lucky, Zohra." Jamilla rested her withered arm on the edge of the olivewood mixing bowl and regarded her cousin with glowing eyes.

Zohra did not look up. *Lucky. Yes, that's me. My mother's dead, my father's mad, my little brother's a murderer, my house is a shambles, my heart is wrecked and it's all my own fault. So very, very lucky . . .*

She had made the foolish error of mentioning Nathanael to her cousin in a moment of weakness a few weeks earlier, before Ummi's death. Not by name, of course. Nor had she referred to him as Jewish, or called him "the doctor's son." All she had said was that there was someone, a man, who had shown her some kindness and brought little treats from time to time. As soon as she had uttered these hints about him, she had regretted it deeply, even though she knew Jamilla would keep her secret. But her heart had been bursting with the need to talk to someone about the extraordinary emotion that gripped her. She had stolen from Nat's room a small volume by the poet Ibn Hazm and learned one of the poems by heart, whispering it into the dark air before she slept:

I would cut open my heart
with a knife, place you
inside and seal up my wound,
so that you could dwell there

Even in the midst of her misery, she felt the rhythm of the words inside her.

With only one good hand, Jamilla still manipulated her dough expertly, and she watched with a small smile Zohra's frowning, fumbling efforts. "I wouldn't mind the attentions of a handsome young man." She chuckled.

Now that Nathanael was no longer in Zohra's life, it would have been a relief to confide in her cousin, but the situation had become so tragic it was impossible to talk about.

"You're welcome to him," she said. "Perhaps you should bake him one of your special loaves." She thumped her ball of dough with a vicious fist, sending a cloud of flour into the air.

Jamilla had set her heart on Malek, and whenever he was home from combat or training she would make him one of her "special" loaves containing a love charm from the sorcerer's market. But Malek showed interest in nothing but his duty to preserve the sultan and fight for Islam. And now that he was, for all practical purposes, head of the family, no one was likely to be arranging a betrothal for him.

It was hard for a daughter with a withered arm in a city over-flowing with marriageable girls to attract the attentions of a suitor. Years of war, even before this latest siege, had winnowed the young men: those left had their pick. Jamilla was not marrying anyone soon, let alone Malek. Reminding herself of Jamilla's situation tempered Zohra's irritation.

"Your loaves are always a lot nicer than mine," she said. "I don't know why, but they are." It was a tiny kindness, the only gift she could offer.

"You don't knock the air out of your dough properly. Look . . ."

After ten minutes of strenuous kneading and instruction, both Zohra's arms ached, but at least the subject had been changed.

They walked down the street to the communal bread oven carrying their cloth-wrapped dough overhead. The line at the oven was longer than usual and included a number of women Zohra didn't recognize. But Jamilla tapped one on the shoulder and they went into an awkward embrace, dipping to kiss each other's cheeks without dropping their bowls of dough.

"What are you doing here, Leila? Are you visiting your relatives?"

The other woman had pale olive skin and lustrous dark eyes that reminded Zohra of Nathanael's striking gaze. A keen jolt of warmth dizzied her: she did not realize she was being addressed until she suddenly became aware that her cousin and her acquaintance were staring at her.

"Was anyone hurt?" Zohra asked, snatching at the threads of the exchange.

Leila shook her head. "They said it was a lucky strike, a freak accident. It's the first time one of the Franj machines has managed to send rocks right over the wall, but now they have the range . . . Well, we decided it was better to be safe than sorry. My sister's house isn't large, but it's closer to the market and farther from the wall. We'll move in with them when my husband comes back from his watch."

Zohra stared at her.

"Didn't you hear? The poor dear baker, two women and one of their children dead, one little girl fighting for her life, less than an hour ago. If it wasn't for the Jewish doctor's lad—"

Zohra's chest tightened. "Nathanael?"

The woman's eyes narrowed. "The son of the doctor from the Street of Tailors," she confirmed with tight lips. "He was returning from seeing a sick woman over near the henna market and some rubble struck him—"

"Was he badly hurt?" Zohra was beyond caution.

Both women were looking at her oddly. Why was she more concerned by a small wound to a Jew than by the deaths of many good Muslims?

"I don't know how he is." Leila turned her shoulder towards Zohra, physically blocking her from the conversation. The line shuffled forward as another batch of dough was taken by the baker, put onto his long shovel and placed on the hot stones inside the big clay oven.

Zohra was seized by a fierce impatience. She must go to Nat, right now, and hang the consequences. But of course she couldn't. She closed her eyes, overcome by the memory of the things they used to do together in the long, hot afternoons—his silken touch, the ridges of muscle bordering the line of black hair that led . . . Her knees felt weak.

"Are you all right, cousin?"

She opened her eyes and they were at the front of the line. Jamilla was reaching up, trying to take the tray of dough from her.

"Here, here, I can do it." Zohra handed the tray to the baker, a small, dark man with a dirty turban and a large moustache. He took the cloth off and handed it back to her. Annoyingly, some of the dough had stuck to it, leaving little craters.

"Never mind," Jamilla said. "At least you'll be able to tell yours from the others when we come back for them."

Well of course I will, Zohra thought bitterly. *Like everything else I try to do, it turns out ruined.*

Back home, Nathanael gritted his teeth as he soaked the last buried scrap of his sleeve, pulled it out of the wound and pressed hard to

stem the fresh flow of blood. It would need stitches. He had managed to bandage and succour the other victims, hardly even noticing his own pain. The sight of the little boy with his head caved in
had driven him into a different part of himself, one in which a cut
on his own arm no longer existed. Now, though, examining the
damage, he started to shake. Delayed shock—he had seen it before
in others. It was as if once his body registered the damage through
his eyes, the pain began to make itself known, throbbing and local-
ized, then radiating in nauseating waves into the rest of his body.

You are lucky to be alive, he told himself, and tried to believe it.

He sewed up the wound, the needle biting through living flesh
and the fine gut drawing and pulling like a thread of fire. The
arm felt heavy and dead now, a lump of useless flesh. He knew he
had crushed some nerves. Were they irreparably damaged, or just
bruised? How he had managed to go about his work, tending to the
other victims of the strike, he did not know. It was amazing how the
body staved off shock when it had to. He had saved the life of one of
the injured women, stemming the gush of blood from her head and
making sure her breathing was steady. He had swiftly bound the
wounds of three others, and had tended to the little girl who even
now lay pale and unresponsive in the little salon off the courtyard.
The others had been beyond help. The first boulder had crushed
the oven, the baker and one of the women in a single impact; the
second had carried the two women it struck several yards, causing
such terrible injuries it was clear they would not survive. The other
casualties, including the unfortunate boy, had, like himself, been
struck by flying detritus from the smashed clay oven.

He went to check on the girl. No one knew her name, or the
name of her dead mother, and no one had taken responsibility for
her. They all had too many mouths to feed and troubles enough of
their own. One by one, the onlookers and survivors had sidled away.
Amidst the wailing of the baker's wife and those who had come out

of their houses to gaze at the carnage, the little girl had lain peacefully with her hair spread out on the muddy ground and the rain pattering steadily onto her closed eyelids, as if the skies wept for her. Nathanael, checking for signs of life though he expected none, had touched her neck and been surprised to find a pulse. "She's alive!" he'd called out. "Will someone help me with her?"

No one stepped forward. Instead, they began to drift away, until he was left alone with the child. For long minutes, he had tried to lift her over his good shoulder, but with only one working arm his efforts had been pitiable. At last a big, quiet man in a dark robe and a faded green turban had stepped forward and offered his services. He bent and scooped the child up and followed Nat without a word through the winding streets of the medina.

When this man had brought the girl in and laid her on the cushions in the shady salon, he said, "Your father eased my mother's passing, God rest her soul. He is a good man, and I can see he has taught you well. My name is Mohammed Azri and I have a smithy near the east gate. If ever you need me or my son, Saddiq, you will find us there. *Bes'salama*." Then he had dipped his head, touched his hand to his heart and walked back out into the dreary day.

. The girl was still unconscious, though her breathing was regular. Nat laid a hand on her forehead, then on her neck, felt her heart beating steadily. He could find no obvious injury to her head or body. Perhaps the shock of what she had seen had rendered her insensible and she would come to in her own time. Poor little thing. In what sort of world did a child have to waken in a stranger's house to the news that her mother was dead?

When Yacub came home, he knelt down and brushed the girl's hair from her forehead, but the child just lay there, her chest rising and falling. He levered himself upright with a grunt as his knees creaked, and looked at Nathanael. "She seems to be physically unharmed. Let us hope she will wake up in her own time. You, on the other hand . . ." He cocked his head. "Let me have a look at that arm."

Nat waved him away. "It's fine, I've stitched it."

His father gave him a long, steady look. "You may be a doctor now, but you're also my son."

Yacub unwound the bandage carefully and regarded the arm with a blank expression. The old doctor gently touched the inflamed skin around the wound, got his son to flex the arm; he touched each finger and manipulated the shoulder joint. Then he went away and came back some minutes later with a sweet-smelling ointment, and he offered Nat a cup of something so strong it made his eyes water.

"Drink this."

"What's in it?"

"I'll tell you when you've drunk it."

Nat knew what that meant. He also knew his father's uncompromising tone. Reduced to being a child again, he took his medicine without complaint and let the poppy take its effect.

The next day there was a knock at the door. Nat opened it and found Zohra Najib there, in a headscarf, reticent, with the rain pattering down around her. "I heard you'd been hurt," she said, and then just stared at him.

"It's nothing. Much. I'm fine, really."

They stood apart as if a fence divided them. "Come in out of the rain," Nathanael started, at exactly the same moment Zohra said, "Well, I must get on."

They both fell silent until Zohra dropped her amber gaze, mumbled something about the fish market and ran away down the alley, her basket bumping on her back.

It was the first time they had been in one another's company since that terrible day when they had found Nima Najib dead. He watched her go, and it was as if his heart were being dragged down the street after her, drawn through the mud and bashed against the walls. Then he went back inside, walked quickly past the kitchen where his mother was crushing chickpeas and sesame seeds with oil, out into the farthest corner of the courtyard under the shelter of the vines, where no one but the bees could see him weep as he had not done since he was a child of three.

After that, he shut all his memories of Zohra away, sealed them off, just as his father had cauterized his wound.

The little girl slept on. On the sixth day, Nathanael went out into the streets to see if he could find a clue to her identity. But no matter where he asked no one knew who she was, or the name of her dead mother. No one had heard of a family seeking a lost child.

When he got home, he found the child was sitting up and that his mother was tempting her with some little pastries. He stopped in the doorway. It was like a small miracle.

Crossing the room, Nat dropped to one knee before the girl. He took one of the cakes and held it out to the child. Honey dripped languorously from it to pool on the plate below. He watched the girl watching it. She glanced up as if questioning the gift, then slid her eyes away hastily. At last she reached out and popped the sweet-meat into her mouth and chewed solemnly, her regard rapturous.

"Can you tell me your name?"

The child shook her head.

"We have to call you something. Zinab?"

Another shake of the head.

"Rachel?"

The little girl glared at him.

Nat ran through half a dozen more names, receiving blank looks or fierce head shakes and was about to give up when suddenly the child said, "Nima."

A prickle ran down his spine. The first word the girl had uttered and it had to be the name of Zohra's dead mother. He caught his mother's gaze over the top of the child's head. Sara gave him a wavery smile. He knew exactly what she was thinking, what she wanted to say.

He forced himself to a cheeriness he did not feel. "Nima? That's your name?"

The little brows drew together. Then the child stuck her finger into the pooled honey, raised it to her mouth and sucked thoughtfully. "Nima," she said again.

Nathanael swallowed. "Nima, can you remember your family name?"

A look of consternation.

"Your father's name?"

Tears began to well. He knew he could not mention the dead mother, her chest all crushed and ruined.

"Nima, well that's good, then," Sara said brightly. "That's a lovely name. Are you from Akka, sweet? Do you live in the city?"

Nima shook her head.

"Did you travel here by boat, on the sea?" Nat asked.

"No." A very emphatic denial. After a pause, she added, "A donkey. It was brown."

"Little dove, all donkeys are brown."

"Some are grey. It had kind eyes and it did this." She shook her head in parody of an animal beset by flies.

Nathanael laughed. "Did it do this?" Throwing his head back, he hee-hawed till both Nima and his mother were giggling uncontrollably.

So that was the key, then.

The next day Nat came back to the house with a tabby kitten— *al-tabiya*, for the markings on watered silk—and like silk its fur was cool and smooth and fragrant. Nima dubbed it Kiri. She buried her nose in its fur, and the little animal squirmed and purred, and from then on it was love and babbling and Kiri this and Kiri that until it was hard to believe the child had ever been mute, and Nat half wished she still was.

Soon Nat was able to take up his duties again, administering medical aid to the garrison. It was hard work, and bloody, but it kept his mind away from his personal pain.

One evening, after finishing his shift, he dropped into the tea house on what had once been called Templars Way but since the retaking of the city had been renamed Martyrs Avenue. Inside, old men sat or squatted, their hands cupped around glasses of hot tea. He took his usual seat just inside the awning and leaned back against the cool wall to watch the rain patter down into the muddy puddles outside.

It was not long before he was recognized. His father was something of a local celebrity—he had brought innumerable children into the world, saved grandmothers and sons and tended to the odd infection picked up in the bordellos by the dock without a word of censure—and Nat had taken on a lot of Yacub's work when he was not working on the wall, now that his father was so occupied at the citadel. It meant he rarely had to pay for his drinks.

Three of the men brought their cushions closer, inquired after his injured arm. Hamsa Nasri, a grocer from close to the Friday Mosque, poured him out a fresh glass of the steaming tea. "Get it down you, lad—it'll warm you through."

Tea was running short. Ships were reluctant to chance the double peril of the enemy fleet and bad weather. And it wasn't just tea, either: sugar, fresh meat, fruit and vegetables were all scarce, for all the farmland beyond the walls had been enveloped and destroyed by the besieging army. Everyone's diet was becoming monotonous.

"What's been going on up there today, then?" Nat nodded his head vaguely in the direction of the city walls.

Younes the barber wore a patched-up version of the garrison uniform, though still with his white crocheted skullcap over his neatly cropped hair. Nat suspected he had volunteered because he liked being first with the news and was missing the gossip from his barbershop. "Nothing much. They're having a worse time of it than us, the Franj. Their trenches are full of water and shit, the mud is knee-deep and no one can be bothered to man the ballistas."

Driss leaned across the table. "I remember when we—"

The rest of them groaned. "No more of your old war stories, Driss!"

Driss was a veteran of the last campaign. A huge scar bisected his eyebrow and carried on, after the interruption of the orbit, down the cheek, to disappear into his grizzled beard. He shrugged. "Just giving the boy the benefit of my extensive knowledge." He patted Nathanael on the shoulder. "You should come back with me, have a good home-cooked meal and let me tell you about Ramla. My Habiba makes a fine lentil soup. Why, you could even bring some of your meat ration, make a proper feast of it."

That got them all talking about the rationing. "I've had to close my stall," Hamsa Nasri said with a sigh. "Now that most of the stock's been commandeered by the citadel to stop all the panic-buying and profiteering, there's just no point staying open. It's bad luck for those of us who were selling at a fair price."

"Tahar the baker was grumbling away this morning," Driss said. "The authorities have set a price on his loaves. He says it's impossible to turn a decent profit. But I swear the loaves Habiba bought off him this morning were smaller than yesterday's."

"Well, that's one way of making money," Hamsa said sourly.

"How long can the bloody Franj keep this up?" Younes said. "Surely the sultan will chase them off before it gets much worse."

"They were there for the taking, the Christians. You could see they were in chaos," said Younes. "Taki ad-Din had them on the run. Salah ad-Din should have pressed on when he had the chance."

Driss agreed. "Another day of battle and we could have driven them right into the sea."

"I heard the sultan was ill," said Nat. It was common knowledge that Salah ad-Din suffered maladies that would send any other man to his bed.

That quietened them. "God give him health," Driss said fervently. "*Insh'allah*."

"*Insh'allah*. Even so, you'd have expected the war divan to act when it had the advantage."

"That's the trouble when your army is made up of squads from as far apart as Mauritania, Harran and south of the Tigris," Driss said. "There are so many factions involved it's a miracle they ever agree on anything."

"If there's one thing they seem to agree on, it's not being here for the winter." The barber laughed.

"There seem to be fewer of them every day," Younes agreed. "The hillside encampments have been getting sparser. But the Franj army is just as diverse—and they don't even speak the same language. At least all of our army speaks Arabic. God knows how the Christians keep order and make their different battalions work together."

Driss laughed morosely. "It's a lot easier when they can't run away. Once the Franj are here they're stuck here, aren't they? Their homes and comforts are thousands of miles away, whereas for our lot, even if their families are far away, there's plenty of women to be had a few days' ride away. That's why so many of them have gone: the sultan had no choice but to let them go, for fear they'd simply leave and never be seen again. Besides, there's not much anyone can do out there at the moment."

"They're soft bastards, those Persian lords. Too used to their luxuries," said the grocer.

"Missing their harems, you mean," Driss said dismissively.

"And their dancing boys." Younes smiled.

It was said that Younes himself kept a painted dancing boy down near the docks. Nat didn't think any the less of Younes for his preference. He just found it rather odd, when the city was so full of prostitutes, to choose to keep a boy. But he supposed everyone needed someone to love. The thought of Zohra's golden eyes made his heart squeeze. He drained the last drops of his now cold tea. It tasted as bitter as death.

Pushing himself away from the table, he stood up. "Good health, gentlemen. May God keep you." It did not matter that their versions of God were different.

As he walked home he saw an old woman begging at the corner of the road, her outstretched hand painfully thin. He imagined Zohra reduced to such a state, and the image horrified him so much that he ran to the bakery, bought the two small loaves that were his family's allowance and, returning, pressed them into the old woman's arms. Then he walked quickly away before she could thank him.

The Romans used starvation as a siege tactic, he thought, remembering Josephus's account of the ancient siege of Jerusalem, when the inhabitants died in droves from famine, ate one another, slaughtered their children because they could not bear to see them suffer. He could not imagine that this modern Franj army would be any more merciful than the Roman besiegers.

PART FIVE

Fire from Heaven

19

John Savage, Bay of Biscay

❀

APRIL 1190

It takes an eternity to muster, provision and organize an army. We did not sail out of Dartmouth harbour until Easter day 1190, blessed by Archbishop Baldwin the Pious himself: ten warships bound for the Holy Land under the flag of King Richard.

When we rounded the cape known as Finisterre, the End of the World, never did a name seem more apt or wished for. I'd been heaving my guts up day and night since we set sail. The other members of the troupe found my condition highly amusing: of all of us—Savaric, Quickfinger, Ezra, Hammer, Saw, Little Ned, Red Will—it seemed I was the only one who'd failed to find his sea legs. Most of them taunted me cruelly, for they were bored, the whole army being banned by edict from gambling, dice games, fighting and swearing. You would think a man born a maid might have been a bit more tender, but Ezra (once Rosamund) was the worst of all. She chuckled at the sight of me all asweat and trembling, planted her feet wide on the deck, grinning as my face got greener. "Ah, poor John, truly you are a creature of the land," she opined, bobbing and swaying in front of me. "Whatever possessed you to board a ship that'll be weeks and months at sea?"

It was a fair question, and one I kept asking myself.

We all wore Savaric's livery. The symbol on it was a hawk in a tree. Little Ned said the device was Savaric's own invention, but if that was so, I was sure he was not the only noble to fabricate such a vanity. There were all sorts proclaiming themselves to be gentry after Richard dispossessed most of the old regime of his father's barons and lords of their goods and land. Some, you could tell in a second, were lords of no more than a dozen sheep and a tumble-down cot. As Saw said, "If they speak English you can bet your arse they're no more noble than me."

Those with the power were all French. French was the language you'd hear spoken on board the ship. We'd all had to learn a bit just to get by. We were on our way to Lisbon to, as they say, *ronday voo* with the rest of the Christian forces and together sail between the Pillars of Hercules and into the Middle Sea before the weather got worse. Though it was hard to imagine what "worse" might entail.

I didn't have to wait very long to find out. A few days later a big wave hit the ship broadside and knocked me flat. I managed to push myself to my knees, hands clasped to my chest as if to force down the furious turmoil within me, turmoil that matched the roiling sea beyond.

"Yes, let us pray, my good man," someone said in English, and when I turned my head there was Baldwin of Ford, wearing no mitre or vestments, just a snowy robe. God alone knew how he kept it so clean on that filthy vessel. His watery blue eyes shone with fervour in a face that was far too pink and hale for such an old man at the mercy of the ocean, and for an instant I felt a surge of hatred for him.

"Let us pray to the risen Christ, whose blessed Ascension we mark this very day."

I said nothing. I couldn't, for nausea had me in its grasp. The archbishop spoke to me in Latin and then in French, but still he got no word from me. I could hear his disapproval in the way the prayers sped up, and he snapped off the words as if he would rather not waste them on such an ingrate. "At least say amen," he spat at last, and the pressure of the air between us was too much for me to bear on top of all else, and "Amen" I croaked out.

Unfortunately, it was not all that came out. A flood of foul bile went everywhere. Not just over the deck and my knees, but also splattering over that snowy robe and even into that snowy, snowy beard.

The archbishop laid hands on me and, shaking me, violently intoned, "Holy Lord, snatch from ruination and from the clutches of the noonday devil this human being made in Your image and likeness. Let Your mighty hand cast him out of Your servant . . ." He glared at me, the watery blue of his eyes sparking cold fire. "What is your name, man?"

More spew threatened. I choked it down. "John Savage."

As if the name confirmed all his suspicions, he shook me harder. "Let Your mighty hand cast him out of Your servant, John Savage."

He shook me so hard I couldn't help erupting again, proof, if proof were needed, that I must be demon-possessed. Anyone normal would have backed off at that point, but I saw the outrage harden into something . . . martial. He tightened his hold on me, his bony old fingers digging into my shoulders.

"Out, unclean spirit! Out, spawn of Beelzebub!" He shook me so hard my teeth rattled. "Begone, enemy of the faith, in the name of our Lord Jesus Christ!"

"Are you out of your mind?" Suddenly, Savaric was there beside me, his hand on Baldwin's arm. "Leave this man alone, for God's sake!"

The archbishop turned his mad blue eyes on the newcomer. "This man is possessed by the foul fiend!"

Savaric tugged the old man's clutching hand free of my shoulder. "Don't be a fool. He's afflicted with nothing worse than seasickness—he's been like this ever since we passed Start Point. There's no devil in him, just a sorrowful heart and a weak stomach." His black eyes were amused. "Isn't that so, John?"

"Aye, sir." I nodded gratefully.

Baldwin reattached his claw to my shoulder. "This man must undergo exorcism. Fell forces are at work here. Look at that sky." He indicated the lowering clouds, great anvil-like thunderheads. "There is nothing natural about such furious tumult! See the anger in the waves that pile up against us! This is a storm raised in fury at the presence of the Fiend."

Over Baldwin's shoulder I could see the sails of the other ships dipping wildly, disappearing into deep troughs between the waves. Wind was whipping foam off the tops of the waves, sending streamers of spume into the air like battle-banners. Then it began to rain so hard it was as if the two elements of air and sea were attempting to reconcile one with the other to make a single watery hell.

With the rain thrashing down upon him, Baldwin roared on. "I cast you out, Demon, in the name of He who stilled the seas and the wind and the storm . . ." A great growl of thunder overhead: a personal message from God. "You see!" Baldwin cried triumphantly. "By all the saints, by the archangels Michael, Gabriel and Raphael . . ."

A wave walloped us, sending men staggering like drunks. Even the archbishop couldn't keep his feet in such conditions, but it didn't stop him. "Saint Thaddeus, Saint Matthias, Saint Barnabas . . ."

Another blast of thunder, as if the skies were splitting apart, and then lightning struck the mainmast. There was a wrenching sound. Men screaming and crying out for protection, for God, for their mothers . . .

Wind wailed and water crashed and the ship's timbers creaked and shrieked. Savaric had rivulets of blood running down his face. Hammer and Saw helped him up, their hair plastered to their skulls, making them gaunt and ethereal, like starved angels. I made out Rosamund with her arm hooked hard around an upright timber. Red Will was on his knees beside her, carroty hair as dark as a rat's, his mouth open in a howl.

Savaric's voice boomed out. "Dear God, humbly we beseech Thee to guard Thy servants on this ship . . ."

"Oh blessed Saint Thomas!" old Baldwin roared now. "Intercede for our souls, most holy of the holy saints, in whose name a multitude of miracles has been achieved. Thomas of Canterbury, aid us in our terror—"

"Saint Thomas!" someone else cried out, and then other crewmen and soldiers were down on their knees, their ghost-like faces turned up to Heaven, all crying upon the name of the celebrated saint.

"Saint Thomas, I will always pray to you if you save me now," moaned one man.

"I promise to visit your shrine!"

"I will pay two silver shillings . . ."

The ship pitched suddenly downwards. Men were screaming and sliding down the deck. One of the skiffs came loose from its fastenings and went flying through the air, tossed as lightly as a leaf, before disappearing into the murk, followed by two of the crew who had been taking shelter beneath it. Above the tall forecastle of our ship, waves towered like black mountains. *If they break and fall upon us we're all lost*, I thought.

". . . in the unity of the Holy Ghost, world without end . . ." Savaric's voice fighting with the thunder.

My hand went to the pendant around my neck and I clutched the Nail of Treves in my palm. The only light left in the world in that dark moment seemed to be the light I remembered in the

Moor's half-moon eyes as he laughed at me for my fears, and that light engulfed me, flooded through me. *If this is how I must go, it could be worse, far worse . . .*

On and on it went, the noise, the chaos. I held fast to the side, feeling the ship bucking beneath me. The next wave hit. For a moment it was as if the sky had fallen; then there was a shivering of the air, a change of pressure. My whole being trembled, inside and out, and suddenly we seemed to have passed through some barrier between worlds and were out the other side with light streaming down through a hole in the clouds like a beam from the Eye of God.

My knees felt weak; I was dizzy, with elation and relief. Looking down at my palm, I found a dark red mark clearly impressed in its centre. A mark like a cross. Tiny, but a cross.

It's just a nail, you numbskull, I chided myself. *There's nothing supernatural about it.*

"Saint Thomas, you have saved us! Thank you, thank you!" Red Will pressed his palms together in fervent prayer. Then he turned to the archbishop. "He appeared to me, wreathed in white light, and said, 'Be not afraid, for I, Thomas, have been appointed by the Lord as guardian of this fleet.'"

"Amen!" Baldwin seized upon this dubious endorsement with gusto. He fell to his knees in dramatic style; you would not think such an old man could be so robust. "A marvel! A wonder! Saint Thomas à Becket, blessed martyr, we praise your name!" He kissed the ampulla of holy water he wore around his neck, held it aloft. "Blessed Saint Thomas!"

"Saint Thomas, Saint Thomas!"

"A miracle!"

The cries rang out around the ship, and other clerics came up from where they had been huddling below decks like frightened mice to hear about the wondrous manner of our salvation. Before long several others attested to seeing the remarkable apparition. And soon our deliverance from the storm was officially declared a miracle worked by Saint Thomas of Canterbury.

It was a tatter-sailed fleet that made its way down the Portuguese coast, heading for Lisbon. There was no more talk of exorcism (though Archbishop Baldwin gave me a hard stare whenever our paths crossed) but much talk of miracles. Soldiers and crew, even nobles and commoners, were talking to one another in halting bursts of English and French, brought together by shared disaster, telling how they had been convinced of their own death until they saw the golden glow of Saint Thomas, his hand held over the ship in protection, anxious to be part of the miracle themselves. Within days, everyone was telling the same tale, the discrepancies forgotten, the other saints invoked in their time of need conveniently passed over in favour of the great English martyr who, like a storm himself, had carried all before him, leaving nothing but debris in his wake.

The doubts I had about the "miracle" I kept to myself, remembering the hysteria of all those desperate people in the churches of England, clutching at the thinnest straws of hope, convincing themselves that magic existed, that dead people were looking down from Heaven and singling them out for special favour.

What was really strange, though, was that after the storm I had no more seasickness. I made my way round the ship, marvelling at this welcome change in my fortune, enjoying the unfamiliar freedom of movement, even taking in the view. The sea! It was huge, stretching uninterrupted to the horizon. The sunsets were spectacular: I couldn't get enough of the sight of that ball of fire sending out streamers of scarlet and gold into the darkening waters, night after night, only to rise again over the land every morning. It was a bigger miracle for me than our survival of the storm. The darkest of hours, followed by a glimmer of golden light.

By the time we arrived at Lisbon we'd been at sea for over two months. We were all wild to rove after being confined to the cramped quarters of the ship, and it looked a sort of paradise, this city. Dry land! Taverns! Ale! Proper food! The castle atop the hill appeared fine and sturdy and benevolent, the authoritative stamp of man's hand on the landscape after all these weeks of being held in nature's thrall. There were tumbles of flowers on the cliffs, bright sails on the boats in the inner harbour, a forest of masts in the sheltered waters of the outer harbour; people milling about the quays, women amongst them . . .

The excited chatter became lewd. Quickfinger grinned. "I never had a Spanish one, but I warrant after dark they're a' the same."

"Who's waiting till dark? Not me!"

"Hope the whores are cheap."

Quickfinger scoffed. "I've never had to pay for a woman in my life!"

Hammer and I exchanged glances. We knew this to be untrue, but who would want to point that out?

Red Will, that's who.

"No decent woman would let you lay a finger on her!"

"It ain't his finger he's got in mind!"

"Aye, it's a bit bigger than a finger, Will No-Dick. Warn't that what Mary called you?" Quickfinger's mobile, expressive face twisted into a sneer.

"You aren't fit to speak her name!"

"I done a lot more than speak her name, little boy, and she would moan mine, over and over. *Oh, Enoch, ooh Enoch, yes, yes. More, oh yes, you're so big, Enoch!*"

Will's move took him by surprise. The ginger head hit him right in the gut, knocking the wind out of him. He went down in a heap, and Will kicked him viciously with every ounce of his hatred. There was danger of real damage. Tempting though it was to let Will take his revenge, Hammer and Saw and I hauled him off and held him till he stopped struggling.

Quickfinger got to his feet with difficulty. Clearly Will's heavy boots had found their mark. Despite being the troupe's joker, Quickfinger didn't like to look a fool except by his own design, and the look on his face was one that promised a violent reckoning in a dark back alley.

"You two, I want you to keep an eye on Will," I told Hammer and Saw. "Don't let him out of your sight once you're ashore, right? And keep him away from Quickfinger."

They looked at one another and shared one of their silent twin communications. "We ain't shepherds," Hammer said mutinously.

"And I'm no lamb." Will was furious.

"Savaric has charged me with keeping you lot out of trouble. You're his men now and he's got a reputation to uphold." The Moor would have given me a sardonic look. I felt like some sort of lickspittle.

In the end I needn't have worried, since Savaric himself appeared to instruct us as to our conduct ashore, telling us that if we thieved we'd be tarred and feathered, and that if we got into a fight he'd leave us to the local authorities. Kill one of our own on land and we'd get tied to the victim and buried alive with him.

"Fuck that," said Quickfinger, not really under his breath. "I ain't getting tied to one of your stinking corpses."

"Better kill a nice clean noble, then," someone chuckled.

Savaric roared for quiet. "Don't insult the local women, they're keen on their honour here, and their menfolk will take you apart. If you must go with a whore, treat her properly and pay the price she asks, because I am not coming to bail you out of gaol. And if you catch the pox, that's your own lookout too. Any man coming back on board showing signs of disease will get thrown in the sea. Remember that you're wearing the de Bohun livery, and that we are on holy business, and that if you sin having taken the cross, God's balance will weigh such sin twice over."

I looked around at the faces of his retinue. Most were men bred to do as they were told: servants and peasants, sons of servants and peasants. Then there were the mummers, the dregs of England, people who didn't fit in anywhere and didn't like being told what to do. There was a distinct difference between the two groups: the first were attentive; the others shuffled, making faces at one another. I could see there was going to be trouble once we were on dry land.

Of the rest of the retinue, apart from the guards Savaric had taken on, there was a falconer, a keeper of armour (paid purely to keep it clean and polished), a horse-caparisoner, a steward, a dresser and three body-servants. Ever determined to put on a good show, Savaric had paid as much attention to his turnout as to the matter of war. "People take you at your own valuation, John," he'd confided to me as we made our way from London to Dartmouth to begin our passage. "Appearances are important. If you don't look as if you take yourself seriously, why should anyone else?" He'd patted the big ruby he always wore. "People see this and take me as a man of means, an important man with enough money to waste on a bauble I can afford to lose at sea or at war."

"But you are a man of means."

"It's all a matter of degree." He fingered the gold chain around his neck and I remembered him breaking the 'ruby' on it open in Rye as he renounced his sins.

"Well, it's a lot more means than I'll ever see."

"This chain is probably the most valuable thing I'll ever own." He shrugged. "The stone's just a piece of glass that I got in Venice.

Clever fellows, those Venetians. They know the value of artifice. It'll come in handy if I ever get taken prisoner. A perfect ransom, right here, around my neck."

"Aren't you afraid someone will try to steal it?"

"Let them try. Makes it seem even more valuable if they do. And if they do, well, I've got you lot to keep me safe."

Another fakery, I thought. A bit of glass posing as a priceless jewel and a bodyguard of ne'er-do-wells and thieves.

Perfect.

At the docks were merchants and sailors from a dozen countries, all speaking different languages. A group of local men—and women— were mending nets and packing pilchards into barrels. Take away the foreign chatter and the vibrant colour of their clothing and we might have been in Cornwall.

After two months at sea none of us could walk properly. My knees had become unreliable; it was as if the whole world was on the move beneath me. Others amongst the crew were more sea-soned sailors; they strode past with barely a wobble, eager to be the first to avail themselves of the fleshpots of Lisbon. Quickfinger attached himself to a contingent of them, having learned the words for "whore" and "whorehouse" in French, Portuguese and Spanish, just to make sure. Little Ned staggered after them.

I pushed Hammer and Saw towards Red Will. "Remember what we agreed."

Hammer stared despairingly at the backs of the men disappearing through the crowd.

"I'm sure there's more than one whorehouse." I sighed.

Saw took Will by the arm. "Tavern first."

"Not going with them . . . Ezra?" Savaric winked.

She grinned. "I could murder an ale."

"I thought we'd walk up to the castle."

"We?"

"You two are my bodyguards with the rest gone off to soak themselves in sin."

Up through the steep winding streets we went, past women hanging their washing out to dry and gossiping. They watched us come and some whisked the corners of their headscarves over their faces so that only their glittering eyes were visible. As we passed they fell quiet, their expressions assessing. Savaric made the sign of the cross—acting like a churchman—and uttered a benediction, and at once they were piety personified, heads dipped in prayer.

Up at the castle, squadrons of soldiers marched in and out, guards in shining armour at the gate. In the chilly shadows under those towering walls the fortress looked less benevolent than it had with the sun shining on it, from the sea. It was built with massive blocks of stone, impregnable.

"Now that's what I call a castle," Savaric declared. "Strategic position, too, superb vantage point. You could hold a place like this against any enemy."

"You'd think so, wouldn't you?" The newcomer, a sturdy man, speaking French, pronounced his name *Robairrr*, Robert de Sable, come from France for the muster. Dark hair shot through with silver, tufts of white in his beard, white crow's feet around the eyes. He was well but not flashily dressed. Still, there was something arrogant about him, unpleasant. Maybe it was just me, disliking Frenchmen.

"It was taken back from the infidel forty years ago in a three-month siege during the Reconquista."

This was a word I was unfamiliar with, but Savaric seemed impressed. "You appear to know a good deal about the history of the place."

The man smiled, showing sharp dog-teeth. "My grandfather was one of those who fought to win it back. The Muslims had a stranglehold over the whole peninsula, spreading their lies and poison, but God sent a storm to drive the fleet of Christian knights on their way to the Holy Land in to Porto for repair. And there, the King of Portugal convinced them to help him retake Lisbon. Ah, yes, God took a hand in events that day." He crossed himself and we all obediently muttered "All praise to the Lord." Ezra looked at me, out of sight of Savaric and the newcomer, and rolled her eyes.

"What people don't understand about sieges is that it's not all about the castle walls," Robert continued. "They look at a fortress like this and think it can't be taken. But you can have the strongest fortress in the world and if its defenders do not have the strength of God in their hearts, they do not have the '. . . something . . .' to hold it against besiegers with God on their side."

"*Volonté*—what does that mean?" I asked, and they both turned to stare at me, a commoner interrupting two nobles.

"The will," Savaric supplied, glaring.

"If the defenders don't have the will to maintain a siege they'll capitulate. They lost heart, the Muslims who tried to hold this castle. They're like that, the Muslims: shake their confidence and you break their will. And once they have lost hope they are yours." He closed his fist as if crushing a fly within it.

The merchants' houses in this city appeared plain on the outside—nothing but mud walls and sturdy, iron-hasped doors—but they opened onto courtyards alive with running water and cascades of bright flowers from galleries where birds sang and bees buzzed. Savaric was given quarters in one such, and his chosen retinue was billeted with him. It was like a palace to me. The sound of the water tumbling from the little fountain at the heart of the courtyard reminded me of the streams by which the Moor and I had slept on the Saints' Way after leaving the priory.

"You look like a child, asleep, John," he'd told me. I'd near bit his head off, shouting "I'm no child!" It had taken time to understand he was putting into words the peculiar familiarity between us: sleeping out in the open in his company felt a thousand times safer than the confines of a monastery dormitory.

The constancy of the little fountain smoothed the rough edges off my tumbling thoughts—till Savaric's voice boomed out. "Put your best clothes on, John, we are going to church!"

Best clothes? Did he think I had five chests of outfits, like him, and a dresser to array me? I put on my livery, though it was rather the worse for wear.

He looked me up and down. "That won't do. Come with me."

His "dresser," an ample Welshman with a bald head and a wicked tongue, took one look at me and declared, "Silk purse time, eh?" then delved into one of the huge cedar chests and came out with a cloak of midnight blue, trimmed at hem and facings with silver. This he whipped about my shoulders with a practised gesture. "And this should hide most of the rats' nest," he declared, slapping a cap on my head to tame my springy black hair. "Better, boyo?" he asked, though not to me.

"Much better." Savaric nodded his satisfaction.

A moment later Ezra joined us, neatly turned out as usual. Women have that knack, even when they're being men. The dresser gave a little sly smile and I sensed he knew exactly what she was.

The church was like no other I'd seen, except in my visions. I stared about in wonder. Tall pillars in rows, each pillar meeting the next in a graceful, pointed arch. Light streamed in from all sides.

I looked around, and I was not the only one enchanted, for everywhere I looked, other men had their faces tipped up to the soaring vaults when they should have been turned down in contemplation and prayer.

I found myself wondering, had Saracens built this place? Or if not Saracens, the Moor's Babas? Like the house with the courtyard, I'd have sworn it was built by no Christian, but daily we were told the Saracen was a monster, savage and ignorant, as dark of heart as he was of skin, fit only to be slaughtered like an animal. How could such soulless creatures have constructed something so wondrous?

We were all quiet as we came out into the bright sun and baking heat after mass. Savaric, Ezra and I walked down into the central square where we took watered wine, warm bread and honey at a table outside a baker's and watched the world go past, still wrapped in the serenity of the church. I slumped on the bench and thrust my legs out, tilting my head back, my eyes slitted against the hot light, and wondered how I might contrive to stay there forever, to slip away when the warships put to sea again, to melt into the shadows of the narrow streets, to spend my days like one of the feral cats that begged so slyly in the square, cadging food from strangers.

Then a shadow fell over me. I opened my eyes and there was a man, bending low to speak into Savaric's ear. He was brown-skinned and dark-eyed, dressed in colours too bright for an Englishman: definitely foreign. Savaric leaned forward, intent. I saw Ezra jump to her feet, knife in hand, but our master motioned for her to sit down. "It's fine, all fine. No need for that."

Savaric drained his wine swiftly, licked his lips, then got up, all in a hurry, as if some bargain had been struck. "Come on," he said, and strode off with us, following through the crowds after the dark man. In an alleyway a band of brown-skinned children tagged along behind us, begging in different languages for money. I chased them off, roaring like a lion, which pleased them mightily.

We moved into a quarter full of stalls selling produce. Our guide dived down an alleyway so fast we nearly lost him. There were little windows high up over the alley, grilled with curled iron, movement behind them, someone looking out; sometimes a white hand, beckoning. Ezra caught my sleeve and, "Whores," she mouthed, and rolled her eyes.

Savaric turned to us. "Not much for you here, Ezra. But will you stand guard at the door, just in case? John, you come in with me."

"It's all right," I said quickly. "I'll stay outside with Ezra."

"Nonsense. Men have needs." He grinned. "Come on, lad, don't dawdle—my treat."

And so I entered my first whorehouse. It was obscure inside, corners lit by candles, cheap ones; their smoke had blackened the walls and ceilings and there was a strong whiff of animal fat, even though there was incense burning in a brazier trying to mask that and other more unsavoury smells. As my eyes adjusted I could see four women lounging on couches, wearing slips of cloth that didn't cover much.

Savaric looked from one to another like a starving man at a banquet. "That one," he said, indicating a girl whose long black hair hung loose to her waist, hiding only her breasts beneath the thin shift she wore. I looked away.

"John, pick your lady or I'll do it for you." He was already dragging his "lady" to her feet. I watched as she shot a look at him and read in it, even in that low light, contempt and revulsion. I could only stand there, mute and frozen, wishing that I were outside, away from the smells, the fug, the women.

"For heaven's sake, man!"

Suddenly a warm body thrust up against me, a soft breast pressed into my arm, and I was propelled into a side room. The door closed fast behind me. The woman Savaric had thrust at me pulled away and we stared at each other like two animals unexpectedly finding themselves in the same bear-pit. She was very young and her eyes were huge and wary. She began to shrug out of her robe.

"No!"

She stopped, one arm out of the dress, and said something in the local language.

I shook my head. "No, I don't . . . I don't want . . ." I backed towards the door.

Her chatter became an insistent gabble—panicked, maybe even angry.

The dress was off now, crumpled on the floor. She lay back on the pallet that was the room's only furniture, placed her feet flat with her knees bent, spread her legs and waited for me to join her.

I had never seen a woman naked before. I couldn't help but look, but all I could think was that she looked incomplete, strangely unfinished. There was no stirring in me; quite the opposite. It occurred to me that I must be a very unnatural sort of man that the sight of a woman's naked cunt made me want to run.

My bewilderment must have showed on my face for the girl began to cry, which was the last thing I had intended. Ashamed, I handed her her dress and she covered herself with it, and we spent the next half hour sitting at opposite sides of the room, not looking at one another, trying not to listen to the noises from the adjoining room.

Walking back to the billet, the three of us were quiet. We were passing through the quarter where the market traders were selling food when suddenly Ezra exclaimed, "What are those?" She pointed at a stall laden with little orbs as bright as the setting sun. I'd never seen anything like them, even in the London markets, and they must have been unfamiliar to the people there as well, for quite a crowd had gathered.

Ezra tugged at my sleeve. "Oh, buy me one, John, please. Please!"

"You can buy one for yourself."

"I can't. They speak foreign here."

"I hate to break this to you, but they'll be speaking foreign wherever we go."

She made a face. "Go on."

Savaric encouraged me. "Buy her one, John. After all, you've had your treat."

I approached the stall, and though I'd picked up none of the local lingo I found my bastard French worked. The man selling the things told me they were "*naranja*," some sort of fruit, apparently, brought out of the east. He sounded a little like my Moor but looked nothing like him. He asked a ludicrous amount for the fruit. I suggested a price that made him bellow with laughter; he lowered the number a little. On we went, spiralling inward to the point we knew we would both reach eventually. When we finally agreed on a price, he nodded and smiled and said a word I'd heard the Moor use.

"Where are you from?" I asked him, handing over the money.

"Here and there."

"Where's there?"

He laughed. "Marrakech."

"Where's Marrakech?"

"Across the water." He gestured vaguely towards the sea.

"Are you a Baba?"

He wrinkled his brow at me and I repeated the question, trying to form the word the way the Moor said it.

"*Al-barbari*, Berber, originally. We call ourselves Amazigh." It sounded like *Ama-ʒir* the way he said it, the "r" rolled the French way, like *Robairrr*. "The free people, it means. Now that's a laugh, stuck in this shithole, trampled by the Franj." He spat in the dust.

In the end he gave me two of the *naranja* for the price we'd agreed for one. I thanked him, bowing my head and pressing my hand to my heart the way the Moor would do, and this made him grin.

I took my prizes back to Ezra and Savaric. Ezra took hers in a kind of wonderment, stroked it as if it were a precious object, sniffed it, squeezed it, squealed at the perfume it left on her hand, then squirrelled it carefully away in her pack. "I'll eat it later," she promised, "when I'm alone."

Wiping the skin clean on my tunic as I would an apple, I bit deeply into the fruit, then exclaimed in shock, "Oh, it is horrible, horrible!" and added a few choice words in Cornish for good measure. Bitterness shrivelled my tongue. I spat out the offending pulp and it lay there bright in the dust.

A gale of laughter—the stallholder and his friends, highly amused. "You don't eat the skin, you barbarian! Like this." The man from Marrakech picked up a fruit, dug his thumbs in, tore a hole through the thick skin and proceeded to peel it.

Mortified, I copied him, but just as I was about to bite into the naked flesh a pair of big Templar knights barged past and confronted the man. "What have we told you about selling here?" One grabbed the stallholder by the throat and, being a good head taller, lifted him off his feet.

"We don't want your kind in this city," the second knight added. He was a big man, with a meaty face, and for some reason familiar to me.

"In this *country*," the first Templar corrected him. "Or anywhere else in Christendom. Stop trying to rip off decent Christians! Take your produce and stick it up your arse!"

"Or we'll do it for you, then roast you over a fire like the pig you are!"

"He wasn't doing anything wrong, I just—"

I tried to intervene but the first Templar shot me a look of pure disgust. "Don't stand up for this infidel bastard or you'll get the same treatment!" He turned his attention back to the stallholder. "Get down on your knees and pray to Jesus Christ the Saviour for your black soul!"

Behind the stall, other Amazigh were gathering, drawn by the rumpus. They looked militant, angry, like men who'd been subjected to this sort of harassment one time too many and were determined to make a stand. When the *naranja*-seller did not immediately do as the Templars asked, they tipped his stall over, sending bright fruit tumbling. Then they casually stabbed the trader in the gut and kicked him as he writhed.

"No!" I couldn't help myself. I should have remembered the beating I took in London, but in the heat of it I grabbed the first Templar by the arm, and when he turned I punched him in the face once, twice—short, hard punches that did the most damage. He went down groaning, clutching his broken nose. The second came at me, sword in hand. I was trying to draw my blade but the midnight-blue cloak—so unnecessary in the heat—got in the way, tangling around my blade.

All at once Ezra was in front of me, darting at the knight, dagger in hand. She stuck the blade into his forearm and twisted. There was a sound like wood splintering, then a shriek. He dropped the weapon with a clang and clutched his ruined arm.

All hell broke loose. Infidels were pouring into the street with meat cleavers and other makeshift weapons, to be met by a stream of Christian fighters, some of whom I recognized as shipmates, and before long we were in the middle of a pitched battle and blood flowed among the cobbles.

I caught hold of Ezra but she gave me a mad look and tried to tear herself free. I very much feared that if I let go of her she would lay into the Templar knight again.

"No, leave him, come on!"

Savaric was running off down the street, never one for a fight. Ezra struggled but I managed to drag her away, and together we merged into the tide of men converging on the little market.

"Geoffrey de Glanvill!" I said it like a curse.

Ezra gazed at me, said nothing.

"That man," I went on, "the one whose arm you just skewered, he was one of the men who . . . ah . . . in Winchelsea—"

"You don't forget the man who raped you," she said calmly.

"I wish I'd severed more than his arm, and if I see him again, I bloody well will."

We found Savaric back at the house looking pale and sheepish. He spread his hands apologetically. "I'd have just been in your way."

What had started with the murder of the *naranja*-seller escalated to a riot as the sailors and soldiers bound for the Holy Land on a sacred task put their Christian zeal into practice and started slaughtering the remaining Saracens and Jews of Lisbon. For days the rampage continued. Whole quarters of the city were burned, shops and homes looted. The skies were thick with smoke, the streets sticky with blood.

Memories of London on that terrible coronation day returned, leaving me sweating and trembling like a sick child. I found it hard to sleep. I was seized by nightmares. Every day members of the troupe returned with fresh tales of horror. A group of knights had been set upon and decapitated by Muslims in the alleys; by way of retribution the Templars had set fire to their mosque, their place of worship, at first prayer and slaughtered dozens as they came running out. Muslim women were hauled out into the streets and raped in the name of Christ. No one could keep order—certainly not the local authorities, who were unprepared for such an eruption of violence, or even the commanders of the fleet, whose charges had been cooped up for far too long aboard ship to show any restraint or discipline. In the end, battalions of soldiers were brought in by the Portuguese king to restore order. Many hundreds of our army were thrown into prison to sober up and repent of their wrong-doings, amongst them Quickfinger—taken in a drunken brawl—and Red Will.

"You were supposed to keep an eye on him," I reminded the twins.

"He got away from us," Hammer lied.

In the end we found they'd been thrown into the same cell with a load of Frenchmen. Savaric reported that when he came upon them they were sitting together playing knucklebones on the floor of the gaol, laughing like brothers. "Best place for them," he said on his return. Which meant that not only would they be kept out of further trouble, but also that while they were in custody he wouldn't have to pay their upkeep.

The mayhem continued, despite reinforcements to the Lisbon garrison. There was an uneasy atmosphere wherever you went. Before we came there had been a working truce among the different elements of the populace, the different cultures rubbing along without much friction, but ancient animosities had been rekindled, dormant grudges acted upon.

Savaric told us to keep our heads down and to stay out of trouble, which coincided neatly with our own inclination. For a long while we remained confined to the area immediately adjacent to the merchant's house, our only exercise being to accompany our master between there and the church, with the occasional visit to the ship to help board supplies. At least this meant no repeat visit to the bordello.

I'd started taking my drawing things with me, as much to ward off boredom as to practise my sole skill. Down at the quays I drew an old man gutting fish. He came to see what I was doing and stared blankly at the sketch, unable to make any sense of the flat image. I drew children throwing a wooden ball under their mothers' watchful care, and a woman weaving at a loom set up in a sunny courtyard. A group of black-clad women came past, chattering like jackdaws. When they saw what I was at they made the sign of the evil eye, as if they thought there was some sort of dangerous magic in my sketches. After more instances of this, I decided to stick to drawing buildings, which were unlikely to have an opinion of me or my work.

Towards the end of the third week in July, after attending the morning mass, I told Savaric I'd like to remain behind. I waved my leather draftsman's satchel by way of explanation.

He nodded. "I am sure Reginald would like to see your impression of this church, since he cannot be here in person."

The canon, with whom I had managed to exchange a few words, told me that the little church had once been a mosque. He said it quite matter-of-factly, without any shame or awkwardness, and added, "We all worship the same God," which took me greatly aback. Until then I had been under the impression that Muslims revered some other deity, and this confused me mightily. Why were we crossing seas and continents to fight people who believed much the same as we did? I decided the old priest had meant something different, or that I had misunderstood.

I wandered about the church, drawing a detail here and there, taking in the elegant pointed arches, the striped pillars, the friezes of carved lettering. Some of the latter had been recently painted over, since they were Islamic writings, but what caught my eye was a small portrait of a holy figure on the eastern wall. Dark-skinned, dark-eyed, hollow-cheeked, with a golden halo that radiated out towards the top corners of the icon. Something within me flipped over at the sight of it, a strange yet familiar flutter. But no matter what I did, I couldn't reproduce on paper the arresting face on the wall. The rest of the church receded as I tried to capture this one image, but failed again and again: the nose too long, the eyes too close together, the jaw too broad . . . One last try, from memory this time.

And then, quite suddenly, there it was. The expression in the eyes, endlessly patient and wise, maybe a little sorrowful, maybe—in another light—a little wry.

My breath caught, my vision hazing at the edges. "I told you we would meet again, John," I heard.

In the shadows was the Moor. I jumped to my feet. Quills, ink, paper flew, and I cried out in despair. The little pot of ink shattered on the floor, spreading in a ruinous black pool across the drawing and the mosaic tiles beneath my feet, like spilled blood.

When I looked up again, the Moor had vanished.

20

✿

It was fearsomely hot for so early in the year, and the news was bad. Malek was on duty inside the door of the sultan's war tent. In there, apart from the pages and the sultan's scribe, Imad al-Din, were two men. Once was a spy. The other was Al-Mashtub, one of Salah ad-Din's senior generals, a warlike Kurdish chieftain who had fought alongside the sultan for much of his life.

"How many ships?" the scribe asked the spy.

There was a pause, as if the man was calculating. "Ten, maybe more."

An uneducated man, Malek decided, unable to count beyond the fingers of his hands. They had to rely on all manner of spies nowadays, things being so disordered. The Christians had broken their supply lines, disrupted their communications. Increasingly they were reduced to passing messages via Akka's swimmers, men who would brave the blockade of enemy ships, as well as the treacherous currents and tides on this part of the coast.

"And these huge timbers—tell me again, for it is hard to believe such trees as you have described can possibly exist."

"I swear on my faith, sir, that they are as I said—giants among trees, the like of which I have never seen. Not just tall but massive in girth, too."

"Can you be more exact?" Imad al-Din's voice was as sharp as his nose.

"Eyes deceive when fear has the beholder in his grip," rumbled Al-Mashtub. But the man was adamant: the timbers were almost the full length of the ships that had brought them, and they were not small ships, either, but good-sized Italian merchant vessels.

Malek saw the sultan's eyebrows shoot up. "Thank you for your news." Almost immediately he regained his equilibrium. "Take this reward, which you will find, I trust, equal to the value of the information you have brought us."

The man scurried past Malek, his face already bent over the open pouch, his fingers assessing the contents. A paid informant, then, motivated by profit rather than by faith. And one well able to count dinars, if not ships' masts.

"The Franj will use those timbers to construct siege towers, towers that will top Akka's walls," Salah ad-Din said.

Al-Mashtub snorted. "We will burn them if they try."

"The caliph's *naft* has failed on that score thus far." The caliph of Baghdad had sent a quantity of the combustible substance and five alchemists from his city to make more and oversee its use— rat-faced men with shifty eyes and a language they had developed to speak secretly amongst themselves. They were embedded in Akka, but so far the artificial fire they manufactured had not managed to do significant damage to the Christian war-engines.

"They need to make larger pots, then," Al-Mashtub declared. "It's obvious, is it not?"

At the door, Malek bristled: this was no way to address the Commander of the Faithful. Al-Mashtub might have been loyal and brave in battle, but he could be blunt.

"It is not the size of the vessel that counts," the sultan said, looking at his general pointedly, "but the contents. The *naft* doesn't burn fiercely enough to get a hold."

"Nonsense." The general contradicted him with a cheerful disregard for protocol. "Make 'em bigger. It's a matter of scale."

"There's not enough clay in the whole of Akka to make fire pots that large," said Imad al-Din. "Nor mangonels with sufficient power to fire them."

Salah ad-Din added, "Let us talk of this no longer. Friend, go take some rest. We shall look forward to your refreshed presence this evening." It was as abrupt a dismissal as Malek had ever heard the sultan deliver.

Al-Mashtub got to his feet, made his obeisances and tramped out of the tent, his fingers tangling in his huge beard, a habit he had when discomfited.

The sultan began dictating letters. He had been sending them out regularly for the past few months across the entire caliphate. Begging letters, Malek's father, Baltasar, would have deemed them, Malek thought. Letters to princes and emirs requesting men and money—to Harran and Mosul, Egypt and Nisbin. Receiving no useful reply, he had then sent his friend, the qadi of the army, Baha ad-Din, the only man he would entrust with the task, to whip up support in person from the princes of Mesopotamia. The qadi had not yet returned.

Reinforcements had arrived with the spring, but they were greatly outnumbered by the Christian troops that had flooded in, ship by ship, ever since the winter storms had dispersed. And that was before the arrival of the vast German army rumoured to be on its way. Malek had heard terrifying numbers mentioned: hundreds of thousands of men. He felt his fear for his family like a burning coal in his stomach.

The sultan rose now to pace the tent, still dictating. "I do not believe you have grasped the extreme gravity of the situation. I must humbly inform you that the army that marches upon us—that is even now approaching Constantinople—is a great dark flood that will destroy everything in its path. How shaming is it that where the Franj of the West have acted in concert at the behest of the popes of Rome to take back the Holy City, our call to jihad has been all but ignored? Is it not shaming that there should be such apathy among the Faithful when there is such zeal among the Polytheists?

"The Franj army is supplied by ships more plentiful than the waves, and for every one of their soldiers who falls, a thousand spring up in his place. We are desperately short here not only of men, but of weapons, food, forage, equipment and the money with which to pay for all of these things. If we do not receive what is necessary then Akka will surely fall, and with it will go all hopes that our sacred endeavour will keep the infidel at bay and prevent the spread of their shadow over all we hold dear."

It was only the use of the word "humbly" that gave Malek a clue as to the recipient: the missive must be to the Caliph of Baghdad. That the sultan had taken such a tone with such a man was proof indeed of his desperation.

Within weeks the siege towers of the Franj were constructed: tall enough to overtop the city walls. Great teams of men wheeled them under cover of darkness. Sheltered by the crenellations on the towers, Franj archers duelled with the garrison bowmen to deadly effect, while beneath their cover other men filled in the great ditch surrounding the city with brush and waste and rocks, and the bodies of the dead—both the Christians shot by the Muslim bowmen and the corpses of those who had fallen from the walls—and inch by inch the towers crept closer. Soon they would be close enough to drop their bridges onto the walls and the enemy would flood from them into Akka.

True to the sultan's observation, fire pots hurled from the city made little mark on the monsters: the Franj had mantled them with hardened leather, off which the pots bounced harmlessly. Where they did strike, all they managed was char and smoke.

Malek watched helplessly. He thought of his family and his friends and neighbours and his heart clenched. But what could he do?

"What on earth are you up to?"

Malek stood up and away from his handiwork, wiping his hands on his tunic. He turned to find himself confronted by the sultan's younger brother, Al-Adil.

"It's a pigeon cote, *sayedi*," he said. "A place where the birds can roost."

"Pigeons? Good heavens, doesn't my brother keep you busy enough?"

Malek sighed. "It was the sultan himself who asked me to build it. For messenger pigeons." He explained how he and his father and brother had developed a system of flying pigeons back and forth between the city and the hills beyond. "My father loves his birds. More than anything else, I sometimes think. But now with Akka cut off we can use them to keep in contact with the garrison."

Al-Adil lifted an eyebrow. "I thought we were using divers to bring messages."

"It's a dangerous business," Malek said.

The sultan's brother tugged at his beard. "But what if the enemy shoots one of your birds down and intercepts the message?"

Malek took a roll of paper from his pouch and handed it over. The older man bent his head over it. "Ah, I see. Some sort of code?"

"My brother Sorgan and I developed it, yes."

"So what happens—God forbid—if one of you dies?"

This was not something Malek dwelled on. It was for God to give and take life at will. "There is my younger brother as well," he said defensively. "Young Aisa. He's learned the code too."

"Well, we must pray that they survive. *Insh'allah*."

"*Insh'allah*."

Towards the end of the month Malek watched the Lord of Dara arrive with troops and contingents of light cavalry, so it seemed either the missives or Baha ad-Din's embassy had had some effect. They moved camp closer to the enemy, the better to survey their movements. Every day there were skirmishes, every day deaths and small triumphs; the hospital tents were kept busy. And still they came, the Franj, new arrivals day by day, and daily the towers moved forward.

Breaking out from time to time from Akka's inner harbour, the Muslim fleet made sorties in an attempt to escape the Christian blockade. The vessels shot *naft* at each other, burning the decks and sails where the viscous stuff stuck, but few of these encounters were conclusive. Then one day a Muslim galley was separated from the rest of the fleet and driven up on the shore. There it was set upon by a ravening band of Franj camp-followers who were butchering pigs on the beach. These women set upon the unfortunate sailors, dragging them from the wreckage, out of the surf and up onto the rocky beach, chopping and stabbing them with the same knives they had used on the livestock. The noise of the slaughter carried as far as the Tower of Flies. From their lofty viewpoint the guards there had looked on helplessly as—out of bowshot—their colleagues were massacred by these harpies, and the surviving pigs squealed and stampeded and shat on the dead and dying. The story spread far and wide. If the women of the Franj were so ferocious, Malek thought, what were their menfolk like?

❄

Every morning, between dawn prayer and his first stint of duty, Malek moved the grain he laid as an incentive to the pigeons a little closer to the camp. Soon they would find the wooden cote.

It was a particularly lovely morning. The sky was an unblemished blue, and a crisp onshore breeze cooled his skin and stirred Asfar's chestnut mane. She pawed the ground, eager for exercise, and so he allowed her to canter down through the tussock grass to the margins where the dunes began. Gulls side-slipped and shrieked high above: if he closed his eyes he could imagine this to be nothing more than a pleasant morning ride and the world a peaceful, stable place in which people loved and laughed and went on with their lives without fear of violent death.

When he opened his eyes again, it was to see a figure emerging from the water, a slender silhouette against the sun-bright sea. Messengers from Akka often came in at this point, having braved the waters of the outer harbour and the open sea beyond the Tower of Flies, where the Christian vessels patrolled. But this was neither Saif nor Mahmoud, both big men with beards and long black locks. As the figure came closer, picking its way between the rocks, he realized with a start that it was his little brother Aisa, and at that moment Aisa saw him and his face broke into an enormous beaming smile.

Malek dismounted in haste and they embraced. Malek came away damp.

"I'm an official messenger now!" Aisa crowed. He thrust his chest out so that his ribs showed. "I've got a message to deliver to Salah ad-Din from Karakush."

Aisa was thinner than he had been when Malek had last seen him, almost a year ago. He was taller too now, more man than boy. Something about that change in him, the time apart and all that had filled it, made his chest tighten.

"Here," he said, throwing his cloak around his brother's shoulders. "Let's get you to the sultan so you can deliver your message."

He leapt up into the saddle and swung Aisa up behind him and the lad chattered out all his news: how he had come to be a messenger; how Kamal had disappeared, no one knew where; how Sorgan and his father were managing to breed the pigeons, and he was teaching Sorgan his letters; how they kept a pair of goats in the rear courtyard, and had learned to grind flour out of date pits—really, the news was endless.

But as they rode back through the lines Aisa went quiet. The sight of all the fighting men, their tents and banners and equipment, the trenches and churned ground where there had been orchards and farms, took his words away.

At last they reached the summit of Tell Ayyadieh and the sultan's war tent. Malek dismounted and helped Aisa down off the big chestnut mare. The boy was shaking. Cold from the sea? A reaction to the long swim? More likely it was the sight of the enemy, so very many of them. Then he wondered if it was simply nerves at the idea of speaking to the sultan.

"Don't be afraid," he said to Aisa. "The sultan isn't a fearsome man, except to his enemies. Greet him humbly, and when he asks you to rise, deliver your message and look him in the eye as you do so. If he asks you your name, tell him without hesitation. And cherish the moment, for you'll remember it the rest of your life." Gently, he brushed a strand of hair out of Aisa's eyes, straightened the cloak and pushed him towards the guards at the door, who checked him for weapons and then let him through.

Aisa managed to prostrate himself with a certain grace, and when the sultan bade him stand he looked the commander in the eye. Aisa delivered the message from the waterproof pouch he wore wrapped about his waist, and Salah ad-Din unrolled the furl of paper and bent his head over it. Then he rolled the message up again and placed it on the table and returned his gaze to Aisa.

"This is the first time you have come as a messenger," Salah ad-Din observed.

Aisa nodded.

"And what is your name, lad?"

"Aisa Najib," Aisa replied without a beat.

"Are you by chance related to Malek, my burning coal, and to Baltasar, who was injured at Ramla?"

Aisa flushed with pride and admitted as much. Malek, watching as unobtrusively as he could from the flap of the tent door, was proud of his brother, too.

The sultan smiled. "Then I am indeed well served by your family. Go now and take food and rest. Return after third prayer and I will have a message for you to take back to Karakush." He paused. "Though it will not be one he much likes."

Aisa bowed and left. Malek ruffled his hair and took him to the field kitchen to eat some mutton, flatbread and dried fruit. After his initial excitement, Aisa went quiet again.

"Why so downcast, little brother?"

And now it all poured out: Aisa's suspicions about their mother's death; the odd way Baba was behaving, forgetting things, and raging one minute and then carrying on as if nothing had happened the next; how he would sometimes look right through you as if you were a stranger, then cry for you not to leave his side, not ever. Malek listened, feeling himself go colder by the minute.

That afternoon Malek was back on duty at the door of the sultan's tent. The debate was heated: half the war council was present, and as usual there was discord. The content of the message Aisa had carried was clear: that the city was hard-pressed and Karakush feared the garrison would not be able to hold out against a full-scale assault. Some of Salah ad-Din's commanders were arguing for storming the

Franj army and somehow destroying the towers; others for diverting the enemy away from Akka to defend themselves.

At last the sultan held up his hands. "In silence there is greater eloquence." Everyone quieted. Salah ad-Din gestured to his page to fetch a bowl of rose-scented water and a clean cloth. He washed and dried his hands, then reverently took his Holy Qur'an upon his lap. Opening it at random, he quoted aloud from Surah 67:5: "And we have (from of old), adorned the lowest heaven with lamps, and we have made them missiles to drive away the devils and for them we have prepared the doom of torment in the most intense blazing fire."

For several long moments he bowed his head in private prayer. Then he called for Malek, who came at a run.

"Go fetch the boy from Damascus, the coppersmith's son."

21

✼

T he "boy" from Damascus was hard to find. Malek finally
tracked him down to an area on the other side of the
encampment that smelled like the opening to Hell. Fires
burned under bubbling cauldrons, and a young man in a leather
apron and gauntlets stood over one of these, watching intently as
the liquid inside changed colour. When Malek explained that the
sultan had requested his presence, his widely spaced black eyes
regarded Malek with anguish.

"Can it wait for twenty minutes? I'm at a critical point in the
experiment."

"I think not."

It was with great reluctance that he was persuaded to go with
Malek, but once he had removed his protective gear and turned his
back on his experiment it was as if he had stripped away his alchemist persona and become just an ordinary person. He was a year
older than Malek and also, he ascertained as they made their way
back across the encampment, a distant cousin on Baltasar's side
of the family. It seemed at first a ridiculous coincidence, but by
the time they had the sultan's pavilion within sight they'd worked
out that the closest they were related was at six removes. "And

pretty much everyone is related to everyone else at that rate." The Damascene laughed.

The sultan greeted the lad cordially and introduced him to the gathered war council. "This is Ahmad al-Rammah. He came to us a week ago, claiming to have discovered a new, more combustible form of *naft*." He turned to Ahmad. "Would you be so good as to tell my generals something of the work you are engaged in?"

Ahmad nodded to the gathering. "*Salaam aleikum*, good sirs. I've been adapting the traditional formula for *naft*, Greek fire. As you've no doubt seen, it's not as effective as it could be, especially against larger targets. The old recipes are well guarded by the alchemical fraternity, but I'm confident I can give you a substance that will burn more explosively, and many times hotter, than the sort you're using at the moment."

"So you're an alchemist, are you?" Keukburi, an emir from east of the Euphrates, said scornfully. "We have another name for alchemists where I'm from." He paused, turned to the others. "Charlatans."

"I don't consider myself an alchemist, sir. I'm a brass-worker by trade, son to a coppersmith. But it's not my metalworking skills that have brought me here. My uncle recently returned to Damascus from the far east with some . . . remarkable information."

"A spy, is he? A thief?"

Salah ad-Din turned to his emir. "Let the young man tell his tale, Blue Wolf."

Ahmad looked around the pavilion. "I believe the *naft* we have made will burn the enemy's war machines. It'll go right through a leather mantlet, the hides they use to protect their towers, soaked in piss—beg pardon, sirs—well, piss and vinegar act as no defence against it. It's also more viscous, so it will stick to the target better."

"Doesn't that make it more difficult to propel?" This from Al-Adil, brother to the sultan.

Ahmad was unperturbed. "I believe I've also developed a delivery system that will overcome the difficulty of propelling the thicker liquid while maintaining its explosive properties."

"Sounds dangerous!" Taki ad-Din laughed.

Ahmad smiled. "It must be handled carefully, that is true."

This provoked further discussion, until the sultan held up his hand and said quietly, "A contingent of men will accompany Ahmad al-Rammah into Akka before dawn, with all he requires for the making and propelling of his Greek fire. And, Malek, you will go with him, and take your brother, the messenger, back with you. It will afford you the chance to see your family."

Malek nodded dumbly and gave thanks, but in his heart he pondered the sultan's words. Did he mean a chance to see his family . . . for the last time?

Aisa peppered his older brother with questions about the stories that had reached them behind the walls over the months of the siege. "We heard one of the Franj got an arrow in his arse when taking a shit outside the trenches!" he recounted gleefully. "Is it true?"

"I really don't know," Malek said, in a flat tone meant to discourage further discussion. It didn't work on Aisa.

"And they have shipped hundreds of women in from across the sea to . . . ah . . . for the soldiers."

This was true: Malek had even heard of soldiers from their own side sneaking over the lines into the brothels on the outskirts of the Franj camp, coming back with lurid tales of women with pearly skin and long red hair who were just as happy to couple with a Muslim as with a Christian, as long as their coin was true. And it seemed there was no prohibition amongst the Franj about the use of such women.

"I know nothing about that," he said. It wasn't entirely true. In Jerusalem he had visited one of the city brothels and there bought himself an hour with a woman whose hair shone like beaten gold, whose eyes were like the sea on a clear day, speckled with yellow and green. He thought of her too often for comfort. But according to Aisa, there were men of Akka slipping out of the city to avail themselves of the Franj whores' services—as if there weren't enough brothels behind the city's own walls. It seemed when you came down to it men were men first of all, Muslim and Christian second. For a brief, unsettling moment he wondered why they were at war at all.

Before dawn the next day they assembled: a battalion of light cavalry, three great carts to bear the Damascene's equipment and chemicals, and a contingent of mounted archers and foot soldiers, selected for their fleetness and courage by Taki ad-Din himself. Malek found Ahmad fussing over the loading of three ironbound barrels. "It's delicate stuff," he kept reminding the men who were loading it. He appeared very nervous, Malek thought, pale around the eyes, with the lairy, concentrated look of a man who had not slept. "The barrels must not be roughly handled."

Malek laughed. "Tell the Franj that!"

It was still dark as they made their way down out of the hills. The embers of the enemy's campfires still glowed: scarlet dots in the gloom. He caught a pungent whiff of the Christians' latrines as they passed the edge of their camp. A horse nickered and was answered by another on the picket lines; the sound seemed piercing in the quiet air. Malek saw Asfar's ears prick up and felt her tense. Was she in season? He'd have to pay attention to that when he got back to camp. Dealing with a mare in foal would be a problem; he'd have to tether her well away from the stallions. Had the Franj sentries been alerted by the horses' calls? Asfar's tension transmitted itself to him and he felt his back prickle as they passed close to the enemy lines, imagining the sudden flight of arrows, invisible against the pre-dawn sky. But there were no cries, and still the sun did not crest the hills behind them to light their progress.

They were within sight of the north gate by the time the cry went up from the Christian lines, and at once all attempts at stealth were abandoned. Taki ad-Din gave the command and they sped downhill towards the city walls. The carts lurched across the uneven ground, and Ahmad got paler by the moment as he sat on the last of these, his arms around the barrel. Malek had seen what a small amount of his "Greek fire" could do. If an entire barrel were to erupt . . .

Malek set his heels to his mount's flanks, told Aisa to hold tight and lie low and urged Asfar on. Arrows pursued them as the Franj bowmen came spilling from their billets, but they had not yet got their range. The quarrels fell mercifully short, and by the time the crossbowmen had reloaded they were long past.

Christian foot soldiers scaled the embankment and came storming out at them, but Taki ad-Din and his cavalry doubled back and rode them down. Scimitars rose and fell as the first rays of sun came over the Toron range, gleaming redly on their blades. A man in a dirty surcoat came at him with an axe and he wheeled the mare aside, avoiding the blow. Behind him there was a cry, but whether it was the man with the axe or another he could not tell, for now the walls loomed over them.

"Open the gate!"

The garrison watch was more vigilant than the enemy: the gates were thrown open and in they swept beneath the tall arch, into a city that had been at siege for the best part of a year. Behind them, the gates thudded shut and the great iron bars clanged into place, just as the muezzin's call to prayer shivered through the air.

In Artillery Square, Taki ad-Din clapped Malek on the shoulder and dismissed him. "Take your brother home. Your family will be worried to death about him. I'll take Ahmad al-Rammah to Karakush and we'll see what his Greek fire can do. After all this effort it had better not be a damp squib!"

Malek stabled Asfar and paid a lad to feed and water her and take care of his equipment—only then would he leave to seek his home. He was looking forward to seeing his family again after this long gap, despite all that had happened. His sister, so sweet and pretty; Sorgan, with his big, slow smile. Even his father . . . But his spirits were soon dampened. Even as Aisa chattered inconsequentially about friends and games and how they'd had competitions diving for shells, he stared about in dismay at the familiar streets. Near the outskirts of the city, houses had been abandoned, their walls gone to rubble; some were burned out. Weeds grew in the once pretty gardens. The fountains had been turned off to conserve precious water. No children played outside; those he saw kept close to their mothers' skirts. The women walked quickly past with their heads down, intent on their errands, where before they would have greeted him and smiled at his uniform. The little market close to their home was closed, and there was no sign of the Armenian sisters who used to sit on their doorstep, gossiping. He wondered where they were now, if they had moved in with relatives, if they were still alive. But there was the Widow Eptisam, at her window, her teeth protruding more than ever out of a face gone worn and thin.

"*Alhemdulillah!*" she cried when she saw them. "God keep you both safe!"

He almost passed Brahim, the baker's son, without recognizing him, he had lost so much weight. "Tahar, his father, died during the winter," Aisa told Malek after they'd salaamed one another and walked on.

"Is Brahim the baker now?"

Aisa shook his head, laughed. "He tried, but he was hopeless at it. Jamilla and Zohra make all our bread now."

Truly, the world had changed shape if his sister had turned to baking.

Aisa chattered on and on: Jamilla this and Jamilla that—he was clearly very fond of their cousin. And how there had been gifts of honey and peppers from the Jewish doctor's family. How Fatima, the grim-faced imam's daughter, kept calling on the house and snooping around corners, no doubt hoping to catch a sight of something untoward, but she never would . . . He fell silent.

"Why not?"

Aisa looked uncomfortable. "Zohra's . . ."

"Zohra's what?"

But Aisa had become uncharacteristically uncommunicative. They arrived at the door to the family house in unaccustomed silence.

As soon as he set foot inside, Malek could feel some spark of life had gone out of the house. He noticed that dust had fetched up in the corners by the stairs; there were grease marks on the door and a stale smell in the corridor that made his nose wrinkle. But someone was singing in the kitchen, and when he opened the door it was to find sunlight pouring in and their cousin Jamilla thumping bread dough on the table with her good arm.

As he entered, she stopped and stared at him as if he were a djinn. Her mouth fell open and she went red in the cheeks. Then she saw Aisa behind him. "Oh, Aisa, Aisa! What a relief."

"You were singing," he said accusingly, though his eyes shone with the mischief of teasing her.

"I didn't mean to." She was even more flustered now. Her eyes darted back to Malek, sweeping over his cuirass and the sword at his side, down to his riding boots with the dagger strapped inside, back up to his face and quickly away again.

At that moment Zohra stepped into the room. She looked older, and a lot like their mother . . . or rather, how he remembered his mother from when he was a child. His eyes pricked.

"Malek?" she said. Then she saw who was with him: "Aisa! We thought we'd lost you. I've been watching the sea all night!" She wrapped him in her arms until he fought free. "Allah be praised! You'd better run up and see Baba at once. Sorgan's with him."

Aisa turned a full circle. "Look, I'm wearing Malek's hauberk! It's heavy! He said I had to wear it in case the Franj fired arrows at us when we rode in, and they did! But they are hopeless shots: they missed us. Malek's got a horse. She's a mare, all reddy brown, and she's called Asfar, isn't she, Malek?"

His brother acceded with a smile. "She's a very fine animal. Even the sultan says so."

"I met the sultan!" Aisa gabbled. "He spoke to me! When I told him my name he said, 'Are you related to Malek?'" He grinned at his brother. "He called you 'my burning coal'!" And then he was off into the corridor, his footsteps slapping noisily on the stairs.

Jamilla clasped her withered arm to her chest. "Well, my goodness, what an honour." She gazed at Malek with all her heart in her eyes, but as soon as he looked back at her she looked away and started energetically kneading the dough again.

Zohra crossed the kitchen to him. "Brother. It's so good to see you at last."

Malek put his arms around her and held her tightly, and felt the fragility of her shoulders and ribs. Had things really been so hard in Akka?

At last his sister stepped away. "Come along," she said. "You should see Baba and Sorgan. Let poor Jamilla concentrate or we'll have no bread." And as their cousin protested, she led her brother into the dim corridor beyond.

On their way up to the terrace, Malek put a hand on his sister's arm. There was something he needed to say to her in private. "Aisa said something that worried me. Something about gifts of food . . ." He felt Zohra stiffen. "Times are hard, I know, and you must all get by as best you can when there are shortages. But I would not want to see your reputation . . . damaged in any way."

She pulled her arm away from him. "Damaged? What in hell are you saying?"

"It's just that such gifts could be . . . misconstrued. Especially from a Jewish family."

She drew herself up, golden eyes fiery. "What has Aisa been saying? Nothing is going on that is 'damaging' to my reputation. Whatever that might mean!"

"All right, all right," Malek said. "But there is no need to look beyond the family for anything you need. Tariq will ensure you need never go short—"

"Tariq?" she spat the name out. "I don't want anything to do with Tariq!"

"He's your betrothed."

"Well, no one consulted me."

"Why should we consult you? Our parents chose Tariq for you when you were a little girl."

"Tariq is a pig. And a coward!" Zohra's face was flushed with a sudden passion Malek could not comprehend. "I will not marry him! And if I want to spend time talking with my friends, I shall!"

"The Prophet says that when a man is alone with a woman, Satan is the third in the room with them!" Malek cried. The force of his fury took even him by surprise.

"What did the Prophet know of a woman's duty? Men! You are all the same." Her hand flew to her mouth, too late to retrieve the insult.

Malek watched his arm rise to strike her, but she did not flinch.

Upstairs on the terrace, he could hear Sorgan and Baltasar welcoming Aisa back; it was jarring to have such happiness just a few feet above their heads. With all the restraint he could muster, Malek drew back his hand, took a deep breath, then pushed past

Zohra. "I am going to see Tariq and Uncle Omar," he declared. "Someone needs to take charge of this family."

Zohra busied herself about the house, her movements jerky. She was shocked to find so many little caches of piled-up dirt and dustballs. There might be a war on, but Nima Najib would never have accepted that excuse for skimping on the housework.

She got down on her knees and scrubbed the tiled floors. For a while the work stilled her mind, but as it became ever more repetitive she found her sense of dread descending. What if Malek returned with Tariq and Rachid to drag her away to be married? Usually a wedding took months to plan—the clothes, the feasting, the guests that had to be invited from miles away, the musicians to be booked, the imam, too—but in times of war such niceties were often ignored. Only last week there had been a swiftly arranged marriage on Swallow Street. Gossip had it the girl had got pregnant—it was said in hushed whispers, a shocking allegation. People blamed the war for loosening morals. The mother of the girl was dead, her father and brothers in the garrison. It seemed she could not be trusted to guard her own honour. Zohra did not want people saying the same thing about her. She did not want anyone talking about her at all.

She thought about running away but there was nowhere to run to: a city becomes a small place when every way out of it is blocked. She fantasized briefly about seeking sanctuary with Nathanael, but how could she after putting such a distance between them, after causing such hurt? Visiting the house had brought back too many memories, and seeing Nathanael—paler and thinner, the laughing eyes now sunken and haunted, his sensuous mouth set in a grim line—had brought her guilt flooding back. There was no going back, and some things time could not mend. In any case, she could not leave her father and Sorgan and Aisa to their own devices—they would grow filthy and starve within a month.

Once she had finished cleaning the house, she went out into the courtyard. Where once it had been neat to the point of sterility—pots of flowers and desiccated herbs placed at precise intervals—now there was now a small riot of nature. She had started cultivating zucchini, peppers, peas, beans, aubergines, chilis, lemon trees, espaliered peach trees, grapes. There was a chicken run along the wall, and a small wooden shed for the goats. Zohra looked around in satisfaction. And then it struck her with some force that their courtyard was every day coming more to resemble the courtyard at Nathanael's house, with its rampant herbs and tumbles of flowers. She closed her eyes and was immediately visited by a memory of Nat standing out there with his trousers rolled up and his hair wild with light, with earth on his hands and cheeks and knees and his arms full of young plants, like some sort of pagan deity.

How long she stood there, remembering, she could not say. But when at last she opened her eyes again, her cheeks were wet with tears.

Nathanael had just finished tending to a wounded man in the barracks when someone called out, "Look, it's Sorgan!"

He turned, and there was Sorgan Najib, Zohra's big, simple brother, a head taller than the off-duty garrison soldiers who were coming up to thump him on the arm or back, full of camaraderie. Of course, he looked different from the last time Nat had seen him, hugging his knees and keening like a child as his mother lay murdered in one room, and dozens of his beloved pigeons lay torn to pieces on the roof.

"How are the pigeons?" someone asked now. "Did the last one make it back all right?"

"Lady? Yes, she's fine. Tucked up in her roost, full of grain," Sorgan replied. But even as he responded, his gaze flicked here and there, and he was frowning. "I can't find my brother."

"Aisa? We saw him earlier. He came back with the column the sultan sent in this morning."

"Malek. It's Malek I can't find."

The soldiers looked from one to another. "When we saw him, he was on his way back to your house with Aisa," said one of the men.

"Aisa's home," Sorgan said. "But I haven't seen Malek at all." The corners of his lips turned down and it looked as if he might cry.

"He's probably gone to see the cousins before coming back to eat with you," another suggested kindly, but Sorgan was not to be so easily placated.

"Why doesn't he want to see me?"

"Course he does, you silly sod. He's your brother, isn't he?"

"Kamal's my brother too and he ran away."

Sorgan's logic was unassailable.

"And Ummi left, too . . ."

His shoulders began to shake. The soldiers shifted awkwardly from foot to foot; no one wanted to see a man of Sorgan's great size break down in tears.

Nat got to his feet and crossed the room, his hand already digging in the pocket of his robe. "Hello, Sorgan," he said cheerily. He offered a handful of dates and nuts to him.

Sorgan's frown dissolved. "I remember you!" he said joyfully, and he crammed the treats into his mouth.

The tension in the room lessened.

"We're going up onto the walls to watch some lad from Damascus show those bastards from Baghdad how to use Greek fire," a sergeant said. The caliph's artificers had not made many friends in Akka. "Why don't you come and watch, Sorgan?"

Sorgan looked unsurely at Nathanael, who nodded encouragement. "Yes, why don't you go up to the walls to watch?"

Sorgan scowled. "Will Malek be there?"

"I don't know," Nat said truthfully.

"I miss him." Tears were gathering again.

"I'll come with you," Nathanael offered. It was about time to go up to the wall as the doctor on duty, though there was very little he could do if there was an accident with the *naft*, which would burn through everything it touched.

Sorgan considered this for a long moment, then imprisoned one of Nat's hands in his own vast fist. "All right, then, if you come with me."

They followed the garrison soldiers up towards the Accursed Tower, at the corner where the east wall met the north wall and was exposed on two fronts to the enemy. This was where the Franj had built their three great siege towers.

There was already a great scrum of people up there. It was mainly other garrison soldiers who had heard about the experiment, but word had spread, and there were a lot of townspeople too, pressing through the crowd and being turned back by the increasingly harassed guards.

"Official personnel only. Look, there's no room. It's dangerous for civilians here. Move a bit farther along the wall towards the harbour. If there's anything to see you'll be able to see it from there. Doctor Nathanael, this way—"

"Sorgan Najib is here to help me," he told the guard.

The guard looked up from Nat to the man looming behind him. "Oh, it's you, Sorgan. Come on through, we'll find a place for you up here. Make way, you there, make way! Garrison soldiers coming through!"

And suddenly they were up on the wide walkway behind the wall. There were a lot of people up there Nat recognized, but many more he did not. Among these, in the middle of a space into which the crowd did not intrude, was a young man near his own age, his face lit by the glow from a giant brazier. He had an odd sort of face, with eyes as wide apart as a fish's. He was tending to a contraption suspended over a brazier.

"It looks like a huge lamp," Sorgan said in wonder. He turned to Nat, pointing at the long spout, from which vapour issued in a noxious cloud. "Is there a djinn in there?"

Nat turned a calming face. "Not a djinn, no. But it could be dangerous, so let's move away a little."

Nat could feel the heat coming off it in waves. In the occasional lull in the noise of the crowd, the enemy missiles striking the walls, the foreign chatter of the black-robed men with beaky faces and crows' robes watching the fish-eyed man and his lamp, he could hear the crackling and popping inside the great brass vessel, and sometimes an ominous rumble. Two men worked a bellows and the brazier flared and spat, and then the noise in the lamp redoubled.

Nat turned with Sorgan and tried to push his way back towards the steps, but there were more soldiers coming up and the press of bodies was almost impossible to negotiate. Eventually they were pushed up against the wall itself, and still the soldiers came, and the pressure became greater. It was hard to breathe and the air was hot. Beside him, Sorgan began to gasp, then to sob. Nat tried to placate the big man with more dates, but as soon as he got his hand out of his pocket they were dashed to the ground by the crush of the crowd and lost underfoot.

Sorgan was staring now, over the heads of the soldiers and other onlookers, out at the Franj siege towers. There were three of them—immensely tall, creaking and grinding and . . . howling. "They're full of ghosts!" Sorgan wailed.

"No, Sorgan, they're not ghosts." Nat had to shout to make himself heard.

"They have no *beeeeards!*"

It was true: many of the Franj were clean-shaven, and the new-comers were paler than the men of Akka, who were the only people Sorgan had for comparison.

"They're enemy soldiers, Sorgan. The Christians: flesh-and-blood men, not ghosts."

"It's like that story from the mosque. The tower full of voices." Sorgan's dark eyes were round and fearful.

Nat frowned. Then he realized what Sorgan meant. "Oh, the *Migdal Bavel*." The Tower of Babel. He tried to remember what the Muslims called the thing, failed.

"The *Burj Babil*. And it's coming right at us!" A soft wail came out of Sorgan, rising in volume to a bellow of fear. The cacophony was unbearable.

Nat reached to put a comforting arm around the big man. "It's all right, Sorgan, it's all right."

But just as he said this the brass vessel gave a vast belch, and suddenly, at the Damascene's command, a great bolt of fire came scorching out of its long snout. The gout of burning *naft* arced across the space between Akka's city walls and the first siege tower, striking it at mid height and splattering wide. For a long moment nothing happened. Inside the tower the enemy soldiers began a ragged, taunting jeer. But then, with a ferocity none could have imagined, the entire midsection of the tower caught fire. And not just any fire: the *naft* burned with such an intensity that the flames seemed white at their heart, then red, then violet. Like rampant flowers they swarmed up and down the structure. The taunts became cries of terror as the blaze ate through the treated hides mantling the engine, then through the wood beneath, hungry for the men who now used their shields to ward off the ravaging fire. Soon the interior of the first tower was ablaze with a steady orange blast, as hot as the inside of a baker's oven. Pieces of burning debris began to rain down, setting fire to the brushwood in the fosse below, and everything else with which the Franj had stuffed the ditch. A terrible acrid stench rose as corpses caught alight, burning with a curious greenish flame, as steady as candles.

The Franj inside and out shouted in their many and various languages for the mercy of their god, but it seemed he was not listening. The top of the first tower, burned through, tilted suddenly and then tumbled backwards, trailing banners of flame, spilling dead and burning men left and right. The second tower took the brunt of the falling timbers, and soon it, too, was alight.

All along the walls of Akka the men who had been defending the city with increasing desperation raised their voices in triumph as below them the enemy fled in terror or were roasted alive.

"Come away," Nathanael said to Sorgan, fearing the sight of such horrible death would upset him even more, but the simple man was gripping the wall with both hands, leaning out towards the blaze, his expression rapacious, yet rapt: with all the innocence and savagery of an avenging angel. He would not be moved.

"See!" he said, his eyes never leaving the hellish scene. "See how the djinn is killing the giants. He is destroying them!"

Nat could not bear to watch the staggering figures down below, their armour gone, their swords melted, their skin crisped black, their heads still afire with an uncanny violet flame, as if their departing souls had taken on visible form. The man from Damascus primed his monstrous cauldron again; the bellows-men worked it up to pressure and applied the levers, which sent more gouts of death shooting out. Behind him, the Greek fire caught the third tower, and all along the walls the cry went up: "God is great!"

Nat saw someone catch the man at the brazier by the shoulders and whirl him around in an impromptu dance. "You have saved Akka, my boy! You're a hero!"

The young man's grin was as wide as the sky. "I knew it would work."

The caliph's artificers stood in a disgruntled huddle, muttering in their secret language, casting dark glances at the parvenu.

Now the city's archers sent down a barrage of arrows on the unfortunate survivors. There was no return fire: the Franj, so shocked at the disaster that had befallen their towers, had even abandoned their incessant bombardment. The mangonels were being towed out of range before they, too, were engulfed. Between the arrows of the Akka bowmen and the Damascene's Greek fire, it was a massacre. And Nat had no work of his own to tend to: there was not a single casualty to the defenders on the wall.

Nathanael and Sorgan walked together in silence along the winding street known as Martyrs Avenue that led to his favourite tea house. From time to time the young doctor cast a glance at his companion, only to find that same expression of unholy glee on his face. Nat found it deeply unnerving.

Inside the tea house was the usual assortment of loafers and greybeards. Word of the Greek fire had not yet spread to this usually reliable bastion of gossip. Hamsa Nasri was fetched from his house to share the celebration; he brought with him old Driss, hobbling painfully from an infected toe. When he saw Nathanael and Sorgan he grinned, the huge old scar running down his face making his expression even more alarming. "Burned the bastards, have we? That'll teach 'em, building their infernal engines. Akka's walls will never fall to such infidel tricks!"

Younes the barber had lost his crocheted white skullcap. Now his bald patch was clearly on display. He looked older. "Who's your friend?" he winked at Nat. "Given up on the girl with the lion eyes, have you?"

Nat gave him what he hoped was a warning glare. "This is Sorgan," he said stiffly, but Younes was not to be so easily diverted.

"Next best thing, eh? Good size, too." He grinned at Sorgan, and the big man, knowing no better, grinned back, spilling pastry crumbs.

Nat got to his feet. "Come on, Sorgan," he said.

But Sorgan was hard to shift once he got settled, and Younes was pressing more of the little honeycakes on him. Nat remembered the stories of the dancing boy he kept.

"Come along, Sorgan," he said more firmly now. "We must get you home."

Sorgan stuffed the cakes into his mouth. His tongue laboriously gathered in the honey that had smeared his face; then he licked his fingers one by one, and then the palms of his hands. For fear he would start on the table, Nathanael hauled him upright and turned him towards the door. "I am sure your sister will be preparing your dinner, and if we don't hurry Malek will eat your share." That, at last, got the big man moving.

As they neared the Najib house, Nathanael was filled with trepidation. Would Zohra answer the door? They reached the door just as it was thrown open and out came Baltasar with a tall man in a white cotton robe. His sleeves were rolled up, revealing pale scars beneath the curling, dark hair of his forearms. His hair was slick from the hammam. His gaze swept over Nathanael—from the skullcap, to Sorgan's grip on his arm, back to the skullcap—then locked onto Nat's eyes. His expression was not exactly unfriendly, but watchful and curious.

"Malek!" Sorgan cried happily.

Behind Zohra's eldest brother came two other men, also dressed in their Friday best. They were tall and handsome, well built and prosperous-looking. He did not like the look of them at all.

"I've brought Sorgan home," Nat said quietly.

Baltasar was in a mellow mood: clearly, he had forgotten the traumatic day on which he had last seen Nathanael, or, as became increasingly clear, he did not recognize the young Jewish doctor at all. Reaching out, he engulfed both of them in an embrace. "We're going to the mosque to give thanks for our good fortune."

Nathanael smiled uncertainly. "It really is marvellous about the Greek fire," he said.

Baltasar frowned. "Greek fire?"

"The destruction of the Franj siege towers."

The old man appeared uncomprehending, then said, beaming, "My lovely daughter Zohra has this very day been married to her cousin Tariq."

22

Malek returned to the Muslim camp in a much calmer state of mind. It was good to see some family matters settled and his sister safely married. Tariq would move into the Najib house, so that meant his father and Sorgan and Aisa would be better looked after: Tariq's work at the citadel brought him in a good wage and access to provisions. It might not be fair that his cousin profited from his safe administrative job when others in the city were suffering, but Malek's first care was for the welfare of his own family.

The destruction of the Franj siege towers had added an air of frantic optimism to the wedding celebrations. People said the siege would soon be over, that the marriage represented a better future, that the couple would be blessed with children who would grow up in safer times, with the wicked foreigners expelled from the region and Akka restored to its proper place in the caliphate. Malek found himself carried along by the hectic mood, as long as he did not look too long at his sister's face. Zohra seemed to drift through the whole ceremony, the feast and the dancing, as if she were absent from her body. She did not wail or fight or cry. She just seemed to . . . go away.

The memory of her vacant eyes returned to him on his dawn ride back to camp, tempting him to doubt. But he was determined to believe in the best possible future. His optimism, however, was not to last. The resumption of his duties for the sultan coincided with the return of Baha ad-Din from his expedition to Baghdad and a summoning of the sultan's inner council to his war tent. Gathered there with Salah ad-Din and his qadi were the sultan's secretary, Imad al-Din, and his nephew, Taki ad-Din.

Malek watched Salah ad-Din break the seal of the letter Baha ad-Din had brought back from the caliph, unroll the missive and scan the contents. The sultan said nothing, but his knuckles whitened as he tried to master his temper.

"Twenty thousand dinars?" he said at last, his voice deceptively quiet. "The caliph offers me a loan—a loan, mind you—to be taken from any merchants in the region and charged against the Baghdad treasury." He angled the scroll towards his scribe. "I spend twenty thousand a day conducting this siege! A day! They gave me a million towards the siege of Damietta—gave, not loaned. By the ninety-nine names of God, what is he thinking to offer such an insult? The Redbeard's German army approaches our northern borders and he offers me twenty thousand dinars!" He threw the scroll aside, where Imad al-Din picked it up and gazed at it earnestly, as if close scrutiny might reveal some previously concealed zeros.

The German army. At the door of the war tent, Malek's heart dropped like a stone. Amid the glee of their recent successes, he had forgotten about Barbarossa and his advancing horde.

The sultan sat back amongst his cushions, massaged his forehead. At last he turned to Baha ad-Din. "Send orders to have Latakia and Beirut dismantled."

"Dismantled, sire?"

"Razed to the ground. It is the only way. We cannot afford to let such strategic cities fall into enemy hands."

The look that passed between the qadi of the army and Taki ad-Din was eloquent. "My lord," Taki said, going down on one knee before his uncle. "Let me take the men of Hama and ride north to intercept Barbarossa's horde. We will cut them down like summer corn before they ever set foot upon our lands."

The sultan gave him a wintry smile. "You are brave beyond courage, nephew. But I think even the flower of Hama cannot survive the trampling of a Christian army two hundred thousand strong. No——" he held up a hand to forestall Taki's retort. "I must think upon this longer. Akka remains the key, so I cannot spare you from the siege. The city is the anvil and we the hammer, and the enemy is the sword we must beat into horseshoes."

The war had to be fought on two fronts. It was decided that Taki ad-Din's son would take the troops of Aleppo to intercept the German force, rallying the faithful to his banner as he went. By the time they reached the northern borders it was hoped that their numbers would have swelled sufficiently to make a stand against the enemy horde and hold them at bay long enough for reinforcements to arrive from other parts of the caliphate.

Malek watched them ride out with their apricot banners fluttering and their spears glinting in the hot light and almost wished he were going with them. Anything was better than staying in camp, mired in dread.

Fighting resumed at Akka, as if the Christians had gained heart from seeing the departure of the Aleppans. It was a fierce, bloody affair. At night, bodies were piled high among the Franj trenches, the stench of decomposition rising even to the sultan's camp. So horrible was the smell that Malek set incense burners outside the pavilion as well as within, but nothing could be done about the clouds of black flies that rose, angry and buzzing, from the corpses whenever they were disturbed. Soldiers returning from the front line complained that sometimes you could hardly see an enemy coming at you for the black blizzard of insects.

The fighting lasted for a week, then ceased, a storm that blew itself out. For a month after that there was nothing to be done but rest and bury the dead.

Then one day a Christian woman came into the Muslim camp, weeping and claiming that raiders had carried off her child. No one believed her: what would anyone want with a squalling infant? As it was, the presence of women in the Franj camp was a matter of considerable discussion. Malek and his friend Ibrahim, the Nubian, now promoted from the mamluk ranks to the burning coals, had talked about women late into the night while they stood their watch. Ibrahim boasted of having three wives: "A big one, a small one and one in between—and many, many babies!" How this was possible when Ibo, as he called himself, was constantly away at war Malek did not know. He thought it best not to ask.

"But how do they manage, your family, without you there to fend for them?"

Ibo looked surprised. "They are women, they look after themselves. Women are amazing. Stronger, I think, than men!"

Malek was nonplussed. Then he grinned. "Do not tease me with your strange African humour. You'll be telling me next that your big wife is as tall as you and can lift an ox!"

Ibrahim's grin lit up the darkness. "She is not tall, my big wife, but broad." He stretched his hands apart. "Her hips are as wide as the desert and her mind is as deep as the sea. You do not understand the strength of such a woman, my friend, until you have been crushed between her thighs or tried to best her in an argument. Never argue with women, Malek, for they are always right and they always win. They are as twisty as snakes, with the memory of elephants and the sting of a scorpion. Dangerous creatures, my friend, very dangerous. I swear, if there were armies of women they would sweep the world beneath their skirts and we would all be their slaves."

Malek shook his head, amused. "But they cannot fight like men, with arms and armour. So maybe that is just as well."

Ibo shrugged. "Where I come from, some wield a spear as well as any man. It is not the strength of the arm that counts," he tapped his head, "but the strength of the will. And women have immense strength of will. It comes from bearing children, I believe. They say the pain of that is worse than any wound, and yet they do it again and again."

None of this fitted with how Malek saw the world, but he reasoned that women in Africa were probably different.

In the end, word of the Franj woman reached the ears of the sultan as she wandered the Muslim lines, seeking her child.

"Go fetch her to me," he instructed Malek. "I would hear her grievance." And so Malek went in search of the woman.

He was astonished to find her flagrantly unveiled. Seeing all that yellow hair reminded him with sudden force of the whore in Jerusalem, and so his manner with her was brusque. She was barely older than his sister, he thought as they walked back to the war tent. What was she doing here, and with a child, too? He wondered if she was married to one of the enemy soldiers—he had heard that their wives sometimes followed them on campaign. Then it occurred to him that she might be one of those who took money for the use of their bodies. The idea roused him fiercely.

Salah ad-Din, courteous as ever, rose and greeted the woman, called for cushions where she might sit, for a goblet of iced sherbet, and watched as she sipped it wonderingly. He took no umbrage at her brazen appearance, at the dirt on her face and clothes, or the scratch marks on her cheeks where she had torn at herself in her grief. Quite the opposite: he treated her as if she were Queen Sibylla herself.

Having coaxed her tale from her, by way of Imad al-Din's halting translation, he dispatched men to search everywhere, within the camp and beyond, to look for the infant. And still the woman wept, more quietly now, gazing fearfully around the tent as if expecting these foreign men with their neat black beards, inquisitive black eyes and unnerving courtesy to transform themselves suddenly into the ravening beasts she believed them to be.

At last, one of the guards returned with a bundle in his arms. Salah ad-Din laid a hand on the infant's head. "A war camp is no place for a child," he admonished its mother. "It does not do for children to be exposed to such horrors at an early age, for fear they will become inured to them and think that life is cheap. The taking of a life should never be done without consideration. It is a great shame to us all that we must resort to such wars."

Then he ordered that a guard accompany her back to the Christian lines under white flags of truce, and all the while the woman looked at him in astonishment.

Looking back, it was almost as if this act of grace was directly rewarded, Malek thought, when two days later an exhausted courier on a sweating horse rode in. The messenger gave his name as Theophilus.

"I have been sent by Isaac the King, emperor of Constantinople," he croaked, "servant of the Messiah, crowned by the grace of God, ever glorious and victorious, the invincible conqueror, the autocrat of the Greeks, Angelos, who extends to His Excellency the Sultan of Egypt, Salah ad-Din, sincere affection and friendship—"

"Yes, yes," cried Imad al-Din impatiently, "but now to the nub of the matter!"

"The German army crossed into Cicilia," Theophilus continued with a frown, annoyed that the formal protocols had been curtailed. "The Holy Roman Emperor Barbarossa was pushing ahead of the main body of his troops with his scouts and a small vanguard.

They came to the River Saleph, but rather than wait for the army the emperor was impatient to continue and insisted on fording the river at once. In the deepest part of the current his horse lost its footing and threw the old man over its shoulder. It was the hottest day of the year but the water, streaming out of the mountains, was deadly cold. It may be that the emperor's heart gave out, for he was not a young man, or that he could not swim, weighed down by his armour. Either way, all attempts to revive him failed—"

"What, the Redbeard is dead?" Salah ad-Din cried, rising from his chair. "The greatest king in Christendom?"

Theophilus inclined his head. "We had the news of his demise on the best authority, for Isaac the King, servant of the Messiah, God praise his name and ever lengthen his days, has spies embedded within Barbarossa's army, and all this was witnessed by one of those men."

Since this tumultuous event, he said, a confusion had fallen over the Germans, whose number had already been greatly reduced by disease and hardship. And although it was thought that they would continue south into Syria, the threat they posed was not as insurmountable as it had previously appeared.

Malek could hardly believe what he was hearing: it seemed too momentous, too fortuitous to take in. It was only when the sultan fell to his knees to give thanks to Allah, and the rest of the inner council followed suit, that it sank in. A black cloud had been lifted. He felt like shouting in exultation. But of course he knelt like the rest and touched his forehead to the ground and thanked God for his grace.

Salah ad-Din sent a pigeon to Akka, but since the Christians had taken to shooting them down whenever they could, he sent a boy to fetch "the swimmer." Malek smiled. For once, Aisa would be able to carry good tidings home. What celebrations there would be!

Aisa, arriving some minutes later, fell to one knee before the sultan to accept the message. He already wore, wrapped tight around his waist, the otterskin bags containing the wages to take back to the garrison. At the sight of his little brother, whose shoulders were beginning to fill out with muscle gained from these regular exertions, Malek's heart swelled with pride.

Salah ad-Din gave him the message he had dictated to Imad al-Din and watched as Aisa tucked it carefully in with the money. "You will be hailed a hero for delivering this," he said, with tears in his eyes.

The smile the lad returned to the sultan was rapt, and Malek found his own eyes swimming with tears.

The news of the loss of the German horde seemed to stir up a ferment in the Christian ranks, and waves of men carrying pikes and axes beat uphill against their own army. The attacks seemed random and disorganized, the provocateurs from the lower orders.

"Desperation?" Ibrahim asked Malek on the third morning of unrest, as they armed themselves on the sultan's orders.

Malek shrugged. "Who can know the mind of the unbeliever?"

"Our lord must think there is an advantage to be gained, if he's sending us out with Ala al-Din." The sultan rarely risked his burning coals for no good reason.

Malek went to the farthest picket lines to saddle up Asfar. She nickered at the sight of him, and when he mounted her she danced and spun around and around. Malek looked at the range of hills to the south, sere and brown, baked by the sun, and above them a hawk making slow, graceful sky-circles, the light turning its wings to a blur of golden-red against the unbroken blue. How lovely, Malek thought, to be up there away from the stink and the noise and the flies, the excrement and sickness and death. But then the hawk folded its wings and stooped, faster than the fastest arrow. It disappeared from sight, but a sudden piercing shriek marked the death of its prey. The sound went through Malek like a shaft of ice. Was this the day he would die? Had it long been written? Unshielded by his usual concerns about keeping the sultan safe, he rode into battle sure that something terrible was about to happen to him.

He lost track of the number of enemies he faced that day—of the nameless men who rose up before him, of the number of times his sword rose and fell, of the blows he struck, the cries of horses and men merging into one long, drawn-out death-scream that became a blur of noise in his head. His world had shrunk to this burning arena in which the sun beat down and the enemy became increasingly trapped between the walls, the ocean and the closing pincers of the Muslim troops.

The chroniclers would write of this battle that the bodies of the Franj stretched in nine lines between the sand dunes and the sea, and that in each line lay a thousand corpses. Malek knew nothing of this: all he saw was what was before him—details etched into his memory, to be replayed in jerky, formless repetitions in the dead of night or during unguarded waking moments. And the worst of the nightmares was to come in his final encounter of the day, when he was barely strong enough to wield his scimitar.

If there was anything different about his final opponent of the day, Malek did not notice it. If the figure was slighter or shorter than others he had faced, he did not register the fact. If the blow the Franj landed on his shield failed to jar his arm as he would have expected, he did not mark it, but pushed back with his shield to unsteady the soldier and swung down with his curved blade with all the strength he could muster, catching the fellow a disabling blow on the shoulder, the honed scimitar shearing down through the flimsy layers of cloth and leather, through skin and muscle and bone, where it grated and stuck, threatening to unhorse him.

The scream the man emitted was terrible. Malek yanked the scimitar up and back with all his strength till it came free and was about to ride on when the trumpets blared out the signal to desist.

Wearily, Malek turned to scan the field, only to find none standing but Muslims and mamluks. And then he knew they had taken the day. All around, men lay corpse-still or writhing. Already, soldiers were scavenging, removing weapons and valuables from the fallen. There was booty to be found: it was a practice shared by every victorious army under the sun. Maybe it was the sight of such mutilated humanity, or superstition at being too close to death in case it rubbed off on you in some way, or the fear of dead men's spirits hovering, or the djinns that swarmed over battlefields like crows. Or maybe he was simply weak of stomach. Whatever the reason, Malek could not bring himself to join them.

He turned Asfar to return to the camp, but a detail snatched his attention. His last opponent lay there, helmet askew, the nose-guard knocked sideways. He glimpsed the whole, naked face now—so pale, and growing paler. The fair skin of these people never failed to amaze him, like dough taken too soon from the oven. But this one had skin so pale it was almost luminous, and the exposed throat was smooth, the veins a shadowy blue.

Something was not right; it clutched at his gut, the dread he had been feeling all day long. He felt compelled to go closer. He found himself swinging down out of the saddle, drawing the mare with him as he stood over the fallen Christian soldier. He went down on one knee and pulled the helmet fully off and a mass of red-gold hair spilled out. Hot iron in his palm; cool hair slipping like silk across the back of his hand: a contradictory image he had difficulty holding in his mind, like opposing magnets. And then the fallen soldier's eyes opened and they were blue, a violent, dark blue like the heart of a storm, yet fringed by golden lashes.

The mouth twisted and uttered a word he could not understand. And then the soldier tried to sit up, rising with immense effort onto one elbow. The ruined leather of the soldier's jerkin—soaked in scarlet, already drying to brown in the baking heat—fell away to reveal an impossible wound—an arm hanging by sinew and shattered bone—and a single, perfect, small white breast.

He had committed a terrible sin: he had cut down a woman.

Malek lurched backwards, appalled as the figure tried once more to rise. He watched, gripped by a sort of terror. Her eyes locked on his, and then blood gushed from her mouth and she fell back and did not move again, but lay there, her hair fanned out, just like the hair of the Jerusalem whore against the mattress on which he had taken her, her blue eyes staring sightlessly into the blue eternity above.

Malek buried his face in his hands and wept, and wept, and wept.

23

❄

Zohra woke suddenly with her heart thundering, her robe tangled around her legs. She lay there, disoriented, sweat pooling between her breasts, trying to remember where she was and what had happened. She had been running from something—or maybe towards something—something terrible, something world-breaking. Running, but unable to move, screaming silently.

Beside her, Tariq stirred, raising his head a little off the mattress. In the darkness she stared at him, willing him not to wake, and a moment later he grunted and turned away from her, and his gentle snoring resumed. It was the only gentle thing about him. Her thighs were chafed from his attentions: he was not a thin man, or a tender husband. Sometimes she thought she would break apart under his weight. "God give me the strength to endure this marriage," she prayed. "I am doing my best, but you are not making it easy."

It had come as no surprise that she did not enjoy all that was required of her as a wife. She had always found it hard to accept, as others seemed to without question, that it was natural that her fate be parcelled out by men. She had at first faced the travails Tariq inflicted on her with cold disdain, but that had just made him crueller. When she tried to fight him off, he laughed and seemed to enjoy it all the more. She had learned to give the appearance of compliance but took herself away from him, into a locked room in her head that smelled of amber and herbs, of inks and vellum.

She lay there a while longer, trying to recover the nightmare, but all that was left in her grasp were dark tatters of threat and danger. She ran through all those she loved, one by one, to reassure herself.

Her father had a summer cold and a hacking cough she did not like the sound of, but whenever she mentioned it he brushed her concerns away. "What do you expect when I spend my days knee-deep in pigeon feathers and bird shit?" Every other day he lost a pigeon, either shot down by the Christians or lost because he was reduced to sending out inexperienced birds. It made him permanently bad-tempered.

Her cousin Jamilla had become Zohra's only ally. It was with some shame that Zohra recognized her meanness toward her cousin before, mistaking her determined positivity for ignorance, her care for interference.

Sorgan was like a huge, overgrown toddler, dogging her footsteps, concern for her brimming out of his trusting dark eyes. It was clear he knew she was unhappy but did not know what to do for her. His childlike distress made her feel like weeping all the more. Better to distract him with whatever food came to hand. It was a ploy that worked with heartbreaking ease.

As for her younger brother, she wished fervently that Aisa had not taken it upon himself to swim messages back and forth between the two commanders. He was so young. Every time he left the house she was terrified she would never see him again.

"Promise me you'll send a pigeon from the Hill of Carobs from now on whenever you arrive at Salah ad-Din's camp," she had asked him.

He had laughed at her. "Don't fuss so. Anyway, there may not always be a spare pigeon to send."

Instantly furious, she'd caught him by the arm. "Don't give me that, or I will personally send a message-bird to your sultan demanding that he stops using a boy to do a man's job."

"There are no men left to do this," Aisa said quietly. "And I think if I am doing a man's job that makes me a man too. Besides, no one makes 'demands' of the sultan. But if you are so worried, I will ask Malek to ask him."

And now, of course, a bird arrived each time Aisa safely crossed the water to the Muslim camp. At this moment at least she could rest easy, knowing he was upstairs in the room with Sorgan, sleeping soundly.

Which left Nathanael . . .

Shivering despite the heat, Zohra pushed that fear away.

As she moved silently down the stairs, she felt like a ghost in her own house, a shadow of herself, barely even a person. How had it come to this, that she—Zohra Najib, once described as "a lioness" and "a wildcat"—should be so reduced? They were at war: everyone was reduced. There was no time for such small complaints when they were all fighting for survival, when everyone had to make sacrifices. Hadn't that been what the governor had declared in the central square last week? "Keep strong your faith in God and each other and we shall prevail."

But sometimes faith was sorely tested.

In the kitchen she pottered about, lighting the stove, pouring water from the ewer, setting it to boil. There was no tea left: that luxury had long since run out. They sometimes used chicory, roasted dandelion root or date pits, but herb tea was less acrid— lemon balm and chamomile picked fresh from the garden, sweetened with a teaspoon of honey from Nathanel's hives. There was not much left.

She went out into the courtyard, where the cockerel regarded her balefully. "Beat you to it," she told him. "What use are you if you cannot even crow the time? Perhaps we should put you in the pot and have done." She didn't mean it, but he turned his back on her anyway, shaking his wattled head as if insulted. Then she let the goats out and watched them gambol into the pre-dawn street.

Zohra made her tea and drank it in the courtyard, surrounded by burgeoning life. More aubergines had ripened, and capsicums and chilis shone like jewels among the dark-green foliage. The garden was thriving, but still it could not provide for them for long, especially with an extra mouth, and that a particularly greedy one, to feed. She picked the aphids off the vines and prodded the bean pods, but their contents felt like little stones. Later she would water them with the wash-water from the house. Plants were always thirsty, but they had been told to try to keep water use to a minimum; already a number of the city's wells had dried up in the hot weather. But people had to eat, and creating gardens wherever they could find waste ground or abandoned land had been a great success. Working in the gardens was one of the things that kept her sane.

The muezzin's dawn call sounded across the city. Zohra went inside and washed, then laid out her prayer mat and knelt and prayed that whatever it was in her nightmare that had woken her had no basis in fact and that all the people she cared for—her father; her brothers Malek and Aisa; Jamilla and her aunt and uncle; Nathanael, the son of Yacub—would be kept safe. Then, as she always did, she added a short prayer for her lost brother Kamal, wherever he might be.

Kamal Najib stood amongst the other *fida'i* in the mountain fortress of Masyaf, known as the Eagle's Nest. Like the other adherents, he wore a white robe. Like the rest of them, his expression was impassive. Emotion was nothing but personal weakness: the Almighty had no use for it; it got in the way of the tasks for which they were appointed. As did thought. "You are here not to think, but to obey," the Grand Headmaster had informed them. "Only through me can you find Purification, Enlightenment and Paradise. You are the tools of God, and tools do not question. Tools do not worry. Tools do not doubt. Tools work only in the hand of the craftsman: until they are picked up to be used they have no purpose. I am the craftsman, and you are the tools I employ as I do God's work. What are you?"

"We are the tools of God," they chanted obediently.

Kamal slid a glance to his right to where Bashar stood, face forward, completely focused on the Grand Headmaster. Except that his friend was "Bashar" no more, just as he himself was no longer "Kamal." And neither were they "friends" in any accepted sense, but members of a shared brotherhood that superseded all other connections. None of them had names, or families, or pasts, or a future beyond the task they were allotted. Tools—as the Grand Headmaster told them over and over again—had no identity of their own but were interchangeable, each there to be made perfect for the work it must perform. It was his job to make them perfect, he said: to file away their flaws and weaknesses, to temper them in fire and douse them in water, to harden them and hone them to a perfect, steely point till they were fit for purpose. And that purpose was to kill. "You are the *hashshashin*, the foundation of the faith, God's assassins."

Every day they rose before dawn, washed in cold mountain water and prayed for long hours. Then they studied the Qur'an, learning the hidden (*batin*) meaning that lay beneath the apparent, or *zahir*, text, a level of meaning only the *hashshashin* could fully grasp after years of application, guided by the imam known as the Speaking Qur'an, rendering passages by heart, consuming the words like food. They ate actual food sparingly; they were hungry all the time—for a tool must have discipline, the power of the mind exerted over the base needs of the body.

It was flesh that made men different to one another, the Grand Headmaster said, flesh in which individual character expressed itself, so flesh must be eroded away, worn down to the bone. Kamal had lost a third of his body weight, and he had never been fat. They all looked the same now, their faces masks of skin over bone. The greatest variations came in height and eye colour, which you could not change. But there was much more that you could. During the year in which he had been in the mountain stronghold, Kamal had learned to vary his gait, his posture, his stance. He had learned to blend into the background, to stay still for hours on end. In a *niqab*, he could walk like a woman; in a tattered robe he limped like a beggar; in a leather jerkin he marched like a soldier. He knew how to add mud to his features to fake leprosy sores, to add lines with the charcoal of a burned stick; with ash, his hair became grey; he was growing a beard, but if it was shaved off, he could pass for a girl.

Other skills he had learned: to wield a pen and a dagger with his left hand as well as he could with his right. To climb even the most perpendicular surfaces by applying strength and balance and a refusal to consider consequences. He could go for days without food, even without water. He could throw a blade with his eyes closed and hit his mark. He could walk across glowing coals and feel no pain—for pain was no more than an illusion conjured by the fleshly body to trick you from the righteous path into laziness and disobedience. He had learned words and sentences in a dozen languages not his own, even Christian prayers and songs.

"You must be your enemy to understand your enemy," the Grand Headmaster said. "How can you come close to that which you do not comprehend? For to kill with the hand, you must be close to your foe, as close as a breath, as close as clothes on skin."

One day there had been a small act of rebellion. Someone had stolen a loaf of bread and eaten it in secret. No one admitted to the theft. The Grand Headmaster had taken all the *fida'i* outside the castle, up the winding mule-track that led to the summit. Up there, on the topmost peak, was built a small white cell, a hermit's retreat or a marabout's tomb. "This is where I come to hear the Word of God," he told them. "Up here, where there is nothing but air to separate us and I hear his voice without distortion, hear the instructions he has for me: the tasks for which you are trained." Then he went inside the tiny room and did not re-emerge for many hours, until the sun had passed the zenith and was descending towards the desert that lay below them.

From where Kamal stood, it had seemed as if the rippling undulations of the earth stretched into infinity, that there was nothing in the world but the mountain, the castle on its slopes and the wide, barren desert plain; as if the world had been wiped clean of humanity and all its mess and complications, as in their own way had all the *fida'i*.

When the Grand Headmaster emerged he beckoned to a young man to climb up to the rocky ledge beside the white cell. The adherent scaled the cliff at once.

"Jump," the Grand Headmaster said. He signalled with his hand the yawning void below.

Kamal sucked in his breath, felt his eyes widen, saw the expression he felt forming on his own face mirrored across those of his fellows. But showing not the least emotion, the adherent stepped off the ledge into thin air and plummeted silently past them. All they heard was the distant thud of his body as it hit the cliff far below, then nothing at all but the high, thin call of a jackal.

"That is perfect obedience, perfect fidelity, absolute loyalty. That is what I expect of each one of you." And with that the Grand Headmaster led them all back down the mountain again.

There had been no more thefts.

Now, Kamal repeated the words of the promise of the *hash-shashin*—to honour God, to do his bidding, to follow the path of "*dai*," to purify their souls so that when they died it would be in glory and they would attain Paradise as the martyrs they were destined to become.

He had heard the words so many times, repeated them so many times, they had become ingrained. Repetition led to serenity, serenity to the ultimate peace of the soul. He was no one; he was the tool of God. His mind was as free and as blank as a clean page on which the Word might be written.

All he waited for now was the Word.

So why, when he slept at night, did he dream of another who looked just like him—another boy of the same height, with the same shade of golden-brown eyes, the same wiry build and quick regard? Who ran and laughed and swam through sparkling water, calling his name, "Kamal, Kamal, Kamal . . ."?

Aisa swam on, each stroke a repetition of the stroke before. His arms ached, but he pushed the pain aside. You could not afford to think about such things, for if you did, your muscles would tense and harden and your body would grow heavy and start to sink, and that was how people drowned.

Getting out of the harbour was always the worst—diving beneath the keels and ropes, holding your breath and your nerve, coming up for air only in the lee of a vessel, where a head breaking the surface would be less obvious. Sometimes when he came up through the water he would hear sailors on the foreign ships talking, laughing. He had got used to the sound of their voices all these weeks, could even distinguish one from another, although he could not understand what they were saying. What he did understand was the sound of their dice falling, the shout of the victor, the groans of the rest. It was a comfort to hear them, to know they were occupied, unlikely to spy the pale shape gliding beneath the waves.

Once past the ships, the sea was suddenly colder. You could feel the depths beneath as a sort of inverse weight, pulling you towards it. It was that sensation, that knowledge—all those dark fathoms below you—that made your muscles heavy and tense. It was out here, in the deep sea, where men drowned.

Aisa streamed all his strength into his arms and legs and breasted the water with determination. At least it was calm, the seas flat. When the big rollers rumbled in it took a terrible effort to swim through them, to arrow yourself down through that muscular, solid swell to where the water was more fluid. Worst was when the wind was up, whipping streamers of foam off the tops of the waves, cross-currents sending them clashing together into a chaos that was almost impossible to swim through. And you could not see where you were. It was easy to get turned around, disoriented. He'd only once experienced such conditions and it had been terrifying; he'd been lucky the tide was running with him or he'd have been carried away, never to set foot on land again.

On he strove. It would be harder coming back. Then he'd have the garrison wages to carry. Packed in sealed packets all around his waist, heavy and cumbersome. *Don't think about that, think of something else . . .*

There was a girl he'd been getting to know, down at the docks. When he'd first met her she'd been helping her father with his crab-lines, her long, thin brown fingers clever at untangling knots and weed. When he'd passed, she'd looked up at him with laughing dark eyes, and when her father when to reset his lines she'd given him a big crab out of the bucketful. "Hold him like this." She spread her fingers wide across the knobbly shell, pinching the beast behind its waving claws. "Then he can't nip you."

He'd run all the way home with his prize so that no one could rob him, and Zohra had boiled it for dinner: a rare treat. The next day he'd gone back to the dock with some aubergines and peppers from the garden, but the girl wasn't there, and he hadn't dared give them to her father in case he got her into trouble. Instead, he'd swapped them for a loaf of bread straight out of the oven, which he'd wolfed down till his stomach ached, and only then had he felt guilty for his greed—it wasn't as if he was starving, not like some people.

Since then, they'd spent some time together almost every day. They had even kissed once, not in the passionate, languorous way he had seen the Jewish doctor's son kiss his sister on that fateful day, but even so, it had filled his thoughts ever since. *Rana,* he thought. *Rana, Rana, Rana with the laughing eyes.* He hadn't spoken formally with her father yet, but he ought to soon, he thought. *I'll greet him politely, but not too humbly. I'll say, "I'm Salah ad-Din's messenger. I've brought you some eggplants, and I want to marry your daughter."*

It sounded so ridiculous that he almost laughed, and ended up snorting water. Sharp and salty, it made his nose and throat sting.

Nathanael ran, his arms full of bandages. There was blood on the tiles; he almost slipped as he came around the corner into the hospital. As he put the bundle down, his father glanced up from the man he was working on, and he was struck by how ill the old man looked, his face pale and sweaty.

"You're not well, Abi," he said, for the third time that day.

"How I feel is of little consequence." Yacub applied force to the wound he was treating. "Pass me a needle, quickly." Beside him on a plate was an array of bone needles threaded with fine gut. Nat had threaded them all first thing that morning, with little Nima watching on in fascination. He'd prepared dozens of them; now there were just four or five, and it was not yet midday. With the coming of the new reinforcements the onslaught on the city had redoubled, and they did not have enough doctors to treat the wounded. The hospital was full, and no one was sleeping, and there was another wave of sweating sickness.

"Here, let me. Things you sew fall apart in the street."

Yacub raised a tired smile. For a moment it looked as if he would demur, but after that they worked swiftly together, patching up one man after another, doing their best with crush injuries and arrow wounds. The burns from mishaps with the Greek fire were the worst to deal with: the substance was merciless in its hunger to eat all in its path—skin, muscle, tendon and bone. Sometimes the victims were brought in still smouldering and you had to be careful handling them.

In the late afternoon, Yacub collapsed. One moment he was saying something to Nat about their beehives, the next he was on the floor, unconscious.

Nathanael cried out in horror, then wondered, *Why am I just standing here? I'm a doctor!* But it was his father lying there, not some unknown soldier. His shout brought other doctors running. They had blood on their hands, and then there was blood on Yacub too. He stood there stupefied as the men prodded at his father, rubbing his chest, fishing in his mouth.

"He's swallowed his tongue!"

"He's stopped breathing!"

And all the while Nat felt strangely, shamefully detached. Time slowed, stilled, then raced. And then suddenly he was back in the moment and someone was clutching his arm and saying, "He's gone, Nat, I'm so sorry," and the other two doctors were standing and wiping their hands on their tunics.

He dropped to his knees, mindless of the blood, placed his hands on his father's face, his throat, his chest. "Abi! Abi!" Marigolds. They had picked marigolds out of the garden together this morning—he could still smell the pungent scent of them, bitter and sun-warmed. How could he be dead? Furious at the old man's iner-tia, he pummelled his ribs.

Yacub's eyelids fluttered and a great wheezing breath came out of him. One of the doctors yelped; the other stood there with his hands over his mouth. Saïd had been a portly man only a year ago. Nathanael remembered him coming to the house to take tea with Yacub and steadily eating his way through every delicacy Sara had served. "Zinab never cooks like this. I think your wife must be a sorceress. She doesn't just mix the ingredients, she charms them!" Now his flesh hung on him like old clothes and he was muttering. Nat thought he recognized the words: a protection against witchcraft.

Back from the dead, Yacub of Nablus looked around like a man momentarily lost and tried to sit up.

"Don't." Nathanael pushed him back down. He turned. "I need to get him home."

Saïd looked away. It was the other two doctors, whom he barely knew, who ran out and commandeered a pair of off-duty soldiers to carry the old man back to the Street of Tailors, with Nat running along in front of them, his medicine bag banging his hip, all the way back home turning at every other step to make sure his father was still alive.

Had he been dead, or were the other doctors mistaken? Nat had thought often about death, about the theory and the real-ity of it, even before these grim days, when he encountered so much of it. The forbidden had always fascinated him. Things that other people would not talk about—like what a soul was, where it abided in the body, if it had a shape or weight, had ever been seen or drawn, where it went when you died. He'd once questioned the rabbi on the subject. The rabbi had placed a hand benevolently on Nat's head, this precocious, unpredictable boy of barely eight, and after many vain attempts to change the subject told him a soul was *nishmat*, the breath of God, inseparably connected with the lifeblood, and that when you died it returned to Yahweh, to await the resurrection.

This had not satisfied him. "Yes, but in the Book of Job it says, 'So man lies down and does not rise. Till the heavens are no more, they will not awake or be roused from their sleep.' But people breathe when they sleep, don't they?"

The rabbi had inclined his head, rather wishing he'd not entered the debate.

"But if God has taken your breath, then you can't breathe, or sleep," Nat had insisted. At which point the rabbi had got up and thanked Yacub (now grinning broadly) and left.

But Nat had followed him outside, still chattering. "And Maimonides says there is no resurrection, not really, not a physical resurrection, just an immanence of the soul which perfects itself through the knowledge of God, and I don't understand that, because in Ecclesiastes it says 'a living dog is better than a dead lion. For the living know that they will die; but the dead know nothing.'"

The rabbi had put his head down and walked faster, and after that he'd taken Yacub to task for encouraging his boy to question the holy books, and for letting him read such heretical works as those by Maimonides. He later recounted the conversation to Nat, laughing. "Nathanael reads anything he finds," Yacub had told him, "and besides, Rabbi Mosheh ben Maimon was under our roof, and the child has the ears of a gossip and the memory of a grocer."

That night, watching over his father as he lay quiet, Nat asked, "What did you see?"

Was that a smile that lifted the corner of his mouth, or a quirk of the muscles, brought on by his ordeal?

"Did I see angels with trumpets and choirs singing hosannas? Or the banquet hall of the World to Come, tables heaving with manna? Or the darkness of the pit?" The smile, if that was what it was, was gone. "None of that. Just a sense of crushing pain and a lifetime of regret for my many failures."

"Never a failure, Abi. Never."

"The boy who tore out the hollow reed I placed in his throat?"

"He died, yes, I know. But the next one lived! And what have you always taught me? That it's only from making mistakes that we learn to do better."

"And sometime we don't." Yacub's voice was barely more than a rasp. "Sometimes I think we can't. Or there would be no more wars. And yet there are always more wars. Men are greedy, aggressive and ungovernable, and perhaps that will never change."

Such despair. "You're tired, Abi. You should sleep." Nat stroked his hand; the old fingers closed over his.

"Listen to me, Nathanael. You have to try to make a difference, no matter how slender the chance of success may seem. It's the only way we can change the outcome, even if by the tiniest of increments. And pass on your knowledge, your wisdom, to a new generation so that they may make a bigger step, and their children a larger step still."

Children. Nat gave a mirthless smile. Little chance of that now. He'd not been able to look at another woman since Zohra had crushed his heart. In comparison to her, they all seemed like little clay dolls.

"Promise me, Nathanael."

"Sleep now, Abi.

"Promise." The old man's grip was suddenly fierce.

"I promise."

As the summer passed on, Yacub dwindled, despite all Sara's and Nathanael's care and herb tisanes, despite all the books bought from the bookseller in the market (no one wanted books any more—you couldn't eat a book, could you?) and all the remedies Nat sought within their pages, despite all Nima's tears because her "grandfather" wouldn't get up and play with her.

On a stifling day in late August, he did not wake from his afternoon nap.

Sara, who had seen her husband's hold on life slackening with every passing day, bore his passing with the sort of dignified acceptance that Nat could only admire, and fail to achieve. He found himself full of seething anger, but he could not disturb Nima with his primal fury, so he took to wandering down to the port, to the serene, impassive wash of the sea, where the boats bobbed quietly at anchor in the little harbour and the seabirds roosted, and there he beat his hands on the stones of the harbour wall and growled like a wild animal.

Even when the storm of his grief had passed he continued to go there. It became his place to sit and think in those rare moments he had between tending to the sick and wounded, looking after Nima and working in the gardens. And it was there that Rana, the crabber's daughter, found him late one night.

"You're the doctor, aren't you?"

Startled, Nathanael turned. "I am." He had taken his father's place at the hospital, had even tended the governor, Karakush the eunuch, up at the citadel. He recognized the girl from his many visits to the port, where she was often to be found, working with her father on the nets and pots. He had marvelled at her dexterity, had once even jested with Rana that she'd make a good doctor if she could handle a smaller needle than the one she used to pass cord back and forth through the netting. She was a sunny creature, always smiling. But she wasn't smiling now.

"Please . . ." Rana couldn't get the words out. She just took a desperate grip on Nathanael's arm and pulled him along at a run.

At the end of the inner harbour a small crowd had gathered. Rana screamed at them to step aside. As they parted, Nat saw a young man lying on the stones, his skin gleaming like pearls in the moonlight. Seaweed was tangled in his hair. A thickly wadded belt was tied around his waist.

"We were going to get married," Rana sobbed.

"Were you now?" A burly man with a great black beard stepped forward.

Rana shot him a look, half guilty, half defiant. "We are. He asked me weeks ago, but I only said yes two days ago, before . . . before . . ."

Nat knelt beside the swimmer, remembering with a suddenly tight heart a sultry day last summer, a figure stepping out of the shadows as he had pulled Zohra back and kissed her forcefully in the doorway. Aisa Najib.

"When did you find him?" he asked of no one in particular.

"Just now—he washed in with the tide, got caught up with the mooring ropes. I don't think he's breathing," said a man in the grimy, salt-stained tunic of a fisherman. "Rana went straight to get you. She said you bring people back from the dead. That's what she said."

Nathanael ran a hand down Aisa's face, feeling the stiffness setting in. His throat swelled; his eyes pricked. He blinked several times before turning to meet the girl's beseeching gaze.

"There is nothing I can do."

"No! No, you must—you must bring him back. You must!"

The crabber pulled his daughter close. "He's gone, pet."

"The lad's a hero," someone declared. "That's a martyr's death he's died, in the name of Allah, the Prophet and our lord Salah ad-Din."

"Aye," another man agreed. "It'll be the first time a dead man's brought the garrison wages in. You can't ask more than that."

"He was only sixteen," Nathanael said, removing the seaweed from around his neck.

"He . . . he . . . told me he was eighteen," sobbed Rana.

"Someone needs to let the family know," a woman said uncertainly.

It would have been so easy to keep his mouth shut and let someone else do it. But he could not.

"I know his family," Nathanael said at last. "I will go."

PART SIX

Warriors of God

24

John Savage, Holy Land

❄

1190

I t was October before we reached the Holy Land. Half a year to cross what felt like half the world—it seemed about right. Putting into the port of Tyre, everyone was keen to get ashore. You could feel the heat coming off the land, as if it had been stored up all summer and was now warding off the coming winter. There was spice in the air and the aroma of fried fish—our noses twitched like dogs'.

Ezra tugged at my sleeve. She was at my side all the time now. "What's that bird there, John?"

It looked to me much the same as any bird back home—brown feathers, beady eyes. "I've no idea." *The Moor would know*, I thought for the hundredth time.

"And that one?"

"Seagull, Ezra."

"I knew that." She grinned. Freckles peppered her nose. She looked like the cheeky boy she purported to be. Ashore, she wolfed as much food as any man, and drank as much ale.

But in Tyre, except for wine, there was no alcohol to be found, much to Quickfinger's dismay. "What, no ale? What sort of shithole is this?"

The twins, Hammer and Saw, chattered away like jackdaws, sometimes in their own language that none of the rest of us could understand, staring around at all the dark-skinned and dark-eyed robed and turbaned men.

"Damn me," Ned said, charged more than he liked for food so spicy it burned his mouth. "I thought we'd come to fight these buggers, not get fleeced by them."

Quickfinger kept his hand on the hilt of the fine sword he'd won at dice in Marseille, where we'd missed King Richard by some weeks. He'd cheated to win it, of course, and the next time he tried the same trick got into a fight and nearly ended up in gaol again. He'd given me his old weapon for saving his skin, but it was not much recompense—a clumsy old falchion, all the weight near the tip for hacking, like a butcher's blade. No finesse there, nor in me as a swordsman: the combination was not pretty.

Besides, I had no zeal to fight the Saracen. The idea of killing another man was not something I'd given much mind to, and I intended to put it off as long as possible. But they had us out of Tyre faster than you could say God's teeth. A fleet full of men who'd been at sea for long weeks—who'd want us in their town for longer than was necessary? I'd barely shaken my sea-legs before they had us marching out again. In my foolishness I was thinking we'd be marching straight for Jerusalem, but instead we found ourselves heading for a town called Acre—or Akka, in the local tongue—a march of a day or so south down the coast. It was a port like Tyre, but held by the Muslims, despite a siege by Christian forces that had—according to Will, who hung on the knights' every word—already lasted a year and more. A siege. I remembered Robert de Sable speaking of such at Lisbon. "The will," he had said. It was all about the will.

"How have they held out for so long," I asked Savaric, "against the flower of Christendom?"

He waved his hand dismissively. "We have God on our side, and King Richard coming any day. We shall prevail in no time. And then it will be on to Jerusalem, where we shall sweep all before us, and the pickings will be rich."

We set out just after dawn, and our company made for a brave sight with the knights astride their big horses, the beasts all caparisoned in bright colours, the men in shining plate and mail, banners flying above. Robert de Sable rode with the Archbishop of Auxerre and the Bishop of Bayonne, talking in French too fast to follow. Ahead of them rode Baldwin, Archbishop of Canterbury, and Hubert, Bishop of Salisbury, the one bearing the sigil of Saint Thomas à Becket, the other a great jewelled cross.

"Bet that's worth summat," Quickfinger said quietly, eyeing the cross.

"Wouldn't like to see you trying to prise that out of the bishop's grasp." I grinned. Hubert Walter looked more like a soldier than a man of the cloth. "He'd pick you up and snap you in two."

"Aye, and eat me for breakfast when we run out of that lot." Quickfinger hiked a thumb back over his shoulder to where a mile of ox carts trundled, piled high with tents and equipment, supplies to feed thousands: cheeses and hams, flour and salted beef, ale and wine, beans and barley and an entire flock of sheep bought in Tyre's huge market.

We sang as we marched:

> *Lignum crucis, signum ducis,*
> *Sequitur exercitus, quod non cessit,*
> *Sed praecessit, in vi sancti spiritus.*

Behind the wood of the Cross, the banner of the chieftain,
Follows the army which has never given way,
But marches in the strength of the Holy Spirit.

Even we foot soldiers had polished our helms and honed our weapons, said our prayers and washed our faces. We looked like God's army, clean in body and spirit, even though the wood of the Cross lay in the hands of the heathen.

But our first sight of the siege city the next day was not auspicious. Black birds were circling: crows? I knew what attracted carrion-eaters. And it was telling that Ezra didn't ask me what birds these were; indeed, within minutes, as we approached closer to the tawny-walled city, all our words had ebbed away.

"What is this place?" Red Will turned a horrified face to me, as if I should know. He had caught the sun in just a few hours' march and his face was already beginning to peel.

He might well have asked. We were marching through a wasteland: acres of turned earth, pitted and burned and stinking. Was this what we were fighting over, this ruined ground? Everywhere there were rags and shards and rubbish mashed into the earth. Looking closer, I saw scattered bones and nameless pieces of rotting flesh where bodies had been rooted up by some rummaging creature.

And the stench—my God, the stench. It hurt the nose.

"What is this hell?" asked Little Ned.

"Who are these people?" asked Ezra.

These people regarded us dourly as we passed, faces weathered to the colour of old wood, more like the infidel we were there to fight than the flower of Christendom we thought to join. They were gaunt and sullen-eyed; their filthy clothes hung on them like rags on scarecrow-sticks. We had thought to have cheers and welcome, but all we heard were catcalls and insults. They laughed at us, sneering at our bright banners and our clean surcoats, at the knights sweating in their armour in the hot sun, at the pennanted lances and our well-ordered marching. But there were other expressions, too, even less pleasant. Avid eyes followed the passage of the warhorses and the ox carts piled with provisions.

As far as the eye could see this wasteland stretched, studded with ragged tents and makeshift lean-tos, striped with earthworks and barricades, spiked palisades, tatty enclosures. Men sat listlessly on the bare ground playing dice and knucklebones. And there were women here too, though it took more than one glance to ascertain their sex, for they were as scrawny and ill-kempt as the men, even those with their dugs out on show. Though our lads had been relishing the chance of a visit to the brothels of Tyre and, due to our swift departure, had never fulfilled their wish, none of them made a lustful comment, but instead looked away in horror. "Women, Jesus," Hammer breathed. He made some odd folk-gesture to ward off evil.

They gave us the filthiest quarter in which to pitch our tents. Savaric protested, and was derided by the lords who presided over the camp. He muttered, "Just wait until King Richard arrives," as if the king were some living saint who could command miracles at will. Well, perhaps he could. For the time being, we pitched our tents where we were told, and set guards on the animals and the provision wagons.

Within days, of course, one of the horses went missing—the mount of a French noble from Aquitaine—along with the lad whose job it was to guard it. The man was almost in tears, for without his horse, what was a knight? As Hammer put it, "Just a fool rattling around in a tankard."

Questioning of the lords in charge of the camp did not go well. The Bishop of Auxerre preached a furious sermon on the subject of theft, exhorting the horse-thieves to confess. Since it had just been announced that any man caught whoring, drinking or thieving would be hanged, unsurprisingly no one stepped forward.

A few hours later and there was still no sign of horse or boy. Savaric sent for me. With him was a man I had not met before, tall, gaunt, with dirty yellow hair and beard, and equipped with more weapons than I'd ever seen on one man. Savaric said he was one of the "*raptores*," which did not fill me with confidence, for in Latin that meant "plunderers." The man—Florian—told me he preferred the French term "*routier*," man of the road.

"A sell-sword?" I asked.

"We don't use that word. Or mercenary, either."

Ordered to make a search, we trudged along in silence for a while after that, looking over the few horses left in the camp, but there was no sign of a dappled grey with feathered fetlocks and a plaited mane.

The *routier* snorted. "We should inspect the roasting spits, and not just for the horse."

I stared at him, and he gave me his quick, feral grin, part of his face static where a sword had at some time bisected his left cheek.

"Is it really so bad here that men have to eat horses?"

Florian turned to me. "What, you never ate horsemeat?"

My expression answered him.

"My God, you people have no idea. There are men here who haven't had a proper meal in weeks. They've been eating frogs, seagulls, rats, anything they can lay hands on. Oh, the nobles do all right, but they don't give a damn about their own people. And the merchants are making a killing. A bushel of wheat for thirty, even forty gold bezants. And with a horse's intestines selling on the black market for eight soldi, can you imagine how much an entire horse is fetching?"

That gave me pause.

"Why do you think I'm working for your lord now?"

I didn't try to answer his question; he was going to tell me anyway.

"Paying me twice as much, and he's brought fresh supplies." He smacked his lips. "Mutton, God's bollocks, I've missed the taste of mutton."

We passed a particularly grim camp and Florian's nose twitched. He pulled me away. "Flux," he said. "If the air begins to smell sweet to you just keep walking. Ain't no horse in the world worth catching the bloody flux for. It's a killer. Twelve thousand Danes and Frisians came out here a year ago." He turned to me. "You know how many are left now?"

I shook my head.

"Maybe two hundred. The flux is doing Saladin's job for him. All he has to do is sit up there in those hills and wait till it kills us all." He nodded towards the horizon, a ragged, tawny line punctuated by far-off banners and the pointed tops of tents. He strode on, pointing out the landmarks of our own camp: a banner here, a banner there.

My eyes wandered to the hills. It was hard to imagine your enemy when they were so far out of sight. The garrison soldiers who manned the walls of the city, we saw them every day, they held no terror for us. But an invisible foe was a different matter.

We passed a heavily guarded enclosure with a fine tent in the middle of it flying a flag with five gold crosses—one large, surrounded by four small—on a white background. Florian nodded towards it.

"The King and Queen of Jerusalem," he said. "Guy de Lusignan and Sibylla, the sister of the Leper King. Once we take Acre they'll make it the seat of their kingdom. Your lot are supporting them."

"My lot?"

"The English, the Angevins."

"Who are they supporting them against?"

He laughed. "You don't know much, do you? Conrad of Montferrat, of course, from the Piedmont—he's claiming the Jerusalem crown.

He's the very devil, is Conrad. A cunning man, brave, too. He held Tyre against the Arabs, against Saladin himself—and that's some feat, for the sultan is another wily man. He took Conrad's father, old Marquis William, and called to Conrad that he'd have the old man killed if he didn't give up the city. But Conrad, he took up his crossbow and pointed it at his father and cried back, 'Stand aside, I'll kill him myself and save you the trouble!' Conrad's a bastard. Well, they both are, but Conrad's a hard bastard and Guy's a weak one. He's only king through his wife, but he's one of your King Richard's vassals and some sort of cousin, so your lot are bound to support his claim. The French and the Germans, they're behind Conrad."

I'd seen a fight already between some German soldiers and some men I recognized off one of the ships that had sailed with us, but I had put it down to traded insults. Now I wondered if this was the cause.

"I thought we were here to win Jerusalem back for Christendom," I said. "Not to get involved in some fight between rival kings."

Florian shook his head wearily, as if he had been saddled with a halfwit child. A sword for hire had to be alert to all manner of alle-giances and manoeuvrings, I supposed. He had to be well enough informed to choose the noble most likely to survive and prosper in order to pay the best wages. But I had little hand in my own destiny, and so I let my mind wander, my eyes upon the grand tent with its gold-and-white banners set amid the same mud and shit as the tents of the commonest soldier. Imagine being the King of Jerusalem, reduced to this. It seemed to me that if God existed he had surely abandoned these people.

I said as much around our campfire that night, and Florian said, "You aren't wrong. What with the flux and the weather and empty bellies and the sheer bloody pointlessness of the whole endeavour, me and the boys would have cleared off long ago if it weren't for the booty."

"Booty?" Quickfinger stopped poking the fire with a bone and his eyes fixed on the *routier*'s scarred face. "What booty?" This was what the troupe had come for, what they had been promised.

"All sorts, if you're up for it." Florian pulled the neck of his tunic aside to reveal three gold chains, each bearing a chunky crucifix.

Ezra pursed her lips; Hammer and Saw exchanged a glance. Ned sucked his teeth thoughtfully. But Will—ever the innocent—could not stop his mouth. "You mean you rob our own dead?" His outrage was almost comical, but no one laughed.

"Until we break these *putain* walls down and get at the treasure inside we're here for nothing. Of course we rob the fools who are stupid enough to go out and fight the enemy."

"But you're paid to fight them too," Will persisted. "And they're infidels. We're morally bound to fight them."

"Oh shut up, Will," Quickfinger growled. "This treasure, tell me more."

"There's a hoard of gold behind the walls of the city, all the gold that came out of Jerusalem. Why else do you think we've spent a year besieging the wretched place? Saladin's got his armoury in there. Why keep it there unless you're defending something valuable?"

"It might just be relics," I suggested smoothly, though my heart had begun to skip. "They're a holy lot, these Muslims, or so I hear."

"Relics!" The *routier* snorted. "Who wants a load of bones *et merde*? No, it's gold they've got. Gold and gems, pearls and rubies—all the riches they robbed out of Jerusalem. Why'd you think King Guy attacked Acre in the first place? It's the contents of his treasury Saladin's stashed in there, looted from the coffers of the Holy City."

"I thought the sultan's palace was in Damascus," Hammer said suddenly, surprising us all.

Damascus? The name rang a bell. I remembered the Moor and Bishop Reginald talking their endless talk of church architecture, the Moor declaring, his eyes burning with passion, that he dreamed of visiting the great mosque in that city. I was so sure I had spied him that day in Lisbon: was he on his way to Damascus, pursuing his dream, even now? A thrill ran through me. I turned a bland face to the mercenary.

"Perhaps Saladin robbed so much treasure from Jerusalem that he decided to spread it around. Better to have two sheepfolds if the wolf's on the prowl."

"Exactly. There's something in that city worth saving, and it ain't the poxy inhabitants."

I went to relay the nub of this conversation to Savaric. Despite the filth of its surroundings, his tent was a handsome one, patterned inside and out in different colours. He called it a pavilion. Baldwin of Canterbury had come past while we were putting it up and Savaric had had the misfortune to emerge while the archbishop was still there and caught the brunt of the old man's contempt.

"What does a man of God have to do with such ostentation? Oh, vanity, vanity, thy name is Savaric Fitzgoldwin!"

Savaric's chest had swelled as if he might explode. He watched the archbishop go, a sour look on his face. "Sanctimonious old bastard. I bet his pavilion's twice the size of my poor dwelling."

But it wasn't. We passed it later that day: plain canvas, marked out from the common soldiers' tents only by the bright standard of Saint Thomas pitched outside. Savaric skulked past it like a beaten dog.

Being Savaric, he soon recovered. I found him that evening lounging in his great wooden chair, his feet propped on a stool, a brazier warming his soles. Beside him was a small, round wooden table in the local style, bought in the market at Tyre, all pretty wooden patterns and shell inlays. On it sat a flask of wine. He waved me to sit down, and with a grunt moved his feet from the stool. He saw me eyeing the wine but did not offer me any.

Thus it starts, I thought. *As soon as there are shortages, it's the poor who go without.*

I told him what the *routier* had said and watched as he took it in. His thoughts were obviously the same as mine, for he nodded and sat up straighter, suddenly alert. "Makes sense. Why else tie your army up here for more than a year?" His black eyes gleamed. "Remember what the Lady Eleanor told Richard in London: 'Recapture the True Cross, my son, and the whole Christian world will open to you as easily as a whore spreads her legs.' Imagine the king's gratitude to the man who saved the True Cross from the Saracens and put it in his hands. Imagine the debt that king would owe, the rewards he would give to such a man—or men. Enough to make them rich beyond dream! Enough for Reggie to build his cathedral—and surely there would be no better church in which to house the world's greatest relic? Just think of the queues of pilgrims who would come to venerate it—"

"Enough!" I cried. "We don't even know it's in there."

He wagged a finger at me. "Spies. That's what we need, from inside the city, who know their way around."

I laughed, largely out of relief. "But no one goes in or out. That's the whole point of a siege, as you explained it to me."

The look he gave me was similar to the one the routier had given me earlier: an incredulous adult to a naive child. "Believe me, John, there are those who pass between the camps." I had no idea what he meant by this. But as long as it didn't mean me, I didn't care.

The weather worsened, and even our own food supplies began to run short. A combination of gluttony, poor husbandry, pilfering and rot had done for us. The mud had deepened and the flux had us by the throat; every day there were more deaths. Every day, raiders from the army on the hill harried our lines, forcing watchfulness and rebuttal, but I had yet to draw my weapon in anger. Life was dull and grim, but at least it was life.

More troops poured in, but there was still no sign of Richard. We began to wonder if he would ever arrive. There were calls for reinforcements to the front lines to hold off the Saracens, but Savaric kept us back: we were there to guard his person and enable him to impress the new king with his valour and resourcefulness. What was the point of heroism if Richard was not there to witness it?

The longer we spent in the besieging camp the clearer it became that it was no unified army of God but a fractured and bitter collection of rival lords who would rather be at each other's throats than unite against the common enemy. The Germans hated the English; the French hated the Anglo-French; the Pisans and Genoese hated each other so much that they had to be kept at opposite sides of the encampment. The French and the Germans had allied with Conrad of Montferrat, but we were supporting Guy, the ousted King of Jerusalem. Until recently, Conrad's supporters had greatly outnumbered Guy's, but English ships were blowing in day by day. And so was the rain.

One morning, Ezra and I were sitting outside the billet trying to get a brew going over a recalcitrant fire. The little fuel we had was soaked through; it smoked but refused to burst into flame. Eventually I leapt to my feet in frustration, with the intent of booting the pot up into the sky. A pair of men on big horses came lumbering into view—one in the bright white surcoat of the Templars, the other older, slab-faced . . .

"Shit! Turn your head, Ezra!"

"What?"

"It's Geoffrey de Glanvill!" I moved so that I was shielding her. "Put your helm on."

She jammed the iron cap on her head; the noseguard made for

anonymity. Their gaze swept over us: just common soldiers, beneath their regard. Then Savaric's voice boomed out a greeting to us.

"Christ's teeth!" I swore at him. "Look, it's de Glanvill."

"Oh . . . *merde*."

Over his shoulder I saw the Templar stare hard, turn and say something to his companion. And then suddenly I recognized the first chevalier as Ranulf de Glanvill, Geoffrey's brother, once the King's Eye.

"Go away, Ezra," I whispered. "Just get up and walk away. Fast as you can. Find Florian, make sure he keeps you out of sight."

Ranulf de Glanvill turned his horse's head in our direction. Savaric, black eyes hooded, turned to meet them.

"Good day, Ranulf. A pleasure to see you join our siege. Sorry about your . . . troubles with the king."

Enthroned upon his impressive warhorse, the slab-faced man drew himself up. "The king and I have reconciled our differences. All is very well between us now."

"Though I hear your coffers are somewhat lighter," Savaric said, and I am sure I was not the only one who caught his gloating tone.

"Who was that man with you?" Geoffrey demanded, squinting at the retreating back of Ezra.

"One of my sergeants," Savaric replied, as if he were a man of great substance. "Recently taken on."

"He was not with you in Lisbon?"

"No," Savaric returned smoothly. "I acquired him here. Part of a dead lord's retinue. The nobility are falling like flies in this place, it's a most unhealthy environment. Best take care of yourselves. And your mounts—there's plenty here have a taste for horseflesh: good men starving while others ride."

The air was charged with violence. The black eyes gave us a hard look. Then Ranulf barked some dismissive response and they moved off, their horses picking their way between the pits and ruts.

Savaric looked drained. He sat down beside me where Ezra was sitting before, as if his legs had given out.

"Why must you taunt them?" I asked.

He gave a small, mirthless laugh. "They're bullies, the pair of them. If you let men like that bully you they will destroy you."

"It's not me I'm worried about," I said. "It's Ezra."

There was soon more to worry about than the de Glanvills. The Archbishop of Besancon had constructed at great personal expense a huge battering ram. Acre was not his objective, but it stood between him and the Holy City. Not a subtle man, he had decided to take matters into his own hands and batter down the doors to the besieged port so that he could get on with the business of winning his place in Heaven.

Massive beams of timber had been strapped into a monstrous, sharpened head of iron. The thing would take hundreds to shift it, up over the filled-in ditches to the great east gate. We had watched smaller rams have no effect against these sturdy walls and gates, even those with "sows" built over them to provide shelter for the men who wielded them from the missiles hurled from the walls. This ram had no need for such shelter: the archbishop had declared that he would stride along beside it bearing the relics of some obscure French saint, roaring prayers and exhortations, which amused us until we heard that we were to be among the men subjected to this harrowing. Even Savaric was not sure, or claimed not to know, how we had been volunteered for this suicidal task.

"I've never seen a prayer stop an arrow," Hammer muttered.

"And we know all about the efficacy of saints' bones." I sighed.

But there was no avoiding the task. We donned our fighting kit in unaccustomed silence: padded leather jerkins to slow and stop an arrow, bits of mail scavenged from the field, steel caps and helms, shields strapped across our backs. By the time I was fitted out I could hardly move, but still I felt naked.

Red Will appeared, looking ashen, his hair dripping. He stank. "Christ on a stick!" Ned blasphemed. "Did you fall in the latrine?"

"It stops Greek fire taking hold," he explained. "Florian said so."

"Aye, and shit'll stop an axe blade." Quickfinger guffawed.

Ezra was drafted to the company of archers. As she was about to leave, she grasped my hand. "Be careful, John." And then she was gone.

We pushed that monster up to the no-man's-land between the encampment and the walls of the city. If I looked up I could see all the defenders' bright banners flying and even make out individual faces among the men on the walls. I was oddly reassured to see they did not all resemble the Moor but were each as different to him as were the fellows around me—stout and thin, light-skinned and dark, though all of them bearded.

Their archers started to wind their crossbows. "Shields!" the officer in charge of us cried, and we swung our shields overhead, trying to interlock them with our neighbours' as we'd been told. Bolts rattled down, mostly harmless, though a man three ranks in front of me cried out and fell down. "Now, PUSH!"

We had a minute or more while our archers kept them busy and the Muslim archers recharged their crossbows, and so we pushed, and the wheeled monstrosity moved ponderously forward. The archbishop roared out some Latin prayer and I found myself hoping the next round of quarrels would stop his bellowing. *If I am to die, please don't let it be in this awful place with some mad French bastard chanting gibberish in my ear.* Such a pettish entreaty, but fervently meant.

Then other engines were moving up alongside us. *Good*, I thought. *More targets for those wretched bolts, better odds for me.* It was an uncharitable thought, but I was sure I wasn't alone in thinking it.

When the bombardment started it was thunderous. The great ram swung back and then we propelled it forward. What could withstand the impact of such a monster? Apparently, the gates of this godforsaken city. Three times the ram struck with such force that the whole earth seemed to tremble; three times it recoiled, leaving no more than a dent in the iron-bound doors. Rocks were falling around our ears—misfired by our own side or cast down by the garrison's own engines, who could tell? A rock was a rock when all was said; if one fell on your head it didn't matter who was hurling it.

This is hell, I thought. I'd thought the same about the Mount, about being in the charnel pit, about waiting to hang; in the middle of a sea-storm; in this filthy wasteland with mud up to my knees and my belly, howling for food. It just went to prove that each time you thought your life had reached its grimmest point, Fate showed you worse, for suddenly there was fire raining down upon us and men were screaming and tearing at their hair and beards, which were in flames. Their hands came away coated in the sticky stuff propelled from the walls, and then their hands were on fire too. The noises they made as the conflagration ate them alive were the worst noises I had ever heard.

Then the ram was afire as well. I watched in horrified fascination as the searing stuff crept up the beams towards me. Choking black smoke engulfed me and we were all coughing, tears running from our eyes.

"Fook, I'm out of here," said Quickfinger, abandoning his post beside me with all the conscience of a jackrabbit.

Why did I not follow him? I don't know, but when the officer yelled at us to push, I pushed as if I were a donkey trained to push a millwheel, without question, without thought, even though a voice in the back of my head chattered at me to drop everything and run.

The ram rolled forward again, gathering speed all the time, and then suddenly there was no resistance and we were hurtling forward . . . through the gate!

Through the billows of smoke suddenly I could see the interior of this foreign city: ochre buildings, square and flat-roofed, distant slender spires rising over the heads of the men swarming out. And abruptly it dawned on me that they had opened the gates. Confusion swept over me. Why would they do this? But there was no time to dwell on this question for the garrison of Acre was now barrelling out of the city, curved swords raised and glinting in the tainted light.

It was a lot harder to run away now. I couldn't see anything but bodies and smoke, and wherever I turned there was someone in my way. And then there was a man right in front of me—black hair, wild black eyes. If he had a helmet he'd lost it—and he was yelling, something I couldn't understand. I wrestled with the horrible falchion, sure that any second he was going to split me from shoulder to hip, but it was impossible to get it free, there was no room, and something was caught up with it, my jerkin, or something else: another man, a body, the ram. For a moment I closed my eyes, expecting death to come for me, and felt piss run down my leg. Not the way I'd expected to go, amidst chaos, ignominiously, without a weapon in my hand. But all that happened was that someone shoved me out of the way and I stumbled and almost fell, and as soon as I got my feet under me again I turned to find the ram disappearing—between the open gates! Pushed and dragged by the city's defenders with the strength of the truly desperate. Moments later, the gates clanged shut and the garrison was gone, and the ram, and those of us who had been manning it, found ourselves standing in a void. In front of me was Will, his face blackened by smoke, but otherwise apparently untouched, his blue eyes stark in his sooty mask. So maybe the urine had saved him after all.

Without a ram to push, I reckoned I'd done my bit. Turning away from the city, I made my way back to camp, sidestepping knots of fighting men, ducking when arrows flew overhead. Back there, I found Quickfinger.

"You took your time."

I had no words.

He sobered. "Tell you summat, we're in for a long haul. They're hard bastards, these Saracens." It was the highest praise I'd ever heard him offer.

❀

Two days later we were sitting around, bored half to death and frozen by the wind that had decided to rush in at us off the sea. It was Saint Martin's Day, we'd been told by Savaric, Saint Martin being one of the great saints of France, a holy man much given to mortification of the flesh.

"He'd be right at home here, then," Little Ned grumbled, lack of good food having caused several of his teeth to fall out.

Hunger was cutting deep. Many of the nobles were hoarding, making little or no provision for their men: the poorest ended up eating grass, worms, even their own boiled boot leather. To avoid mutiny, a supply run was being made to Haifa, led by Henry of Champagne and Conrad of Montferrat.

Between sharp showers, we swore as we tried to get the wet timber to light.

"I thought it was all going to be glory and treasure," Saw complained.

Red Will looked as if he might weep—or maybe that was just the perennial ague he had, his eyes pink-rimmed, his nose dripping.

Hammer blew on his hands. "Could have stayed at home if I'd wanted to starve and freeze and stink."

His brother grunted. "So much for exotic climes."

"Aye, a grand opportunity to travel overseas, meet new folk and kill 'em." Quickfinger laughed humourlessly.

"I didn't think it was going to be like this," Ezra said. She'd lost weight; her eyes looked huge as she hunched over her knees.

"You'll be wishing you'd stayed at home and married your farmboy," I teased her.

The gaze she turned on me was unsettling. "Never," she said. "Never, never and never."

Further discussion was curtailed by a messenger galloping in from the forward column, crying for reinforcements. "Our troops have been set upon by that devil Saladin. They're facing each other off down at the Spring Head, six miles south. Muster quickly and get down there!"

Savaric volunteered to stay behind and guard the camp and engines, but our commander was no fool. "You'll go with de Lusignan's force. We've set the Flemings to guard the camp."

I felt sick, remembering our last outing.

Ezra checked the string on her bow a dozen times, counted her arrows, got Hammer to sharpen her knives. The twins bristled with all manner of mismatched weapons, some French, mostly foreign. We would be fighting on foot: we were down to three horses, since there wasn't enough food to keep the great beasts alive, and so only Savaric and the *routiers* would ride.

A hasty mass was held before we marched.

"That means they expect us to die," Little Ned muttered.

"Best confess our sins, brother," Hammer said to Saw.

"We'll be here till Christmas!" They laughed—graveyard humour.

Savaric rode out in style, determined to make an impression on his fellow nobles. He had even brought along his falcons and the falconer, in case there was game to be had on the way. He was himself adorned in red and gold; red and gold was the caparison of his warhorse. The rest of us wore his livery, rather the worse for wear now, but we were resplendent in comparison with our fellow soldiers, many of whom had dwelt in filth and hardship a year and more. I felt a fraud, and also terrified, never less so than when Baldwin shrove our souls, en masse, and sent us on our way.

Hubert of Salisbury had armed himself with a greatsword and a giant stave. The Bishop of Rouen took him by the arm. "A shepherd of the cross should preach, not fight!"

Hubert shook him off. "Heaven has been taken from us by violence; only by violence may we seize it back."

I fell in beside Quickfinger and was surprised to catch him crossing himself. "Do you believe our souls will be weighed in God's balance?" he asked.

"The Moor used to say that every act of kindness we do in this world will outweigh a sin in the next."

The corners of Quickfinger's mouth turned down. "I wish I'd led a better life," he said quietly. "I should ha' treated Mary more kindly."

By the time we reached the Spring Head we found ourselves meeting the retreat. The men falling back looked like walking corpses: faces gaunt as bone, empty eyes, blood all over. Some limped; others were carried by their comrades. I saw Savaric in animated discussion with Robert de Sable and for a brief, heady moment believed we would turn back too, but no, on we went. *Why are we doing this?* I thought in sudden desperation. *Are we all such sheep?*

Then the noise of the battle ahead of us became distinct: cries and the clash of weapons, screams and screeching steel. My guts felt like water. I looked back over my shoulder, but even if I could have brought myself to break rank suddenly there was nowhere to flee, for back the way we came I could now see Muslim cavalry—men in spiked helmets and coloured robes, their small, round shields and curved swords catching the last light of the sun. Up on the inland hills there was a sea of them, a tide rushing down upon us. Thousands of them, ready to drown us in our own blood.

My God, is this how I will die? In the mud of this foreign place? This thought perversely put some backbone in me, and when at last I found myself facing my first Saracen, who came hurtling down upon us shrieking like a demon, I raised my heavy falchion and hacked and screamed in a sort of frenzy until he was down, to be replaced by another, and another. I fought without any sophistication and with terror bubbling beneath my skin. Just hacked and parried and pushed and dodged and kicked and cut and brained like some mindless beast, dealing horrible wounds to others for fear of the horrible wounds they would otherwise deal to me.

As the sun set we fought on; as the light died we fought on; and as the moon rose, until there was not enough light to see who was enemy and who not; and then the Saracens were moving back into the hills above and we were hastily regrouped and marched out. I did not recognize any of the men who surrounded me, and not just because they all wore masks of blood that glittered strangely in the moonlight. Where was the rest of my troupe? I should have looked for them. But I feared what I would find.

I felt battered from crown to heel, but at least I was still in possession of all my limbs, which could not be said for many of the fallen, whose bodies and bits of bodies we were too tired to bury and flung instead, with no ceremony, into the river. None of those I handled looked familiar, and anyway the gloom made them all alike. Too exhausted even to feel relief at my survival, I trudged in silence back towards Acre with my head down, breathing heavily, trying to make an inventory of my pains, then giving up as they all merged into one. Numbed as I was by my ordeal, still, I could not help but feel a tightening of dread as I neared the camp in the small hours of the morning.

I found our quarters empty save for Ezra, who was sitting outside the tent with her legs straight out in front of her like a poppet thrown down by a bored child. She looked up, her drawn features illuminated by the dancing light of her lantern.

"John!"

And then she was laughing and I was laughing. She got to her feet and launched herself at me and we engaged in a ridiculous, lumbering jig with the mud sucking at our feet and Ezra chanting, "You're alive, alive, alive-o!" And there was such glee, such mad triumph in my own survival surging inside me that I thought, *I will kiss her.*

And just as I was about it, fool that I was, there was a commotion and she broke away from me with an appalled look on her face, and when I turned it was to see Quickfinger and Hammer carrying a slumped form between them, and Red Will limping along behind.

It was Saw they carried. It was clear he was dead, for no one could survive such a wound. Cleaved through shoulder almost to his waist, the body was obscene in the detail it revealed, things that should be inside and kept in, secret and contained, left out in the air. Beneath the gaping jerkin, bones glinted, viscera gleamed. Laid across his ruined chest, his fingers were curled around the hilt of a dagger. And then his eyelids fluttered and I almost fell down in shock.

Will went running to find a chirurgeon while Hammer knelt beside his twin, tears making clean runnels through the gore that covered his face. He mumbled and nonsense came out: their strange twin-talk, like childish babble. But Saw's face twitched into a grimace, or maybe a smile, and he tried to say something. An awful noise came out—a sort of gurgling rasp, followed by a pinkish froth that bubbled on the lips.

Ezra burst into tears and buried her face in my shoulder. Quickfinger shifted awkwardly from foot to foot, alternately staring around for Will's return and gazing down in horror at his friend. Then he got on his knees and put his hands together and started fervently praying, calling on every saint whose name we'd ever taken in vain to perform miracles, to knit up Saw's broken body, to restore him to if not health, then life, at least.

There was such anguish in his eyes I couldn't say what I was thinking: namely, that he knew as well as I did what nonsense it all was. That nothing could save Saw now, not prayer, not doctors, nor relics or miracles. But instead I turned to walk to Savaric's pavilion, only to come upon the disgraced churchman heading our way with Will—with no doctor in tow, but carrying a box which I recognized as one of the Glastonbury reliquaries.

"I will call upon the power of Saint Beonna," Savaric told us. He was half in, half out of his battle gear; he clanked when he walked. He went with difficulty down on his knees beside our stricken friend, laid a hand upon his filthy brow. Then he gently uncurled Saw's fingers from the hilt of the dagger and laid it aside, wiped the blood-covered hand clean on his own tunic before placing it upon the carved reliquary and intoning solemnly, "O Beonna, most ancient father of the monks, look with favour on this poor soul who has done much to help honour your memory and cherish your remains. Let the grace of your divinity flow out upon him and restore his body to this world so that he may fight on to restore the Holy City to Christendom in your name. *In nomine Patris, et Filii, et Spiritus Sancti*. Amen."

We all said "Amen" and waited for the body to bloom forth, smoothing the organs back into their casings, knitting up the shattered bones, resheathing them in unmarked skin. And when the body twitched suddenly, we all gasped. But the gasp became a moan, for all that issued from Saw was a gush of fresh blood that spilled from his mouth. And then he was entirely still, as if all that Savaric's prayer had done was to violently free his soul from some cord that was keeping it anchored inside.

Savaric uttered the prayer for the dead over him, then had to be helped to his feet. I retrieved the remains of Saint Beonna and followed him back to the pavilion, leaving Hammer to grieve over his lost twin with the rest of the troupe.

"Did you really think that would work?" I asked him.

He turned a weary face to me, his black eyes empty of thought, empty of hope. "It was worth a try."

It was only later, back in camp, when Saw had been decently buried and his brother's grief dosed with the strongest brandy we could lay hands on, that I asked the question that had been niggling at me.

"Where is Little Ned?"

Will said, "He was just in front of me. I turned away for a moment and . . . we got separated. I didn't see him again."

Ned was an odd one: never popular, being a bit secretive, shifty, unforthcoming, always on the outside of the group. Now we felt guilty that we had not thought of him sooner, distracted as we had been by Saw's demise. I remembered the beating I gave him after he thieved the steward's purse back in Somerset. It seemed a thousand years ago.

We asked around; we visited the hospital tent. God, there were sights in there I never wish to see again. But of Little Ned there was no sign

It struck me later, as I tried, and failed, to sleep, that of the eight of us who had set out with glad hearts to gull the willing populace of England to sign for the cross and come fight on this hellish expedition, there were only four left. I could only hope that Plaguey Mary and the Moor were still alive, in a safer place than this. But I couldn't help but feel that we were paying a heavy price for cozening the poor folk of our land into paying a part in this infernal war.

The supply run to Haifa having failed, conditions in the camp worsened daily. By comparison with many, we were living well: there was still some cheese left, salted beef and flour. But our cook had died of the flux, and Savaric's Welshman had been deputized to do his best with the meagre contents of our provisions wagons. He'd been surprisingly creative: we found ourselves eating better than we had before, though when Savaric asked him what was in a particularly tasty stew he'd served up he was evasive.

Quickfinger stared at the pale meat in his bowl. "You don't think—?" He picked out a bone, held it up. It was about the length of his little finger. He wiggled it as if it had come off his own hand, then made us all dig the tiny bones out of our own bowls.

"Definitely not human," I said. I could have sworn he looked disappointed.

The next day we found out exactly what we had eaten. The falconer was in the hospital tent, slowly expiring from wounds he had sustained at the Spring Head. The two birds he kept with him had vanished.

We were detailed to take turns guarding the wagons. Every morning and every night Savaric's steward took an inventory of what we had left. Even so there was pilfering. Men had been hanged. The usual punishment was a thrashing, which proved to be an insufficient deterrent; after that, the loss of a hand. But what was the point of keeping a man who couldn't fight? He was just an extra mouth to feed. Every day we heard of men who had climbed the earthworks and gone over to the enemy, "turned Turk."

"They say it's better to be taken captive by Saladin than to starve to death here," grumbled Savaric's horse-caparisoner. "They've got all sorts up there in those hills: deer and sheep and goats and swans and cameleopards; fresh cakes baked with honey, new flour and fruit from Damascus." I watched a globule of saliva drip from the corner of his mouth.

"They cut your cock off if you go over to them, the Saracen," Quickfinger offered helpfully.

The caparisoner quailed. "What?"

"Aye, they do." He turned an earnest face to the man, then a dissembling face to me, a discreet wink. "Summat to do wi' their religion."

The caparisoner went pale and took himself off to rethink his future. I could not help but think of my own gullibility concerning the eating of babies.

Famine continued to bite and the rain continued to fall. Death stalked the Christian camp, picking victims at will: a lord here, a peasant-soldier there; camp-followers, servants, archers, cooks. One day we heard a terrible wailing from the camp of the Latin Kingdom. Florian went out to investigate and came back with the news that the two small daughters of the king and queen of Jerusalem were dead in the night, succumbed to the bloody flux, and that their mother, Sibylla, would not let their bodies be buried, but clung to them weeping with no thought for her own well-being.

Two innocent children brought into this hell to suffer and to die, for nothing. What sense was there in a world where such things happened?

One night, a week or so later, I was sitting with Ezra on guard duty. We didn't often find ourselves on the same watch, and maybe that was because I had been avoiding being alone with her these past weeks, after that almost-kiss. Of course I'd said nothing, and neither had she, but I felt her eyes on me all the time when we were in company, as uncomfortable as a touch. In the dark, sitting our watch, it was easier to bear.

We talked about nothing in particular—about the weather, the food, the general discomforts; about poor Queen Sibylla, who had herself now sickened of the same disease that carried off her girls—and then she said to me, quite out of the blue: "When the war's over and we go back to England, we should marry. Each other, I mean. Get a little piece of land, some animals. I can look after them, make butter and cheese and suchlike. Have some chickens, for the eggs, raise some up, sell some chicks at market, that sort of thing."

There was a long, panicked pause as I tried to think how to respond to this proposition, and into this silence she added, "Because I know, you see. We're like each other more than you think. I don't want babies and you don't want a wife, or any woman, really. We'd suit one another well enough and no one would fuss us."

I stared out into the darkness, where the fires of a thousand campfires like our own burned in the night. Had she seen to the heart of me, just like that, Ezra-who-was-Rosamund, with her solemn, unremarkable brown eyes?

"I . . . ah . . ." I could not frame the words.

"I saw the way the Moor looked at you," she went on. "And how you looked at him. And Mary said something once—"

"What? What did she say?"

"'They're made for each other, those two.' That's what she said. 'Made for each other and they don't even know it, or at least John don't. The Moor, he knows all the world has to offer: he's seen it all, just one look at him and you can tell. But he's waiting.'"

My mouth was so dry I could hardly speak. "Waiting? Waiting for what?"

"For you. To know yourself. That was what Mary said. And I've been watching you too. How you don't go after the whores. I saw your face when Savaric pushed that one at you in Lisbon, and it was right about then I remembered what Mary said. And . . ." She paused, then said in a rush, "I've seen your drawings, your secret sketches of him—I'm sorry, I didn't mean to pry."

There was a distant agony inside me, worse than any arrow wound: an emptiness, a loss. I shook my head in the darkness. "Then why would you ask me? Knowing what I am?" It was the first time I had made such an admission, even to myself.

I could feel her smile, but when she replied her tone was melancholic. "People are contrary, en't they? Not being able to have something doesn't make you want it any the less."

We ran out of words then; the weight of thoughts hung heavy between us. We were still sitting glumly silent when Savaric chanced by. He sat companionably by our fire, warming his hands. After a few minutes Ezra excused herself for a piss.

"When will King Richard come?" I asked Savaric.

"Not till the spring now. They say the storms that ravage the coasts of the Middle Sea in winter can be severe, and we wouldn't want to lose him to shipwreck. But when he comes . . ." He made an expansive gesture. "When he comes we'll bring this damned siege to a close in no time. The whole world goes in fear of our Lionheart."

And then we can go home from this dreadful place, I sighed to myself. "And no sign of Philip Augustus, either," I said aloud. "Florian says the French nobles are fretting, and some are even talking of leaving." I wondered how important this war could be that we were here and those two potentates were wherever they were, attending, no doubt, to matters more important in the eyes of a king.

"What was that?" Savaric was suddenly intent, looking around.

"What? I heard nothing."

We sat in the flickering light, listening like a pair of owls. Then I heard it, a rustle, a distant thud against the hollow wood of a wagon. I made a sign to Savaric—*quietly, come with me*—and drew my dagger. Together we crept around the back of the stores, in time to see a faint glow and the shapes of two men, one inside the wagon handing what looked like a side of cured gammon down to a fellow outside.

I gestured to Savaric—*stay here*, meaning, catch them if they run. Then I hurled myself at the back of the nearest man, hauling him down into the mud. He landed in a heap and my fist connected solidly with his head, and he groaned and stopped struggling. But the second man leapt out of the wagon and pushed past us, dodged away from Savaric and was gone into the night before either of us had a chance to give chase. I held on to the first robber, thinking that Ezra would have had the runaway down in no time; she was both tough and quick, whereas our master had spent too long sitting on his backside eating the same stores we were trying to guard.

I dragged the miscreant closer to the fire so we could get a better look at him. When the light fell upon his face, Savaric roared: "You!"

I stared at the man for some seconds before it came to me: Geoffrey de Glanvill, thinner than last I'd seen him, riding around the camp in his Templar surcoat with his brother at his side, as if the pair of them had come to conquer the world and divide it up between them.

Savaric grabbed him by the throat. "Steal my food, would you? So you're a thief as well as a rapist, are you?"

De Glanvill blinked up at him, frowning. "What did you say?"

"You raping, thieving bastard! Just wait till de Sable hears about this, I'll make sure you swing for it, so help me God!" Savaric was raging now, unaware of the implications of what he had just said. Too late, I tried to head him off.

"Yes, you *thieving* villain!" I cried, emphasizing the "thieving" with all my might. But Savaric was too furious to take my meaning. And then, if it were not enough that our master had made it clear that he knew all along that de Glanvill had attacked the young woman in Winchelsea, and that Savaric therefore must have had words with her, hidden her and lied about it, "Ezra" appeared, bareheaded, the light from the fire burning rosy across her face.

De Glanvill's eyes widened in disbelief. "You! You're the little whore who tried to murder my cousin!"

Ezra snarled and flung herself at him, lacerating his face with her nails.

"Christ!" Savaric hauled her away before she could rip his head off, and thrust her in my direction.

She was a handful, fighting me with every ounce of her strength. I remembered a jackrabbit I'd once caught on Dartmoor, every fibre in its body bent on escaping me. Eventually I'd let it go, appalled by its will to live. But Ezra I hung on to.

Then suddenly there was a blur of movement and a cry, and Savaric was swearing. Over Ezra's shoulder, I saw him fall, clutching his side, and then de Glanvill was running, stumbling through the mud and away.

"John! Get after him! If he gets back to his brother, Rosamund is lost."

I ran. As a foot soldier I was used to the mud; De Glanvill, a horseman, was less so. His feet slipped and he fell to his knees, then hurled himself upright again. More surefooted, I made up the ground between us. I saw him twist his head round, his face pale through the gloom, then he was dodging sideways, heading for the tents, splashing heedlessly, making poor progress. He was a lord, been brought up in castles lit by a thousand candles, but I had spent my early years as a feral creature, the stars my only light in darkness. I saw the guy rope he tripped over even before he did, and then I was on him, hand clamped hard over his mouth to stop his noise. My dagger went in under the ribs, and beneath my hand a long moan escaped, like the lowing of a cow.

It never fails to surprise me how fragile we are, we human beings, our soft outer skin so inadequate, so vulnerable. That first stroke was almost certainly a killing stroke, but I couldn't stop. I withdrew the dagger from the sheath of his flesh and plunged it in again, and again, the memory of what he did to Ezra making me savage.

I don't know how long I was there, on my knees, stabbing and sobbing till long after there was no more moaning but my own and at last I became aware of rain pattering down on me. Then thunder rumbled overhead and the rain fell harder, each drop like a stinging rebuke from Heaven.

Back at Savaric's pavilion, I found him in the chair he called his throne, naked to the waist, with Florian applying a field dressing to his wound. They both stared at me in horror as I entered. I was all over mud and blood, like some demonic creature.

"Is he dead?" Savaric asked.

I nodded.

"Well, it had to be done," Savaric said. You could tell he wasn't badly wounded. "He'd have gone straight to Ranulf and told all, and after what happened in Lisbon it wouldn't only have been Ezra's neck at risk."

Florian looked at him curiously, and I wondered how much, or little, he knew. Then Savaric turned to me and laughed. "So, you're a proper soldier now!"

A proper soldier, yes—a red-fisted murderer who had not only taken a man's life, but relished the deed. The bile that had been threatening now scoured the back of my throat and came pouring out.

The horrible irony was that I needn't have killed Geoffrey de Glanvill after all, for the next day word reached us that his brother Ranulf had died of the flux. Some days after that, Archbishop Baldwin's ancient life ebbed away, to be followed by half a hundred other nobles. How many of us commoners perished I could not tell you. Death walked amongst us, swinging his scythe: it was a high harvest field day for the minions of Hell.

✳

Nathanael watched the man close the door behind him and move off down the street. Tariq walked with his shoulders hunched and his hands curled inwards, a man guarding the generous swell of his belly from jealous eyes. Even if Nat had not known who he was, he would have hated him for his self-satisfied swagger. Imagine, feeding yourself out of the citadel stores and bringing nothing out to feed your wife, her father and brother. The man was a monster on that count alone. Nathanael wished him dead.

He waited until Tariq was out of sight, checked to make sure there was no one marking his presence, then crossed the road and rapped on the door, once, twice, a pause, then once again. Footsteps on the tile floor, then the door opened and he stepped quickly inside.

"Did he see you?"

"No."

"Good."

Nat handed the covered basket over and Zohra took it. Inside was the very last of their store of tea, some lentils and chickpeas scraped from the cellar floor, a small packet of rice that would make maybe two meagre meals, some raisins from last summer's grape harvest and a handful of the final dried onions. There was hardly anything left to give. Soon they would be like the very poorest folk, forced to boil old hides and shoe leather for broth, to search for weeds among the ruins, to lie in wait for the few rats or wild birds left within the walls. Some people had made a sort of tea out of ground-up palm fronds, which proved to be poisonous. He watched Zohra move quickly towards the kitchen with her treasures.

"You must not live in fear of him," he chided, following her into the kitchen. "He cannot forbid you to go out."

Zohra sighed. "It's easier to do as he demands. Don't be angry with me, I can't bear it."

Ever since Aisa had drowned, something had gone out of her, some essential spark. Little sign of the lioness now, more like a feral cat that snatched at food then ran away. Tariq, noting this, had pressed his advantage, every day taking greater control of the household, and of his wife, introducing rules governing her behaviour—not to venture beyond the communal oven at the end of the road, not to walk abroad without either himself or Rachid, not to allow anyone beyond the immediate family into the house when he was not there, to go veiled at all times, never to look any man directly in the eye.

"He never said anything about other parts," Nat had teased upon hearing this, and Zohra had promptly burst into tears. So now he tried not to add to her burdens by making remarks or jokes, though it was difficult to see Zohra so reduced. And gradually, once the storm of grief over the loss of poor Aisa had lost some degree of its force, he had tried increasingly to bring a little kindness into her life—a pot of honey, packets of herbal tea put together by Sara, some grain for the pigeons begged from a merchant in exchange for his services, a piece of turquoise silk he had found in a chest at home with which Zohra might bind her hair beneath the hood of her djellaba. He had never seen her wear it, no doubt out of fear her husband would demand to know where it had come from. He seemed to take pleasure in denying her.

"Little bird," he said now, "you haven't been eating."

Zohra shook her head. "I eat enough."

"Enough to survive, not enough to thrive."

"There's not enough to go around. The men need more than I do."

Nathanael cut off the bitter words that welled up inside him. "Sorgan gets little treats up at the garrison, and Tariq gets fed at the citadel," he pointed out. "You must not let them take your share. What would they do without you if you were to fall sick?" He watched as Zohra took this in. He took Zohra's hand in his own, turned it over. "See how every bone is visible? That's too thin." It was a thrill to touch her, even innocently. "If ever you run out of food you must come to me, there is always something I can find. You will, won't you?"

Zohra looked down at her hands and said nothing.

How had she become so passive? To see her like this gave him a physical pain, a pang of loss. *Little wraith*, he thought, *little ghost*.

"Promise me."

"Your first duty is to your mother and Nima," Zohra said quietly.

Duty? The word *love* teetered on Nathanael's tongue but he bit it back. *Each day a little more*, he vowed to himself. *I will win you back. I will save you.* He hoped his fervour didn't show in his eyes.

"There is always honey, little bird. Always honey for you. And when that is gone, there is always me."

Zohra looked confused. "What?"

She does not remember, Nat thought. *She does not remember that afternoon when I offered my whole self to her, to love, to destroy, to be devoured—eaten if ever she was starving.* The remark had been made half in jest, but he meant it fully now. *Perhaps she does not remember how we were*, he thought again. *Perhaps she doesn't remember any of it at all.*

But Zohra remembered it all: every word, every touch. And that was what frightened her so much.

A fortnight later, Nat was sitting in the tea house, staring into the glass of liquid before him on the table. You could not have called it tea; he did not know what it had been made from.

"It's all there was," Hamsa Nasri said, apologetically.

Around them the usual babble of gossip and chatter dipped and rumbled. The tenor of it grew more sober by the day. There had been some excitement at the arrival of the new commander the previous week, a fierce Kurd with a huge black beard by the name of Al-Mashtub, who had given a rousing speech about pride and ancestors. But it was clear to Nat as he listened to the conversations around him that folk were losing what little optimism the Kurd's arrival had initially provoked.

"The sultan sent him because he knew what was coming," said Younes, who'd just come down from a shift on the wall. "He'll have had spies out all down the coast, and when they reported back what they'd seen heading our way he knew our defences would need stiffening. He's an old warhorse is Al-Mashtub. He's seen it all. He'll put some backbone into the garrison."

Six great ships bearing the blue silk banners of the French king, Philip Augustus, had sailed blithely into view the previous week, entirely unchallenged. The Christian blockade was so tight that no Muslim ship could approach without being destroyed or turned back miles from Akka's port. From these ships they had watched a small army of new warriors in full armour disembarking, warhorses with ribbons braided through their manes, horns blaring, troops singing in chorus. They seemed happy to be at war.

"They want to kill us," Younes said. "They cannot wait."

"I've never seen such monsters as those siege towers they brought," said a thin young man who pulled up a stool to join their group. "I never knew trees grew so high."

Younes leaned over and pulled him into an embrace so tender that Nat realized the young man must be his dancing boy, Iskander. He looked as frail as a cricket, as if he had not eaten in weeks. There was probably not much trade at the moment, Nat thought.

"I heard they have massive battering rams, too," Hamsa said, at his most doomy. "Those towers will overtop our walls, and while they've got us pinned down they'll send the rams in to batter down the gates."

"I heard our supplies of *naft* are running out," Younes said. "Even the lad from Damascus can't magic it out of thin air."

Nat had been up on the walls earlier in the day, in his usual capacity as a doctor to the wounded, but also—though it went against every precept of his training—as a combatant. There was hardly a man in the city now who did not put in a shift with a crossbow, if he could shoot one, or simply hefting rocks to the catapult team to lob down at the enemy. The Franj had set up a number of vast catapults, the largest of which the garrison had named The Bad Neighbour. They had set up their own mangonel, The Bad Kinsman, opposite. Daily, the two traded boulders. A large chunk of the wall near the Accursed Tower had been badly damaged. They had repaired it as best they could, beneath a hail of missiles. The enemy were mining deep inside the sturdy walls now; it was only counter-mining from within that stopped them breaking through. By night the Franj continued to fill in the moat, bringing earth and stones from their camp, building up a great rampart topped with iron breastworks, behind which shield their bowmen fired upon the garrison night and day.

"They are inexorable," Younes said, his eyes dark with exhaustion. "They are like the sea: every day they come up closer and wash away a little more of our defences. And they just keep coming, God damn them." Then he told them how the man beside him on the wall had fallen to the ground as if arrow-struck. "I looked for a wound," he said, "but there was nothing. He was quite, quite dead. Even Nat here couldn't have brought him back."

There was muted laughter at this old joke.

"I thought perhaps he'd fainted. I mean, no one's getting any sleep with this bombardment. But no, he'd just died. Just like that— on the spot. From hunger, we reckoned. His body was all skin and bone." He shook his head, and turned his attention to Iskander.

Nat watched as Younes stroked the boy's cheek, oblivious to the gaze of others, and he saw how the lad turned his face to his lover, and for a moment he felt a twinge of jealousy. When he looked around, he saw the same looks of sympathy and tenderness on other men's faces as they watched the pair. There was no disapproval or disgust; no one had the energy for it. They were all teetering on the edge of survival—lost and grieving, damaged and alone.

"Nathanael!"

Nat looked around. It was the veteran, Driss.

"Thank the Lord you're here." The old man touched his hands to his heart. "Can you come see my Habiba? She's taken a turn for the worse."

Nat made his farewells swiftly, swung his great leather doctor's bag over his shoulder and followed the fierce old soldier down the street, trying not to wince at his pronounced limp, which must have been all the more painful when forced to such determined speed.

The house didn't look like much from the outside; Muslim culture enshrined modesty at its heart. But once inside Nat looked around the salon with some surprise. As far as he knew Driss got by on a veteran's pension, which wasn't much. Yet shining Venetian vases sat on carved tables inlaid with mother-of-pearl; there was a good quality carpet beneath his bare soles. Driss had been most insistent about the removal of shoes at the door, which was the case in most houses, but in times of sickness and hardship people didn't always remember such niceties.

He attended the old woman in the cool room at the back of the house where she lay in shuttered darkness, went into the small but immaculate kitchen and made up tinctures for her from the simples he carried in his bag. It was clear, though, that she wouldn't last out the year, and there was little he could do for her condition. Not that he said as much. There was no point in taking hope away from the devoted couple, and sometimes people rallied miraculously. But when it came to the matter of payment he refused to take anything for the visit or the medicines.

"I can't take money from a friend," he said. "And you're always paying for my tea." Which was true.

Driss was implacable. "I can afford it," he insisted, as he always did, and Nat realized it was not just the iron pride of a soldier speaking, but simple, honest truth.

Nathanael was less shy than others when it came to matters of money—you had to be when you were a doctor, in and out of people's houses, in and out of their lives. Indicating the lavish furnishings, he asked, "Did you come into a fortune or something?"

"Or something." The veteran tapped the side of his nose, but his eyes glinted. Nat could sense he was dying to tell his story to someone, a story he could not tell in public.

"So . . . ?" he encouraged. "What was the something?"

"You must tell no one. I was sworn to secrecy."

Nat placed his hand on his heart. "I promise."

Driss leaned in close as if the walls had ears. "I saved the sultan's life once," he said in a hoarse whisper.

Nat raised his eyebrows. "Did you now? And which battle was that in?" He almost dreaded asking, for the old man's war stories were famed for being interminable.

"Not a battle. Someone tried to kill him." He pulled aside the neck of his frayed brown robe, a garment that wouldn't have seemed out of place on a beggar in the central square.

Nat found himself looking at a big, pale scar, a depressed and puckered circle, much more wicked in appearance than anything produced by a simple knife wound. He sucked air through his teeth. "Nasty, that. Looks as if you lost a fair bit of flesh there."

"They had to cut it out," Driss said matter-of-factly. "The blade was poisoned."

"Poisoned?"

"It was the Old Man."

"What old man?" Nat frowned.

"The Old Man of the Mountains, old Sidi ad-Din Sinan. The Lord of the *Hashshashin*."

"He really exists?" Nathanael was skeptical. People in power often put about tales of assassination attempts to bolster the legend of their capacity for survival. Though from what people said of the sultan, he did not sound like a man much given to embellishment or lies.

"He's tried to murder Salah ad-Din three times to my certain knowledge. The first time was in '74 when I got in the way. Then a while later some fellow who'd managed to win his trust enough to be made a personal bodyguard attacked him. That was a close shave. Luckily the sultan is a cautious man—he was wearing a mail coif under his turban at the time and the blade grazed right off it. It's said he wears a steel cap at all times now. And on the last occasion, when he'd gone to beard the old lion in his den at Masyuf itself, they say he woke to find an assassin's dagger and some cakes on the pillow beside him, the cakes still warm from the oven."

"But why would the Old Man want to kill Salah ad-Din? Surely they're on the same side."

Driss shook his head. "These fanatics, they have no side but their own. Can't see beyond their own noses. The world they inhabit is a distortion, a fantasy, an abomination of all that is right and decent. There's nothing godly about them. They'd side with the Devil himself if they thought it would bring about the domination they seek. It wouldn't surprise me to find them in league with the bastards beyond these very gates."

The pig had almost touched him! With a thrill of disgust, Kamal Najib pressed himself back against the side of the ship until the hard wooden rail bit into his spine. He watched the unclean creature skittering crazily down the deck to join the other half dozen that had also been let loose from the crate, and felt nothing but contempt for a captain who had thought such a facile stratagem could deceive the might and intellect of the infidel.

Everyone had shaved their beards off just before they set sail from Beirut on the *Crescent Moon* (and the name of the ship had been painted out): if challenged they would claim they were Christian sailors come to relieve the hardships of the besieging army. He had barely even started growing his own chin-hair, but even so the cool sea breeze on his naked skin felt strange, adding to his general sense of discomfort. He hated being on board a ship, hated the idea of the heaving sea beneath the hull. He had never learned to swim. When Zohra and Aisa had been competing with one another as to who could dive deepest and swim fastest, Kamal had always stayed on the beach, crying with fear at the thought of someone pushing him in. He had learned ways to control fear during his training in the mountains, but beneath the Grand Headmaster's chants he could still sense the cold profundity of his dread.

For months now he had been plagued with nightmares of drowning from which he woke gasping in terror. It seemed cruel of Fate to decree that he should be sent on this particular mission. Or maybe—and this seemed even more likely—the Grand Headmaster knew his greatest fear and was determined he should face it head on.

To get out of the way of the revolting hogs, he climbed the steps up to the high forecastle. The Grand Headmaster had drummed into all of them how the sultan was no true Muslim, that he was a man bent on power for his own pleasure and ambition. After all, he was not a true Arab but one of those troublesome Kurds, barely more than savages. That Salah ad-Din had come to prominence in such a far-flung region of the Ummah, the cradle of debauchery and corruption that was Egypt, whence came that abomination the eunuch Karakush, further emphasized the wrongness of the situation. Twice, the Order had attempted to assassinate Salah ad-Din; twice, he had eluded them.

But this had not stopped the sultan from sequestering the goods of the Nizari sect. And so the Old Man had declared him their enemy. To the naive it might seem illogical to support the efforts of the infidel against a man leading the troops of the Ummah, he'd said, but the ways of Allah were mysterious, far beyond the comprehension of ordinary men. He—Sidi Rachid ad-Din Sinan—was one of the few to whom such understanding was vouchsafed. One day his disciples would take pride in having played their small part in the great scheme.

It had not been hard to persuade Kamal of the sultan's iniquity; after all, he had heard his father deriding the man often enough. Bashar, though, had owned up to private doubts in the beginning of their training. He had left Akka to emulate his dead elder brother, who had died in the service of the *hashshashin*, and who had always said Salah ad-Din was as close to a saint as any man he had ever met. But the Grand Headmaster was a highly persuasive man, able to quote the Holy Book at will to back up his every utterance, and in the end Bashar had forgotten everything he had ever believed in his former life. Where his mission had taken his erstwhile friend now, Kamal did not know. What he did know was that when he had completed this, his own first mission, he would be a fully fledged *hashshashin*, beloved of the Order.

From the top deck of the *Crescent Moon*'s forecastle, Kamal could see the foreign ships bearing down behind them—one handsome galley and three smaller craft. But even the big galley was tiny compared to the *Crescent Moon*, which carried six hundred and fifty fighting men, a hundred camel-loads of weapons and ammunition, thousands of bottles of Greek fire, and large ampullae filled with poisonous snakes to be hurled from the walls of Akka. The hold was stuffed with provisions for the starving inhabitants of the city—distantly visible as a line of pale ochre beyond the Christian naval blockade. The warriors on board would bolster the beleaguered garrison; the supplies would feed the city for many months, long enough, it was hoped, for troops to muster from across the caliphate to answer Sultan Salah ad-Din's call to arms.

If they could run the blockade and force their way into Akka, it would surely be the downfall of the Franj. The siege would fail and the sultan would once more be victorious, confirmed in his power and potency.

But that was the last thing the Old Man of the Mountains wished for. As soon as the Grand Headmaster had heard from his spies about the great ship being provisioned at Beirut, he had sent Kamal to infiltrate the crew and thwart the attempt. Kamal hoped he could complete this part of his mission successfully. His stomach contracted, he thought he might throw up, but once more his training came into play and he forced himself to calmness.

A smaller craft was approaching them. When it came within hailing distance of the *Crescent Moon*'s mighty prow, a man stood up and challenged them, inquiring as to their identity and the port they had set sail from. The captain was ready for this—but so was Kamal, well schooled in the various tongues of the Franj. The Beiruti captain spoke, and Kamal translated his words for the captain of the foreign ship.

"My captain says we have come from Genoa and are bound for Tyre with supplies for the Christian army! But you may tell your master this is not the full truth." He knew he could not mention the word Beirut—even the dull-witted captain would be suspicious if he heard the name of his home port mentioned.

Kamal watched the foreigner's smooth face take in this information. "You fly no Christian flag," the man called back.

He translated this for the captain, who cursed. "Tell them we left port in a great hurry, knowing the army's need for provisions."

It was a feeble response, and Kamal duly relayed it, grinning his contempt. "If you take me back with you," he told the officer in the skiff, "I can tell your master a great deal more. Demand me as a hostage. You will not regret it."

And so it was that he climbed nimbly down the rope into the enemy skiff and was rowed swiftly away, his eyes firmly shut against the proximity of the terrible sea.

Once safely on board the foreign ship, he relaxed a little and looked around. The crew seemed very organized, very workman-like. They went about their tasks quickly and with discipline. Sidi ad-Din Sinan would have approved. Kamal relayed all his information to the captain of the vessel in the presence of a tall, red-haired man, relating how they had come from Beirut on the sultan's command, listing the goods contained in the hold, the numbers of men stowed below.

Perhaps they would not believe him. He must make them believe him, for this was only the first part of the plan. Whatever danger he put himself in did not matter. All that mattered was the Way and the Grand Headmaster's will.

Kamal watched the *Crescent Moon* plough on towards Akka, heading for the blockade of Christian vessels lined up across the entrance to the harbour. Not too fast, but with purpose, as they had been proceeding before the challenge had come from the other vessels. He knew they would use the oars to power the ship through the blockade once they approached the city, but that they would reserve the rowers' strength for that final push.

Beyond the *Crescent Moon*, Kamal could clearly make out the Tower of Flies rising like a spear past the breakwater of the inner harbour, and the pale-gold walls that bounded the seaward face of the city. He had never before seen his home from the sea. It looked beautiful, serene. The minarets of the mosques extended gracefully towards the sky. If you ignored the Christian ships and the swaths of enemy forces stretching for miles outside the walls, it looked untouched by war. For a moment he experienced a pang of nostalgia for his lost life; then he tamped it down ferociously.

Suddenly there was a cry. "Get after them! Stop them reaching the blockade!"

And now it was a race. The galley he was on was big, but it was nowhere near as powerful as the *Crescent Moon*. At top speed that ship might well bully its way through the blockade and into Akka's harbour, but the pursuing vessels were faster and more nimble. They sailed alongside in no time, and their crews rained missiles on the Arab vessel. The crew of the Arab vessel—ordinary sailors, untrained for war—took cover, but the game was up now.

Kamal watched from a safe place behind a bulwark as the Muslim troops swarmed up onto the deck and returned fire. But now, as if to confirm once more the Order's righteous plan, the wind suddenly dropped, threatening to becalm the *Crescent Moon* if the rowers did not prevail against the tide. Down on the rowing decks the overseers would be lashing the oarsmen for all they were worth, but now the foreign galley he was in came around in the *Crescent*

Moon's path. He watched as some of the Franj threw themselves into the sea, ropes slung across their backs. *They are better men than me*, he found himself thinking. *Even if the Grand Headmaster himself ordered me to leap into the sea, I could not do it.*

Somehow they had got their ropes around the prow and were pulling the *Crescent Moon* around. And while the smaller ships harried it, ramming its sides with the iron beaks attached to their prows, the ship he was on came up on the Arab ship, and its crew hurled grappling irons over the side and hauled themselves closer, till the two vessels collided broadside. And then suddenly the main deck of the *Crescent Moon* was swarming with foreign soldiers, and there was a chaos of hand-to-hand fighting as the Muslim soldiers met them in force, and the pigs charged and squealed.

Even at a distance, Kamal could smell the foul stench: pigshit and blood, and the sweat of terrified men. The ship gave a shudder as if it too felt Kamal's disgust, and then one of the foreign vessels staved a hole in the *Crescent Moon*'s starboard side. As the iron beak withdrew, taking splintered planking with it, he saw the water rush in. He imagined it, a boiling sea filling the hold, weighing it down. He watched while the ship began to list as water filled the hold; and then men were throwing themselves off the decks down into the waves, giving themselves up to the sea rather than be taken by the Franj. Kamal felt a frisson of horror, mixed with a nasty, small stir of satisfaction.

Again and again the Christian galleys attacked, ramming their monstrous beaks into the *Crescent Moon*'s sides. The greedy sea rushed in and suddenly the mighty vessel foundered. Just moments later the *Crescent Moon* sank, taking to the bottom its precious cargo—men and weapons, and the food to sustain the city and its inhabitants.

For the briefest moment Kamal thought of his father, of his brother Sorgan, of his sister Zohra and his twin, Aisa, no doubt slowly starving to death or dying of pestilence, like everyone else in the doomed city. And then he remembered what he had done to them, and shut all his feelings away as the Grand Headmaster had taught him to do.

The red-haired man strode to the prow of his galley, smiling with satisfaction. Beside him stood the captain of the *Trenchemere*, and beside them both was Kamal Najib.

They stared intently at the ochre city beyond, now close enough to see the blackened scorch-marks made by Greek fire and the scars made by the rams and mangonels on the east wall.

"I see Philip has kept his promise not to take the city until I arrived," the red-haired man said cheerfully.

The captain grinned. "If that ship had made it through our blockade, our task would certainly have been made a great deal tougher, sire."

Sire.

Kamal stared up at the red-haired figure: a giant of a man. He had felt in his bones the identity of the man even as he had given up to him his information. It was similar to the way he felt when he was in the presence of the Old Man of the Mountains, that corona of power, as if God had crowned them both in some intangible yet unmistakable way.

Well trained in the ways of the Franj, he went down on one knee.

"King Richard, I am yours to command," he said, with hardly any trace of an accent.

27

"Christ! Another one." Quickfinger fiddled in his mouth, grimacing foully, pulled out a tooth and brandished it at us.

Our gums were bleeding; we had sores on our tongues and the insides of our cheeks. We were scrawny and aching in limb and joint, in no fit state to fight a determined foe.

"Yah, get away with that thing!" I scrambled to my feet. Black stars and nausea: the ground met my face. I felt so weak it was like dying, but Ezra got me sitting up.

"Ah, look at the two of you. Ain't it sweet?" Little Ned gave us both a nasty look, then spat a brown streak of phlegm onto the ground between us.

We had found him at last—or rather, he'd found us. He had been wounded in the battle near the Spring Head but had been dragged on a litter back to camp with two or three others, and on the return journey he'd taken a random arrow in the back. We'd missed him when we made our rounds of the hospital because he was face down and unconscious. How he had survived I had no idea, but it had not made him any more cheerful, and sometimes I caught him watching us with slitted eyes, as if he blamed us for leaving him. I suppose he had a point.

Ezra brought me water and gave me a bit of jerky to chew on till I got some strength back. "I'll fetch you something from Savaric's secret stash later," she promised.

I gave her a sideways look. "Secret stash?"

She put a finger to her lips. "I know where he keeps it."

I chewed on the jerky; it was so tough and my gums were so sore that it hurt like fire. It was like trying to eat my own boot, and at the rate we were going I suspected I'd be down to that soon. The winter had been terrible. I'd seen men eating grass, men gnawing on bones they had to fight the feral dogs for. The merchants profited, but didn't they always? One of the Genoans had his stores set on fire when he refused to sell at a reasonable price. You could understand the anger, but what a waste of food!

It had been better since then; ships were making it through the storms with necessaries. Still, the good stuff vanished at once and we always ended up with the leavings.

King Richard had arrived on the Saturday before the Feast of the Apostle with galleys full of warriors, weapons and war machines, and a ton of huge boulders brought all the way from Sicily. My, how we laughed to watch his crew unloading that lot, staggering up from the beaches, or trying to roll the things uphill, as if they had no idea we had plenty of rock already. They said he also brought all manner of provender with him—flitches of salted bacon, white flour, a herd of Sicilian sheep. No doubt Savaric was stockpiling it against greater disaster, or eating it secretly himself. Ezra was appalled, but I just took this for granted: it was what the nobility did, thinking they had a God-given right to survive while the hoi polloi starved.

The king also brought his newly acquired wife, some Spanish princess with an unpronounceable name. We were curious about this Berengaria. Who in her right mind would choose to come to this hellhole, let alone a sweet girl from Navarre? Quickfinger took himself off to get a look at her and reported back that she was a "reet eyeful."

"It's all right for the fooking gentry, they get a nice piece of arse while all poor Enoch Pilchard gets is his own right hand." He contemplated his palm mournfully. And off he went to find a quiet spot.

Ezra caught my eye and I looked away.

There had been jubilation throughout the camp when King Richard arrived: we built bonfires on the shore, barrels of wine and spirits were broken out of the stores of the newly arrived fleet and we all drank our fill and sang and danced and toasted his health and our own. Richard the Mighty would huff the walls of Acre down like the wolf in the old tale, and then, laden with the fabled treasure of the siege city, we'd be on our way to Jerusalem the Golden.

But it had already been a fortnight and still the wretched garrison was holding out, even though we were smashing their walls by day and night with the hundreds of catapults Richard brought with him, as well as the great tower—Mategriffon—from which the archers rained death upon the soldiers on the walls. Trouble was, no matter how many of them we killed, there were always more of them manning the walls the next day. And still I couldn't manage to hate them.

"I seen a woman up there yesterday, I swear," Red Will told us. "And sometimes there are children." He shook his head. "It ain't right, killing women and children."

"It's war," Hammer said. "Everyone dies." He'd been angry as a banked fire since the death of his twin. On the battlefield, he was remorseless, hacking and stabbing with such loathing you could see he was killing each man as if he were the man who murdered his brother. It was a personal vendetta, a blood-oath between Hammer and the entire Muslim army. If we'd had an army of Hammers we could have stormed the world, left it bleeding and writhing on the ground.

The big *routier*, Florian, came over. "There's a prisoner exchange going on," he said. He was looking particularly splendid: a new surcoat, or one newly washed; his biggest sword; and his helm all sanded to a high polish. Was he was out to catch the eye of a greater noble than Savaric now that the taking of the city was coming closer, one who would guarantee the best looting rights?

"Why exchange the bastards?" Hammer said. "They should just execute the lot of them."

Florian merely shrugged. "Some of these men are valuable, fetch good ransoms. And war is business." The way he said this was like "bees knees."

Hammer leapt to his feet, fists balled. "My brother's dead, and you call it 'business'!"

Florian held his hands up as if to say "nothing to do with me, mate" and looked to me for backup.

"Leave it alone, Michael," I said.

The use of his real name had some sort of magical effect on Hammer—he looked more like a boy than a man.

"I'll come with you," I told Florian.

A delegation of Saracens had come down from the sultan's camp under a flag of parlay, a big contingent of archers amongst them, with their neat little horses and spiky helms and gleaming round shields, pennants fluttering from their lances as if they were out for a day at the lists. They had a hundred or so prisoners with them, all immaculately clean and glowing with health.

The prisoners we had for exchange were a motley collection: some warriors, others crewmen and merchants. Even stripped to their underclothes, they bore themselves bravely. Our men looked rather less delighted to be returned, truth be told. "Better to be taken captive by Saladin than to be in this place," I said to Florian, and he grinned and pointed some noblemen out to me. They were all French—big-boned and arrogant—and it didn't take me long to get bored. I was just turning away to trudge back to camp when I saw him.

His profile was unmistakable. Long, straight nose, angular cheekbones, hooded eyes, taller than the rest of the Saracen captives, carrying himself straight and upright. All at once, the dizziness returned. I clutched at Florian's arm to stop myself going down. I missed my mark and ended up grabbing his sword. Florian pushed me away with an exclamation.

The captive turned his head. His eyes widened, he took a step towards me—and one of the Templar guards lifted his mailed fist and beat him down. There was an outcry from the Saracens, who surged forward. A scuffle broke out, and then King Richard himself waded in, conspicuous by his short red hair and height, bellowing, separating one man from another, sending them flying.

I recovered myself and was running, my knees shaky, my heart thundering. I was making good progress until someone caught me by the shoulder and spun me around. I lost my footing and went down hard.

"I know how you feel," Florian said, helping me to my feet. "Fuckers. See them up close and you just can't help yourself. You want to kill them, like cockroaches. But the deal's done. They're all bought and paid for by the sultan."

I stared at the retreating backs of the Saracens, but they were too far away, and already I was questioning what my eyes had seen. But my body knew; my body was quite certain.

It was the Moor.

Malek stared down from Tell Ayyadieh at the scene of devastation below. The Christian campfires stretched far and wide, even down to the sea. It was as if the whole valley was on fire. They were inexorable: they stopped for nothing, not for holy days, nor sleep, nor darkness. How the gates and walls of Akka were still standing seemed inexplicable, and yet they had withstood the bombardment.

Men and women were standing shoulder to shoulder on the walls, he had heard, as everyone took a turn to relieve the exhausted garrison. They said that children ran about gathering up fallen enemy arrows, rolling unbroken boulders that had flown over the walls to the city's own trebuchets to fire back at the Franj; that women hurled pots of Greek fire down upon the siege towers and ladders, screaming at the invaders with such venom it put a fire in their men's hearts.

Were his aunts among those women? Was Sorgan? All he knew for sure was that Aisa was not. The realization of that loss yet again made him want to weep. A new swimmer had relayed the news. "A martyr," he kept telling Malek. "A true hero of Islam, like his brother."

Malek did not feel like any sort of hero, not with his family dying beyond his protection, not with women fighting on the walls of his city. Was Zohra up there? Would he lose her next? He closed his eyes against the welling tears and felt again the slip of the dying woman's silky hair across the back of his hand, the hot iron of her helmet in his palm. That image invaded his dreams at night: thick metal, fine hair, too tangible, except that sometimes the two transposed their qualities in a nightmarish way so that the hair became as thick as rope, while the armour floated as fragile as a bird's wing, and his mind tried to wrestle the concepts back into their rightful places.

What courage the defenders show, he thought, and felt ashamed. Ever since he had broken down over the Franj woman he had unknowingly cut down, the sultan had kept him by his side, as if it were his duty to take care of his burning coal rather than the other way round. "When the generous man stumbles, God takes him by the hand," he'd said, which humbled Malek further.

Their army was depleted. Taki ad-Din had left a couple of months earlier, selfishly to see to his own lands in the north-east, on the promise of a swift return, but he had not yet come back. The men of el-Adil, the sultan's youngest brother, who had been there since the very beginning of the siege almost two years before, had also been granted leave. A fresh force had been called up from Egypt, but they had not yet arrived. Daily they lobbed pots of deadly *naft* into the Franj camp, causing destruction and chaos. It was to do with distraction, the sultan explained quietly to his impatient generals: to give respite to the garrison, and enable running repairs to be made to the damaged walls. It was all they could do while they waited for reinforcements.

"Some tea?"

He opened his eyes with a jolt, and turned to find his friend Ibrahim carrying two glasses of steaming liquid. He took one gratefully, relieved that the darkness hid his weakness.

"What news, brother?"

"They say the infidel lord, Malik al-Inkitar, is sick."

"The English king?"

Ibrahim nodded. "Our spies say he has leonardia: his hair is falling out, and his teeth and nails are loose. He is in great pain, they say, his mouth full of ulcers, and his muscles are as weak as grass. He cannot even walk, they say, let alone fight. The French king is suffering too, not as badly, but he is of a weaker constitution."

Perhaps they would die, as the German king did. It was an uncharitable thought, but sometimes all Malek wanted was an end to this war, to lay down his arms and walk away. To be an ordinary man again, rather than a butcher of men. And women . . .

"Salah ad-Din, may God bring peace upon him, has asked Damascus to send fruit for him. He says it will aid his recovery." Ibo shook his head. "We've been spending all this time trying to kill the enemy, and yet our lord would preserve them."

Malek smiled. "He is the finest war leader the Faithful have ever seen, and yet he has too gentle a heart. I've served him a long time but I don't pretend to understand him."

The next day, Malek was back on duty at the door to the sultan's war tent when a man came running, his face and clothes covered in dust and grime, blood and filth on his hands. "There is something Salah ad-Din needs to see!" he panted.

Malek looked him up and down. "You should know better than to come to the sultan's tent in this state."

The man laughed bitterly. "I have come out of Akka." When he spread his arms his ribs were visible through the thin cloth of his shirt.

Malek apologized, humbled. "How are things in the city?" It was a stupid question; he regretted it at once.

The man cocked his head, took in Malek's immaculate tunic, his polished shield and helm, his clean boots. "It is worse than anything you can imagine," he said. "We're dying in droves. Disease is rampant, and everyone is starving. There's hardly a bean left to eat, even in the citadel storehouse. It's said that it's best not to walk in some parts of the city at night: people go missing, and feral dogs—the canny ones that haven't yet been eaten themselves—fight over bones that never came from any creature that walked on four legs."

Malek could not imagine his genteel neighbours so reduced, let alone his own family. Chills ran through him.

Suddenly the man prostrated himself, forehead to the ground, and Malek turned to find the sultan standing at the entrance.

"Please, get up." Salah ad-Din reached down and caught the filthy man by the elbow, helped him to his feet. "Tell me your name," he said gently.

"I am Iskander, son of Nahr," the man said.

When he raised his face to the sultan Malek saw that he was younger than he had originally thought, barely more than a boy. But his eyes—his eyes were older than any eyes he had ever seen.

"Before the war I earned my living as a dancer. Now, well now . . ." He looked away. "Now I do what we all must do to get by. I am sorry to come before you in this condition. Even water is limited in Akka."

The sultan called for a page, but the man shook his head. "You must see what we have brought out of the city."

Iskander led Salah ad-Din, with a number of his emirs and Malek following behind, to gather around a giant boulder. The men of Akka had rolled it out of the city, it was explained, all the way uphill to the camp.

"This rock killed twelve people in one strike in the central plaza," one of the Akka men said.

Malek did not recognize him. They were all so thin: he might have walked past a cousin without knowing him.

"They have a monstrous weapon called God's Stone-thrower. It was that machine that sent this missile into the city. Usually anything that flies all that way and strikes with such force is pulverized on impact. And yet, as you see, it is hardly damaged."

Keukburi, the Blue Wolf, ran a hand over the boulder, which stood as high as his waist, and shook his head wonderingly. "How do they even load such a missile?"

El-Adil said grimly, "This rock does not come from the area."

"We saw the Franj unloading such boulders from their ships," one of the Akka men said. "We laughed at the time to watch them struggling through the surf with their cargo. We thought they were mad."

"The English king brought them from Sicily," said a tall, thin, dark man whom Malek recognized as one of the redeemed prisoners. "They are of an exceptionally hard granite, harder by far than

Akka's walls of limestone." He spoke very pure Arabic, but with an accent Malek could not quite place. Since his arrival just a few days ago he had been singled out by Salah ad-Din and often sat with him late at night, talking about scripture and architecture. No one seemed to know who he was, and yet everyone seemed to like him and judged him both courteous and learned.

"They brought them all this way for this purpose," Iskander said, awed by such cold-blooded planning. "They are intent on destroying us."

"We thought you ought to see what we are dealing with at first hand, sire," another man said. "We are proud to play our part in the struggle against the infidel. But it is becoming harder every day, and we do not know how long we can hold out."

The sultan nodded, his lips a thin line. "God wastes not the hire of those who do well. Be steadfast: we are awaiting reinforcements. Islam thanks you for your service. I thank you."

The men were led away to be fed and cared for. All but two of them returned to the city, even though they were offered the choice of remaining in the camp.

"Those are brave men," Ibo said, watching them go. "They are going back to their own deaths, and they know it." He bit his lip as Malek took a sharp breath. "I am sorry, my friend. Your family, I know. May God preserve them."

Later that day a bird arrived from the emirs of the city. It was a grey pigeon, wild of eye, and it refused to settle on the cote or to rest long enough for any to catch it and retrieve its message until, at last, attracted by the grain they put out for it but exhausted by evading them, it fell dead to the ground. Malek's heart sank when he saw that the message it bore was not tied with red silk; nor was the message encrypted in the code they used.

"Greetings to our commander and our imam, the glorious Salah ad-Din," Baha ad-Din read out. "If this bombardment continues much longer the wall around the Accursed Tower will surely fail. We have run out of supplies and cannot hold out much longer. Forgive our weak words, we are desperate. We beg for your succour and your aid. Blessings be upon you. Karakush."

Karakush, Commander of the City of Akka, groaned and pressed the cold cloth to his head. "It's the noise I can't stand. It never stops."

The rumble of boulders smashing into the walls of the city was clearly audible even above the strumming of the oud player in the musician's niche.

"Drink this." Vapour from the steaming cup diffused the perfume of ginger and feverfew into the room. Nathanael cupped the eunuch's hands around it so that he inhaled the fumes even as he drank. Nat had added a dose of skullcap for good measure: the emir's headaches were getting worse, which was unsurprising.

When Karakush had drained the tisane he struggled to his feet. "I must go up to the wall, I must see how much the damage—"

Nathanael pushed him back down. "You won't do any good up there, not in the state you're in. Don't let the people see you weak and in pain, it won't put them in good heart."

"I have failed. It was a strategic error to leave the city standing, but I thought it could be made strong."

Nat frowned. What madness was this? Sometimes when the herbs began to have an effect, the emir's mind would wander as the tension was released in him.

"I don't know what you mean," he said quietly, hoping it would calm him. "Hush. Just close your eyes and breathe deeply and let your body absorb the medicine."

He needed to collect Nima from Rana the crabber's daughter and see to his mother's dressings. Sara had been knocked down by a panicked crowd avoiding a fire in the medina. She had sustained a broken arm and abrasions that had gone septic, despite all his best efforts. Lack of food meant that none of them had the strength to fight infection, and his mother was suffering. He worried she would lose the arm. It would not be the first amputation he had carried out, but to have to do it to your own mother? He was not sure he could.

The eunuch's grip tightened. "I feel responsible for this city, not just because of my position. He was going to destroy Akka, Salah ad-Din, after he took it back, did you know that? He said it was too strategic a port to be allowed to fall into the hands of the Christians. It was badly damaged—hardly worth the repair. But I saw the possibilities, how to strengthen its defences, to rebuild it stone by stone. I argued for us to save Akka, and he put me in charge of the renovations, and then of the treasury, of the infidel cross we captured at Hattin, and then of his armoury—and finally of the entire city and all its people!" He gave a small, mirthless laugh. "The Orientals have a saying: *Be careful what you wish for*. It was hubris to think I knew better than the sultan. And see where my ambition has got me, has got us? He knew it was vulnerable to siege—hadn't he taken it himself by such a method? Had I only listened to him, the people would be safe, moved inland to Damascus, or down the coast to Haifa, and our army would not have been tied up here these two years, enforcing this pointless double siege. And my friend Salah ad-Din would be safe in his palace, being tended by his wives, or by good doctors like your poor dear father, rather than suffering from fevers and colic amidst the filth and disease of a stagnant army camp." He breathed out, long and slow, a great sigh. "We cannot continue. If we try we will all perish."

Nathanael stared at him in horror. "I hope this is your headache talking. You can't possibly surrender Akka. Not after all we've been through."

Karakush looked unhappy; Nat could see his reaction had taken the governor by surprise. The eunuch put his hands to his head. "I believe we shall have to surrender. I can see no other choice."

They were so intent they did not notice the huge shape filling the doorway.

"What, you would discuss our plans with a foreigner?"

The man who had entered the chamber was as large as his voice, hulking, and with a bush of a beard. Al-Mashtub, made grand emir by the sultan, glared first at Karakush, then at Nathanael.

"He's not a foreigner, he's my doctor," Karakush told him defensively.

Nat's eyes glittered. "I was born in this city," he enunciated. He laid his palm on the eunuch's forehead, then pressed three fingers flat to the side of his neck and stared off into empty air, counting silently. "Elevated," he pronounced at last with something approaching satisfaction. He turned to Al-Mashtub. "Do you know what I was doing before I was summoned here? Throwing stones at Christians, that's what. I was up on the north-east wall risking my life with everyone else up there, men, women and children— hurling boulders and fire pots, gathering arrows, piling up whatever ammunition we could find. We're all inhabitants of this city, most of us born here. For some of us it's the only home we've ever known. People have grown up here, made friends, built houses, raised families. It's our city: it belongs to us and we'll fight to the death to save it. Have you talked to those people? Have you asked them what they want? Whether they care that all they've suffered these past two years may go for nothing?"

What he meant was: *It's you who is a newcomer, a Kurd. And the Black Bird is a eunuch out of Egypt. What do either of you know of Akka?*

The Grand Emir looked put out. "I do not ask," he growled. "I tell."

Karakush winced, but Nat had seen too much to be outfaced by such bluster.

The eunuch spread his hands, apologetic, helpless. "Akka will be razed to the ground if we do not come to terms. The walls will fall to this incessant battering—there are only so many repairs we can make before they give way. And these kings are the flower of Christendom: men of honour, famed for their chivalry . . ."

"Men of honour! I'll tell you what my father, God rest his soul, would have said to hear you speak of surrender to such men. My father was a man of peace, but he was also a scholar and a man of knowledge who said we never learn anything from history, of which he would have reminded you with just one word: Jerusalem."

The emir and eunuch exchanged a puzzled glance.

"These 'men of honour' come of the same stock as those who torched the synagogues of Jerusalem with my grandfather's father, his sister, her husband, their children, his grandmother and my great-aunt Miriam inside. They were all burned to death, screaming for mercy, while outside the flower of chivalry hooted and cheered and fed the flames. And outside they butchered every Muslim they found—except those rich enough to earn them a fat ransom—and raped the women and cut the throats of the children. The streets ran knee-deep in blood, and yet you would surrender to such people?"

A long silence followed this outburst; the oud-player had stopped strumming.

Al-Mashtub looked to Karakush, prompting him to bid his wayward "doctor" still his tongue.

At last the eunuch took a deep breath. "We are all people of the Book, sir. There is an understanding between us, no matter how brutal these wars become. And this English king, this Malik al-Inkitar, is greatly respected as a courtly warrior. Times have changed since Al-Quds fell to the Christians. Our enemies behaved like barbarians then, but now we are dealing with great kings, and the eyes of the world will be upon them. If we must sue for peace—*insh'allah*, the reinforcements our sultan has promised will arrive—but if they do not, then we must come to terms that will not shame the brave people of this city, or demean their suffering."

Nat wanted to stay, to argue, but it was clear there was nothing more to say.

"No! No, you can't take them!"

The birds made a noise Sorgan had never heard before as Tariq took them from their roost. When he or his father handled them they cooed gently, a soft trilling that made him feel warm and comfortable inside. There was a panic in this noise, though. As his brother-by-law straightened up with one pigeon grasped in each hand, the birds stretched their necks up and away from the engulfing fingers, their eyes bulging.

"If I want them, I shall take them. Everything in this house is mine," Tariq pronounced.

Sorgan frowned. "But the pigeons are not in the house."

"Get out of my way, idiot!"

Sorgan knew that this word was a sort of insult. People with mean eyes and laughing mouths used it about him. But Tariq was not laughing now. His eyes were small and mean—narrowed to a glare—and his face was getting red.

"Put them back!" Sorgan shouted. "They aren't yours. They are Baba's, and this is his house, not yours."

But Tariq kept moving forward, head down like a bull ready to charge. He must have squeezed the birds as his body tensed, for one of the pigeons gave out a sort of squawk.

Sorgan did not like Tariq. He ate too much and made too much noise. And he had heard muffled cries from his sister's room in the night, and sometimes in the morning Zohra's eyes were red-rimmed and too bright, and there were bruises on her arms. Like some sort of epiphany, Sorgan now suddenly made a connection between Zohra and the pigeons, a connection that had to do with pain.

"You're hurting them!"

Tariq laughed. "You're soft in the head, you are. And so's your father, keeping perfectly good eating like these when people go starving."

"They take messages to the sultan." Sorgan wasn't entirely sure what a sultan was but he knew it was important.

"The sultan! What more does he need to know? He knows we're starving to death and still he does nothing. So I'm going to take these two birds and wring their necks and then your sister is going to cook them for me. Can't do my job if I'm hungry, can I?"

Tariq made to push past Sorgan, but Sorgan blocked the doorway.

"Get out of the way!" Tariq said.

"You can't take the pigeons!"

"I can, and I will!" Tariq thrust his sweaty face at Sorgan. "What's more, I'm going to EAT them, and no one—least of all a moron like you—is going to stop me!" He barged into Sorgan with his shoulder, putting all his weight into it, and gained a yard of space so that he made his way towards the stairs. "I'm going to have Zohra stuff them with ground almonds. And dates. I know there are some left—I found a parcel of them tucked away behind some sacks. She's been trying to hide them from me, sly bitch."

Sorgan's giant hand grabbed the back of his robe and Tariq's feet went out from under him. He hit the stairs hard, first with his spine, then his head, which bounced up off the stone with such force that a piece of his tongue went flying, blood spraying from it. He splayed his fingers wide and the birds flew free. Nothing could stop his fall, or his yelling. Not until he hit the wall where the steps turned the corner.

The pigeons fluttered wildly in the stairwell, their wings clattering. Then they alighted on Tariq's unmoving form and all was quiet. Sorgan smiled.

Many of the houses Nathanael walked past were deserted, the doors locked, the windows shuttered. But others stood open, violated and looted. Poor leavings lay scattered in the dust outside—scraps of fabric, shards of pottery and glass. He bent and picked up a curious piece of wood, only to find it was a discarded toy, a little dolly, its limbs all twisted and broken. It didn't look as though he could repair it: a shame, or he would have given it to little Nima to replace her lost cat.

The tabby, Kiri, had disappeared a week ago. Nat had a pretty good idea of what had probably happened to it: you didn't live in a starving city without seeing people eating things they would never have considered edible in better times. He'd done his best to keep the little animal in the house, but of course you couldn't easily confine a cat, and when he'd tried Kiri took it as a challenge, fleeing between his legs out into the courtyard and climbing the vine up onto the wall. She sat there for a moment, watching him reproachfully, before disappearing onto the neighbours' rooftops, only to reappear at her usual time in the evening for food and petting. After that, he had given up and hoped the little cat would have the sense to avoid danger. Day by day Kiri had proven herself a skilful survivor, but Nima cried herself to sleep the first night the tabby didn't come home. The next day she made Nathanael walk the streets with her, calling its name. They even knocked on doors, with Nat making apologetic faces at the neighbours while Nima asked if they'd seen her cat, describing it in loving detail.

Some people were sympathetic, and one or two even gave the little girl a piece of food—bread made with ground date pits, a piece of dried fish—that they could barely afford to part with. But most were short with them, and a couple were openly derisive and angry. "A cat? If that's the most you've lost you're very lucky." One man even said, "I tell you, *habibi*, if we'd seen a cat, there'd have been kebabs that night!" After that house visit, Nima was very quiet.

Nathanael no longer walked near the central plaza, where the bazaar had once spilled into the square. The sight of the abandoned stalls, the empty crates and canvas covers, the shattered boulders, cratered ground and gaping reed roof over the *qissaria*, and the dust over everything simply depressed him too much. The little Henna Souq, where he had first encountered Zohra Najib, was all closed up: no one cared much about how they looked or how they smelled when they did not know where their next meal was coming from.

He was luckier than most: Rana and her father looked after Nima when he was working, in exchange for his treatment of Rana's little brother, who suffered from intermittent shivering fevers. These Nathanael could never quite eradicate, but he could at least relieve them with warming possets and tisanes. Rana's family also gave him small fish and crabs from time to time. They had also, till last week, provided Nima with fish heads and tails with which to feed Kiri.

Nathanael sighed. If it had not been for the crabbers and the fishermen at the quay, they would all have starved to death long ago, though even the little harbour was not safe from the Franj missiles. Only last week a boat had taken a direct hit and gone to the bottom, and any vessel attempting to slip out into the open sea was immediately set upon by the ships in the enemy blockade

Rana and her father lived in a row of little mud-brick houses close to the docks. It had been a poor area at the best of times, and now it was little more than a slum. He reached the crabbers' door and knocked. Sad to see doors shut, he thought: in times of peace folk were so much more trusting, in and out of each other's houses, sharing food and gossip, borrowing pots and ingredients, doors left wide open. Now it seemed people trusted their neighbours even less than their common enemy, the Franj.

"Hello! It's me, Nathanael!" he called, and Rana opened the door and ushered him inside.

"Look, Nat, look!" Nima held something out—an earthenware pot full of water. Nathanael took it from her and raised it to his lips.

"No, silly!" The child giggled so much she almost choked. "It's not for drinking, look, look!" Inside the pot there was a small, multicoloured fish swimming around in a dull, endless quest for the non-existent exit from its earthenware prison. "Rana says you can't eat this sort, so I'm going to keep it. But if Kiri comes home we'll have to hide it away or she'll eat it and get sick."

How long before she would forget the cat, Nat wondered, then felt ashamed of himself. Nima's adoration of the tabby was as ardent as his for Zohra: as a child, you didn't make the distinction between differing values of objects of desire.

He treated the boy, examining his tongue and his eyes, but found little sign of recovery. If he was honest, he did not think the lad would survive the summer, war or no war. But you couldn't take people's hope away from them, and so when Rana's father asked he said he was no better but no worse, which was the truth.

"Perhaps they're right to surrender," the crabber said, shocking him.

"What?"

The man shrugged. "A swimmer left for Salah ad-Din's camp this morning with another message from the commanders asking that they be allowed to call a truce and discuss terms."

"Another?"

"That's at least the second message. He sent back a flat no last time, and I don't suppose it'll be any different this time, more's the pity." The crabber paused. "I just hope the lad makes it, he looked so tired and thin—" Too late he stopped, and his daughter's face was closed and still.

To hear of the commanders of the city discussing the possibility of surrender filled Nathanael with a righteous fury: they had no right to decide the fate of the inhabitants of a city in which neither had lived for any time, to which they had no emotional ties. But to hear the crabber welcoming the idea sobered him. Perhaps, he thought—a rare admission—he was wrong.

On the way back to the Street of Tailors, he barely paid attention to Nima's chatter, and so wrapped up in his thoughts was he that he did not respond at first when his name was called. It was Nima who cried out, "It's Zohra, look, it's Zohra!"

Zohra Najib had obviously left the house in a hurry, for she came bare-headed, her black hair snaking like the Medusa's. She clutched Nathanael's arm. "You have to come, quickly. You have to help me, Nat. There's no one else I can ask."

It was immediately clear that there was no doctor on earth who could do anything for Tariq. He lay in a heap at the foot of the stairs on the first landing, his neck at such an angle that it was obvious it had been broken. Sorgan sat at the top of the stairs like a statue.

"We have to get him out of here, hide him," Zohra said.

"I killed him," Sorgan added, with what seemed to Nathanael to be gloating satisfaction. "He hurt the pigeons. He hurt Zohra, too."

Nat felt the old fury fire through him. Damn the man: he wished he'd killed him himself.

"Hush!" Zohra implored her brother. "You can't say that! What have I told you?" She gazed helplessly at Nathanael. "They'll take him away, put him in gaol, maybe even hang him. After Mother and Aisa, and Kamal . . ." The amber eyes welled with tears. "People go missing all the time," Zohra said. "They slip out over the walls, giving themselves up as prisoners to the enemy, or trying to make it to Salah ad-Din's camp. And Tariq was never known as any sort of hero."

"They're going to ask questions anyway, my love."

"Yes, but without a body . . ."

Nat rubbed a hand over his face and sighed. "Let me see what I can do."

The area of the city near the east gate was worse than anywhere he had yet been. The houses were cratered, burned-out ruins, and in the midst of them a pair of huge mangonels had been set up, broken masonry from the houses used as ammunition to fire at the enemy over the walls. The sound of the enemy bombardment was loud here, and sometimes he could see clouds of mortar-dust blooming above the walls as their missiles struck.

"I'm looking for the smith, Mohammed Azri," he shouted to one of the soldiers on duty, but the man shook his head, and so did the next dozen people he asked.

But farther down the road he found the ruins of a forge and a young man salvaging bits of pig iron.

"I'm looking for Mohammed Azri," Nat said.

The man straightened up, extended a hand. "I am his son, Saddiq. We've moved the smithy to a safer place." He was young and tall, gaunt in the face. The way his robe hung on him suggested he had been well-muscled before the famine took hold.

He led Nat through alleys towards the centre of the city, to a street that led onto the bazaar. Of old, it had been a tranquil area, occupied by bookbinders and perfume-sellers. The minaret of the Friday Mosque rose up behind it. Now, there was the usual array of boarded-up doors and stalls and a strong smell of burning. They made their way through a throng of folk and workers ferrying barrows of wood and charcoal.

In the space occupied by the new smithy, soot-covered boys fed the fires and wielded the bellows while a group of men heated metal and hammered it out. A pile of household pots, horseshoes and braziers were being fed into the fires to emerge as arrowheads, swords and spearheads, which were, as they cooled, gathered eagerly by waiting soldiers and garrison volunteers. They did not look like people ready to give up the fight, Nathanael thought; they looked impatient and determined. He recognized the tallest of the hammering men as the one who had carried an unconscious Nima back to their home after the missile strike had killed her mother at the baker's.

Nat hung back, waiting for a chance to speak with the smith, watching the rhythmic rise and fall of the hammers, the searing brightness of the fanned flames. But after a while one of the men missed his blow and stood swaying; then he went down like a felled ox. Others dragged him away from the heat of the furnace and the hammering recommenced.

Nathanael gathered himself. "I'm a doctor, let me through."

The man was not unconscious, but he was groggy. "Have you eaten anything?" he asked him at last, and the fallen man cocked an eye and croaked out, "Have you?"

There was not much humour to be had in the midst of the siege, but that provoked some laughter. Someone brought the man a piece of flatbread and some lentil paste, another gave him water, and soon he was back on his feet again.

Mohammed Azri came to Nat's side. "I recognize you," he said. "You're the doctor's son."

"I'm the doctor now."

"Have you come to claim the favour I owe you?"

He admitted as much. "You may not want to do it when I tell you what it is."

Mohammed Azri led him away to the back of the smithy where a small brazier bore a steaming samovar, and he poured out a bowl of some pale brown liquid. It did not taste like any tea Nat had ever drunk, but he sipped it gratefully. He kept his explanation to a minimum and the smith asked few questions.

"I will do this thing because it is you who asks," he said at last. "I will meet you by the Little Mosque in the small hours."

Nathanael had straightened Tariq's limbs before they stiffened, but even so it took all five of them to move the body, they were all so weak and the corpse so heavy.

"He has not stinted himself during this siege." Saddiq grimaced.

Zohra gave a bitter laugh. "No. Tariq did not believe in stinting himself."

Baltasar, wakened by noises that echoed off the tiled walls, cried out from his bed, and Zohra ran to give him more of the valerian Nathanael had brought to quieten him. After that he slept till past first prayer, by which time the shrouded corpse of Tariq Assad was in its final resting place, the open grave near the east wall where all the poor dead were being interred. Nat stared into the mass grave, then around at the desolation, feeling a long-denied anger. This was his city, his home. These were good people, decent people, who had not sought conflict but were simply caught in the middle of two warring forces.

As they came away, the smith bowed his head and intoned, "O Allah! Grant this man protection and have mercy on him, and pardon him, and wash him with water and snow and hail and cleanse him of faults as a white cloth is cleansed of dirt."

Nathanael gazed at Zohra, who held his glance for one piercing moment, then looked down at the shrouded body. "I am a widow," she whispered. She started to tremble.

Then Sorgan's stomach grumbled loudly. Saddiq clapped him on the shoulder. "That's the trouble with being a giant," he said. "It sounds so much emptier than anyone else's stomach."

"It is emptier," Sorgan complained.

Mohammed Azri turned to Zohra. "I will bid you farewell, lady."

She clasped his hand. "I do not know how to thank you."

He looked at her hulking brother, then back to her upturned face. "I do. We are in desperate need of help at the forge. Could he help us sometimes?"

"You should ask him."

The smith smiled at Sorgan. "Tell me, young man, do you like fire?"

Sorgan's eyes lit up. "I love fire."

28

❁

They had been telling me about Hell all my life. From those first weeks when I entered the Priory of St. Michael on the Mount as a wild boy, they'd set about beating it into me. In the book of Saint Matthew, Hell is described as a place where both soul and body could be destroyed. Acre defined the idea of Hell for me now.

Outside the walls there was a constant background noise of souls in agony, always an unquenchable fire was burning, and at night a storm of darkness. What it was like inside, God alone knew. We had been battering at the walls by night and day, hurling Greek fire over the battlements. If it went on much longer soon there would be nothing left of Acre but a burned-out shell. And maybe that was what they wanted, those kings we fought for: for, like angels armed with savage weapons, they were merciless in their destruction.

King Richard was so determined to take the city before the French king, Philip, that he was defying even the illness that ravaged him and had risen from the bed to which he had been banished by his doctors. He'd had a kind of hurdle-shed constructed for himself, and from there—too weak to stand upright—he would lie on his back to fire his mighty crossbow, and thus claim the glory.

Meanwhile, King Philip's diggers had burrowed almost through the thickness of the wall beside the Accursed Tower, and, having set fires below the tower, they had weakened the structure. But still it had not fallen, and still the defenders held firm. And so the bombardment went on.

Our king declared that he would personally pay a week's wages to any man who brought back a stone from the wall with his own hands. Four gold bezants! The heralds who brought the decree were almost trampled in the rush that ensued. Of the troupe, only Quickfinger succeeded in the task—by stealing a stone from a man who was having trouble dragging his boulder out of the trench with him, and running back through the smoke to claim his reward. Ezra was stationed with the other bowmen, and so I had seen little of her these past weeks; Little Ned spat at the idea of putting himself in harm's way—"You can't spend your wages in Hell, can you?"; and Hammer had stared at the herald as if he wanted to kill him.

I just remembered what the Moor had once told me. "In the end, *habibi*, money has as little value as the dust of the earth."

I was assigned to supply boulders to God's Stone-thrower, the massive trebuchet King Richard had taken over. It was trained exclusively on the wounded area around the Accursed Tower, while the other two great machines—in the control of the Templars on one side, and the Hospitallers on the other—weakened neighbouring parts of Acre's walls. Some of the stones we brought were huge Sicilian boulders that had come off the king's ships. It took several men to roll and to load them. It was easier but less effective to bring the rocks out of the damaged walls themselves, those that had been wrenched by hand by the reckless and the desperate and piled up in the king's camp, worth more than their weight in gold.

One way or another, we kept up a constant barrage, but the city's garrison maintained their defence: we had to shelter from arrows and bolts, from stones from their own machines, and worst of all from the fire pots they lobbed. Time and again we beat out the flames and avoided getting the sticky substance on us. When men were set afire there was nothing anyone could do save to save them from torment. Their corpses burned on and on, like wickless candles, till there was nothing left of them but stench. I had also seen others, still burning, fed into the trebuchet bucket and hurled over the walls along with the other missiles. The first time I'd witnessed this, I could not believe my eyes, but within a week I was inured to it: just another atrocity among so many others.

A man could not take too much of this. I had seen men go mad and run for the sea, tearing off their armour and clothes, shouting that they would swim home. I would have joined them, had I been able to swim. I had also seen figures hurl themselves from the walls of the besieged city. God knew what the conditions in there were like that they would choose to destroy themselves so.

But then the next day the strangest thing happened. In the middle of the day, quite without warning, the sun disappeared and darkness fell across the battlefield: an unsettling, penumbrous light like no other I had ever experienced. Some men fell to their knees and started praying. Others, who had been watching the sky as this odd phenomenon occurred, were struck blind. People were crying out—on the walls, as well as down in the field—calling on their gods for mercy.

"God is angry with us!"

"We are all damned!"

But then, just as quickly as it had left us, the light returned, flooding the heavens. The Bishop of Salisbury raised his hands to the skies. "And the sun shall be turned into darkness and the moon into blood before the coming of the great and awesome day of the Lord!"

Hammer screwed his face up in disgust. "Moon of blood tonight then, lads."

We were reluctantly resuming our trebuchet duties when a page came running to fetch me. "John Savage. His lordship, Savaric de Bohun, demands your presence."

It was almost with relief that I followed him to Savaric's tent.

Unfortunately, the relief was not to last for long.

"Come with me, John," Savaric said. "We're going to see the king."

If you had presented the man in the great pavilion as King Richard of England to me I would have laughed in your face. That hale, dangerous lion who had crowned himself in London, where was he? The man who sat there, hunched among cushions, looked half his size, his eyes too bright in their hoods of bone, the bright red hair lank and dark. He stared at me when I followed Savaric inside his pavilion, and when given my name he leaned forward and gripped my arm with a clammy hand. Ginger hair sprouted from huge knuckles.

"You have to go into Acre, John Savage," he told me in a hoarse whisper, and when he drew his lips back to pronounce the city's name I could see the blood leaking from his gums. We were all ill, all reduced in body and spirit, but to see this monster of a king in such a state was a shock. I had to force myself back to his words.

"The darkness—it was a sign, a sign that the Saracens are preparing to destroy the True Cross. We have been sorely tried, but this is the great test. If we do not save His cross we will all be damned, and our war will fail. The Church does not pray for the damned soul, did you know?" He was rambling. I was terrified.

"I have a spy who comes from the city, and he knows where they keep the cross. He will guide you to it, won't you . . . boy, boy, what's your name? Come and meet John Savage."

A slight, dark lad came out of the shadows at the back of the pavilion and prostrated himself to the king in some strange oriental fashion. Then he got tidily to his feet and stood, hands at his sides, unblinking.

"Kamal, my lord. My name is Kamal."

He had large, black eyes and a delicate bone structure, and just the lightest fuzz of beard. In the chancy candlelight there was something about him that was unsettling: he looked more like a girl than a boy.

What could I say? You can't refuse a king—not to his face—and expect to survive it. I managed to bow and mumble some nonsense. But as soon as we were out of that tent again, I turned on Savaric.

"I'm not going into Acre to fetch out some old relic."

"You could make yourself a rich man, John."

I folded my arms. "I'm not doing it."

"I didn't want to resort to this, John, but . . . well, I would hate to have to explain to the king what happened to Geoffrey de Glanvill."

"It's hardly as if I was alone in that . . . venture."

"And whose word do you think they will believe, if it comes to that, John?"

I closed my eyes. I was a dead man, one way or another.

To my great surprise it was not difficult to persuade the troupe to go on this fool's mission: they'd all heard the tales of the gold squirrelled away by the Saracens in the city treasury, the jewels and coins. Such an audacious mission restored their sense of being the canny outsiders conning the gullible and the slow. After that, the talk was all of treasure and what they'd do with it: the women they'd buy, the land they'd own, the houses they'd build and, most of all, the food they'd eat.

"Roast ox, every night," Ned said. "Smoking and hissing over a fire with two well-built wenches to turn the spit."

"Four," grinned Quickfinger, "stripped to the waist, because of the heat."

"Swan," said Will. "Stuffed with all sorts of other birds, like the king's feast you told us about."

I was made to rehearse yet again the entire contents of those laden tables while the troupe groaned and sighed and made themselves impossible promises. In the end, once they'd exhausted their fantasies, it was Quickfinger who asked the only sensible question.

"How do we get out? Getting in, easy enough. But getting out, laden wi' treasure?" He waggled his eyebrows meaningfully.

"There's a boat," I said, and couldn't blame them for being dubious. I certainly had been when Savaric explained it to me.

"All you have to do is to get out past the Tower of Flies, the tower that guards the city's harbour," he'd said. "Get past the harbour chain and one of our ships will pick you up from there. I've already paid the captain a retainer."

"You make it sound so simple," I'd said to Savaric.

He'd nodded earnestly. "But it is, my boy, it is! That's the beauty of it."

He was so convinced that he'd almost convinced me. Almost.

This time the message came with a swimmer, a young man much exhausted by his ordeal. Malek aided him into the sultan's war tent as the sun was dying. Bare-chested, he had patches of salt drying in a white crust on his skin, and all within took note of the stark geometry of his ribs. His prostration was more a collapse than a courtesy.

Salah ad-Din raised him up with his own hands and took the oilcloth-wrapped message from him. Baha ad-Din read it aloud:

"To our beloved sultan, Salah ad-Din Yusuf ibn Ayyub, Commander of the Faithful and hope of Islam, greetings from your faithful servants Saïf ad-Din Ali al-Mashtub and Beha ad-Din Karakush. It pains us to tell you that we are so utterly reduced and exhausted that we have no choice but to surrender the city. If you do not effect anything for our rescue, we shall offer to capitulate and make no condition but that we receive our lives."

The sultan—never outfaced by anything—put his head in his hands. When he raised it up again, he looked deathly, his skin grey and his bright black eyes dulled. Malek felt a sharp pang of sympathy for his commander.

"Do they not know that we have received reinforcements?" Salah ad-Din asked of no one in particular. A few days before, more troops from Sinjar and Egypt had ridden in, followed by Ala ad-Din, the Lord of Mosul.

"My lord, they will surely have seen the levies arriving," his brother, Al-Adil, said quietly. "But we have not yet been able to break through the enemy lines, and the emirs will be aware of that failure."

"The Emir of Shaizar will arrive imminently, and my nephew, too, will soon be with us. They must hold out, just a little longer. They must!" The sultan turned to the messenger. "Are you able to swim? No, don't answer that. I know you will say you can, but it is clear to me that you are exhausted. We will send a pigeon."

There was a quiet muttering at the back of the tent, then Imad al-Din coughed politely. "I am afraid to report, sire, that we have no pigeon to send. None have arrived from the city this day and there are none roosting in the cote."

The sultan took up his copy of the Qur'an and opened it at random. He read silently for a moment, then quoted aloud, "'Do they not look at the birds, held poised in the midst of the air and sky? Nothing holds them up but the power of Allah. Verily in this are signs for those who believe.'" He looked up and now his face was serene. "We will have faith and wait for the pigeons to arrive."

Sure enough, two birds settled on the cote just after sunset.

The cavalry sprang into their saddles, and Malek patted Asfar's flank. For once they were not holding back to watch the battle from on high. This time they would ride at the forefront of the army, and the sultan and his brother, in their desperation, would lead them.

Down from the hill they charged, one battalion after another, with the drums thumping and the trumpets blaring, with the orange silk banners flying and with cries of "For God and Akka!" The noise of their coming was immense, a thunder in the ground and in the air, and seeing their attack, the Franj manned their defences determinedly, setting flights of arrows to fall upon them, spears and pikes to keep the cavalry at bay. Again and again the Muslim army attacked, and every time they were repulsed, the Franj infantry standing as solid as a wall.

The sultan rode tirelessly, as restless as a mother grieving for a lost child; tears stood in his eyes as he charged from battalion to battalion, urging his men on.

Malek saw a huge Franj warrior hold a parapet on the ramparts against all comers, although pierced by dozens of arrows. It was only when one of the *naft*-throwers hurled an ignited pot of Greek fire at him that the warrior fell, his body engulfed by flame. In response, the Christians killed several prisoners, covering them in Greek fire and hoisting them up on the ramparts that guarded their trenches, so that they burned like torches. Malek, horrified, said a prayer, but could not stop looking. There was a cry behind him and to his horror he saw his own people do the same with a Franj prisoner: the smoke from the two pyres mingled, rank and acrid, making Malek's eyes water. At least, that was the excuse he told himself for the tears running down his face. And all the time the great machines bombarded the city.

The archers darted in and out of the cavalry, sending flights of flaming arrows over the earth ramparts towards the stone-throwers and the soldiers who manned them, but the Christian archers who stood their ground seemed to have greater accuracy. One figure in particular, wrapped in a green cloak, took a bold stance atop the rampart, shoulder to the fore, a narrow target, and sent bodkin after bodkin into the ranks of the faithful from his odd long bow, each one unerringly finding its mark. Malek whirled his horse around, beating off enemies, but every time he looked back the archer was still there with a small forest of arrows planted in front of him, letting fly, bending, taking another bodkin, nocking it to his string. *What coolness*, Malek thought, half-admiringly. Then a Franj foot soldier came up under his sword arm and tried to haul him out of the saddle and his attention was returned to the crucial matter of staying alive. Swinging hard, he struck the man with his shield until he fell beneath Asfar's stamping hooves.

To his right, he could hear the sultan's war cry. He turned in time to see an arrow graze the commander's turban, carrying a clout of cloth with it as it flew, straight into the burning coal behind him. With horror, Malek saw his friend Ibrahim fall with a shout.

"Ibo!" he cried in despair. "No, Ibo!"

Digging his heels into Asfar's barrel, he surged towards his fallen comrade, but the press of bodies was too tight, the tide of the fighting too fierce: it was as much as he could do to keep his seat. Another arrow fell close to the sultan, then another. Malek looked up and saw clearly that the green archer was the culprit, again. Suddenly wild with anger and grief, he forced Asfar through the fighting, cutting a bloody path through the Franj infantry who swarmed towards him, his sword arm rising and falling in a fury all its own.

"For Ibo!" he shouted. "For Ibrahim!"

He soon found he was not the only one to have identified the green archer as a menace. Malek saw another man draw back his arm and then the graceful arc of the lance as it flew through the air and found its mark. The green-cloaked figure toppled with a scream.

That scream drove a bolt of ice down Malek's spine. Before he even knew what he was doing, he had spurred Asfar on towards the foot of the berm where the archer's body lay. He saw the figure try to rise, using its bow as a crutch. Bringing the chestnut around, he leaned down out of the saddle and grabbed the archer, hauling him up and over the horse's withers with an ease that surprised, and yet did not surprise. Then he turned and charged back through the ranks towards the sultan and his cadre.

He had never taken a prisoner before: as one of the burning coals, he had more pressing duties that banished thoughts of personal gain or strategic captive exchange, and by the time he caught up with his fellows he was already having second thoughts about his rash venture.

But Salah ad-Din looked at the figure draped over Asfar's shoulder and nodded his approval. "He wears the colour of the Prophet. God give him grace for he has fought valiantly, and if he must die let him do so in the ease of our hospital."

Twilight was falling, purpling the air, but still the Franj defence was fierce and the bombardment of the city continued. Wearily, the faithful drifted back to camp, called by the muezzin, retrieving their fallen comrades on the way.

The burning coals delivered the sultan into the waiting hands of his anxious physicians, but still he would not rest. He paced to the edge of the bluff and stared down at the city that he would soon lose, at the fires and the stone-strike besetting its walls, at the sea of Christian besiegers awaiting their chance to sack and rape, and tears made runnels in the dust on his sunken cheeks.

Dismissed, Malek led Asfar to the hospital tent. His captive still had hold of the deadly bow that had wrought such havoc and no one could persuade him to part with it. At last, a tall, dark man detached himself from the other caregivers and spoke to the archer quietly in one of the Franj languages. The archer's eyes went wide with shock and he tried to rise, but the other pressed him down gently and without struggle took the bow from his stiff fingers. The archer subsided, feebly pulling his bloodied jerkin close.

"You have done a good deed in saving this . . . man," the dark man said.

He had a western accent, Malek noted again, and for a moment wondered if that was why he had hesitated. But something in him knew it was not the reason.

"It's a woman, isn't it?" His eyes travelled over the archer's spare frame, lingered on the torso. There was no clue there, since the blood of men and women flows the same colour, but he knew he was right.

Half-moon eyes regarded him enigmatically. "Who knows what any of us are? We are just people, good and bad, women and men, strong and weak, believers and unbelievers—sometimes all at once. We waver constantly between the boundaries others set for us: none should judge another. But yes, this is Ezra, who once was an English woman called Rosamund, and a brave fighter in every sense of that word. Take her bow, for it is her pride and joy, and keep it safe while I treat her wound."

Malek took the bow in his hand. It was very different to the bows with which he was familiar, which were short and recurved, compact enough to use on horseback. This one was long and straight, as elegant as a woman. He looked from the bow to the woman on the pallet, taking in the set of her jaw, the smoothness of the exposed throat, the curve of her cheek, and felt a warmth rise in him that had nothing to do with lust. Suddenly, he felt intensely pleased that he had saved her from the battlefield, even though she had killed his friend.

He turned and found himself face to face with Ibrahim, his arm in a sling, his face split by a gigantic grin, one eye closed from swelling. They embraced like brothers. Over Malek's shoulder, Ibrahim caught sight of the green-cloaked archer. In two strides he was at her bedside, staring down.

"That is the devil who nearly killed the sultan!"

"The one that shot you, yes!" said Malek, feeling almost light-headed.

Ibo stared down at her. "I have sons older than this one." He looked to the tall man. "Will he live?"

"I think so, yes."

"Make sure he does." A new speaker: a familiar but unexpected voice.

Suddenly there were people prostrating themselves all around, foreheads touching the ground; even the groaning of the wounded stilled.

The sultan ignored them. "If I had an army of men as brave as this one, nothing would withstand it."

Ibrahim and Malek exchanged glances. How much braver did they have to be?

The sultan continued to gaze at the prostrate, barely conscious, archer. Then he frowned. A moment later, he bent and ran a finger along the archer's jaw, then withdrew his hand as if burned. "A woman," he said. He shook his head, disbelieving. "A woman?"

Ibrahim stared and stared. Then he laughed. "You see what I mean," he said to Malek, "about the strength of women?"

Now the sultan's physicians arrived, all a-bustle: Salah ad-Din had obviously outpaced them. They milled about the commander, tutting and fussing until at last, under their stern instruction, he removed his helm, turban and all, and they examined the damage impassively. The cloth was torn; the steel beneath scratched.

There was a general intake of breath. Then, *"Alhemdulillah!"* cried one of the physicians fervently. "All praise to Allah for preserving your life!"

"It seems my death is not yet written," the sultan said, exhaustion graven in the deep lines of his face, "though I would give it gladly to save Akka. But it will take a miracle now to give the defenders sufficient heart to hold on until my nephew arrives. A miracle."

The tall, thin man stepped forward. "If it's miracles you're after, I may be able to help."

29

✻

I went to look for Ezra to say farewell before my suicide mission into Acre, but she was nowhere to be found. I asked after her and people shook their heads. "Don't know, mate, haven't seen her since yesterday."

But one man took me aside. "I saw her fall."

I stared at him. "What do you mean 'fall'?"

"Big black horseman chucked a lance at her and she fell. Off the rampart."

"Show me where."

"No point. All the bodies have been buried."

I turned on my heel and ran to the hospital tent. But she wasn't there either, and the lad they led me to when I described Ezra looked nothing like her. Sick at heart, I trailed back to the others.

"No luck?" Quickfinger was sincere in his inquiry, but Little Ned gave a twist of the lips—a small satisfaction. I wished we'd never taken him on. Or that he'd never come back from the Haifa mission.

"No sign of her," I said.

Hammer looked stricken. "Not Ros—not Ezra," he said. "I can't believe it."

Red Will burst into tears.

"Christ's sake," said Ned, disgusted.

Quickfinger shook his head. "She can't be dead. Not Ezra. If she were, we'd know."

"You never 'knew' whether I was dead or not," Ned said sourly. "You all looked at me like you'd seen a ghost when I turned up."

"Like a bad penny," Quickfinger muttered. He turned his attention to me. "What time we off, then?"

"Hour after sunset," I said. "Be ready."

I tried to put all thought of Ezra out of my mind. Like Quickfinger, I could not imagine her dead. In any case, it hardly mattered, since we would surely be dead ourselves in a matter of hours.

Our quiet passage through the camp provoked little notice, but the mood of the troupe sank at the sight of the fierce fires burning within the walls, the ragged tumble of debris beside the Accursed Tower where the breach had been made the day before and the fierce defence that continued into the night as our forces pressed their advantage.

"What if the city falls while we're inside it?" Will asked nervously.

Quickfinger laughed. "We'll just have to run faster'n the rest of the bastards heading for the treasury."

"Aye, and get hanged for our pains," said Little Ned.

"You can go back now if you don't want to come," I told him sharply.

He gave me a nasty look. "What, and see the rest of you rich and lording it about? No thanks."

Kamal, the young spy who had been in the king's tent, led us past the north-east salient and around into the French quarter of the camp where Conrad of Montferrat had his pavilions before quitting the siege a week earlier, having got what he wanted. As soon as poor Queen Sibylla succumbed to the same illness that had carried off her girls, he had set about pressing his claim to the Jerusalem throne, and now had reinforced it by marrying her sister Isabella. After that, Acre didn't matter to him, he'd take the long view: sit back and let it stand or fall. "One cunt in, one out," as Hammer had put it succinctly.

Here we had to show Savaric's ring to pass beyond the camp, and I had to have a heated discussion with the Frenchman who tried to pocket it, which ended with some pushing and shoving until another officer recognized our livery.

"De Bohun," he laughed. "Upstart."

I didn't much feel like defending Savaric's honour, especially in French, so I ignored the insult.

"We're on a reconnaissance mission," I told him. "The boy says there's a weak area of wall down near the marsh. We've been sent to take a look."

He eyed Kamal suspiciously, then transferred his narrow gaze to me. "We use deserters for target practice round here," he said, showing his teeth.

"We're not deserters."

"If you're not back this way in an hour we'll come looking for you. We still have a horse or two. Don't think you can turn Turk," he sneered. "You may be happy to give up your foreskins, but you'll end up losing your heads." And he brandished something at me that looked suspiciously like dried ears threaded on a string, worn like a baldric across his chest. I wondered how I'd not noticed it before.

Once out of sight of the lines we darkened our skin with some gall-ink mixed with oil, donned the hooded cloaks the men of the region wore and wrapped lengths of coloured cotton about our heads—the boy showed us how. Under the cloaks we had sacks for the booty. We carried daggers in our boots and tucked into the back of our belts, and Little Ned had his throwing knives. The disguises took us back to our mumming days: we looked at one another and laughed. You'd not even have recognized Red Will under the soot and the scarf and the soot-darkened beard—even with his light eyes he looked like some sort of demon, till you saw his hands trembling.

While Kamal was rewinding Hammer's turban, which had already come undone, I took Quickfinger aside. "I don't trust him, but since he's the only guide we've got and none of us know the city or speak the language, we can't afford to lose him, so keep your eye on him. If he tries to run off—well, you know what to do."

He nodded.

At this point the city walls were too high to scale and the good land gave way to marsh that wouldn't support war engines. We could see the sea now, glittering dimly under the light of a quarter moon.

"What we going to do, then, swim?" Hammer asked the guide. I hoped he was joking; I had never learned.

The lad turned a blank, flat-lidded stare upon him, as unreadable as a cat's gaze. "No. Now you follow me, do as I say."

Hammer looked at me. "Can we trust him?"

"You can trust me." His expression did not change. "There is tunnel leading into what was Templars' Ward, from when city was held by the *Franj*."

A moment later, the sliver of moon fell behind the clouds and the night became darker. I shivered. This was madness, being led by a traitor into a besieged city in which the survivors had been starved down to the bone, hating the enemy with a fierce passion. *If they find us*, I thought, *they will kill us. And probably eat us.*

We had to feel our way along the wall, for we could not risk a light. Kamal located the tunnel and we ducked inside into utter darkness. It was so narrow we had to go in single file: first our guide, then me, then Quickfinger, Hammer, Ned and finally Will.

I have never liked enclosed spaces. It comes of living wild on the moors with no roof but the sky, and of being trapped in the chapel with the door shut and no way out. It was a relief to emerge on the other side, even if it was into an enemy town. We came out into some sort of cellar, cavernous but man-made. Even in the dark I could feel the space around me, and when I squinted I could just make out a great branching arch of brickwork overhead.

"Which way now?"

He pointed upwards.

We ran up stairs, our steps echoing forlornly through empty corridors and halls, and eventually emerged into a wasteland. All around were the shells of abandoned or burned out buildings, crumbling, weed-covered, blasted.

Kamal, shaken out of his usual torpor, gazed about, his eyes like the holes in the masonry. He muttered something to himself.

"What?"

"Everyone gone." He gestured to an uninhabited house on the right. Roofless, now; the door hanging by one hinge. "Bashar family lived there. And next Ahmed the shoemaker, wife and daughters." He turned at the junction with a narrow alley and paced towards it. It was lightless, lifeless. Not even a rat stirred.

We were all sobered: this was what a two-year siege reduced a city to. And in the background, a dull rumble, the attack on the walls went on.

Kamal had us put our hoods up and walk apart from one another so that if we were to encounter anyone we would be less conspicuous. "You two hold hands," he told Will and Quickfinger.

"Why?"

Kamal frowned. "Is what cousins do here."

"We aren't cousins," said Will, at the same time as Quickfinger muttered, "Fook that."

"Friends, brothers, cousins, what it matter?" The boy's eyes sparked with something—anger?—but in the end we left Hammer and Ned lurking at the back, with Will on his own in the middle.

Quickfinger and I walked alongside Kamal, who strode quickly, head down, as if he feared to be recognized. Why would a man leave his hometown, returning only as a traitor, to bring enemies within its walls? It was a question I should have asked before. But it was rather too late now.

We reached a junction where the road gave out onto a larger highway, and we got an up-close sight of the enemy. As yet we'd seen only their soldiers—you didn't have the luxury of taking in the humanity of their features when you were trying to avoid being split in two.

"They're like walking corpses," Red Will said in a horrified whisper.

Even Quickfinger was shocked. "I thought we had it bad."

I remembered what the Moor had said about lack of imagination being necessary to those who conducted a war, and suddenly I feel dirty and ashamed. That day I had eaten meal porridge and bean stew with a hunk of salt beef, a tankard of ale and some stale bread, and complained. I was part of a Christian army that had brought starvation to these people, and for what? Some golden city none of us had ever seen, heart of a religion that had done nothing but oppress us with a fear of punishment beyond death. In the face of such obvious suffering, going in to search for a bauble like the True Cross seemed an obscenity.

We found the gates to the citadel missing. "Taken to be melted down for weapons, mebbe," Quickfinger said.

"Where are the guards?" I whispered to Kamal.

He shrugged. "Dead. Or on wall."

"Who'd leave a great treasure unguarded?"

He glanced at me, and the quarter moon was reflected in his eyes so that he looked inhuman: like a demon or a risen spirit. "You cannot eat gold."

Kamal led us to a ramble of buildings that must once have been stables, judging by the stale, animal smell. Of the horses there was no sign—no doubt long since eaten. We crossed a yard strewn with wisps of old straw to a side door. Kamal pushed at it but it stayed closed. He ducked and put his eye to a small hole on the right, then took a hooked stick from his belt and poked it through, fiddled; then with a click we heard the latch lift.

We passed through arched doorways and along deserted corridors decorated with carved plaster friezes until we reached a staircase and heard voices. Kamal waved us back. We ducked inside the first darkened room, glimpsing opulence within: Turkish carpets, silk hangings, vases that gleamed in the gloom. There we waited, with the door closed to a crack. Soon light spilled along the bottom of the door; footsteps passed, the sound of them diminishing second by second until at last Kamal stuck his head out, then beckoned us to follow. At the staircase, once again he gestured for us to stay in the shadows while he checked the next floor. He ran fleetly up the steps without making a sound, disappeared down a corridor. We waited, trying to still our breathing. And waited.

I found myself frowning. Had he abandoned us?

"Little bastard," Quickfinger hissed. "Where is he?"

I put a finger to my lips and watched the balustrade above as if by sheer will I could make our guide reappear. At long last there was movement, and then Kamal waved us up, quickly, quickly. Up the stairs we went; even with care our boots were scuffing and our breath hissing. There were lights lit up there. Kamal led us past gorgeously decorated rooms stuffed with rich furnishings. Hammer and Ned stared in avariciously; Quickfinger licked his lips, looked shifty. One moment he was there, the next he had ducked inside, only to re-emerge seconds later with a fat silver candlestick in his fist. "Booty," he whispered cheerfully.

At last the boy stopped outside a pair of grand doors. "Wait here," he told us. "Guard door. Kill anyone who try come in."

He made to turn away, but I collared him. "What are you talking about? We're not here to kill anyone. Now, where's the treasury?"

"Let go. Do what I say, *keffir*, or I tell you nothing. You do what I say, guard door while I kill the eunuch, then I take you down find your filthy relic."

I did not know what he meant by the word "eunuch." I gave him a hard shake. "You kill anyone here and we'll have the entire garrison down on our heads! Get us to the treasury and then you can go about your own bloody business."

"Take hands off me, dirty infidel!"

"Why, you little bastard!" Suddenly Quickfinger had a knife at Kamal's throat.

The knife seemed to give the boy strength. He twisted like a rat and was out of my grip and into the room.

Of all the chambers I had seen, this was the richest—candles and sconces illuminated pillars joined by horseshoe arches, and at the far end of the chamber were two men. One lay on the couch. He was fat: even recumbent, his belly stuck up like a hill. The other was pressing a cloth over his eyes, bent over him, his back to the door. Neither saw Kamal as he darted out of the shadows. From one pillar to the next he ran, ducking behind carved furniture, slipping between billowing silks. A glint as something caught the candle-light: from somewhere two daggers appeared in his hands, even though he had been searched thoroughly before we left. I recognized the weapons—Little Ned would be feeling two blades lighter.

I opened my mouth but the shout that echoed through the room was Kamal's: a warbling battle cry. As he launched himself at the man on the couch, the other man turned. Seeing the assassin, he threw himself between Kamal and the man on the couch, hands grabbing for the daggers. He caught one wrist, but the assassin's second hand snaked out of his grasp. With a twisting move as elegant as an acrobat's, Kamal bent away from the man who had got between him and his target. His free arm arced down and in a flash embedded the blade in the other's side. Connected now at two points, the pair staggered together in a clumsy dance. A tray clattered off a side table. The man on the couch sat up, groaning, pulling the cloth from his face. Seeing the assassin tangling with the man who had been tending him, he yelled fit to wake the dead.

"Shit!" said Little Ned. "That's done for us." He turned and legged it down the corridor, and the rest of the troupe pounded after him. But without our guide, what chance had we of finding the cross, let alone getting ourselves out of this maze of a city?

Cursing, I strode into the room. I made it to the first set of pillars in time to see the fat man leap from the couch with far greater agility than any man so corpulent had a right to possess. From somewhere, a scimitar had appeared in his hand and it scythed down.

"No!" I shouted.

But it was too late: as the wounded man tried to hold Kamal at bay, his hands scrabbling at the assassin's wrists, blood pouring from him, the blade of the scimitar sheared through the muscles of the boy's back, and down he went, with the other man beneath him.

I came to a dead halt and the fat man stared at me, now resembling not at all a soft glutton, his eyes like agates. Without taking his gaze off me, he kicked the assassin hard. Getting no response, he set a foot on the body and jerked his sword free and pushed the corpse so that it rolled off the dying man, who tried to rise. He got as far as his knees before crumpling so bonelessly that I heard his head strike the floor.

I started to back slowly away, my eyes flitting from the bodies and the spreading pool of blood to the fat man's scimitar. Then I heard voices behind me and turned to find two large, bearded men coming through the door.

The fat man cried something that sounded like "*Hash shash een!*" and the men drew their swords.

I reached around for the dagger in my belt and it got caught up in the cloak. I never was any sort of fighter. By the time I had wrestled it clear they were on me, and in any case, what could a man with a small knife do against trained soldiers wielding long blades? But as the first one raised his scimitar to cut me down his expression changed from violent intent to shock, and then he collapsed at my feet. As if in a dream, I noticed a knife in his back. A moment later the second soldier was clutching his head. Quickfinger grabbed me by the arm and hauled me away. In his other hand he carried a bloodied candlestick. Behind him was Little Ned, grinning savagely, the last of his throwing blades at the ready. This he hurled at the fat man coming for us with his scimitar. Whether it struck him or not I had no idea; we bolted for the doors. Once outside, Ned slammed them shut, and Quickfinger thrust a spear he had got from somewhere into the frame, barring them from opening from the inside. "This way!" he shouted at me as I stood there like a sleepwalker.

We ran pell-mell down corridors and steps, feet slapping on the stone, no subterfuge left to us. At the bottom of a staircase we found Will and Hammer.

"More guards that way!" Hammer shouted, pointing.

"Down," I said, remembering the assassin's words. "We go down."

Hallways lined with columns, shadows between, doors closed and open, but the chambers all appeared empty: where was everyone? We turned a corner and suddenly there were rough-hewn steps leading down into darkness.

"Stay here," I told the others.

At the bottom of the flight was a thick wooden door with an ornate handle. I set my hands to it, expecting it to be locked, but it gave before me and I fell inward, landing on my knees in the gloom. I looked around, my eyes adjusting quickly: a jumble of boxes, sacks, chests, fallen statues, indistinct objects.

On hands and knees, I made my way farther in. The first box I opened contained what felt like chunks of crystal. The second was empty except for a spill of coins across its base. The third yielded a casket full of bones. Christian relics: my mouth twisted in a wry grin. I made my way back to the stairs, where Quickfinger was looking down expectantly.

"We're going to need some light."

We'd passed a lit sconce in the previous hallway: Hammer slipped off, and we saw the light of the liberated torch jagging across the walls as he came running back. The other three followed him down the steps.

"Not you," I told Will, placing a restraining hand on his chest. "You stay here and keep watch."

"Why me?"

"I trust you to keep your eyes open," I lied. I knew the others would disobey me. "Give me your sack. We'll fill it for you—you'll not lose out."

He gave it up with bad grace and went back up the stairs.

By the time I re-entered the ill-named treasury, Hammer had stuck the torch in a tall vase and was opening chests at random— swearing because they were empty, or all but. Quickfinger kicked a statue and its arm fell off with a clatter. Little Ned ferreted around silently. On and on we searched, feverish in our disappointment. But a few minutes later at the back of the room I heard a cry: "By 'eck, Enoch Pilchard, you're a rich man!"

We crowded around the chest he had forced open and gazed in at the tumble of chalices, dishes and monstrances, church candle- sticks, caskets and something that looked like a crozier. These were surely the treasures sacked from Jerusalem the Golden.

While the lads stuffed their sacks, I went from chest to chest, feeling my way between the boxes, against the walls, where there was no light. I had reached the farthest corner of the chamber when I felt a sudden hot pain against my throat. Somehow, without noticing, I had broken the crystal that enclosed the Nail of Treves, and either a shard of the casing or the nail itself had caught in the fabric of my tunic and turned inward, pricking me hard. When I looked down, I saw a bundle wrapped in sacking, jammed against the back wall. Pulling aside the rough cloth, I saw gold gleam through the gap.

"Bring the torch!"

Light jumped and flared. I unwound the sacking and gasped. Huge jewels embedded in a thick casing of gold within which, visible at the shorn ends, was wood. Not new, blond wood, neatly sawed, but gnarled, dark wood almost black with age, close-grained, jagged and lighter where it had been roughly broken off. No one would wrap gold around a bit of old wood, unless . . . ? Feeling a sudden superstitious fear, I drew back.

Quickfinger, Little Ned and Hammer stared over my shoulder.

"Aye, that'll do," Quickfinger said. The torchlight reflecting from the gold, from the rubies and the pearls, illuminated his expression of awe. He fell to his knees with his palms joined and whispered, "Sweet Jesu, forgive me my sins, of which there are many, Christ who was nailed to the cross to save our souls, have mercy on this sinner . . ." over and over, and for a moment—just a moment—I became a believer.

Little Ned broke the spell, kicking Quickfinger on the thigh. "You soft bugger, get off your knees." He looked at me. "Where's the rest of it? You could hardly crucify a man on that, could you? Not unless he were a dwarf."

"It looks as if it's been broken up," I said, feeling uneasy. I didn't want to touch it. I fought down my superstitious side: we had a job to do. "Come on, help me wrap this thing. We need to get out of here."

But even as I bent towards it, I hesitated once more. I, even I, felt something like belief tremble through me, if only for a moment. But then the candle flame guttered and I could see that it was just a piece of wood jollied up in precious metal, and when I bent to run my hand over it, I felt nothing special. I felt a profound disappointment, a falling away, like stepping into an unseen hole. Didn't I know well enough there was no magic in this world: just grit and grime and blood and fakery? *Come on, John,* I told myself fiercely. *Get out of here, give the wretched thing over to good King Richard and you'll be made for life, a hero, a rich man.* Yet I kept seeing the pool of blood spilling upstairs in the rich chamber.

Quickfinger gave me that crazed grin of his, the one he used to fox those he robbed. "By 'eck," he said. "We found the fookin' needle in the haystack!"

With the cloth covering up the gold, the remnant of the cross looked nondescript, but when I hefted it, by God it was heavy! I staggered and almost fell. It was almost as if it did not wish to be moved, like a mule that had dug its heels in, or a recalcitrant dog. The others were too busy cramming precious objects into their sacks to see my difficulty, and by the time we made it back up the steps we were all similarly laden.

No one stopped us as we ran through the citadel corridors. We emerged into the darkness of the gardens and still there were no guards. "Don't run," I told the troupe. "Don't draw attention to yourselves." We drew our cloaks around us and walked with our heads down into the streets.

There was hardly anyone around. At a crossroads we came upon a child by the side of the road; as we passed he looked up, automatically put out a hand, begging. He said something in a high, reedy voice, and Red Will turned around and, digging into his sack, pulled out a charger of pure silver and thrust it into the boy's hands.

"What the hell are you doing?" demanded Little Ned, glaring at him as if he would like to kill him.

Quickfinger cuffed Will around the head. "You soft idiot. He weren't beggin' for treasure, he were beggin' for bread."

The child stared uncomprehendingly at the shining item, then cast the silver plate into the dust. A woman picked up the charger and shouted at us, and angry-looking people began to appear out of the shadows. A man grabbed Red Will and pulled his hood down, exposing his light eyes, and suddenly there was a crowd, pushing and shouting. Someone wrested the sack of booty from him and upended it, gold and jewels spilling across the ground. A few people dropped to their knees, even in their starvation lured by the tawdry thrill of gold, but the rest were intent upon the interloper.

I saw Hammer clutch the dagger at his waist, but then he seemed to think better of it and, without a word, turned and walked smartly away.

Red Will cried out. The crowd was pushing him from one to another now, grabbing at his clothing. There was the sound of cloth tearing and I saw his pale skin gleaming. "*Franj!*" someone shouted, and there was a scream, and Will went down in a flurry of fists and knives.

With a cry of "Enoch Pilchard!" Quickfinger launched himself into the fray. He had the crozier in one hand, a dagger in the other. Like a whirling demon he set about the attackers and the crowd parted before his fury, then closed in around him.

30

They beat us with sticks and whatever else came to hand, then surrounded us and pushed us through the streets and up onto the ramparts, screaming at us in their guttural language. They were thin—so thin—but hatred gave them strength as they pushed people out of the way, shouting at the tops of their voices to be heard over the hellish noise. Quickfinger was in front of me, the pre-dawn light making a silver corona of his wild frizz of hair. Little Ned stumbled along beside me, swearing and lashing out. I looked behind me, and there, unconscious, carried by his hands and feet, his long, thin body making a bow, his tangled red hair trailing in the dust, was Will. A rusty stain spread across his robe; the hilt of a dagger protruded from his side.

"Will!" I cried.

Someone grabbed hold of Ned and shoved him at a team of men loading rocks into the missile-basket of a massive catapult. The officer—at least he seemed to be the man in charge—looked at us. There was no fellow-feeling in his expression, just a sort of exhausted mirth, as if he were enjoying a joke with the powers that be at our expense.

Ned fought like a demon, but they knocked him over the head and piled him unceremoniously into the sling of the trebuchet, on top of its load of rocks. "For fook's sake!" Quickfinger breathed. "They're going to chuck him over t'wall."

I had not believed they would do it. I had seen corpses and body parts of animals and men sent over their walls by our own catapult men, hurtling overhead to burst and spatter on the ochre stones of the city, spreading brains and gore and disease where they landed. But I had never seen a living being hurled to destruction. I hadn't much liked Ned, but to die like this—streaking towards your death, terrified and powerless in the face of the inevitable, agonizing obliteration—was something I would wish on no man. And yet, when they released the mechanism and Ned's screams trailed away into the general cacophony, I could not look away.

As Ned arced towards the Christian lines, they started hauling on the winding mechanism of the trebuchet beside it, drawing back the counterweight. I shrank reflexively. It was Red Will they handed forward. They slung him unceremoniously into the sling, and I prayed silently he would not awaken suddenly to his awful fate.

Quickfinger broke free of his captors and confronted them like a wild animal, hands like claws, curses spilling from his mouth. "You bloody bastards, leave him be!" It did no good: he was soon held back. When the sling was released for a second time, he wept and bowed his head, and started to recite the Lord's Prayer.

I had never been able to pray without feeling myself a hypocrite, until then. I watched as Will soared gracefully, the rising sun making an angel of him, illuminating his billowing robe as if he had unfurled invisible wings. On reaching the top of its arc, Will's body plunged towards the darkness of the Christian camp. Then I lost him in the distance and the gloom. Any last cry he might have made was swallowed by the racket of the great engine as it rocked and recoiled.

They came for me next. I bit and scratched. I used every trick I'd ever learned, but none of them had ever done me much good—in the monastery on the Mount; beaten by the mob in London—and of course they did me no good now. Up into the catapult basket they hauled me until I was sitting astride a great boulder like some champion on his tourney horse. I stared out over the walls to the beauty before me—of the Christian army campfires punctuating the gloom, the red eye of the sun peeping over the distant hills. Was this the last sight my eyes would see? *Only if I close them now*, I told myself with gallows humour.

But what in hell was that?

At the western edge of the battlefield, something stirred in the foothills leading from the Muslim camp. I shouted out and stared, and all of a sudden everyone was doing the same, craning their necks, pushing forward for a better view. I had the best view of all.

A green cloud had materialized on the outer reaches of our lines, accompanied by a blare of trumpets, a throb of drums and great explosions of light. On it came, gaining definition until I could see a band of charging horsemen enveloped in an uncanny cloud of green smoke, hundreds of them, in green cloaks, with the crescent banners of Islam flying from their lances.

All around, I could see our soldiers falling back in fear, abandoning their positions, some even abandoning their weapons. Many fell to their knees as if in terror and awe as the spectral horsemen careered past. Many died, seeming to realize too late that this strange green cavalry was more corporeal than they had imagined.

The defenders of Acre crowded forward, their hands raised as if to bless God. They beamed at one another, hugged each other, laughed, even danced.

"*Alhemdulillah!*" cried the man who was holding Quickfinger. He fell to his knees, pressed his forehead to the ground.

All around, the other soldiers were doing the same. There were a lot of cries of "*Allahu akhbar!*" They seemed to be praying.

I gazed out at the bizarre scene beyond the walls. What was I seeing? It defied the imagination, and yet, and yet . . . that green vapour . . . I had seen coloured smoke, and incandescent lights, and heard cacophonies like this before . . .

Quickfinger caught my arm urgently, hauling me from out of the trebuchet. "Wake up, man! Run!"

We stumbled down the stairs up which we'd been dragged into the deserted streets below just as the first rays of the morning sun crept into the city. We had lost all our treasure. All that remained to us was the wretched lump of wood jammed hard against my ribs. How I had managed to hold on to it through all this I didn't really know, given how cumbersome the thing was, but strangely it had felt lighter with every step we'd taken. Or maybe I'd been so distracted by our circumstances I'd paid it scant attention. I didn't even know why I was bothering to carry it any more, for it had caused the deaths of Will and Little Ned. I thought, *If we ever get out of this godforsaken place, King Richard can take his Wood of Life, his* lignum vitae, *and stick it up his royal arse.*

Wearily, I looked around. Ochre buildings everywhere in various states of ruin, a maze of streets, and downhill, impossibly far away, a glint of liquid silver. "There!" I pointed. "The sea."

Quickfinger shook his head. "Too far. Let's head back for the tunnel we came in by."

But the streets towards the north were filling with soldiery heading for the walls, no doubt to view the miraculous presence in the field beyond. At last we were forced to move downhill towards the sea after all, through ruined neighbourhoods and burned buildings, through abandoned marketplaces and open spaces gone to baked clay and dust. As we went, the cloaking darkness faded, and all of a sudden a wailing rent the air, right overhead. Shocked, I craned my neck towards the crying voice. Picked out by the first rays of dawn light was a man standing on the gallery of one of those tall spires they called minarets. He was not looking down at us but pointing out over the walls, and I realized that his raucous cries were not the usual melodic call to prayer but a summons to witness what he was seeing, what we had just seen for ourselves—the cloud of green horsemen charging out from the Muslim lines.

Suddenly a mass of people were surging up the hill towards us.

"Fook!" Quickfinger's eyes went wide with panic.

I grabbed him by the arm and bundled him ahead of me up some wide steps and into an open doorway, from which we watched the crowds pour past. I don't know what made me turn to look into the building. Perhaps it was the faint scent of roses . . .

Inside was a marble-floored hall, and through a tall, horseshoe arch at the back I glimpsed something that made my knees tremble. Without thinking, I stepped towards it.

Hard fingers hauled me back. "Where do you think you're going?" Quickfinger glared at me.

I found myself wordless, unable to frame even the thought to answer him. The scent of roses had become overpowering. I pulled away from him as though he were not there, my feet dragging me to the space beyond the horseshoe-shaped opening. And there it was. The vision in my head, the towering, arcaded pillars linked by a succession of beautiful pointed arches. And above them a sky of gold: a soaring, gleaming cupola, bounding an immensity of light. I staggered, and sat down, dizzied, the Moor's sonorous voice like a deep bell in my head: "A place where earth touches heaven" . . . and then I blacked out.

I must have lost consciousness for only a few seconds, for I came to with Quickfinger bent over me, fumbling at my cloak as if to find a heartbeat. His eyes were wet. It touched me that he should show such emotion for me: then I realized it was not my plight that had caused him to blink so. He had pulled aside the cloth and was gazing down in awe at the True Cross.

"Well fook me, John, I thought we'd lost the lot." All of a sudden his dagger was in his hand, and for a dizzying moment I thought he was going to stick me with it and leave me bleeding on the marble floor in the place of my visions. But instead he dug the point into the casing and prised out a red stone, which he held up so that all the light in the mosque seemed to funnel through it. His fingers closed over it, but I could still see the light between them, as if it had eaten the sun. "My fee," he said grimly, "for this fools' chase." He stashed it carefully away from prying eyes and hands, then helped me to my feet, and together we stumbled back through the marble hallway.

Outside, the streets were deserted, and I blessed the natural curiosity and superstition of people, which had always been our stock in trade, for taking them up onto the city walls and out of our path. We continued our passage towards the sea, keeping the rising sun over our left shoulders. Downhill we ran until at last we glimpsed a gleam between alleys stacked with empty crates, and there was the harbour, shining in the rosy light. There were little boats and skiffs aplenty, pulled up and overturned on the quay. We selected one, found oars and were beginning to push it down the ramp into the water when a voice behind us shouted, "Wait!"

Quickfinger spun, ready for a fight, but it was Hammer, belting towards us, his dark eyes wild with joy, the first time I had seen him smile since his twin died.

"I thought you were all dead!"

"Aye," said Quickfinger. "Didn't stick around to find out, I noticed." Then his long, pale face broke into a grin and he grabbed Hammer up and spun him around, losing his turban in the process. I swear the carpenter rattled—and when he was on his feet again I saw why: under the cloak was his bag full of ransacked gold and silver plate.

"Ha!" cried Quickfinger. "That's where me loot went, then."

We had just got the sack stowed in the skiff when there was another shout, not such a friendly one this time. Men were running towards us waving sticks and knives overhead, shouting threats.

The boat rocked dangerously as we leapt aboard and shoved off into the harbour.

"Can you row?" I shouted.

Quickfinger and Hammer both shook their heads. "But if it means getting out of here, I'll learn bloody fast!" Quickfinger grabbed an oar and set about throwing up enormous jets of water with it, to little effect. We made an untidy job of getting into any rhythm, not helped by Hammer squatting in the bow, screaming at us to hurry. I could already see the danger: my eyes were trained on the quay-side, where a dozen or so men were leaping into the little boats and coming after us, gaining all the time.

A huge splash a yard away sent a gout of water into our skiff as a lobbed rock just missed us. With a howl, Quickfinger dug his oar into the water as if hoeing carrots and immediately we skewed to the right and threatened to turn a complete circle.

"Give me your oar!" I roared at him and banished him to the stern. "Just lie low and don't move!"

It was hard work but terror lent me strength, and soon we were out of range of missiles from the shore and heading towards the open sea and the Tower of Flies jutting out from the end of the breakwater. Beyond it lay three warships: surely one of these was the vessel detailed to pick us up. I checked our course over my shoulder and then put all my effort into the rowing, but even so, it seemed the thin, dark men in their small fishing boats were catching us stroke by stroke.

"Oh God!" cried Hammer a few minutes later.

"What?" There was a splash away to my left. "What was that?"

"Crossbow," said Quickfinger succinctly.

I risked a look back and saw that we were heading too close to the tower. The red morning light twinkled on the helms of the men up on the tower battlements. This time I saw the crossbow raised, pointed right at me. It took every ounce of willpower I possessed to turn back to my task and ignore my coming death. I heard the quarrel whistling through the air towards me, and closed my eyes, even as I drove the oars into the water and heaved with all my might. There was a dull thud and a heavy vibration, and when I opened my eyes again a crossbow bolt stood in the stern between Quickfinger's splayed feet.

"We're never going to make it!" Hammer shouted. "Look, they're gaining on us!"

Over Quickfinger's shoulder I saw the little flotilla of boats coming right at us now, could make out the features of the two men in the leading skiff as they turned while they rowed, their sharp noses and dark beards jutting from beneath their head-wrappings.

With immense effort, I dug the right oar in and hit something hard. A rock? I stared down to see the dark outline of a massive chain just below the surface. The keel of our little boat grazed over it, and then we were free of it. My left oar skimmed the surface so that a silver feather of water flew off the top of the blade, and we skewed away from the Tower of Flies, across the bows of the pursuing boats and into the open water. I prayed the warships would see our plight and come for us, but they didn't appear to have seen us.

"Take my turban!" I yelled at Quickfinger, who just stared at me, mouth open like an idiot. "Unwind it and wave it to attract their attention."

I could see the nearest ship flew English colours, and that lifted my heart, but only for a moment, as there was a rough, shearing sound and a hole appeared in the cloth through which the sky shone for a second, and a clout of red fabric traced the arc of the crossbow bolt that then buried itself in the sea.

Quickfinger sat down again, looking ashen. And then suddenly there came a shout from the warship, and a moment later it was coming towards us, at a barely perceptible pace, until you saw the banks of oars rising and falling in what seemed from such distance a languid precision. I saw the men in the boats chasing us gesticulate and stop rowing; two even turned tail. Relief swept over me, but it was ill timed, for just as the warship hove into sight a bolt struck Quickfinger in the shoulder and knocked him overboard.

"Shit!" I shipped the oars and scrambled after him. There he was, just below the surface, yellow hair waving gently in the tide like some great sea anemone, a dark wash of blood blooming on the water. Bracing my chest on the side, I leaned over, reached down into the chill water, wrapped my fingers in his hair and hauled with all my might. Up he came like a cork out of a bottle, and as soon as he surfaced curses and water flew from his mouth with equal force. I did not let go. Together Hammer and I landed him like a huge fish. The bolt was lodged in the top of his shoulder. I didn't think it would kill him, but he was paler than I had ever seen him.

Even so, as soon as he could reach it he swarmed up the rope ladder the warship dropped for us, using one hand and the crook of his elbow, and his feet like monkey's hands, as if Paradise awaited at the top. Between us, Hammer and I managed to get the treasure sack, the cross and ourselves onto the ladder, despite the chop of the waves carrying the skiff away from under us, and the rope bucking and snaking like a live thing. Falling over the side of the ship onto that solid deck made me feel like weeping with relief.

This euphoria was not to last long. Barely had we confirmed our identity to the captain—a ruddy-faced man who stood as four-square as a bear set to worry terriers—when there was a scream of "'Ware Greek fire!"

Looking up, I saw one of the warship's great sails catch, and within seconds it was blazing with a heat so fierce I could feel it scald my face half the deck away. The captain ordered men up the mast to cut the sail down and dump it overboard, but it was already too late: the flames were running from top to bottom of the sheet, ravenously searching for more solid fuel to feed upon. I saw a man beat at the fire that touched the deck and come away with his hands aflame, then his face and hair as he beat at himself in panic. The sail came crashing down a moment later, to be shovelled overboard, along with a sailor caught up in the lines and burning like a torch, and suddenly all was mayhem.

We had come within range of the Tower of Flies' ballistas: the soldiers of the Muslim garrison were hurling fire pots at us—no doubt delighted to have a target to aim for after weeks of inactivity—and now two more landed, spraying their lethal contents across the deck.

"Sand!" the captain roared. Men staggered across the deck to spill sacks of sand over the tarry mixture, but although it smothered the flames for a few seconds, nothing could quench them. They burned with a salty sea-flame—green-blue, blue-green—

"Christ!" I experienced a sudden hallucinatory flashback of the smell of burned chemicals.

Quickfinger turned a questioning face to me.

"That green smoke we saw around the Muslim cavalry galloping towards the city? I've seen it before. Remember those experiments on the road to Exeter?" In my mind's eye I saw the Moor blowing on his chemical compounds, coaxing them to life as they cast weird green light on the sharp planes of his beautiful face.

Quickfinger's expression was a picture of amazement. "The Moor! Well fook me sideways," he said at last. "Now that's what I call a reet good miracle."

There was a scream behind us. Turning, I saw the green flames bursting back into greedy red life, and soon there were holes in the planking through which you could glimpse the lower deck and the rowers beneath, screaming and scrambling as gobbets of the Greek fire dripped down upon them.

The captain sent men to whip them back to work. "If we don't move out of range we will all perish!" he shouted at them, but the sight of the enemy fire eating its way through everything it came in contact with was too terrifying for logic to prevail, and within minutes all the rowers had abandoned their oars and were running in all directions, many with their clothes and hair afire. The stench took me back to that day on the battering ram when Acre's defenders had rained Greek fire down on us. At least on solid ground there had been somewhere to run—as Quickfinger had done—but here there was only the sea, a great stretch of deep, dark water, between us and the other warships, who were keeping their distance. And even that wasn't safe, for where the fire pots hit and shattered, the liquid they contained merely floated on the surface and burned and burned, creating murderous islands of fire that crept to join with one another.

Soon there were men choosing the sea over the doomed ship. I saw that those who dived off in order to swim beneath the burning surface and come up farther out survived. But I knew I could not do it.

Hammer had no such hesitation. Without a word he clambered up onto the side and leapt off, vanishing from sight beneath the inky waves below.

Quickfinger turned a long, lugubrious face towards me, and with his good arm reached for my hand. "You saved my life, John. For about ten minutes." He gave me his lopsided grin. Then he reached into the treasure sack, selected a likely piece and stuffed it down inside his tunic. "Come on, lad. Time for another unlikely escape."

"I can't swim."

"Hold on to me. Reckon I can swim well enough for two, even wi' only one arm."

I shook my head. "I'll drown us both." I mustered a wobbly smile. "You go."

He regarded me sadly. "Aye, well, I'll see thee in Paradise, John. It's been . . . interesting."

And then he was gone with a great splash. The dandelion head showed for a moment amid the roiling water and smoke, and then sank without trace. I strained my eyes to watch for his re-emergence somewhere beyond the chaos but saw nothing.

The hills of the far land stretched hazy and serene beneath a blue sky indifferent to the fates of men. Somewhere up there was the Moor. My heart yearned towards him with such force I almost cried out. Had I been able to fly, I would have made my way up there as fast as an arrow, calling his name. Except that I did not know his name. The absurdity of that almost made me laugh, even as I raked those distant hills with my helpless gaze. But at that moment a great cloud of choking black smoke came billowing up from the lower decks and engulfed me, obscuring my view like a personal message: I would never see him again, not in this life.

Why had I not followed him that day in Rye? I should have gone with him, wherever he went, told him my feelings could not be denied, that I would travel to the ends of the earth just to be by his side. I had not understood my heart then, fool that I was. But I understood it now. It was love—pure and simple—and I had been too weak to see it, too much of a coward to embrace the truth.

Tears burned. My life had been a lie from start to finish. I masqueraded as a man, but really I was just a wild creature taken off the moors. I walked in clothes and spoke the words men used, but I was no more than a shaved beast. I had lied and faked and led my troupe to an evil war and then to their deaths, one by one, and for what? A dream of treasure and misplaced glory: lies, both. I had let myself be pushed and pulled by the tides of men and had failed simply to turn and say "no" before it was too late. I would never see any of them again—Saw or Ned or Will, Mary, Quickfinger, Hammer and Ezra. Savaric and Reginald. And finally, always, the one to whom my thoughts turned last thing at night and first in the morning: the Moor. And I had no one but myself to blame.

Well, there was no time for regrets now. Now I would give my lying corpse up to the tides not of men but of the great sea itself. And in my arms, the greatest lie of all: a portion of Christendom's greatest fake.

I clambered awkwardly overboard, clutching the relic close— at least its weight would carry my soul straight to the bottom—and reminded myself that drowning was said to be a fair death if you didn't fight it. Certainly it had to be better than burning alive. I fixed my mind on the memory of a pair of laughing, half-moon eyes and jumped.

The sea hit me like a cold wall, driving all the breath out of me. Then the water closed over my head and tried to press itself in through my mouth and nose. Burning above; burning within. I took one last look upwards in that strange, cold, dark green world.

Overhead, the hull of the ship was a great black whale, and the fiery waves a flare of orange like the promise of Heaven.

PART SEVEN

The True Cross

31

ohra brushed a hand across Nathanael's curly black hair. Such a thrill to touch him again, a private heaven to feel him warm and breathing, when she had thought him dead.

She closed her eyes, remembering the icy blast that had gone through her when Sorgan had come back from the barracks babbling about an attack: a doctor fatally injured by *hashshashin* trying to kill the emir. How could she have known he meant Nathanael when he did not even know himself? She could not say, she just knew. Or maybe all lovers at once leapt to the conclusion that it was their own beloved to whom Fate had dealt the cruel blow. It did not matter: she had run all the way to the citadel with no other thought in her head, had had to plead with the guards to let her through, had used both Malek's name and that of her despised dead husband in order to be admitted.

Seeing Nathanael lying there, pale as paper, had almost stopped her heart. All pretence fled at that sight. This was the person she loved most in the world, more than her father, her brothers, her cousins; more than her own life. How could she ever have thought otherwise? How could she have denied those feelings? She knew a strange, conflicting shame that she had done so out of fear of what others might think and say. Out of the fear of being cast out, condemned. It seemed absurd in the face of monstrous loss to have allowed such pointless conventions to make her turn away from the truth in her heart. Such a calmness had come over her then as she accepted the truth that it was as if she stood in the still point of a storm.

"I will take him," she had told them, the fussing women, the grave-faced men.

And so an unconscious Nathanael had been brought to the Najib house to occupy Zohra's own room. Without Nat to take care of them Sara and little Nima had been persuaded to come, too: they were in her mother's old sickroom. Downstairs, Baltasar and Sorgan shared the salon. The old man said little about this sudden influx of residents. Since the last of his pigeons had perished—lost to an arrow, to starvation or weakness, to the sea or stray air currents, no one knew—he had hardly said a word, but had lain rolled in a blanket on the divan in the half-dark most of the time, like an animal in its lair, stirring only to take whatever poor food was to be had, or to sit in the courtyard telling his prayer beads with his crippled hands.

But the arrival of Nathanael and his mother had wrought a great change in Baltasar. On the next day, he had got himself up and, commandeering Sorgan, taken himself off to the hammam for a steam. There was never any lack of wood in the city. So many houses were empty now; their doors and broken furniture lay stacked outside the bathhouses as firewood to heat the water. He had sat down to dinner with them that night in a clean robe and turban. He had been polite to Sara—more than polite, *courtly*, Zohra had thought at the time, passing her the best scraps from the poor dinner they shared, filling her cup with water, as if she could do nothing for herself with only one arm. Never once had he complained that there were strangers in his house, and one of them a young Jewish man, lying wounded in his daughter's room.

This very morning Zohra had seen Sara join him out in the courtyard garden, and these two bereaved, frail people had sat in companionable, accepting silence until inevitably it was broken by the chatter of the child with some new discovery to show them. They had turned to her as one and exclaimed over the pebble or the leaf she had brought them, and for a few minutes it was as if she had turned a sun upon them, a golden light that banished pain and memories and deep-graven lines.

Zohra had found herself welling up. This was how it should be. This was what mattered, even though all around them the world was falling apart. What did it matter that they each came from a different family, from a different culture? Jewish, Muslim and in Nima's case who-knew-what? This was how the world should be—people brought together by love.

Except that a small voice reminded her it was not only love that had brought this motley gathering together, but violence, hatred and death.

She allowed herself the luxury of cupping Nathanael's cheek tenderly. When he stirred, she almost cried out.

His eyelids fluttered, then sprang open. "How long have I been here?" he whispered.

"Three days, my love. Three long days."

"Where's Nima?" He tried to struggle upright, subsided.

"Nima is down in the courtyard with your mother. They are sitting in the sun playing some game with black and white stones." As she peeled the bandages away to change the dressing, she explained what had happened, as best she knew it, and Nathanael lay there quietly, taking it all in.

At last the stab-wound was bared. Zohra winced, though the patient did not. He was so thin: the comparison with the young man who had charmed her at the perfume stall more so long ago struck her every time she saw his body, every time she touched him. When she had attended to his wound, she had almost wept at the thinness of his once-sleek torso, before forcing herself to the task of closing the bloody gash. The stitches she had sewn in her lover's flesh seemed outrageous. *I did that with a needle*, she thought again now, with a sort of horrified fascination. Was she really the same woman who had retched each time she cleared her mother's bedpan, who had balked at even looking at a naked body as she washed it? It had been a long journey between then and now. A long journey for all of them.

Nathanael raised himself with effort, craning his neck. "You made a good job of that." He sounded surprised.

"I didn't know what to do. The healers up at the citadel were hopeless, just left you bleeding."

"Healers," he scoffed, sounding more like himself. "They aren't healers." He lay down again with a sigh. "You'll need to make a salve to go over the stitches or it will heal too tight. Bring my doctor's bag and the herbs and liniments from the cupboard in my room."

This was more like the Nathanael she knew: ebullient, peremptory. Zohra smiled to herself, then picked something up from beside the bed, removed the stopper and held it under his nose. "What, like this?" She grinned at his expression of amazement. "Your mother helped me. She told me where to find everything, and Nima helped me mix it." She laughed. "Well, Nima dripped honey on the floor and broke a dish, but she wanted to be involved. She loves you, you know." She took his hand in her own and raised it to her lips, feeling his bones beneath an inadequate layering, like an old man's, and added softly, "As do I."

Nathanael squeezed his eyes shut, but still tears escaped. Silence bound them for several minutes until Nat said suddenly, as if remembering something too late, "Karakush!"

"He's well, well enough to surrender the city, or at least that's what everyone is saying. I don't know, I haven't really been paying attention to anything beyond this room. It hasn't happened yet. Perhaps it won't." Zohra bit her lip. "They said there was an assassin, just a boy . . . ?"

Black eyes, narrow face.

With a sudden realization that made him go cold all over, Nat remembered where he had seen that face before. Running past them, blood-covered, on the day Zohra's mother had died. The younger brother, the one who had smothered her with a pillow . . .

Should he say anything? If the boy had lived, Zohra would soon know from others, and if he had died . . . well, the body would already have been buried. What was the point of adding to the woes of this unlucky family if his identity was not known?

Making his decision, he reached up and pulled Zohra down to him and kissed her till they both ran out of breath.

In the old tea house, Nathanael was sorely missed. But now they had a newcomer to talk to about him, which was almost better than having the quiet, polite doctor's lad with them.

"So how is he today?"

Baltasar Najib put down his cup and coughed, the eruption racking his thin frame. "Are you sure this stuff is made from roasted date pits? It tastes more like roasted rat droppings to me."

Driss laughed. "How I've missed your cheery presence, my friend."

"He's not doing badly. My girl's taking care of him." If Baltasar noticed the swift glances exchanged around the table, he did not remark on them but drew himself up. "He took the assassin's blade and saved the life of the governor. Didn't he, eh, Sorgan? Sorgan was the one came running home with the news."

Beside him, Sorgan eyed the last piece of stale bread with avaricious eyes, too hungry to say anything at all.

Driss snorted. "Just in time for him to receive the English devil's demands."

"I still don't understand why the Old Man would send his *hashshashin* to kill Karakush." Younes the barber shook his head. "Surely it would have been better to kill Malik al-Inkitar?" He used the Arabic name for the English king.

"The Old Man is a mad dog. He bites at random." Hamsa Nasri, the grocer, drained his tea and made a face. "May as well drink hot water."

Driss stared into the bottom of his cup as if it held the answer to all questions. "I reckon," he said, "the Old Man wants Akka for himself."

"What, and he's done a deal with the Franj?" Younes sounded skeptical.

"It's not beyond him. Think about it: he takes control of the port trade, taxes the goods in and out, gets back some of his lost revenue. It's one in Salah ad-Din's eye, too—he wouldn't mind that. Remember how I got my wound," Driss said.

There was a general groan. "Not again," Hamsa said.

"Show more respect to an old soldier," Baltasar growled. "Some of us were fighting for your freedom before you were born."

"Freedom." Younes shook his head. "The freedom to sit here and starve." His gaze shifted to the table in search of the remnant of bread, but it was gone. Sorgan's jaw moved ruminatively, his eyes glazed with a certain private pleasure. Younes opened his mouth to complain but was distracted by the arrival of a man coming through the door.

"The Franj have offered us safe passage and the right to remove all our property!" He grinned broadly, as if at some sort of joke.

There was hubbub at this. "For the surrender of the city?" someone asked.

The man wiped a sheen of grey dust off his face. "For the surrender of the whole Latin Kingdom!" He took a seat at a table close to where Baltasar and the others sat. "That's what I just heard."

"The entire Latin Kingdom?" Hassan asked, disbelieving. "They must be joking!"

"That's what he said, Malik al-Inkitar. He demanded all the cities of the Kingdom of Jerusalem as it was in the time of the French King Louis. And all the Christian prisoners taken by the emirs, and by the sultan's army, too. Oh, and that relic we captured at Hattin, the one they venerate as the cross the prophet Isa Christ was crucified on."

"Well, they can have that!" someone shouted, and everyone laughed. Then they sobered.

"Salah ad-Din will never agree to such outrageous terms," Driss said fiercely.

"I heard Al-Mashtub lost his temper and swore we'd all die fighting before we ceded the city. 'We will not yield while there is breath in our bodies,' that's what he said," declared the newcomer. He wore a battered garrison uniform.

Must have been one of the first to volunteer, Baltasar thought approvingly. "Aye, well, he's a warrior to his core, that one," he said.

"And then the English king said, 'The ransom of your bodies shall be your heads'!" the soldier went on.

"I'd rather have my head, to be honest," said Younes, running a hand over his bald patch.

"You would not give up the city so easily?" Driss rumbled.

"Easily? It's been two years. We've nothing left," said the barber. Loose skin had gathered beneath his eyes, on his neck; he looked twenty years older.

"But if we surrender now it will all have been for nothing, all the death, all the hardship." Driss's eyes were suddenly wet.

Baltasar clasped his old friend's shoulder, and felt the bones there, as fragile as a pigeon's. That was alarming, for he remembered

Driss as a big man, bound with muscle, tough as an old boot, until, like himself, he'd been invalided out of the army. And like him, Driss had lost his wife. Baltasar had found out only yesterday that Habiba had died weeks back, while he had been struggling with his own demons. It was clear the veteran was not doing well on his own. They had joked together as young men that they planned to die before their wives; it was the best way, since neither man could imagine life without them. But now he was living that life, and it was harder than he had ever thought. He knew what Driss must be going through; it brought his own pain back to him twofold. Feeling his own eyes prick, he said hoarsely, "There's a time for all things: a time to resist and a time to give way."

"The outer wall is down. The only thing holding the infidel out now is sheer force of will, and we've got less of that every day," the soldier said.

"But what if reinforcements come?"

The soldier shrugged. "Reinforcements have come and gone. But the caliph doesn't care about us. It's a long way from here to Baghdad."

"There are some who say he'd like to see Salah ad-Din taken down a peg or two," said Driss, lowering his voice.

"Yes, well, he's not the one been camped up there through the summer sickness and the winter snows, sick as a dog and hundreds of leagues away from his wives and all the comforts of home," said the soldier.

"Easy to ignore the plight of your subjects when everywhere you look there's peace and plenty and perfumed flesh," Younes said sourly.

No one said anything to this; there was nothing to say. The Caliph of Baghdad might have been the spiritual leader of the Ummah, the whole Muslim world, but it was hard not to be bitter in the face of such indifference.

"He's a tough man, the sultan," Baltasar said grudgingly. "He won't give in." Wearily, using Sorgan's shoulder, he levered himself to his feet. "Come on, lad, time to go home."

The Muslim army had thrown itself into the attack again and again each day, to no avail: the earthworks the Franj had erected had proved to be an effective barrier to their charging horses, and with each assault they had lost more men to the enemy archers. And still their machines pounded the failing city walls, ever widening the breach beside what had once been the Accursed Tower, now no more than a tumbled pile of rubble. How the garrison had managed to keep them from swarming into the city Malek could hardly imagine—or rather, and worse, he could.

The sultan sat his horse morosely, watching the ebb and flow of the battle below. Earlier in the day he had ridden out to battle himself, only to move back from the front line when the white flags were raised and the emirs came riding out of the city to the Templars' tent to parlay once more. They had been in there a long time, but in all that while Salah ad-Din had said nothing; he had simply watched, with his lips in a tight line and his eyes burning, as if his regard could sear away the very fabric of the tent.

Malek could not understand how he was still even able to sit his horse. He had not rested in three days, had taken no refreshment except the herbal drink his exasperated doctors had all but forced down him. "They will come soon, our reinforcements," he had said repeatedly. "Then we shall test the strength of these kings." A great number of reinforcements had arrived the day before under the command of Taki ad-Din, but still they had been unable to breach the earthworks, and still the emirs had ridden out to meet with the enemy, without taking instruction from the sultan.

"My lord, my lord!" A pageboy, covered in dust, threw himself down, heedless of the stamping hooves around him.

"Get up, Mohammad!" The sultan swung himself down out of the saddle with the grunt of a man in pain and raised the boy to his feet. "What is so urgent that it cannot wait for my return?"

"My lord, a swimmer from Akka!"

The man was as thin as a stick and could not stop coughing. He looked as if the tides had carried him from the city like a piece of flotsam. For a while it seemed he might expire before he could deliver his message. A hacking fit brought up blood. Eventually, shivering even though wrapped in a heavy woollen blanket, he spluttered out his unwelcome news.

"The emirs have met the Franj kings, my lord. They will surrender the city this very day—"

"What? No, we will fight on," the sultan interrupted him. "The Prince of Hama has returned, and with God's good grace more will surely come in answer to our call to arms. Return to them at once . . . no, after you have rested, of course. Forgive my haste. Return and tell the emirs I will not cede the city. They must hold out a little longer. All is not yet lost."

The swimmer's trembling increased despite the thickness of the blanket. He could not meet the sultan's eye as he said, in a voice barely above a whisper, "My lord, it is too late. Terms have been agreed and an accord has been signed."

A dumbfounded silence fell. No one could bear to look directly at the sultan, but all could feel a quiet inner wrath beating off him in waves. After a long, long moment he said, "Well, we shall see about this."

Malek and Ibrahim followed at a safe distance as he stormed about outside the war tent, sometimes with his head down, muttering, at others with his eyes raised to Heaven as if seeking divine inspiration.

Malek looked at Ibo, who shook his head. "How could they do this without their lord's instruction?"

Malek was at a loss. "I do not know." He could not blame anyone for surrendering after so long, after such privation, but he hated to see the sultan faced with both insurrection and defeat. He gazed unhappily towards the distant city. Out there, on the walls, there appeared to be some activity, though it was hard to make out precisely at such a distance. He frowned and squinted against the hot sun. No! It could not be . . .

"My lord." Interrupting the sultan when he was thinking was never advisable, but Malek could not bear that he be made a fool. "My lord," he said more quietly as the sultan turned to look at him, eyes as black as old blood. "They have taken down the crescent and raised the enemy's banners over the walls of Akka."

There, waving on the breeze that came always at this time off the gleaming sea, flew the azure, crimson and green banners of the kings of the Franj.

"Even from the Friday Mosque," the sultan said in disbelief.

Yes, even from the slender minaret of the city's great mosque there now flew an infidel banner, a great fluttering ribbon of blue and gold.

For a moment it looked as if Salah ad-Din might collapse. He swayed where he stood, put a hand to his face. Malek and Ibrahim readied themselves to catch him if he fell, but then he took a great breath and drew himself upright. "What is done cannot be undone and we must make the best of it." He raised his hands to the skies. "It is written. God grant me the strength to save our people." And he strode back into the tent with a face like thunder.

The messenger looked up with fear in his eyes. But Salah ad-Din took his seat once more and, after a few moments in which he simply took breaths in and let them out again, said calmly, "Tell me the terms the emirs have agreed to."

The swimmer blinked rapidly. "In exchange for the lives of the inhabitants and for their property they have agreed on a sum of two hundred thousand gold bezants—"

This time it was Baha ad-Din, the qadi, who interrupted. "How much?" he cried. "That's outrageous! Are they mad? They know full well our coffers are empty. Do they think our alchemists can conjure gold from thin air?"

"Gently, my friend, let the poor fellow continue," the sultan said with deceptive mildness. "Two hundred thousand gold bezants, and what else?"

The messenger looked at his hands. "And the return of five hundred Christian captives, including all the nobles taken prisoner, a list of which is being compiled." He drew a shuddering breath and then coughing racked him for several minutes while all inside the tent gazed at one another in despair. The sultan commanded that a hot drink be brought for the man, suggested exactly which spices should be added to it, and waited while it was brewed and the swimmer drank it down and was able to continue.

"One hundred of the most eminent men in the city, including the grand emir, Al-Mashtub, and the governor, Karakush, are to be held as hostages against the completion of the agreement. The kings have also demanded the return of the relic they call the True Cross, in the selfsame condition in which it was seized after the Battle of Hattin."

Now Salah ad-Din visibly lost his composure. "But the cross was broken up! Karakush knows that full well. He has part of the wretched object in the Akka treasury. The rest was . . . scattered, as befits the worthless symbol it was. The caliph has a small portion, and much of the gold was stripped and melted down." He tugged on his beard, a sure sign of perturbation. He sighed. "Well, there's not much we can do about that. Go on," he told the man. "Is that the end of your message?"

"My lord, all this is to be rendered to the kings of the Franj within one month—the money, the Christian captives, the cross. They will hold the lives of half the surviving inhabitants of the city, including all its fighting men, in surety."

At this, the sultan's face became dark with blood, and it was a long time before he mastered himself sufficiently to be able to speak. "By God, you are trying me sorely. How could they have agreed to such an accord? There has to be some way to vary these terms."

Again he got his feet and began to pace, but this time Malek stood rooted, sweat breaking out down his back and under his arms. A rank smell rose to his nostrils and he recognized it for what it was: the stench of fear. Fear for his family, worse than he had ever felt before. What would happen to them if the sultan could not meet the terms? He had seen the captive Muslims burning like candles on the battlefield. Had seen bodies mutilated where they lay, the wounded dispatched even as they cried for aid. Templars had even massacred pilgrims making the Hajj. These people had no honour, no mercy. He felt burning bile rise into his mouth and black stars danced before his eyes. Turning unsteadily, he fled outside and fell to his knees on the hard-packed earth. The bile was unstoppable: it came out in a tide, wave after wave, right at the entrance to the tent, so that the sour smell of it wafted in on the breeze, overwhelming the attar in the braziers.

Men inside exclaimed in disgust. Then someone immensely strong picked him up as if he were a child and set him down some distance away from the scene of his crime.

"Here, drink this." Ibrahim's broad, dark face loomed above him, for once unsmiling.

Malek took the mug of water and rinsed his mouth out, spitting the residue onto the ground where the dry red clay swallowed it greedily. "My family. What are we going to do?" he asked his friend, agonized. "We cannot meet the terms. I know we cannot."

"We will," Ibo said grimly. "One way or another we will. We have to."

They had assembled in the central square outside the Friday Mosque, the survivors of Akka, everyone who could walk or crawl. Such silence! The air so still! There had not been such quiet for two whole years. People stood a little straighter, held their heads a little higher, as if the burden of the noise of the incessant battering of the walls and the cries of the enemy army beyond had been lifted from them. It was a wonder to be able to walk easily rather than to scuttle in fear for your life from falling missiles or debris. You could even hear the gulls, Nathanael thought, as they planed on hot air currents high overhead.

He glanced across at Zohra, marvelling now as he always had at the lambent amber of her eyes: today they were full of sunlight, and there were roses in her cheeks; a smile twitched the corner of her lips. Last night they had lain together for the first time in two years, and even though the pain of his wound had been fierce, the pleasure had been fiercer. He could remember every sensual touch, like fingers of flame on his skin.

Forcing his mind away from the delicious wonders of the night, he looked around. Was this really the totality of all who had survived? The square was less than half full and not even tightly packed. *And each of us takes up so much less space now*, he thought.

People wrapped in bandages, people holding themselves up with sticks, people supported by members of their family. Children with the faces of old men; women carrying babes in their arms, looking more like grandmothers than mothers. More women than men. So many had given their lives in defence of the city.

Apart from Zohra and her family there were few he recognized. Sayedi Efraim, the herb-seller, gaunt but hale, and beside him a woman who might have been his wife or his sister. One of the Armenian women who used to sit on the doorstep with her sister all day, every day, gossiping and watching the world go by; of her sister there was no sign. Mohammed Azri, the smith, and his son, Saddiq, with a few of their workers, including Zohra's hulking great brother Sorgan. Some of the black-robed alchemists who came and went from the citadel. There was the crabber and his daughter, Rana, and some of their neighbours from down at the port. Saïd, the doctor from the hospital, less than a third of his original girth.

Little Nima tugged suddenly at his hand and gazed up with her wide black eyes. "Who is that man?" She pointed to the dais that had hastily been erected. "And why has he got half a black sheep stuck to his face?"

Despite the gravity of the atmosphere, Nat snorted. "Hush, little monster, show some respect! That is the grand emir, Al-Mashtub."

The Kurdish lord, his black beard bushier than ever, and the governor of the city, the eunuch Karakush, stood up there on the dais, looking uncomfortable, flanked by Templar knights, their great swords bared, their mail coifs glittering. The knights wore long white surcoats emblazoned with the red cross that all in Akka had come to know and hate the last time the Franj held the city. Enemy soldiers ringed the square—big, pale-skinned men for the most part, in a tatterdemalion collection of leather and mail. Many were looking about in wonder. For some, Nathanael thought, it would be the first time they had ever set foot in a Syrian town. All this way from wherever they called home, and for what? A shell of a city—burned out, dusty, broken, abandoned—and a handful of citizens hating them for what they had gone through and all they had lost. Who would wish to be the victor? How could anyone surveying the ruins of this place and these people not feel shame?

"People of Akka!" The voice of the grand emir, Al-Mashtub, roared out, calling them all to attention. "We have this day surrendered the city to the Christian kings, to Philip Augustus of France and Richard of England, both of whom we know as great and honourable men, worthy champions of their people, God-fearing upholders of their faith and keepers of their word. And that word is—in accordance with the *ius belli*, the rights of war—that the Commander of the Faithful, Sultan of Egypt and Syria, Salah ad-Din shall redeem our lives and our property from our vanquishers for an agreed sum, against the payment of which the governor and I and ninety-eight other notables of the city shall stand as hostage. Our lives are now forfeit to these kings."

People nodded gravely. This was as one would expect: an honourable bargain made between honourable parties. But the grand emir had not finished. He held up his hands for quiet. "In addition, we have agreed . . ." He hesitated, came to a halt and looked to Karakush.

The eunuch now stepped forward and called hoarsely, "Good people of Akka, you know me well. I have been your governor since we took the city back from the Franj—"

A ragged cheer erupted from somewhere in the crowd. Templar eyes darted, seeking out likely troublemakers.

"I love this city as I love my own life—" the governor tried to continue.

"That must be a great deal, judging by the size of him," someone said, and the remark was met with a ripple of laughter.

"Like my own life," Karakush repeated earnestly. "To see it resist so bravely, to see the sacrifices you have made over these two years, each and every one of you. Mothers who have lost their sons, daughters their fathers, wives their husbands—"

"And husbands their wives!" cried one woman.

"And husbands their wives, and children their mothers," Karakush forged on. "To see all this has torn my heart. But there had to come a day when we said enough to such sacrifice, a day when one more life lost to no avail would tip the balance, when the weight of lost souls was too heavy to be borne. This is that day.

"The kings of the Franj have struck a hard bargain, I cannot deny that. To save the lives of those of you here today, and those you have left at home too sick or too young to be present, we have had to agree to a heavy price. It is a price worth paying, and it is a price that will be redeemed, so have faith in our lord Salah ad-Din and the princes of the Ummah to see that it shall be so. Not only the lives of the one hundred will stand surety against the ransom, but one out of every two of you: a half of the remaining population of this city."

What? The gasp was universal. What did he mean?

Nathanael turned to Zohra, saw her look of consternation, squeezed her hand. One out of every two . . . Nima looked up at her, frowning. One out of every two . . . Sara and Baltasar . . .Voices began to mutter; then the mutter became a rumble, and the rumble a roar.

Christian hands fell to the hilts of their swords. Karakush waved his arms, but it was the grand emir's bellow that rose above the tide of noise.

"Hear us out. As God is my witness, the deal is done and we must accept what has been written. By the rough estimate of the tallymen there are almost six thousand souls left in the city, and so just under three thousand of you must be held as hostages. The Christian kings have demanded that able-bodied men of less than forty years of age be kept as hostages, and that the elderly, women and children be free to leave, so long as the rest stand surety."

People began to protest at this stricture. A woman began to wail, "Not my son! Not my beautiful Hassan!"

Nathanael felt a hand grasp his arm and turned to find Zohra gazing at him with her golden eyes blazing, but he could not tell if it was with fear or fury.

The emir held up his hand for silence and at last the crowd quieted.

"I know from looking out upon you that there are not three thousand men of fighting age left in the city, so we will need to seek volunteers from those of you who are entitled to leave. It is a great deal to ask of you, but ask it I must. Those who remain will be well treated, kept in quarters that are being prepared for this eventuality. All will be well fed and looked after, and any wounds or sickness from which they suffer shall be attended to with the skill of the best Christian and Muslim doctors available. I myself, Saïf al-Mashtub, appointed grand emir by the Commander of the Faithful himself, give you my word on this. And if that is not enough . . ."—he gestured to a boy, who handed him up a parcel wrapped in green silk—"I swear it on the Holy Qur'an." Reverently, he took the book from its wrappings and held it aloft. "Place your trust in the honour of these kings and the greatness of God, and all shall be well."

Now Karakush took up the discourse. "I would ask all of you to consider this carefully. The qadis and their scribes will take your names and details, and those who wish to volunteer as hostages should come to the steps of the Friday Mosque."

At this, a surprising number of people surged forward.

"Well fed and cared for," said a man standing in front of Nathanael, nudging his neighbour. "Quickly, let's go to the qadi and pledge ourselves!" For a moment the neighbour, who looked older than the designated age, dithered, then the pair of them pushed through the throng.

"We must complete the roster by midday tomorrow," the governor continued, "so you will have tonight to discuss the matter with your families. But before you go, please form orderly lines and give your names, ages and addresses to the qadis."

Orderly lines were not a normal part of life in Akka, where

no one had ever willingly queued for anything. Already there was anger and incomprehension; before long, there was hubbub and chaos.

That night the occupants of the Najib house cooked up a strange casserole of everything they could scrape together. Nathanael bartered some honey for a quantity of couscous from Fatima, the imam's daughter, and Zohra made bread from flour bartered for a salve. Despite the gravity of the situation, the atmosphere was curiously festive. For the first time in ages there were six gathered around the table in the guest salon. Not the same six as there used to be, Zohra thought, struck suddenly by their losses. No Ummi, no Aisa, and who knew whether Kamal was alive or dead?

Malek at least was well, that much she had ascertained from the swimmer who had carried the surrender terms to the sultan. He had also reported that Malek had broken down in tears of relief to hear that his sister still lived. "It would kill me to lose her, or any more of my family," he had told the man. And he had also sent a personal message to Zohra in the code that he had devised for the pigeon missives, which Aisa had taught her. "Get out," it read. "Leave the city as soon as you are able and bring Baba and Sorgan with you." She had said nothing to anyone else, not even Nathanael, about this. Its implications distressed her too much.

The meal finished, talk soon turned to the decisions they had to make.

"I will stay as a hostage," Baltasar declared. "I am too old to leave the city now, too old and too tired."

"No, Baba, you must take Sorgan. He cannot look after himself."

"I can! I am a smith now. I don't need anyone to take care of me. Mohammed Azri feeds me and Saddiq helps me with fire!"

Zohra placed a hand on his arm. "I know, Sorgan, I know. You've worked so hard. But there may not be much use for smiths any more now that the city has been surrendered to the Franj."

Sorgan glowered. "The Franj. I hate the Franj! I'd like to put them all in the fire and hammer them to bits!" His fists flexed.

Zohra sighed. "You see, we can't leave him here. He'll be in danger."

Her brother folded his arms obstinately. "I want to go with the smiths. I don't want to be part of this family if you won't let me." There was no use arguing with him.

"They are sure to keep the Azris as hostages," Nat said quietly. "They want to keep all the able-bodied men where they can control them. They're the ones the Franj want."

"As slaves!" cried Baltasar.

"More likely to prevent them taking up arms against our enemy," said Sara quietly, clutching the stump of her arm. She did not believe in deferring to the views of men, especially if they were wrong. "Of course they would. But we cannot let our enemies dictate who stays and who goes."

"Everyone will go eventually, won't they?" Zohra said, seeking reassurance. "When the ransom is paid?"

Nathanael said nothing, remembering Jerusalem. He turned to his mother. "You and Baltasar should leave with Zohra and Nima," he said gently. "No one can make you stay."

"Nima?" said Baltasar. He looked up with sudden expectant hope, but then his eyes filled slowly with tears. "Oh, yes . . ." There were moments when he looked up when someone entered the room as if he thought his wife were still alive and was just coming back from the souq. Seeing the expression on his face when he remembered the truth broke Zohra's heart each time.

Her father rolled his thin shoulders. "I will stay," he announced. "Akka is my home."

Zohra felt a familiar frustration rise. "But, Baba, you can leave—"

He rounded on her. "I may not be under forty, but I am as able-bodied as the next man." He looked as if he might hit anyone who contradicted him.

Sara placed her hand over his and squeezed it gently. "I am not leaving either. What would I do with just one arm out there in the world? No. I will go with Baltasar and Sorgan to the quarters they are preparing, where there is good food and treatment for all our ills."

"Cousin Jamilla does very well with just one arm," Zohra said, just as Nathanael said, "I am a doctor! You know you won't get better care elsewhere."

Sara smiled at both of them, and in that smile Nat saw a benediction. She knew all, and accepted all—even blessed them for it. "Nathaniel, you must leave. Anyone can see you are not able-bodied right now. The governor will surely sign your papers. You must take Nima and Zohra and leave as soon as they let you go. I'll hear no more arguments."

"Good, then," said Baltasar. "That's decided. Now, what do we have for dessert?"

All over the city the same discussions were taking place.

The next morning Nat went with Baltasar and Sorgan to their usual tea house: there were rumours of real tea being served, and Baltasar was determined to carry on as if nothing else of importance had happened.

The place was full: neither a cushion nor a stool to be had. But as soon as people saw Baltasar a seat was given up to him; even in the hardest times, the oldest and frailest must be respected. Younes shifted on his cushion to make room for Nathanael, who bent with some pain and took the offered space. Sorgan stood sniffing the air as if scenting something he had not smelled in a very long time.

"Look, Sorgan," Hamsa Nasri said, waving his hand with a flourish as if announcing a magic trick, "proper bread!"

Sorgan gazed at the reed basket on the table, his eyes round with amazement. Younes tore a flat, round loaf in half and quickly handed it up to him before he could make off with the entire basket.

"I'm staying," he mumbled a few seconds later, his mouth stuffed full of bread.

"I want to stay," Younes said morosely. "But Iskander, he wants to go. He says he'll wear women's robes and a veil if he has to. No one's likely to stop him—he's prettier than most women." He gave a mirthless smile. "He's had enough of Akka, he says. I think that means he's had enough of me."

The old veteran, Driss, leaned across the table and patted his hand. "I'm sure he doesn't mean that. Iskander loves you, it's plain to anyone. You should go with him. You're both young enough to start your lives somewhere new."

Younes gave a rueful smile. "Hardly!" He brushed a hand over his bald head. What had remained of his hair had fallen out in the past weeks as if it no longer had the strength to hold on.

"Well, younger than me."

"Everyone's younger than you!"

They laughed.

"We old folk must stick together," Baltasar said grimly. "The young ones should try to get out if they can."

"I shall stay," Driss said. "I can't leave Habiba here on her own."

They all knew what he meant. They had buried his wife beside Driss's two daughters and grandson. It had been a harsh summer.

"There's nothing away from Akka for me," said Baltasar.

"But you've family in Damascus!" said Driss.

Baltasar shrugged. "I haven't seen them in years. Besides, who wants an old wolf like me moving in with them? I'll just make the children cry."

It was clear, Nat thought, that he said this to make Driss feel better, and he experienced a surge of proud sorrow that set a hard lump in his throat. "I will stay, too," he said, mastering himself. "I'll be classed as able-bodied soon enough, and people here need doctors."

Baltasar Najib gave him a hard look. "Driss and I have seen too much of the world to have any illusions left, lad. We've got no lives ahead of us—we've lived well and made families, and it's your turn to do that now. You get out while you can, and take my daughter with you. You promise me now: you'll take Zohra and the child and you'll leave with them."

Nat stared back at him unhappily. "I don't think my conscience can let me."

"Shit on your conscience, boy!" Baltasar roared, and the tea house went quiet. Even Sorgan stopped chewing.

Driss put a hand Baltasar's arm. "Hush now, old friend, you're upsetting poor Sorgan here. Here, son, have some olives with that bread." He pushed a little bowl of gleaming fresh olives in the big man's direction.

Sorgan stared at the bowl as if it were full of eyeballs. "I hate olives," he said firmly. "I want cake."

Younes laughed. "Steady on, son. You'll be asking for roast lamb next!"

Sorgan went very still. "I remember the taste of lamb. My mouth remembers." Spittle gleamed on his lip. He looked around with sudden intent. "I don't smell lamb. Where is it?"

"You'll have mutton soon enough," Baltasar told him, and when Sorgan started to wail like a child they all tried to calm him down with whatever tidbits they could find.

In the chaos, Hamsa Nasri leaned across the table and said quietly to Nat, "You have to leave, you know. You've got to get out. Take this chance to save your own life, and Baltasar's daughter, too. It's the best you can do for this city: survive, and keep it going elsewhere. Keep the memory of how it was, raise your children to remember."

Nathanael stared at him. His wound started to throb painfully. "What do you mean? You don't trust the Franj to honour the terms?"

The grocer looked grim. "I don't trust anyone, son. I'm a grocer and the son of a grocer. You've seen the sign in my shop. I give no credit."

32

✻

"John . . ."

For a second time my eyelids parted to let in the tiniest sliver of light. I did not want to be woken from my dream. Something hugely significant was taking place in it, something I could not quite comprehend. Elements of it tumbled through my head, just as I had been tumbled by the waves. I closed my eyes tight and quested after the trailing threads of the dream. But it was gone now, and anyway it had made no sense.

"John!" More forceful now, a voice I recalled from long ago, from another world: one lost and barred to me now.

A hand shook my shoulder, not ungently.

"John, come back from wherever you are. Come to me. Open your eyes."

That voice. I knew it better than my own. Obediently I opened my eyes. Light flooded in. I blinked and blinked, pinned by the merciless illumination. Then a blissful shadow gave me respite. When my eyes adjusted my heart turned over.

Half-moon eyes. That fine, straight nose. For a long moment I simply lay there and looked at him, and for a long time he lay there without a word and looked at me. Nose to nose, dark and pale, like opposing chess pieces, or a statue and its shadow.

Then a hand touched my brow, cupped my cheek.

"John."

The way he said my name this time, it made something shiver deep inside me. The word was full of . . . what? A tone I had never heard from him or any other. Tenderness. Yes, that was the word for it.

I tried to frame his name, and remembered I had never known it.

Then an arm went around my back and the world tilted and shifted until I was sitting upright, the sun in my eyes, feeling like a straw-filled poppet.

"Here, drink this."

I had thought I would never wish to drink water again, I had shipped so much of it. This was not salty but as sweet as wine. I gulped it greedily.

"Slow down, you'll be sick."

I sipped. I looked around. I was on a beach. The sun was spangling the sea. I was alive! How could that be possible?

I remembered hugging the relic, going down, down through the dark waters with its mighty weight dragging me towards the seabed, getting colder all the time, my ribs getting crushed more tightly with every second of my descent. After that . . . well, I had no memories, just a crazed jumble of images churning around my head.

"It's a miracle," I croaked—my idea of a joke, which I knew would make him laugh.

But he didn't. He just nodded thoughtfully. "Yes, John, a miracle. Truly."

He looked away from me for a moment and his face changed. I had always found the Moor unreadable, even at the best of times, and now he seemed more himself than he ever had before, as enigmatic as a shadow.

"I can't believe you found me," I managed to whisper. "Am I really alive? Perhaps I'm between worlds now. God knows, I deserve to wander in Purgatory a long time for all I have done . . ."

He frowned at that. "You are not in Purgatory, John. You are in the world. Now look, there are soldiers coming down from the camp, so we must get you on your feet, and I shall speak for you. Can you do that? Can you rise, with my help?"

I could. For about three seconds. Then I was down in the shingle again as if I had no backbone. From there, I asked, "Quickfinger and Hammer?" Now it was all coming back to me.

The Moor shook his head. "I'm sorry, John, I've seen no one else alive. Put your arm around my shoulder. Let's try again. There. There we are. Steady, now."

The soldiers reached us then, their footsteps crunching on the pebbles: thin, dark leathery-looking men in pointed steel caps, with curved swords at their sides. Seeing them gave me a start. What was I stupidly expecting—that they would be "our" soldiers, not the enemy? For a moment a chill ran through me. Surely they would kill me on the spot. But they didn't seem very interested in slaughtering me. Rather, they engaged in a lengthy conversation with the Moor, in which I caught only a word here and there.

"Come, John," the Moor said at last. "I'll take you back to camp. The sultan will be glad to see you." He paused. "We need as many Franj captives as we can get," he explained. "Don't we, lads? For ransom."

I goggled at him in hurt disbelief. Had I been rescued so miraculously, found so miraculously, only to be sold back to the king I had failed?

"I do not think he will pay much for me, if anything," I managed to get out.

The Moor turned his face to me, his expression as blank as a cat's. "It's a numbers game, John. Trust me."

I will not pretend it was not daunting, that journey up from the shore to the Muslim camp. I had thought myself a dead man, destined for the pits of Hell, but now here I was, surprisingly ascending, through the midst of a thousands of enemy soldiers, who turned to regard me more with curiosity than hostility. I was in the midst of our foe! Never had I felt so exposed. And yet, at the same time, with the Moor's arm around me and his charged, wiry strength bearing me up, filling me with his strange, engulfing confidence, it was like walking in a dream through flameless fire or silent monstrosities, a dream in which you know you can take no harm.

As my initial terrors lifted, I began to take in my surroundings. Everywhere I looked returned some marvel or surprise. The greatest surprise of all was the general cleanliness of this vast encampment. Where ours was all churned earth, or mud, depending on the season, and stank of piss and shit and rot, up here on the tawny hillsides order largely prevailed. We passed well-dug and well-watered latrines, picketed horses, camp-kitchens from which smells emanated that made my nose twitch. Myriad tents of many hues and patterned designs, pennants fluttering beside them, and everywhere the symbol of the crescent moon, where there were a thousand different devices in the Christian camp. An area where a dozen men, stripped to their breeches, washed and beat clothing in a channelled stream—no sign of a woman anywhere—and above this, where the diverted stream flowed into a neatly tiled area, men performed ablutions, their sleeves rolled high, washing their hands and forearms, their faces and necks, with utmost care.

The Moor saw how I stared at this sight and chuckled to himself.

As we made our way little farther up the slope there came a great, lowing note, followed by a tumble of others that shimmered on the hot air, the chant taken up by other voices on other hills, until there seemed a single great song of summoning, and I noticed that a tide of men was moving in the same direction. While I was puzzling over this, the soldiers in front of us dropped to their knees, facing inland, knelt and touched their foreheads to the ground.

The Moor stood where he was and merely cast his gaze skywards. He raised his hands to his face, closed his eyes and brushed his palms from his forehead, over his lips and down to his heart. Then he opened his eyes and looked right at me, and I felt as if my heart stopped. In that moment I knew he had just thanked God that I was alive.

On the summit of the hill a great pavilion was pitched, apricot banners flying all around it and guards stationed outside the door, big men made taller by their spiked helmets. I thought, *That must be the tent of our chief enemy, the pagan king, Saladin*, and with brief, hallucinatory clarity remembered Hammer capering across the stage with three rag-babies threaded on his lance. Then shame came over me as I recalled the Moor's expression when I had asked my idiot question.

Even though I knew with the rational part of me that the sultan was no cannibal, and probably no other sort of monster either, it was to my great relief that we turned aside before we reached the great pavilion, to another, smaller tent pitched a little distance away. The Moor said something to the soldiers and they debated for a moment, then he ducked inside and disappeared from view. A short while later he came out again and beckoned me inside.

"The qadi of the army, Baha ad-Din," he said to me, indicating a short, stout man with a carefully trimmed beard and bright, watchful eyes.

I bowed as politely as I could manage, for my legs were trembling with the effort of the long uphill walk, and the man shot a number of questions at the Moor, who answered them shortly. I watched as the scribe took a quill in hand, opened a small flask, dipped the quill, knocked it on the rim and then wrote something on a piece of fine-looking vellum, his hand moving swiftly, and oddly, from right to left.

"I've told him your name, your age and place of birth," the Moor said quietly.

I stared at him. "Even I don't know my age."

"I guessed. Does it matter? I also told him you're an acclaimed creator of illusion."

I swallowed an hysterical laugh. "You told him I'm a conman and miracle-faker?"

"Those are not the exact words I used. I said you are an artist, and even that took some explaining."

The scribe interrupted, firing fast questions at the Moor, who nodded and answered smoothly. Then he bowed to the man, took me by the arm and manoeuvred me outside.

"I will bring you paper, inks and some charcoal if there is any fine enough to be used for such a task," he said, once we were out in the sunlight again.

"What . . . task?"

"We need you to draw the True Cross for us."

"What?" The word came out at so high a pitch that it was more of a womanish squeal.

The Moor made a minute gesture with his right hand, one I knew to mean *be calm*. He had used the same gesture in the Lady Chapel, and at Rye. "The True Cross makes up part of the surrender terms to ransom the people of the city. And it is missing." He eyed me steadily. "You were seen fleeing Akka's harbour, you and Quickfinger with his pale blond hair, and another, small and dark, whom I take to be Hammer. And the cross is, apparently, missing from the city's treasury. You can see how we might make a connection."

Panic flared. Was I about to be denounced as a thief and punished—hanged, or worse? But no: I was not thinking clearly, was not thinking at all. Something jagged through my head, a sort of pain, or terror, or guilt.

He kept watching me, his half-moon eyes gleaming. "You are not being accused, John." He held my gaze. "We can overlook the attempted theft. What we need from you is your memory, to draw the True Cross in all the detail you can recall."

"If I even saw the cross—"

"John . . ." His voice was soft. "Don't allow a small crime to stand in the way of the salvation of three thousand people."

I swallowed. "Is there no one else who could do this for you?"

"Those who recall seeing the relic taken from the field at Hattin have given wildly contradictory descriptions—it was, after all, four years ago. The sultan's brother remembers it being about so high." He swept his hands over a yard apart. "And so wide . . ." Almost the same again.

"That's far larger than the piece I . . . saw."

"It was broken up after its capture. The sultan ordered it done after the victory, to show the Christians how little their relic meant, how little power it had."

"What happened to the rest of it?"

He shrugged. "No one seems to know."

"And the gold?"

"Melted down, and long since been used in coin."

"It's going to be expensive to recreate."

The Moor spread his hands. "There is hardly a bezant left in the sultan's coffers. All has been spent on this war. He keeps nothing for himself."

"Well, where are you going to get it from?"

He looked thoughtful. "That is my problem. Your task is to concentrate on the look of the relic, on the patterns and designs, the placement of the jewels."

I thought about that small, heavy object, dragging me down through the dark waters, away from the fires above. Then, out of nowhere, I thought about it in quite a different way: not small, not heavy, but suddenly vast and buoyant. My head breaking the surface. The sun on my face . . .

That couldn't be right—my mind playing tricks on me again.

"Are you remembering?" the Moor asked. He was watching me intensely, a curious look on his face.

"Sort of," I said, trying to shake the odd feeling of immense weight followed by immense weightlessness. Something was nagging at me. Something important. Another fleeting sensation of the trailing edges of a dream, like one of my fits about to take hold. Then the feeling passed. I blinked. "They fired Will and Ned over the city walls. In their trebuchet."

That jolted him, I could see. "May their souls find rest," he said.

"They're all dead, not just Ned and Will," I said, the full horror if it returning to me. Tears fell unchecked. "Saw at the Spring Head, Quickfinger and Hammer lost to the sea, Ezra in battle . . ." Snot began to drip from my nose.

The Moor was quiet for several paces, taking this in. Then he said simply, "Come with me."

Not the hospital tent, I thought, my nostrils twitching as if they could already smell the rot and filth. Memories of our own still haunted my sleep, making me wake sweating in the depths of night. But yes, it was the hospital tent he led me to.

Inside, it was quiet and cool. Men in dark robes ghosted between the beds, carrying instruments and flasks, even a small brass brazier giving off some sweet-smelling smoke. Lines of pallets bearing men in various states of damage—the usual missing limbs and hands, crush-wounds from hooves and maces, holings from arrows and crossbolt quarrels. There was some groaning, but nothing like the hell-shrieks of our field hospital.

"They are dosed with poppy syrup," the Moor said. "It aids

the healing process if the pain recedes—the body relaxes and stops expending all its energy on defending the wound site. Also, every man here knows that if it is his time to die he will be received into Heaven with the acclamation of martyrdom, and his family will be well provided for." He paused, smiling at my expression. "Though they and we would much rather they lived."

He led me through the long tent to a screened area at the far end. As we rounded the screen, my eyes were drawn to the man who sat cross-legged beside the pallet: a striking fellow, his back very upright, with a fine-planed face and large, expressive black eyes, trained with rapt attention on the patient. He wore, I noticed, the same costume as the guards outside the great pavilion; at his side on the ground sat a polished steel helm. In his lap were roses: pale-pink briar roses, soft and incongruous against the heavy leather and chain mail of his armour.

As we appeared he looked up, startled, then shot to his feet as if caught doing something he should not. The roses scattered, shedding their fragrance. Some of the petals fell upon the bed, where the patient reached out to them. I stared. Blinked, and stared again.

"Ezra!"

I think her shock was the equal to my own. She screwed her eyes up as if finding them untrustworthy.

"I thought you were dead!" I said hoarsely.

"So did I!"

Suddenly we were grinning at one another, dizzied by surprised delight. The young soldier began to move away, discomfited. The look he gave me was not friendly.

"Malek!" called Ezra, then followed this with something foreign that made him turn back with a shy smile. He placed his hand on his heart, bowed to us and walked away.

In just these few days she had learned their language? I began to think I was dreaming.

"He saved me," Ezra said, swivelling so that she could follow his progress until he was out of sight. The Moor scooped up the briars and laid them on the bed. "I was on the berm and one of their archers shot me and I fell in the ditch. Thought I was going to die there with all those soldiers and horses, and Malek, well, he leaned down off his horse—it's a lovely chestnut called Asfar—and he hauled me up. And look!" She leaned, wincing, to the other side of the pallet and pulled up her bow. "He saved this, too!"

Such a paragon, I thought. "No doubt he saved you for the prisoner exchange," I said sourly.

"I . . . no . . ." She looked puzzled. "No one's said anything about ransom or exchange or anything." She laughed. "I don't think King Richard's going to be paying to get a woman back!"

"Shhh . . . be careful."

"They dressed my wound, John—you think they don't know?" She grabbed my hand. "But John, how are you here? It's like magic—first the Moor, now you. Next it'll be Quickfinger and Will!"

I looked away from her shining eyes. "I don't think so." I steeled myself to tell her what had happened to them, but she was already chattering on.

"And I met the sultan! He comes to see me every day, despite everything else he has to do, can you imagine? He brings me fruit, to help me get better. They bring him fruit every day from Damascus, wherever that is. Imagine that! Fruit, from his own fruit basket." She grabbed my hand. "They've been so nice to me, John, courtly, like I'm some sort of princess. No one's ever treated me like that before. And Malek . . ." She looked down at the roses, and when she looked up again her eyes were full of some kind of wonder. "Well, he's been lovely." Her grip on my hand tightened. "John, I don't want to go back. You won't make me, will you?"

I stared at her. "You want to stay with the enemy?"

"They're not *my* enemy," she said, snorting out her derision.

"But they're Muslims," I persisted, something bitter in me finding voice, something . . . disappointed. "They're foreign, they have foreign ways, speak a foreign language—"

She reeled off an unintelligible stream of gibberish that made the Moor laugh. He corrected her and she repeated back what he said, twice, until she'd got the strange sounds right. When she looked back at me it was with defiance and a sort of pride. "See? I'm learning. It won't take long. Everyone's helping."

"I bet they are." Jealousy made me sharp. "What about our plans? We were going to find some land, raise animals, remember?"

Her face fell. "I didn't mean to be disloyal, not to you. You're my friend. We are still friends, aren't we?" She sounded just like me with the Moor, I thought.

I shook my head. "Sorry. It's just . . . well, a lot to think about, a lot to take in. I'm glad you're alive and well, Ezra. I really am."

"You can call me Rosamund now. Malek does. The Moor says it's Latin, and means 'rose of the world' or some such nonsense," she said, colouring. "Hence the . . ." Her fingers brushed the flower petals.

I must have looked miserable or embarrassed, for the Moor stepped in now and, businesslike, applied himself to examining her dressing. "Go sit in the sun outside, John," he told me, and, glad to be dismissed, I pushed my way through the tent flap and stood blinking in the bright light, I had been transported to another world, one in which none of the old rules applied.

Why was I so disturbed that Ezra—Rosamund—should choose to stay here, among these foreigners? Had I not myself been distraught at the idea of being sent away when the Moor had mentioned the prisoner exchange? Would I not willingly have traded any chance of returning to England, for staying here—anywhere—with him?

But she's a woman, a small voice inside me prompted. *That's different.*

425

It was different. And yet maybe it was different in ways that mattered even less. What awaited Ez—Rosamund back in England? Returned to the army with her true identity revealed, she'd surely be reduced to a camp-whore; in England, she'd end up on the streets, doing the same thing. I didn't know what awaited her here. Perhaps the respect with which she had been treated by the young soldier who had saved her, and by the sultan himself, would prevail. Perhaps she could make a better life here than she could back home. Or perhaps not. I did not know. But I couldn't help thinking about the hatred on the faces of the people of Akka, what had happened to Will and to Ned, catapulted, screaming, over the walls . . .

And the beaten, burned Jews of London . . .

And the captured Muslims set alight like candles on the battlefield . . .

There is a savagery in all of us, I thought, then caught myself thinking it. Savage. My own name, or at least the one I had been given. Yes, a savage in all of us. But perhaps there were acts of grace that might redeem us.

Later that night, when they brought me the drawing things the Moor had ordered, I was filled with determination to conjure the image of the relic. I forced my mind back to that first glimpse of it in the storeroom in the citadel cellars: the gleam of the gold, the glint of the gems. The strange charge I had felt from the Nail of Treves.

I reached up to touch my charm. It was not there.

You'd think that now I was reunited with my friend, his parting gift would no longer carry the significance for me that it had. But the loss of it struck me like a fist.

And now I could not remember what the fragment of the Cross had looked like at all. Gold encased, yes, with the old wood showing through almost black at one end. But the details? The ornamentation? Gone like smoke. Would it matter? Surely an old piece of wood dressed up in any cover of gold would do the trick. Memories were flawed and chancy things, as even the Moor had said, two people's accounts of the same object or event rarely matching. But all it took was one doubt. All those people . . .

Back to the storeroom I led my unwilling mind. *Look in the chest: remember pulling out the cross, the True Cross, or rather the thing masquerading as it, remember the dancing light of the sconce playing across the gold, flickering in the gems . . .*

It was no good. I could not retrieve the memory. Had I looked at the relic at any other time? No, after it was bundled away inside my cloak it had stayed wrapped, right up till the moment the ocean swallowed me, fire all around, the air choked with the screams of burning men. God's teeth, what was I going to do?

It's a funny thing, the mind. Reach after something, chase it like a dog chases a rat, and it will guard its secrets. It's only when you give up that it teases you with a glimpse of the thing you were searching for. And sometimes a glimpse is enough.

The strange thing is that it wasn't a glimpse of the cross in the storeroom that came to me then. No, the quality of the light was different—brighter, sharper. The detail was still there, though: a ruby at the centre of a ring of bosses in the gold, etched lines connecting it to the next precious setting, and the next. Pearls here, emeralds there: a gaudy, tawdry thing. I almost smiled at the apparent fakeness of such opulence. If I closed my eyes, I could feel the stones, rough and hard beneath my fingertips . . .

I began to draw.

Zohra chose two of her father's best robes and tunics, a warm cloak, a sleeping blanket, and his favourite soft leather slippers, old and battered but perfectly moulded over the years to the shape of his feet, for him to take into the hostage quarters.

He took one look at the slippers and threw them down. "I can't be seen in these! Bring me the yellow ones."

"But, Baba, you always say they hurt your feet, the yellow ones."

"Never! I've never said that. Can't wear filthy old things like that in front of the Franj. They're fit only for the fire now. Like their owner."

"Don't say such things!" She took the old brown *qundara* back upstairs and came back with the stiff yellow ones, feeling unaccountably sorrowful.

When it came time to say goodbye, Baltasar let her hug him, standing unresponsive for several moments before suddenly seeming to remember who she was and what was happening, and then he almost crushed her in his embrace. When they came apart she saw his eyes were wet.

"Oh, Baba!" she wailed.

At last Sara stepped between them. "I'll look after him," she said. "You look after my son for me. You must make him go. Promise me." She leaned in and spoke in a low voice. "Tell him whatever it takes to make him leave the city with you, do you understand me?" The look she gave Zohra was powerfully communicative, and Zohra nodded, the tears rolling down her cheeks. Sara brushed them away with the thumb of her one remaining hand. "I know you will, and I bless you for it." She stepped back and spoke more loudly. "Pack that wound with honey-salve night and day, won't you?"

Nima clung to Baltasar's legs and cried when Zohra pulled her away. She had grown fond of the old bear of a man in the short time they had been together, perhaps because he was the only one who ever had time for her babbling; perhaps because he became, while he was with her, like a grandfather she had lost. Zohra took her upstairs and brought out all the old wooden toys she and the boys had shared as children and left her playing happily while she gathered clothes and a wide-toothed comb for Sorgan, and wrapped carefully in a white cloth a small cake she had made for him with flour and eggs and honey bought from the new supplies coming into the city. Something he would find later when he opened up his things. Something that might make him think of her . . .

But when she tried to give him the bundle down in the hallway Sorgan refused to take it, not wanting Mohammed Azri to see him being treated like a child.

"Sorgan, look at me."

"Want to go now." He pulled away from her.

"I know you do. But, Sorgan, I'm leaving the city. I may not see you . . . for a while."

"All right." For a moment he looked thoughtful. "Will you have lamb to eat tonight?"

Abruptly, Zohra's eyes swam with tears.

Sorgan was alarmed. "Don't cry! I am sure you will have lamb too." Without warning, he seized her in a fierce embrace, and that unexpected gesture caused her tears to spill. Muffled against his shoulder, she gasped out, "You are my brother and I love you, do you understand? Wherever you are, wherever I am, that will never change. Will you remember that?"

Embarrassed, he pulled away from her. "I have to go now. Mohammed is waiting for me."

Silently, Zohra tailed him to the door and handed her bundle to the smith, who took it from her with a wry smile. "I will see you again soon, *insh'allah*," Mohammed Azri told her.

"*Insh'allah*."

Zohra watched them go down the street, merging with the others who had chosen to go as hostages, until they turned the corner and disappeared from view. She had never felt so bereft in her life. To go back into a house that was empty of all its normal inhabitants felt bleak.

That night, she could not settle, could not sleep. She crept about, feeling uncomfortable and out of sorts, then packed away the things that had been left out and set the house to rights so that it was in order for when they returned. If they ever would . . .

It was important not to think about that. Instead, she rehearsed the words she would say to Nathanael when he came back from the qadi's office as she went from room to room, neatening drapes and closing drawers. All the sleeping-blankets she folded and stored away, rolled up the rugs to keep the dust off them, shut the kitchen things into the larder. The pigeon loft she swept and cleaned, locked the door to the terrace.

She stood at the threshold of the room at the top of the house that her parents had shared for so long, remembering. It was here she had first seen the twins, tiny creatures curled at Nima's breast, fast asleep, as pink and hairless as baby mice. She must have been, what? Less than three? Amazing how the mind retained such images with such clarity: she could recall how the light had slanted through the shutters, falling in lozenges on the coloured blanket over the bed. The room had seemed huge to her then; it looked so small now. Small and empty.

Then she went to check on the child in her mother's old sick-room. Little Nima, engaged in some secret game of her own in which she talked to each object in a peremptory, chiding voice, had scattered the toys about with cheerful abandon. Zohra retrieved a rag-ball that had crept half under the low table and caught a flash of yellow as she did so. Bending down, she pulled out the yellow silk cushion she had used to prop her mother up when feeding her. She stared at it for a long moment, then hugged it with a groan. She had never been able to bring herself to throw it away: to do so was somehow to admit that Kamal had hastened her death with it.

"Oh, Ummi. I'm so sorry," she whispered to the empty air.

Nima stared at her. "Who are you talking to?"

"No one, sweetheart. No one at all."

When, some while later, she caught out of the corner of her eye a movement at the threshold of the room, she cried out, but it was Nathanael, returned from the qadi's office. He looked morose, but forced a smile when Nima solemnly offered him the little wooden camel she had been playing with.

"Your hand is dirty!" she chided him as he reached to take it. She snatched the camel back and cradled it to her chest.

Nat gave a small snort of laughter. "That's not dirt, little bird. It's ink." He held his palm up. In the middle of it was stamped a large black cross.

Zohra's heart began to beat wildly. "What's that?" She hardly dared ask.

"I have official permission to leave the city."

"There's someone asking for you, Malek."

His head came sharply up out of the doze. Such a sweet dream had been interrupted, he hardly wanted to be disturbed. "Who? Who is it?"

"Malek, oh, Malek!"

One moment he had been daydreaming about a woman's embrace, the next minute it was happening in life. The woman in the dream had been small but sturdy; the one in his arms felt like a bag of bones. Disoriented, he held her away from him, in doubt as to which world he was in: the dream or the real.

"*Alhemdulillah!* A thousand thanks are due! Thank God you are safe!"

"Cousin Jamilla," he managed at last. When he'd heard that all those not being kept as hostages in the city had been told to leave, on account of there not being enough food to feed them, he had thought Zohra would come to him here. "Thank merciful God you are alive," he said, trying to sound sincere when all he truly felt was disappointment and the edge of a fear he did not wish to dwell on. Surely Zohra had not opted to stay as a hostage? With Tariq working at the citadel it suddenly seemed all too possible.

"You look well," he said. It was a blatant untruth: she looked more like a walking skeleton, something barely resurrected, her good arm as thin now as the withered one, her grin making a death's head of her face. "And the rest of the family?" he asked in the usual polite formula, knowing not to expect the usual polite answer.

She fought back tears. "Baba and Ummi have stayed behind as hostages. I offered but they would not let me." She gazed at him, trying to frame the words. "But they took your father, and Sorgan, too!"

He took this in silently. At least they were still alive. For now. "And Zohra?"

Jamilla looked uncomfortable. "She is well."

"Where is she? And Tariq?"

Her fingers fastened on his arm like claws. "What? You did not know? I'm sorry to be the bearer of sad news."

Malek felt his heart stop. What had happened? "My sister?"

When she shook her head, his relief was so intense he could hardly take in the rest of what she said. "Rachid died of a fever during the rains, and Tariq . . ." Her eyes scanned his face. "We all thought Tariq had come to the sultan's camp. He disappeared one night from the city." She sighed. "Well, he must have been caught by the Christians. He must be part of the prisoner exchange."

"*Insh'allah*. Poor Zohra. How has she managed on her own?"

"She's not on her own," Jamilla said.

Malek's face darkened. "The Jewish doctor."

"Life has been very . . . difficult in Akka these past months. People have been forced into all sorts of odd . . . arrangements."

"War will do that," he said quietly. "To all of us."

And so when Zohra trailed into camp later that day with a pale, stooped Jewish man and a small chattering child, he greeted her with relief and asked no questions.

Soon the camp began to fill with refugees. Everywhere you looked there were sights to break your heart. Children as insubstantial as djinns, women so thin it looked as if a puff of breeze would carry them away over the horizon like chaff. Hollow-eyed, sunken-cheeked, sometimes missing limbs, hopping on crutches, swathed in bandages, carried slung between staggering folk in barely better condition they came. Those who could walk came toiling up the hill with their heads high, in their best clothes, with all the possessions they could carry—which, in their state of weakness, was not much—on their backs. It was horribly sobering. Yes, the army had suffered losses in the battles and skirmishes, but that was the soldier's lot. There had been sickness, but there was always sickness in an army camp in summer, and some privation; it was as nothing compared to what the citizens of Akka had suffered.

He and Ibo and the rest of their comrades had given up their tent to his sister and cousin and some other women and children, and now, off duty, they walked through the camp, taking in the sights and listening to snippets of the conversations around the many cook-fires.

"I tried to persuade her but she would not come . . ."

"My father said the same: he's too old to go anywhere else and start again . . ."

". . . makes me sick to see the Templars in the central square again . . ."

". . . they will pollute the mosque."

"I heard they beat the imam and burned the minbar . . ."

"Franj soldiers rampaged through my cousin's house, smashing furniture, shitting on carpets . . ."

"I cannot find my brother . . ."

"I have lost my husband . . ."

"What will happen to my sons?"

Back at their own campfire, Ibo shook his head. "It is shameful that it should come to this after so much effort. After such resistance."

Malek grimaced. "They could not go on for ever. At least those who live will be saved."

"I heard we do not have the ransom money."

Malek had heard the same. The coffers were empty. The sultan had called upon all the provinces to send whatever they could, had written again to the caliph in Baghdad, not for the war effort this time but to save the lives of his subjects.

"He has not coughed up before," was all the big African said. "I doubt he will this time."

Malek was quiet for a long time.

33

❄

The Moor came to sit with me as I worked. He looked through the pieces of paper I had discarded and pursed his lips. Then he stood behind me and watched as I smudged out a detail. He sharpened a new reed-quill for me. "Try this."

I did. It was satisfying to see the fine line I could manage now. "Much better." I dotted the bosses I remembered around one of the gem settings and sat back. "I don't know whether the pattern is replicated across the whole piece," I said uncertainly. "Or on the back."

"It will have been made to be seen at all angles. Don't forget, the old Bishop of Acre carried it into battle with him."

"He must've been a strong man," I said, thinking of the weight of the fragment I'd carried through the city.

"He was a valiant man. He went down fighting," the Moor said. "But let's concentrate on getting the front right for now."

I worked in silence for a time. Then he said, "Do you know the legend of the True Cross, John?"

"Of course," I said. "Christ was crucified on it, alongside two thieves."

"They weren't really thieves," the Moor explained. "At least one of them wasn't. More of a trickster. But that's not exactly what I meant. Do you know whence came the wood for the cross?"

"Off some tree?" I suggested facetiously.

He smiled. "Some say it came from three trees grown from seed from the Tree of Mercy, seeds collected by Seth, the son of Adam, which he then planted in the mouth of his father's corpse."

"Seems an odd place to plant a tree."

"The logic of ancient myths is not necessarily our logic, John. But there's another tale, more detailed than that one. Do you want to hear it?"

"Can I escape it?" I bent my head to draw the opening in the gold through which the wood could be seen, and no doubt touched by the devout.

"I won't tell you if you don't want to hear. But maybe the telling of the story will be imbued in the drawing you make, and thence into the making of the object. Perhaps it will be the better for it."

I looked up at him. "That sounds like magic and miracles to me. And we all know about the truth of those."

"Such a cynic. Has not life taught you that there are ever more possibilities than those you first guessed at?"

"Maybe." I felt uncomfortable with the turn the conversation was taking. "Just tell me the story, then."

He paused for so long I thought I had offended him, but finally he said, "It is told in other traditions that a cutting from the Tree of Knowledge was planted on Adam's grave, where it grew and flourished until the time of Suleiman the Great."

"I don't know that name," I said, moving the reed scratchily across the paper.

"You will know him as Solomon the King."

I grinned to myself. "Oh, the one who cut the baby in half!"

He chuckled. "You jest. Unless you really didn't pay attention to your teachers at the priory."

"I don't tend to take in lessons if they are accompanied by the strike of a stick."

"It is a poor way to teach," he said, "that much is true. Well, it is said that the great tree was cut down in Solomon's time in order to construct the bridge over which the Queen of Sheba—or, as the Arabs call her, Bilqis—passed on her way to meet with the great king. She was less than halfway across it when she was struck by an extraordinary vision. She fell to her knees in the middle of the bridge, shaking and crying out."

I stopped what I was doing and looked at him. "She suffered fits like me?"

He regarded me steadily. "When did you last fall down, John?"

I could not remember the last time I had suffered a full fit, falling and frothing and speaking in tongues of arches and pillars and angels' wings. Not since . . . well, not since he had left me. "I can't remember."

"That is good, then. It worked."

I gave him a hard stare. "What worked?"

The Moor gave a secretive smile, shook his head a little. "It doesn't matter."

"Tell me."

He ruffled my hair, sending a warmth down my spine that gathered in my tailbone like a small fire. "On with our story, my Savage. In her vision, Bilqis foresaw some extraordinary role for the simple bridge. She babbled about the coming of a new order, the replacement of God's covenant with the Jews, a terrible act of sacrifice. In terror, Solomon had the bridge ripped up and buried deep where none would ever find it. But centuries later the remnants of the bridge were found and dug up and used by Zerubbabel to construct the Temple in Jerusalem, as is told in the Book of Ezra.

"Many generations later, King Herod decided to replace the old temple with a more magnificent edifice, a project attended by sacrificial rituals and the spilling of much blood. It was during this reconstruction that the wood was discarded once more, except this time the pieces were used for a different and crueller purpose—as the crosses upon which Isa Christ and the two men condemned to die beside him were crucified."

"I thought the Muslims didn't believe in Jesus Christ."

"He is revered as a prophet—a great prophet—in Islam," the Moor corrected me gently. "It is only the story of the risen Christ that is disputed."

I laughed. "Dead men do not rise?"

He spread his hands. "Who am I to deny it?"

Salah ad-Din bent his head over the piece of paper, but from where he was, Malek could see nothing of what it contained. Something was going on, something to do with the ransom terms—that was as much as he knew—and it all seemed very secret. Everyone but al-Adil, Ahmad al-Rammah, the coppersmith's son from Damascus, the tall, dark man they called the Moor and Baha ad-Din had been sent from the war tent. He watched out of the corner of his eye as the sultan turned the paper on its side, scrutinized it and turned it back again. He met the Moor's regard solemnly. "I am no expert at interpreting such things," he said.

He passed the drawing to his brother, who frowned and perused it for several long moments. Then he, too, shook his head. "It is a piece of paper," he said. "The distance from this to the object itself is too great a leap of imagination for a plain soldier like me."

"You have some experience in these matters," the sultan said to the Moor. "Do you think it will pass muster?"

"That rather depends on the quality of the casing, of the metal and its workmanship," the Moor said.

"And this . . . mountain copper, what do you call it?" He turned to the Damascene.

"Orichalcum, my lord."

"You can make it look enough like gold to pass scrutiny by the Franj envoys?"

"I believe so, sire."

"Are you able to get hold of enough of the substance for the purpose?" Baha ad-Din asked. "If this metal will pass for gold on even a cursory inspection, I don't imagine that it will come cheap."

"My family have been working a seam of it for generations," Ahmad said. "It would be our honour to supply the material for the salvation of the people of Akka and the glory of God. We will accept no payment for it."

The sultan looked humbled. He raised his hands to Heaven and called a blessing upon the boy and his family. Then he smiled. "It is just as well, for I have nothing left with which to pay you." He turned to Baha ad-Din. "And the gems?"

"That too is in hand, sire. Leave that with me."

The sultan looked back at the Moor. "If this stratagem succeeds, we shall all be much in your debt, *sayedi*."

The tall foreigner bowed. "In matters such as these there can be no debt, my lord."

For the best part of a fortnight, the Moor and his artisans worked on the relic—the wide-eyed young man called Ahmad from Damascus who was in charge of the smelting process, two dark-robed alchemists, a goldsmith and his boy. The smelter, the Moor informed me, had been responsible for creating the Greek fire that had destroyed the ship Quickfinger, Hammer and I were on. So valued was he by the sultan, the Moor explained, that he had been smuggled out of the city on the very night we had found our way in.

I looked at the Moor now in the dim light of the work tent, narrowing my eyes at him. "Was that what all that green smoke was about?"

He looked at me askance. "That did not work quite as planned. In one way it was more successful than I ever hoped. In another, not so much."

"Don't be so cryptic! Tell me what you mean."

"What did you see, John?"

I thought back, suppressing a shudder at how close to death I had come that day. I remembered the view from the basket of the trebuchet, the green cloud full of spectral horsemen, hundreds of them, all in green cloaks, the crescent banners of Islam flying from their lances. I told him what I thought I'd seen and watched as he gave a rueful smile

"The martyrs of Islam, garbed in the Prophet's own colour!" Ahmad said. "I couldn't have asked for a better diversion."

"It was a good illusion, wasn't it?" The Moor was pleased.

"It saved my life," I said.

He gave me a long, languorous look that made the blood rise in my face. "It did, didn't it?" Behind him, the artificer laughed silently and returned to his task.

I wondered how so young and cheerful a man as Ahmad could be responsible for dealing so much death. But now, I supposed, he was working to save lives. Maybe there was some kind of invisible balance at work in the world after all.

Our work tent was set up at some distance from the rest of the army camp, partly because of the noxious fumes we were producing, and partly because of the need for secrecy. There were many times during that week that I thought our task impossible. The bubbling metal in the cauldron was a dull brown colour, bursting into bubbles of red and giving out sulphurous farts and gulps. On the first attempt it emerged almost black, and no amount of alum or scraping made much difference.

The Moor was unfazed, however. "It's a matter of trial and error," he'd said after consulting Ahmad and the alchemists. "Once we hit the right heat to anneal it, the impurities will emerge and can be removed. That will brighten the colour."

I simply couldn't imagine how the dull mixture in that cauldron could ever come to resemble the gleaming relic we'd stolen from the treasury in Acre. In the end, for fear my lack of conviction would somehow magically spoil the process further, I left them to it.

I did not see the Moor for several days, spending my time instead with Rosamund as she recuperated from her wound. Sometimes we were joined by the tall Muslim soldier, and I would watch how his dour, narrow face lit up when she smiled at him, and how her cheeks glowed as she mimed something she could not yet phrase in his language, and I wondered how such tenderness could possibly flower out of the bloody roots of this war.

Then, one day, the Moor came to find me. His robe was spotted and stained and his hands were black to the wrists, his nails as filthy as my own. I had never before seen him dirty. Even on the muddiest of our travels he had always somehow contrived to remain fastidiously clean, making soaps from riverbank plants, using sand or grit to wash with where there was no water. He smelled sharply of citrus, with a bitter, salty tinge. I wrinkled my nose.

He grinned. "We've had to use a cartload of lemons and another of alum, but I think we've done it. Come and see."

The tent was dark after the bright light outside. It took a while for my eyes to adjust to the light, but when they did . . .

"That's incredible."

The goldsmith's boy was beating out a thin sheet of the metal. It gleamed like buttercups. Like liquid sunshine. Like gold . . .

"It'll tarnish and blacken as time goes on, so I've sent word to the sultan. The Christian envoys will be here in two days."

"Two days!"

"Sayedi Soufiane here says that will be time enough to do the work, and that we can keep the oxidation at bay long enough for the metal to retain its colour." He said something rapidly to the goldsmith in their guttural language; the old man nodded vigorously and raised his hands, as if seeking God's aid.

And I had thought our venture at Glastonbury a chancy business . . .

"May I?" I gestured towards the artifact.

The goldsmith was reluctant to let me near his work of art, and I couldn't honestly blame him, but at last he stepped aside. He had been sitting, surrounded by candles at night and with the flaps of the tent up by day, hammering and etching for days with his tiny gold-working tools. What he had achieved in that time was well-nigh miraculous: the back as well as the front of the replica cross was adorned with "jewels"—finely chiselled coloured glass and some real pearls purloined from who knew where—and busy with whorls and bosses and tiny portraits of Christian saints. Some of the latter I'd drawn from scratch: the others I'd recalled from the Lady Chapel. There had been a lot of metal to embellish: we'd had to extemporize. But who, I thought, gazing at this wondrous object, would ever suspect it had been forged by infidels? It was covered with Christian iconography devised by a wild heathen who'd lived as a beast on the moors, and replicated by a man whose religion allowed for no such representations of its sacred imagery.

I picked it up gingerly, expecting it to weigh as heavy as iron. It came away lighter than I'd expected and I almost let it slip. The goldsmith wrestled it away from me and set it back on the table. The look he gave me was not friendly.

"We had to use more wood and less metal in the end," the Moor said, stepping out of the shadows. "Drawing the golden hue out of the copper proved to be . . . challenging. We were not left with enough to make all parts solid, like the original. And maybe

the wood of the relic became denser with age as it dried and contracted over the centuries. But," he bent and swept his fingertips
lightly over the intricate, glowing surface, "it looks impressive to
me . . . pagan that I am." He turned and grinned at me, and the gold
reflected in the half-moons of his eyes.

For a moment my knees went weak. "You have worked magic,"
I told him.

"Jamil."

Malek turned with a start to find Rosamund behind him. Asfar
whickered, annoyed that Malek's careful grooming had suddenly
stopped. *"Jamilla,"* he corrected. "The feminine form takes an 'a.'
And yes, she is beautiful my horse, my Asfar."

"Jamil," repeated Rosamond cheerfully. She touched Malek on
the chest. "You. You look so . . . grand." Not knowing the Arabic
for this, she puffed her chest out and strutted until he laughed.

He took his helmet off and held it out to her. "See, it is only me,
Malek, under all this," he said in Arabic, and then, "Only a man,"
he continued in English, and she almost fell down in shock.

"What? How?"

"Your friend the Moor. He teaches me your language."

Rosamund's grin went from ear to ear. "He is matchmaking!"
She chuckled, and refused to explain the word to him. Instead,
she ran her hand through the chestnut mare's glossy mane and
exclaimed when her fingers came away gleaming with fragrant oil.
"She smells better than me!"

"The sultan has asked us not to shame him," Malek tried to
explain. He mimed polishing his helmet, the harness, his boots,
while Rosamund made appreciative noises.

"Very handsome," she said. *"Jamil!"* and this time he did not
correct her. A faint blush coloured his cheeks.

443

"He cannot be seen to be lacking funds," he went on quickly in Arabic to cover his embarrassment, "when the envoys come." This was what Ibrahim had so perceptively remarked first thing that morning: "He will need to buy more time and to instill confidence in them. It is a dangerous and narrow path between two chasms that he has to walk."

Malek had nodded grimly, thinking of his father and brother, his Uncle Omar and his aunts. He had felt sick then, but now, looking at Rosamund, his heart lifted. Whenever he saw her smile his heart leapt up, and whenever she was with him she smiled. The two things seemed indivisible: a marvellous, miraculous conjunction of events. There was something thrilling about this connection between them. He did not know what it was or what it meant. He did not know where it might lead or how he might be changed by it, but whenever that smile—sometimes shy, sometimes teasing—lit her face, he felt that anything in the world was possible.

I will speak to my father as soon as he is released, he thought. *While he is still happy to be alive.* It would not be an easy conversation. A foreign woman raised by their enemies, speaking only a little Arabic, with no bridal goods and no one to speak for her and, worst of all, an infidel. For a moment his heart seized at the prospect. But the best things in life never come easy—wasn't Baltasar himself fond of saying that?

Malek took up his position with the rest of the burning coals on either side of the meeting place. All the best carpets had been gathered from the princes of the camp and laid out over the parched soil—a gorgeous tapestry of crimson and peach and ochre and rose and blue—leading to the canopy. Beneath it the sultan sat in his plain dark-green robe and his plain white turban, under which Malek knew he wore the steel cap he had always worn since the *hashshashin* had made their last attempt on his life. The scene made a handsome sight. *Jamil*, he thought, and smiled to himself.

The envoys came riding up the Hill of Carobs with their banners flying. Malek recognized among them the blue silk of the French king and the red-and-gold of the English king, and behind them the great gold crosses on white silk of the Kingdom of Jerusalem. Had the great kings themselves come? He craned his neck, intrigued. No, the man whose squire flew the English banner was not al-Inkitar, and the Frenchman also did not look like a king. The third envoy, though, he recognized, barely. Guy de Lusignan: the snake who had started this siege, the man Salah ad-Din had spared after the Battle of Hattin. The intervening four years had not been kind to him. Lank brown hair threaded with grey was bound back from his forehead by a thin golden circlet; deep-set eyes gazed hauntingly from beneath a shelf of bone. They had heard he'd lost his daughters to the plague, and his queen, too; he looked himself like a man on the brink of death.

The envoys dismounted and the sultan rose to welcome them. Refreshments were brought, greetings exchanged. Niceties over, the English envoy waved his men forward. They were burly fellows, chosen for their ability to carry heavy chests. Salah ad-Din waved the men away, as if it was rude to bring business to a head quite so soon in their meeting. Voices were raised, but not enough for Malek to hear exactly what was said. His guts clenched: it was clear that the envoys were unhappy, that their instructions had been to fetch the ransom monies and to return with them without delay. More talking, quieter now. Some prisoners were herded forward and given over to the envoys, followed by four small chests: a down payment on the full ransom.

Even this was not enough to calm tempers. The English envoy shouted again; the Frenchman joined him. Hands went to sword hilts on either side.

The sultan stood and said something to a man behind him. He gestured for the envoys to take another glass of wine. Then, at a signal, the honour guard parted to allow the passage of a tall man in a white robe. It was the Moor, and he carried before him the relic that had been captured at Hattin, the object the Franj called the True Cross.

Sunlight played over rich gold, sparked a fire in the jewels, caressed the pearls. The Moor's sleeves fell back to show arm muscles corded with the effort of bearing the heavy cross aloft. A heady scent of roses engulfed the onlookers.

The envoys stared at the relic, Guy de Lusignan through narrowed eyes, the other two with expressions of awe bordering on terror.

Then, one by one, they fell to their knees before it and began to pray.

34

✻

"**H**old still, John. You're as twitchy as a mule plagued by horseflies."

I tried to still myself beneath his hands and allow myself to luxuriate in the sensation.

"Shaggy as a pony," he said fondly. Clippings of my black hair floated to the ground, as coarse and curly as a dog's.

I closed my eyes and tilted my face up to the sun till the insides of my eyelids shone as red as a *naranja*. "Tell me, were you ever in Lisbon?" I asked, trying to sound nonchalant.

The hands stopped for a moment, then resumed their gentle plucking and measuring and cutting. "Once," he said softly. There was a smile in his voice.

"I . . . I thought I saw you there."

"I was on the road the best part of two years," he said evasively.

"Where did you go after you left us in Rye?"

"From Paris to Cluny Abbey. I followed the pilgrim route to Compostela. After that . . ."—snip, snip—"a little while in Cordoba. Do you know there are eight hundred and fifty-six columns in the Great Mosque? It is a building shaped by light," he said dreamily. "Then I travelled on in search of a special form of arch that will enable us to build our cathedral high, make it light and airy—"

"I have seen these arches!" I could not help but shout it out. People stared, then laughed, thinking the Moor had nicked an ear. I lowered my voice. "In Acre, in the mosque. There were things there I have dreamed of all my life—towering pillars and sharp arches, and a roof all of gold—"

He stopped cutting. "You went into the Friday Mosque?"

I nodded. "While Quickfinger and I were escaping. It was . . . like a vision."

The Moor clucked his tongue. "A pair of infidels in a mosque." He started his snipping again. "I took ship from Lisbon to Amalfi and from there to Monte Cassino, where there are still Muslim masons working. From there I shipped to North Africa to see the Qubbat Barudiyan in Marrakech, and from there to the Qairouan Mosque, and at last to Cairo."

I turned my head to look at him, and this time the shears really did nick my ear. "Ow! But how did you afford it, having left me all your money?"

"Oh, John." He sounded amused. "Reginald sent me to visit the sacred sites where I would find these ogival arches that enable a construction so strong it will allow for the opening of great windows in the walls. I was to find masons who understand the principles required to construct his project at Wells. He gave me a good sum of money to carry out the research."

"Oh. That was very trusting of him."

He bellowed out a laugh. "It was, wasn't it? A trickster, a foreigner, a . . . heathen. I could have taken the money and run. I can't deny it crossed my mind."

"And yet here you are. Faking relics for the enemy."

"God rarely chooses a straight path for us. I was on my way from Beirut to visit the Umayyad Mosque in Damascus when the ship I was on was taken by the Franj."

"So it was you I saw in the prisoner exchange!" I turned to look at him. His face was so close I could feel his breath on me. A wild upsurge of joy welled deep inside me . . .

A babble of noise made him straighten up abruptly. I turned to see who was chattering, and found a young lad of twelve or thirteen, tricked out in the garb of the sultan's servants: dark green with yellow-gold braid, curly slippers on his feet.

The Moor nodded. "*Na'am*," he said. "*Wachha*." He clapped me on the shoulder. "Come on, John, there's another envoy from the English king. They want me as interpreter. I may need you."

I trailed him to the sultan's tent, shedding cut hair as I went.

A squire bearing a lance from which flew the white flag of truce stood awkwardly outside the war tent. Behind him, two big mounted soldiers. I stared at the second one, his face in profile as he looked out over the valley to the city of Acre. It was the big *routier*, Florian. My heart hammered.. "I know him," I said. "He mustn't see me."

"Stay a pace behind me," the Moor said, "and keep your head down. You're swarthy enough to pass as one of us now." He shot me a grin, enjoying my discomfort.

The guard on the door was Rosamund's Malek, who, when the Moor explained I was helping translate the envoy's words, waved me through. Inside, there was a fug of incense, wisps of fragrant smoke spiralling up towards the ceiling. Through them I saw for the first time Sultan Saladin. He was not what I had expected, for he looked neither warlike nor fearsome. Instead he was rather a slight, studious man, his gaunt face set in weary lines, silver threading his neat beard, eyes as dark as spent embers. His attention was trained on his guest—the envoy, I supposed.

The smoke curled and twisted, and then the guest turned to say something to the sultan—a polite acceptance of the glass of sherbet he held in his hands, maybe—and I saw his face full on. It was Savaric de Bohun.

The Moor was ahead of me. All he did was gesture with his right hand. I slipped gratefully into the shadows behind one of the tall censers where the smoke was thickest and watched as the Moor prostrated himself gracefully to the sultan, then straightened up.

Savaric's eyes went round with shock. "You!"

"The world is smaller than we think it sometimes," the Moor said smoothly. "It is a pleasure to see you again, and looking so well, *effendi*." He put his hand to his heart and bowed in the oriental fashion.

"Well, I suppose this makes my task easier in some ways," Savaric mused, "and harder in others." He paused. "Your sultan will not like what I have been sent to tell him."

The Moor inclined his head, then translated this. The sultan said something quietly and the Moor relayed it. "He says the messenger's job is never easy, especially when he carries the burden of heavy words. It is best to empty out your sack of rocks and to lighten your load. Nothing you say will be held against you."

Savaric nodded, his moon-face pensive. Then he said, "King Richard asks, well, actually demands, that all of the agreed monies be paid over right away, the rest of the prisoners released, and the True Cross given up to him at once. Or he will kill all the hostages."

I felt ice form in my stomach. The Moor's face became very still. Then he relayed this quietly to the sultan. I watched anger flare in those sunken, dark eyes. Then the sultan composed himself, turned to Savaric and said something smilingly.

The Moor said, "First our prisoners must be released to us, and then King Richard shall have his gold and his cross. The weight of souls is heavier than the weight of gold, and the sultan has a duty of care for our people."

Savaric shook his head. "The king said the sultan would say that, but I fear he has already discounted this option. Once the prisoners, the money and the True Cross are in his possession, then and only then will the Muslims be released."

Again the Moor repeated these words in Arabic; again the sultan smothered his anger. Then he spoke at length in a quiet and measured tone.

"Our kingdom is vast and far-flung, and not all of our resources are at hand. The sultan fears that he has had to send to Baghdad and to Cairo for the ransom monies, for his own coffers are empty or already in the hands of the Christian kings."

"There was not a great deal in the Acre treasury," Savaric said. "Richard was highly displeased." He shot a look at the sultan, then said softly to the Moor, "This is not for you to translate, but I want to know how it is that the True Cross that was supposed to be in the treasury is now here in the sultan's hands."

The Moor regarded him dispassionately. He translated something to the sultan and then said, "So if King Richard has already assessed the poor state of our treasury he must know that what we say is true: we do not have the resources here to pay the ransom and must wait until the caliph in Baghdad and the vizier in Cairo send the requisite monies. As to the cross—" He smiled, showing his teeth, an expression I knew well. It was the grin he gave another when lying to his face. "Well, it never was in Acre."

Savaric's face fell. "I cannot go back empty-handed. He is not a man to make empty threats, Richard. He is both determined and ruthless."

I saw the Moor hesitate for a moment. Was "ruthless" a word he knew? But he could not consult me without giving me away.

Again the exchange of words, again the Moor's smooth voice. "The sultan maintains he has kept his side of the bargain by paying over the first instalment of the ransom money and a goodly quantity of prisoners, but we have been given nothing in exchange, which was not what was agreed. You must go back to your king and remind him of the terms of the accord."

Savaric looked desperate. "At least let me take the cross. That might mollify him for a while."

The Moor translated this, and the sultan shook his head. "Tell your king he must show patience, that most kingly of qualities, and he shall be fully rewarded in due course."

Savaric became very red in the face. Sweat beaded his brow. "None of you know Richard as I do. You have no idea what he is capable of."

"The sultan has spoken," the Moor said softly. "There is nothing more I can do."

"At least let me see the True Cross," Savaric begged. "For myself."

The Moor relayed this, and a curious expression crossed the sultan's face. He turned and spoke to a man behind him who walked quickly from the tent.

There followed several minutes of tense silence during which sugared pastries were offered and refused. Then the man returned, and behind him Ahmad al-Rammah and one of the alchemists bearing a heavy object smothered in silk. They came to a halt between the door and Savaric so that much of the natural light was blotted out. Then they uncovered their burden.

Savaric's dark eyes welled; tears spilled. His mouth gaped open. He got unsteadily to his feet and staggered a pace towards the cross. Alarmed, Ahmad took a pace back. "It's all right," the Moor said. "*Messhi moushki*. Let him approach."

The tears were streaming so fast down Savaric's face now that I doubted he could see anything clearly. From where I crouched I could see that the back of the relic had darkened already in the day since it was last polished with lemon and alum salt. But judging by the citrus smell that permeated the air, maybe Ahmad had swiftly removed the patina from the front of the artifact.

Savaric reached a trembling hand to the relic, touched it briefly and closed his eyes, his lips moving in silent prayer. He turned back to the Moor. "Let me take it," he begged again. "If I go back with nothing . . . He has a terrible temper, this king. He is a man obsessed with getting his own way. There is no flexibility in him. I fear for the hostages. There is not enough food for all as it is, and there are so many of them . . ." His voice trailed off.

The chill ran down my back and legs. This was a king whose subjects had massacred Jews in his own city and who had done nothing to stop them. "You have no idea what he is capable of," Savaric had said. But I did.

I stood up from my hiding place.

"King Richard has neither patience nor honour," I said. "Savaric, you must do whatever you can to save these people. Tell him he must wait for his payment."

Savaric stared at me as if he were seeing a ghost. The Moor said something quickly to the sultan, who again shook his head and replied quietly.

Meanwhile, my erstwhile master looked me up and down. "John, have you turned coat?"

"I never had a coat to turn," I said bitterly.

The Moor interrupted us. "Remind your king that princes must honour their words," he translated. "The sultan will hold the cross as surety against the welfare of our people."

At a motion from the sultan, the men hooded the relic again and carried it away. Light flooded into the tent in their wake.

Savaric watched them go, shaking his head sadly. "I have no influence, none at all. I am just a messenger." He bowed to the sultan and walked away. When he came to me, he extended his hand. "Good luck, John."

"And to you."

"I fear I will need it more than you."

Some days later, Zohra and Nathanael walked away from the camp, to a pretty spot on the hills above the road to Nazareth, having left

Nima in the care of Cousin Jamilla. They took with them dates and water, and a loaf that was still warm from the oven. It was the first time they had been out of the eyes of others for a long while, for the men's and women's areas were on opposite sides of the encampment: even husbands and wives slept separate from one another. To be alone together was like a huge weight being lifted.

It was afternoon before the conversation turned to the future: they had both been sidestepping the subject.

"Where will we go, beloved?"

Zohra turned her head and smiled up at Nathanael, the blue sky reflecting in her wide eyes. "I don't know. I don't care, as long as it's with you."

A stray curl of hair had slipped from her confining headscarf. Nat pulled at it playfully, winding it around and around his finger till it came free. "Damascus is where you have family," he started.

Zohra rolled up onto her elbows. "You are my family now. You and little Nima. We shall just wait for Baba and Sorgan and your mother to be released and get them to the cousins in Damascus, and then we can go wherever you want."

"Wherever?"

"Wherever."

Nat grinned up at her. "The moon?"

"I will come to the moon with you," said Zohra, deadly serious.

He tugged on the strand of hair to bring her closer. Zohra resisted playfully, then leaned in for a long, final kiss. Then she sat up and dusted the bits of earth and dried grass from her skirts. "We'd better be getting back to camp . . ."

The sun was westering now, casting a brazen light across the sea.

"There are people coming out of the city," Nathanael said suddenly.

Zohra shaded her eyes. "A lot of people." She turned to her lover, suddenly glowing with hope. "You don't think . . . the ransom has been paid, do you?"

Nat said nothing, but a vertical line formed between his brows.

More and yet more figures emerged from the city gates, tiny as ants at that distance.

"Let's go back down to the camp," Zohra said excitedly. "We can see better from there."

Nat put a hand on her arm. "I think we should stay where we are. There will be a lot of fuss and bother around the camp if the hostages have been released."

"But they will need our help—"

"I don't think the pair of us will make a whit of difference," he said grimly. "Let us wait and see what's going on before we move." His voice held a note of foreboding that made Zohra turn to him questioningly. Nathanael shook his head. "All will soon be clear," he said, trying to sound reassuring.

A column of soldiers and a great crowd of people on foot came out and began to move slowly uphill. "I don't know what's going on," Nat admitted after a while. "It does look as if they are bringing all the hostages out."

They sat in silence as the procession filed through the Christian camp and continued to toil up towards the Tell Ayyadieh and the Muslim camp. "It looks as if they're delivering them to the sultan," Zohra said happily. "I do hope so. I've been so worried about Baba. I know he says he's too old to leave Akka and start anew, but he has family in Damascus."

Still they came on, and soon they could see that the prisoners were roped together, their hands bound with thick cords, men and women, even children.

"You'd think they'd allow them a bit more dignity," Zohra said bitterly. "It's not as if they're going to run if they're being freed, is it?"

She started down the hillside towards them. Biting off a curse, Nat went after her fast, grabbed her by the arms and spun her around, but Zohra tore herself free and continued at a run. "Look, look! I can see Aunt Asha in her best red robe, and look, there's Mohammed Azri and Sorgan!"

The sight of people she knew stopped her in her tracks. Nathanael stared at the swarm of hostages in anguish, making out, almost against his will, a face here and there, searching for his mother, Sara. Instead he saw one of the women who had been in the baker's queue on the day Nima's mother had been killed, and Sayedi Efraim, the old herb-seller, supporting as best he could the weight of an elderly, grey-haired woman, who must surely have been his wife. Saïd, the doctor from the hospital; the crabber, and his daughter, Rana . . .

Then he saw the men behind them draw their swords.

"Come with me, my lioness," he said, bundling Zohra backwards. "This is not a sight for those amber eyes."

Zohra fought him. "What are you doing? I'm sure if we look hard enough we'll be able to see Sara and my father, too. Oh——"

A body crumpled, suddenly headless, followed by another and another. Screams rent the air.

Zohra gazed over Nat's shoulder, aghast. "No! No, they can't——"

It had clearly been designed that the slaughter should take place in full view of the Muslim camp. Swords flashed in the late-afternoon light, the sun and worse lending them a red sheen. Suddenly there were soldiers from the Muslim camp careering down the hillside. Christian soldiers rode out to confront them, easily keeping them at bay, while behind them the decapitations continued inexorably.

Zohra wailed and tried to run. "Baba!" she screamed. "Sorgan!"

Nathanael wrapped his arms around her, bore her to the ground. "There is nothing you can do. Nothing!"

Zohra fought like a wildcat, biting and scratching in her fury. "I must see, I must!" Her hair came loose from the scarf, a snaking river of black. She flung herself this way and that, but Nat would not let her go. At last she subsided, tears and dust streaking her face. "It is the least I can do," she croaked, wrenching herself upright. "I must watch. I must bear witness."

Nathanael collapsed beside her, his limbs suddenly as weak as string, his wound throbbing as if it had been made anew. They knelt together in the parched dead grass, tears falling silently as one by one the bodies fell and the earth became red mud, as the soldiers surged against one another and the banners of kings flew in the scream-laden air.

35

*

I did not have much recollection of that day for a long time. The Moor told me he feared me dead. When the killing started I apparently ran screaming down the hillside, without armour, bare-headed and weaponless. When he found me, hours later, I was covered top to toe in blood, none of it my own, and had my hands wrapped around a mace, from which I would not be parted. They say I growled like an animal, could not speak in any human tongue.

The sequence of events on that terrible day came back to me in fits and starts, in the middle of a sweat-filled nightmare, or out of the blue. We left the camp a few days later, striking out into the interior of the country, heading for Damascus. On the road we overtook many refugees previously freed from the city. They had all lost family in the massacre; their tales were hard to hear. There was a young woman who had lost her father and brother in the slaughter, and the rest of her family either prior to or during the siege. That she was still able to eat and speak, and even sometimes smile, after such a loss was to me a greater miracle than any church could boast.

She was travelling with a tall, dark-haired man and a pretty child. Occasionally, I caught the man giving me puzzled looks, which made me feel uncomfortable, scrutinized.

In the middle of the third night we travelled with them I sat bolt upright, sweating. It had come to me: I had seen the assassin stab that very man in the citadel inside Acre, had seen him on the floor of that rich chamber, surrounded by a spreading pool of blood. I had thought him dead, and felt guilty for doing nothing to help him.

Once my heart had stilled I lay there looking up at the swath of stars scattered overhead and wondered at the fact he was still alive. A great weight lifted off me that night: even though we never said anything about it, it was as if I had been handed a gift, a sort of redemption.

Nathanael was a doctor. He and the Moor fell into easy company, comparing herbal remedies, experimenting with the best tisanes to ease my troubled sleep and that of the woman he called his wife, Zohra. And whatever they did, the child, Nima—who seemed drawn by the Moor, as children often are—watched with her big, dark eyes, taking it all in.

"I'm going to be a doctor too, just like both of you," she announced.

"Are you, little bee?" the Moor asked her.

"Yes," she declared solemnly.

Nathanael smiled at him over Nima's head. "You have to make a difference, that's what my father always said. No matter how slim the chance of success may seem, it's the only way to make things better in the end. You have to pass on your wisdom to a new generation, and each time, step by step, things improve."

The Moor held his gaze, then nodded slowly. "That's it exactly."

In Damascus we shared an empty and long-neglected house rented from a distant cousin of Zohra's. They did not seem much pleased to welcome her new husband. I felt a fool when the Moor had to explain to me why; it had not even occurred to me.

"Does it matter so much that he's a Jew?" I asked. Before we had left the Muslim camp, Rosamund had announced to me that she was going to marry Malek. "He doesn't know it yet," she'd added with a grin. "But I am." Christian and Muslim; Jew and Muslim; and . . . well, I had no idea how to identify the Moor and myself.

"People go to war over such things," he said. "But we are all just men."

The Moor and Nathanael and I put our backs into clearing the weed-filled garden, replacing the broken tiles around the rubble-choked fountain, clearing the water-pipes, restoring it to life. But the greatest restorative was to my soul. It felt good and simple to put my efforts into manual labour. It made me feel again that despite all I had seen there was still some small chance of bringing something good into this imperfect world. We planted fruit trees. Buntings gathered at the water's edge on the first day we turned the fountain on, until Nima came dancing out, clapping her hands with delight, and scared them away. Then she acquired a cat, a sly calico tom with mismatched eyes, and after that the birds kept their distance.

One day the Moor suggested I come to the Umayyad Mosque with him.

"But I can't."

He raised an eyebrow.

"I'm not a Muslim. You said I was a heathen and it wasn't allowed."

"What are you, John?"

So much easier to say what I was not. "I don't know."

"Do any of us know? We may call ourselves by many names—Christian and Jew, Muslim or infidel. But how can we know our source or our destination? As soon ask stone or earth or river: we each of us have our own secret way of being a part of the mystery." His eyes glowed as if lit from within. "Come be a part of the mystery with me. I will show you what to do."

There was a great serenity to be found amongst the endless replication of pillars and arches of the mosque. Its quiet beauty surprised me. I was given permission to sketch there, and I did, day after day, which soothed my spirit. To capture that immense impression of space and light would have taken a greater artist than me. Still, it woke in me a sense of greater purpose. I felt as I had in the little church in Lisbon, as if I was questing after the unseen, the elusive capture of perfection. I recalled the vision of grace I had experienced in the Acre mosque. I began to understand what drove Bishop Reginald and his dream for his cathedral, despite all the questionable methods he and his cousin had employed.

When I stumblingly tried to discuss this with the Moor, he smiled. "And now you are ready to travel with me."

"Travel where?"

"There is still much to see, much to discover, before we go back."

"Back where?"

"Back to England. To Wells."

I had come to think of Damascus as home. Almost. Almost it had come to feel like home to me. "I don't understand why you would want to go back to England after . . . after all that has happened."

"All the more reason to do what I must do. There are two kinds of men in this world, John. Those who fear beauty and seek to destroy it, and those who strive to create it, against all the odds, who seek to make sense of the world, to find the truth of it. Beauty is the highest truth of all: to capture that beauty in stone, to the glory of God—whatever name we call him by—is the most perfect expression of man's striving. After all the ugliness we have seen, how much more does the world need beauty?"

A few days later we left Damascus. And so it was that a boy bearing the name of Savage, a wild boy from the Cornish moors, entered the gates of Jerusalem the Golden.

The city still lay in Muslim hands; King Richard's drive to regain the holy city had come to nothing. Deserted by the French King Philip Augustus, dogged by ill health and self-doubt, by concerns about his kingdom back home, he had turned back from the decisive battle, which he might well have won, said the Moor, the Muslim army being so exhausted and reduced.

"All that death and cruelty, for nothing."

"War never solved anything," my friend said. "But it can destroy much. Look around you."

We were inside the Al-Aqsa Mosque in the eastern part of the Holy City, having walked through the remarkable bazaar to reach it.

"When the Christians took the city at the end of the last century, they killed every Muslim who took sanctuary here. Then they turned this place into stables," the Moor told me. "First blood, then horse shit, but even that could not break its beauty. Salah ad-Din had it washed with rosewater, scattered with rose petals when he took it back. And now look at it."

I gazed around at the marble pillars, at the colonnades of arches. I looked at him. The previous night there had been a cloudburst: rolling thunder overhead, rain hammering down; lightning I could see even though my closed lids. Maybe it had reminded my unconscious mind of being rolled in the sea, the thundering of the breakers as they drove me in to shore.

"I saw you," I said. "The day I was washed up on the shore south of Acre. I have remembered now, remembered it all."

He looked at me oddly. "Go on."

I closed my eyes, drawing it back. "The cross. I had it in my hands when I jumped off the ship. It was so heavy, dragging me down to the bottom of the sea, and I was just . . . letting it. I accepted everything: the past, my heart, my sins, my death. I knew it all and I let it all go. Gave myself up to my fate, or to God, or whatever you might call it. And then . . ." I frowned. "It became so light, the cross, and huge. Suddenly it felt . . . immense. And instead of dragging me down, it was taking me up, towards the light. I thought I was dying. I thought it was the end. And I just . . . embraced it.

"The next thing I knew, I was on the beach. I thought I was in Heaven, seeing you there beside me. And then you picked up this piece of wood—just a dull chunk of grey stuff, like driftwood. Except you turned it over and there was a bit of gold, and some jewels, still covering it, and you dug your thumbs into it and . . . peeled it away, just like a skin from a *naranja*, and then you sat back on your heels just looking at it, the wood, I mean. And you brushed the sand off it, and looked at it again, very close. And then you did something strange."

"I did?"

"You did." I creased my brow, trying to separate nightmare from memory. "You took the Nail of Treves from around my neck."

The half-moon eyes never left my face. "I was going to leave it there," he said. "I never wanted to see it again. But I never could leave well alone. It felt hot in my hand. Buzzing slightly, like a wounded bee." His voice was dreamy, far away. "My wrist started to ache in that old familiar way . . ." He shivered. "I knocked the wood against a rock to dislodge the sand and there it was: a small dark hole. I took the nail and put it in. It fit perfectly." His gaze, dark and lambent, burned me. "As I knew it would."

"Who are you?" Suddenly, I was terrified of the answer.

"Just a man," he said, smiling.

He offered me his hand, and together we walked out into the light.

Somerset, England

❖

1239

Standing in the nave of Wells Cathedral, I crane my neck back so far I almost stagger with dizziness. Is it by some act of faith between air and stone that this magnificent masonry is held in place? Why doesn't it all come crashing down? I've seen the effort it takes to raise just a single piece of stone—the slings and pulleys, the teams of strong men—and yet the network of vaulted ribs that interlace the distant ceiling appear to float in shimmering weightlessness with all the grace of a spiderweb spread across a hedge at dawn.

They say this is the strongest structure ever created, that it is the greatest hymn of praise to the divine made by the hand of man. But these pillars of light joined with the arches of Islam represent a marriage forged in blood and war and suffering.

I travelled half the world under the banners of a Christian army to do battle with the Muslim foe, and yet the geometries that have made this cathedral possible were designed by the very people we went to kill. Arab architects dreamed them; Arab masons built them. And somehow a savage and an infidel helped to bring them together.

Gazing up, it seems to me that the vaulted ribs spread high above are like the branches of a tree, delicate yet strong. And suddenly, with a force that threatens to overwhelm me, I remember lying on a Seville hillside, staring up through interlacing branches and leaves at the effulgence of the sky beyond, the earth hot beneath my back and my senses full of orange blossom and the presence of the man beside me.

The Moor.

That unmistakable profile—long, straight nose, angular cheekbone, hooded eye—he turned his head and looked right back at me. The world stood still. Then he said just one word.

"*Habibi.*"

"What does it mean?" All those years and I'd never asked.

He gave me that liquefying smile. "Beloved. It means beloved."

Who was he, this enigma made flesh, and where did he come from? When I pressed him I never got a useful answer. "I am from neither east nor west, land nor sea." It was like a game to him. He did once give me a name I could use for him, but it never fitted how I thought of him. "The Moor" suited him better than any random name.

He died three years ago, just before Reginald's cathedral was finished.

I say Reginald's, but the truth of it is that Bishop Reginald never lived to see his grand dream constructed. In the greatest of ironies, he was elected archbishop of Canterbury after the death in Acre of his old rival, Baldwin of Forde. Sadly, he did not enjoy his crowning glory for very long; he was himself dead by the end of that year, buried in his beloved Bath, where it has been claimed that he performed many miraculous cures of the weak and the sick. It has also been claimed that when he died he was wearing a hair shirt beneath his episcopal vestments.

He managed, just before his demise, to secure the see of Bath and Wells for his cousin Savaric, who came back from the war bearing letters purporting to be from King Richard himself, declaring that Savaric should be elected to that bishopric. And so suddenly the Moor and I found ourselves working for that old fraud once more, now with his hands on all the funds he could ever need to see the great cathedral constructed, especially once he had persuaded King Richard (after helping to secure his release from imprisonment on his return from the Holy Land) to exchange his seat at Bath for that of Glastonbury. Where shortly after he was invested a miraculous find was made, not only of the remains of the hero-king Arthur of the Britons, but also of his wife, Queen Guenevere. And that brought pilgrims flocking from all corners of the kingdom: yet more funds destined for his coffers.

For our part, the Moor and I brought back a dozen masons to help with the project at Wells, collecting them as we travelled back to England: a couple from Jerusalem, from Tunisia and Amalfi, from Cordoba and Cluny. Some were Arabs, others French and Spanish. Muslims, Jews, even a Coptic Christian, they represented our epic journey, and just like the mongrel troupe with whom we had toured the south of England, they were a marvellous miscellany, which was fitting, given the new style of building they had come to create. Not speaking one another's languages, they spoke instead a new language of architecture: one of squinches and domes, of flying buttresses and ribbed vaults, of colonnades and pointed arches stolen straight out of the heart of Islam. Those arches enabled the masons to build higher than ever before, and for the structure to support as much as three times the weight, to allow thin walls to be punctured by tall windows that would let fountains of light spill into the building.

It was a glorious experiment, Wells, and we made it a glorious reality.

And now the light—so much of it, a torrent, not what you would expect in a great cavern of stone—is hurting my eyes. Or perhaps it's the memories. Too many memories . . .

Suddenly I am snuffling and weeping and I cannot stop, and

one of the canons passes me with a sympathetic glance, as if he knows full well that men cannot bear the awe of such a place, that we are too weak and fragile to comprehend its power. If I could, I would run outside, where the world follows its natural order. But there is something I have come to see. And so I dry my eyes on my sleeve and lean on my stick for a moment, and then turn and tap my way back down the nave, counting.

Ah, there it is. You'd never spot it if you didn't know. If you hadn't been there that night. But no one else was there: just the two of us by candlelight, when the masons had gone home and the monks were abed. We levered up a couple of the newly laid flagstones and buried the treasure at the foot of one of the pillars. And then the Moor propped a stolen ladder against the pillar and scratched a little cipher just beneath the decorative capital. Even if you were looking for it you could easily miss it, and even if you didn't you'd probably have no idea what it meant. It's a set of Arabic numerals—not exactly what you'd expect to find in a Christian cathedral. Shockingly, there has been an enemy in our midst: a for-eigner, an infidel, a wolf in the fold.

I think if Reginald had lived, the Moor would have placed that last remnant of the True Cross in his hands; there was a true affection between the two of them, based on their shared dream of beauty. Instead, rather than hand it over to Savaric, who would surely have sold it to the highest bidder, he had brought it here; and here, we had buried it. It was the Moor's little joke, and the greatest gift in Christendom.

Has it worked miracles from its secret hiding place? Does its magic flow out into the world? Or is it no more than a piece of dead wood, cynically encased in rich gold to add to the pretense? To this day I do not know.

One thing I do know: about four years after we returned from the Holy Land I was sitting with the Moor at the window of an inn looking out onto the market square at Wells, our hands cupped around beakers of spiced wine, taking in the sights—the busy merchants and wool-sellers, the cider-makers and the costermongers all doing lively trade—when a couple caught my eye. The man tall and lanky, with a shock of hair like a dandelion clock; the woman richly dressed, her hair up in a wimple, a small child toddling at her side. For a moment I thought I was hallucinating a ghost. Then I banged my wine down on the table and ran outside.

"Quickfinger!"

The man turned with a look of guilt and fear, as if he expected a sheriff about to collar him. When his darting eyes settled on me, I saw his face go slack with shock; then he was running at me with his arms wide.

"By 'eck, John Savage! I thought the sea had taken you."

"I thought the same of you."

"One of the other ships hauled me in." He grinned. "I en't called Pilchard for nowt!"

The woman joined us. I almost didn't recognize her, and when I did I nearly called her by the name I knew her best by. "Pl—Mary!"

She dimpled at me: she'd put on weight and it suited her, especially in those figured velvets.

"You look as if life's treating you well," I said.

She cocked her head at me, then looked past my shoulder at the figure sitting by the window of the inn, looking out at us with his half-moon eyes. "You, too," she said. "I'm glad, for both of you." She placed her hand on the child's head till the lad turned his face up to us. Quickfinger's features in miniature. He was never going to be handsome, but when he grinned it seemed he already had his father's mischievous charm. "We called him John," she said.

It took a moment to sink in. Then I felt absurdly pleased.

Quickfinger leaned in towards me conspiratorially. "That ruby I got out of the True Cross came in reet handy."

Are there miracles in the world, or just the clever toils of fate? Or maybe simply the wise use of opportunity? In a way it really doesn't matter: the outcome is still the same.

But just then it was as if the sun had come out and was shining on us all, washing us with golden light that erased the years and all the blood shed and spilled. It made me smile then, as it does now.

END

Author's Note

Pillars of Light began, as novels sometimes do, with a sudden wild flare of intellectual curiosity and a completely uneducated guess. Following up that hunch led to two years of research and three of writing and revising, a huge amount of work that took me a long way off my usual writing track, which had been closely focused on my adopted country of Morocco. Writing this twelfth-century epic felt at the outset like an impossible task, setting out on a journey into completely unknown territory equipped with only a vague understanding of where I was going, no map and a leaky canteen. I would be crossing ground that many writers had traversed before, but from a completely different direction (as far as I am aware, no one has written a novel about the ordinary people trapped in the notorious Siege of Acre, both inside and outside the walls).

In the end, the book turned out to be not so different from my previous novels in terms of its concerns, though the scope was on a rather more (dauntingly) epic scale. And as with those previous books what started with a quest for knowledge about an obscure subject (the Barbary pirates in *The Tenth Gift*, the desert nomads of the Sahara in *The Salt Road*; and African and European slavery in *The Sultan's Wife*) in this case soon turned into a story about love and war, the clash of cultures between East and West, and the common humanity and experiences people share no matter what their origins or affiliations.

Many of the characters in my tale are real people: the crusading king Richard the Lionheart and champion of Islam, Salah ad-Din, have been heroes for West and East down the ages. Their lieutenants and allies are also well documented in the chronicles and annals of the time and in hundreds of tales about what we call the crusades (a term not coined until the late sixteenth century, therefore not used in this novel). Lesser known, but equally historical, is the young swimmer Aisa, who carried messages between the besieged city and the Muslim army, and was feted for dying as a martyr, bringing the garrison wages into shore on his body, thus fulfilling his task. The rest of the Najib family, and the other folk who inhabit Acre, are fictional except for Karakush and al-Mashtub. Do not ask me who the Moor is, or whether he is real or fabricated: he is an enigma all his own.

Other fully historical figures in the story include Savaric and Reginald de Bohun; and anyone who has read any history about the building of cathedrals in this time, when Church and State were so much more entwined, will know that the funding for their foundation and erection often stemmed from dubious sources. Much of the funding and recruitment for the Third Crusade depended on just the sort of spiritually and financially manipulative methods as the troupe's mumming tour: indeed, the Archbishop of Canterbury (the much-disliked Baldwin of Forde) led a similar progress around Wales to drum up support and funds for the enterprise. Richard the Lionheart was so keen to raise the money required to fund the crusade he said he would have sold London itself, if he could have found a buyer.

Reginald de Bohun did indeed found the cathedral at Wells, which represents the first true expression of the Gothic. But he died before seeing his vision translated into reality. It was his venal cousin Savaric who oversaw much of the construction before being succeeded by Bishop Jocelin, with whom the cathedral is more popularly connected.

The seed for *Pillars of Light*—that wild, uneducated guess—came during a rare period of insomnia. I was reading, but had the television on low as background noise. I glimpsed up from the page, not really focusing on the screen. For a moment, as the camera panned across an interior of serried pillars and soaring arches, I thought I was seeing the Great Mosque in Casablanca (the only mosque I, as an infidel woman, have been allowed to enter). Then the voiceover started and I realized it was Salisbury Cathedral.

The program was, it turned out, part of an Open University course about the building of Europe's majestic cathedrals, the most remarkable achievement of the Middle Ages. I went back to my book. But still the impression of Islamic architecture remained with me, as if superimposed over the images of English Gothic stone, and the seed of an idea took root in my mind. I wondered why I had made such an unlikely leap of imagination. I started to research the origins of cathedral design, not expecting to unearth any significant connection. But I was to be amazed. The more I dug, the more I discovered. There had, it transpires, long been a school of thought that Islamic structures had influenced Christian architecture.

In the early twentieth century French art historian Emile Mâle was convinced that the cathedral at Puy-en-Velay showed a clear influence from Moorish Spain. A few years later, Ahmad Fikry, a student of Henri Focillon, produced a doctoral thesis on the influence of Islamic forms in the French Romanesque, particularly at Puy, noting parallels between the cupolas of the Puy and those in the mosque of Qairouan in Tunisia. Historian Louis Bréhier also noted similarities with the Arab architecture of Spain and believed the architect to have been either a Muslim, or a Mozarabic Christian. But it was the pointed arch which characterizes the Gothic style that makes the case for a link to Islamic architecture most clearly.

The pointed—or ogival—arch had long been used in the orient, in Islamic and even pre-Islamic architecture, linking arcades of tall pillars to give an effect of geometric uniformity, an elegance that soothed the mind and enabled the supplicant to feel closer to God. Utility and beauty often go hand in hand: the pointed arch is more efficient at distributing the weight of masonry above it, enabling the stonework to span higher and wider gaps, supported by narrower columns. But a direct link between Islamic architecture and Gothic cathedrals remained a controversial theory—in Christian eyes, at least—until very recently. A number of leading academics have started to trace the journey the concept may have taken and to date that journey to the fluid movement of people between the Middle East and Europe during the early medieval crusades. As chance would have it, a friend of mine was taking an advanced degree in Islamic art at around this time, and happened to attend a talk in which the lecturer spoke of the first Western examples of pointed arches being taken from the Arab world, through Europe to England, culminating in Wells, the first cathedral to entirely dispense with the round arch in favour of the pointed arch. This was soon followed by a fine article by expert in Islamic architecture Tom Verde in the June 2012 edition of *Saudi Aramco World* precisely delineating the trajectory of the pointed arch from Syria and the Arab world to the West via the medium of the crusades.

It has also been argued that the change in emphasis from the darker, weightier Romanesque to more fluid, light-filled total design of the Gothic came about at around the same time as the introduction of Arabic numerals from Spain in the early twelfth century. Moving from the Roman numeral system to the Arabic numerals we still use today represented a revolution in thinking. Multiplication and division became easier and more comprehensible—and also more transferable—so the greater complexities of Gothic design became possible to encompass, and masons who had been working in the Muslim tradition were able to travel to work alongside European craftsmen and exchange ideas freely, thus enabling the spread of this fusion of East and West. As evidence of this, a set of Arabic numerals used to mark up timbers for assembly were quite recently discovered in the roof of Salisbury Cathedral.

But to my knowledge, no one has discovered the fragment of the True Cross that John and the Moor buried beneath a pillar in the cathedral at Wells: that is my own invention. Indeed, what happened to the large relic carried by the Bishop of Acre before the Christian army at the disaster at Hattin remains a mystery to this day. The bishop was killed and it fell into the hands of Salah ad-Din, who sent part of it to the Caliph of Baghdad, who buried it in June 1189 beneath the Bab en-Nuby, to be trodden beneath Muslim feet. But Baha ad-Din states in his chronicle that it was exhibited at Salah ad-Din's camp in the hills above Acre; and that after the failed negotiation for the hostages it was sent as a gift to Isaac the Emperor of Constantinople (Istanbul). Yet Hubert of Salisbury is said to have been allowed by Salah ad-Din to see it in Jerusalem in September 1192. And then there is the tale of the Franj soldier who went out to the battlefield at Hattin and after three days dug it up. Or the report of Richard being shown a fragment of the Cross by the Abbot of St. Elias at Beyt Nuba before he gave up the crusade (without regaining Jerusalem) and returned (by a circuitous route) to England in October 1192.

There were without doubt many faked relics and fragments of the True Cross. As the sixteenth-century theologian John Calvin famously said: "There is no town, however small, which has not some morsel of it. . . . If all the pieces which could be found were collected into a heap, they would form a good shipload." Even as recently as 2013 there were reports of a fragment being discovered, in a church in Turkey.

I started working on *Pillars of Light* before the revolt against the Assad regime and the arrival of Daesh—the so-called Islamic State group—in Syria and Iraq. Writing the book while the current

tragedy of this riven area plays out has been both painful and apposite. There have been times I've had to stop work, as stories of the
destruction and violence suffered by the ordinary people of Syria
eclipsed the historical events I was trying to recapture. In particular, witness accounts of the siege in Homs paralleled so closely the
worst details of the siege at Acre that it was hard not to despair
at mankind's inability to develop empathy and decency down the
ages. Likewise, the vile beheadings carried out by Daesh in the full
glare of modern publicity, so reminiscent of the crazed fundamen-
talism of the Hashshashin, also mirror uncomfortably the cold-
blooded execution of the Acre hostages by Richard I, deliberately
within view of the Muslim army. Terrorism is nothing new and is
not limited to a single culture or religion. There is a tendency for
the modern reader to look back on people of the past and dismiss
them as less cultivated, less civilized than we are. But if history
teaches us anything it must surely be that we rarely learn from the
mistakes and atrocities of the past.

Jane Johnson, London, July 2015

Source Material

Ashridge, Thomas. *The Crusades: The War for the Holy Land*. London: Simon & Schuster, 2010.

Bagnoli, Martina, Holger A. Klein, C. Griffith Mann, and James Robinson, eds. *Treasures of Heaven: Saints, Relics and Devotion in Medieval Europe*. London: British Museum Press, 2011.

Clark, William W. *Medieval Cathedrals*. Westport, CT: Greenwood Press, 2006.

Derbyshire, David. "Why Irish helped raise the roof on Salisbury Cathedral." *The Telegraph*, March 5, 2003. http://www.telegraph.co.uk/news/uknews/1423739/Why-Irish-helped-raise-the-roof-on-Salisbury-Cathedral.html (accessed June 17, 2015).

Finucane, Ronald C. *Miracles and Pilgrims: Popular Beliefs in Medieval England*. London: Macmillan, 1977.

Gravett, Christopher. *Medieval Siege Warfare*. Oxford: Osprey Publishing, 1990.

Hafiz, Yasmine. "Piece of Jesus' Cross Found? Archaeologists Discover 'Holy Thing' in Balatlar Church in Turkey." *The Huffington Post*, August 1, 2013. http://www.huffingtonpost.com/2013/08/01/jesus-cross-found-archaeology_n_3691938.html (accessed June 17, 2015).

Hindley, Geoffrey. *Saladin: Hero of Islam*. Barnsley, UK: Pen and Sword, 2010.

Housley, Norman. *Fighting for the Cross: Crusading to the Holy Land*. New Haven, CT: Yale University Press, 2008.

Hovedon, Roger de. *The Annals of Roger de Hoveden: Comprising the*

History of England and of Other Countries of Europe from A.D. 732 to A.D. 1201. Translated by Henry T. Riley. London: H.G. Bonn, 1853.

Ibn Shaddād, Bahā' al-Dīn. *The Rare and Excellent History of Saladin*. Translated by D.S. Richards. Aldershot, UK: Ashgate, 2001.

Lane-Poole, Stanley. *Saladin: All-Powerful Sultan and the Uniter of Islam*. New York: Cooper Square Press, 2002.

Maalouf, Amin. *The Crusades through Arab Eyes*. Translated by J. Rothschild. New York: Al Saqi Books, 1984.

Montefiore, Simon Sebag. *Jerusalem: The Biography*. London: Weidenfeld & Nicolson, 2011.

Nicholson, Helen J., trans. *The Chronicle of the Third Crusade: A Translation of the Itinerarium peregrinorum et gesta regis Ricardi*. Aldershot, UK: Ashgate, 2001.

Reston, James, Jr. *Warriors of God: Richard the Lionheart and Saladin in the Third Crusade*. New York: Doubleday, 2001.

Scott, Robert. *The Gothic Enterprise: A Guide to Understanding the Medieval Cathedral*. London: University of California Press, 2003.

Tyerman, Christopher. *God's War: A New History of the Crusades*. London: Allen Lane, 2006.

Verde, Tom. "The Point of the Arch." *Saudi Aramco World* 63, no. 3 (May/June 2012): 34–43. Also available online at http://www. saudiaramcoworld.com/issue/201203/the.point.of. the.arch.htm.

Wales, Gerald of. *The Journey Through Wales and the Description of Wales (Itinerarium Cambriae)*. Edited by Betty Radice. Translated by Lewis Thorpe. Middlesex, UK: Penguin, 1978.

Wheatcroft, Andrew. *Infidels: A History of the Conflict Between Christendom and Islam*. New York: Random House, 2005.

Acknowledgments

I would like to express my gratitude to the many people who saw me through this book; to all those who provided support, talked things over, read, wrote, offered comments, allowed me to quote their remarks and assisted in the editing, proofreading and design.

I would like to thank UCLan Publishing for enabling me to publish this book. Above all I want to thank the MA Publishing students (2016–17 cohort) who worked so hard to bring the book to fruition.

Thanks to Becky Chilcott for her design work and Debbie Williams, Wayne Noble, Alexa Gregson, Stuart Hampton-Reeves, Roger Gray and Molly McDonough for their dedication and belief in the book. Also to Michael Thomas, Vice-Chancellor of UCLan for making all this possible. Finally, thank you to Amber Elliott for her hard work on the social media.